Oni Bushi

By

Mary Anderson

Curious Neko Books

Art by Okaiyugo at Din Animation Studio

ISBN: 979-8-9887955-0-6

www.curiousneko.com

Acknowledgements

First and foremost, I would like to thank my husband for his unconditional love and support.

Big hugs go to my family and friends as well.

Many thanks to those who assisted me with edits – *Oni Bushi* would not be as polished as it is without all of your help!

A huge round of applause goes to Din Animation Studio, the wonderful team of artists who created the visuals for this book. (check out the full-color characters on the Curious Neko Books website! www.curiousneko.com)

And last, but not least, a big thank you to Xris and Mr. MB. You both were unfortunate enough to read the original version over 18 years ago…I hope you'll agree that this story has vastly improved since then!

Dedication

Oni Bushi is dedicated to the person who began this writing journey with me. He is someone who forces me to complete my work, who pushes my imagination beyond its limits, and he is the reason that I continue to write. Without him, *Oni Bushi* would never have made it past a few failed re-write attempts.

Haru, this book is for YOU.

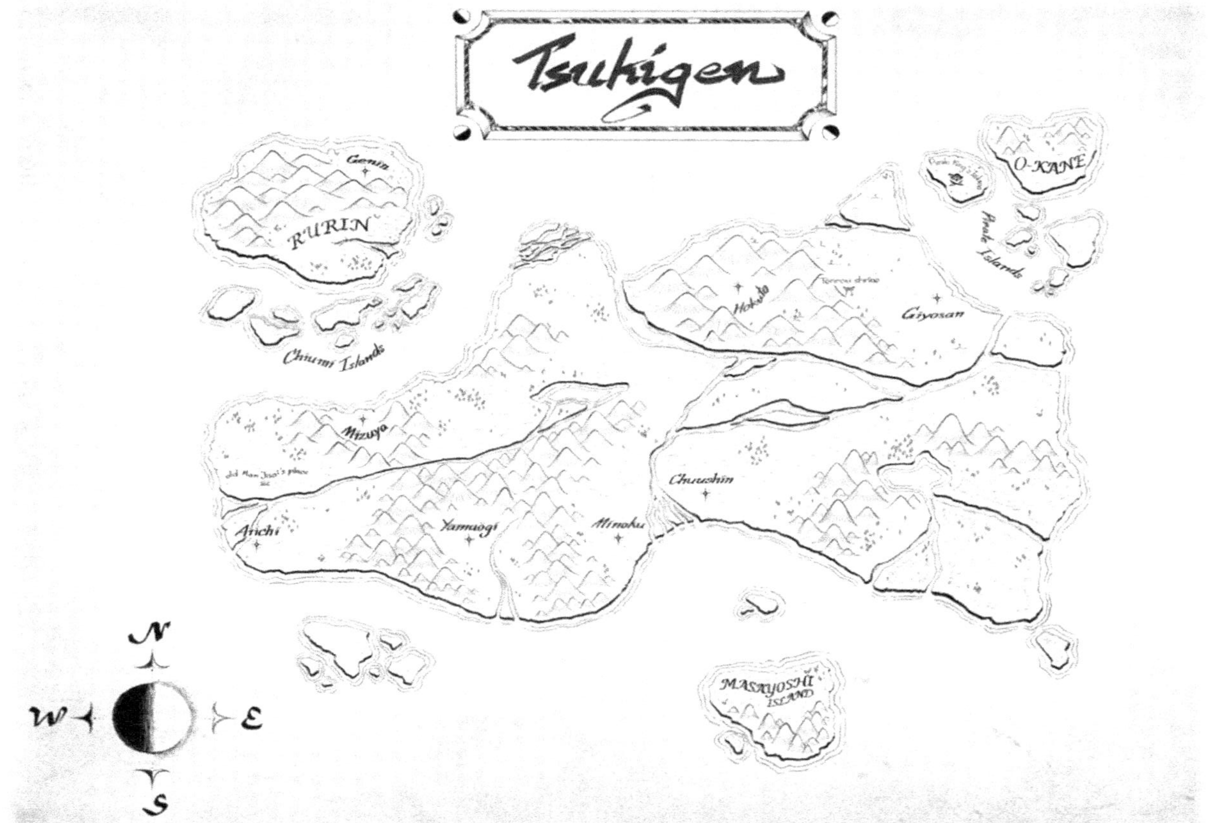

Tsukigen
RURIN
Genin
Chiumi Islands
O-KANE
Pirate Islands
Hokido
Giyosan
Mizuyo
old Man Jiroi's place
Chuushin
Arichi
Yamaogi
Minoku
MASAYOSHI ISLAND
N
W
E
S

Introduction

Blood dripped from the blade as Kazuki slowly dragged it behind him in the frozen dirt. The tearing, scraping sound coming from the tip of the katana barely made it to the boy's ears. Echoing in his mind were the horrible screams of his mother. The boy's body shook uncontrollably, but he continued to walk. Direction didn't matter. *Anywhere but here,* he had thought, and then his feet had begun to move, sluggishly dragging him away from the village. Who knows how long it had been since then? The boy didn't know where he was. His vision had become as dark as the red blood that had splashed across his face.

There was a burning sensation growing in the boy's left arm; the sword was too heavy for him. *I should leave it,* he thought, but his fingers would not relax their grip. There was something in him that told the boy not to let it go. It was more of a sensation than a voice, but it told him: '*That sword is a part of you now. You must carry it with you wherever you go. Never part with it. Never.*' The boy's arm continued to burn with pain as he stumbled over many rocks, before finally falling to the ground.

The ground was cold against his bare skin. If he remembered

correctly, fresh snow had fallen early that morning. Fat white flakes which had reminded him of cherry blossom petals; the same petals his mother had loved so much.

Closing his unseeing eyes, Kazuki clutched a small piece of pink fabric in his right hand. *Mother...*

He stopped shivering. Cold was no longer something he could feel. Even as the icy wind raged, cutting into his skin, the boy could feel nothing.

He did not move. There was no incentive for him to continue moving. There was nothing and no one waiting for him at the imaginary finish line.

Kazuki was alone. And he wanted to die.

Blossoming cherry trees were the first things Kazuki laid eyes on. He frowned. After five years of darkness, the world was too bright and colorful for him. The boy had become accustomed to the world of darkness, and now preferred it.

Glancing around, the boy took in the world around him. It was just as he had pictured; the green grass, blossoming trees, and small wooden house all appeared before him. He had come to know of their existence through his now heightened senses of smell, sound, and touch.

Sight is the most useless of senses, he reminded himself.

The house sat in a small clearing, surrounded by towering trees on all sides. It was a secluded place with only the creatures of the forest as neighbors. The boy enjoyed the relative quiet and had used the sounds of the birds, squirrels, foxes, deer, and other animals as a sort of guessing game for sharpening his hearing. He had tried mimicking a few calls here and there, but he found his imitations rather poor – as did the original callers, who never responded.

A pleasant breeze rustled through the trees and brought with it the sweet and earthy smells of spring. One of the cherry blossoms floated down on the wind and landed on the boy's shoulder. Grimacing, he brushed the troublesome flower off. As he did, his eyes landed on the katana at his side; it was the same one he dragged through the snow five years ago, but he had never seen it until now.

Kazuki untied the sageo from his obi so that he could fully inspect the sheathed weapon. When he held the katana horizontally in front of him, Kazuki saw that, like most katana, the blade was housed in a black lacquered saya. The tsuka, however, was unique in that it was wrapped with a dark red fabric (the same as the sageo) and the ray skin beneath it was black. The menuki, which were partially obscured by the dark red wrapping, resembled an oni mask that the boy had seen during one of his village shrine's festivals.

Turning the katana slightly, Kazuki inspected the tsuba next. While the overall shape was a circle, the inner design looked like thick, swirled clouds. There was also a creature on it, but it wasn't one that the boy was familiar with. As Kazuki looked closer, he was amazed at the detail the creator had managed to etch into the dark metal. The creature, which was leaping around the circle, almost looked like the fabled nine-tailed fox, but the fox's nine tails were represented as snakes – no, they were dragon heads, because each head had ears, horns, and whiskers.

"And finally," the boy remarked as he slowly unsheathed the blade. He was not a katana expert by any means, but since the head of each house in his village owned a katana, he had seen quite a few in which to compare his to. This one was by far the most beautiful. Even solely considering the blade itself, Kazuki's katana was a work of art. Everything about it was perfection: the curve, the angle, the sharpness, and the spectacular hamon – the pattern of which was somewhere between a wave and a mountain. The boy was mesmerized.

"I thought I would find you out here."

The boy quickly sheathed his katana and, as he turned to his left, saw the old man standing in the doorway. He was just as worn-out as the door that he was leaning against; the one that always smelled of damp wood and never slid sideways properly. Multiple rips adorned the rice paper squares, explaining the frequent drafts, while the dark wood framing was splintered and partly rotten. Thankfully, it never got as cold there as it did in his village, otherwise the boy would have frozen to death by now.

A smile was spreading across the old man's saggy face. He, too, looked exactly like the boy had imagined. Short, chopped grey hair hung around his thin, wrinkly face. His greying beard was short and relatively neat. He wore a plain grey kimono with a black hakama, both of which were ragged and stained from years of wear. The katana that hung at his side also had a black lacquered saya, but the tsuka was traditional in its decoration, with black wrappings over white ray skin. He was too far away to see the menuki or the tsuba design.

"It's time for your lessons."

The boy nodded, slid his saya through his obi, and deftly retied his sageo. Following the old man into the house, the boy made sure to kick his sandals off before stepping inside. He turned to slide the door shut behind him, but the old man insisted he leave it open on such a nice day. The boy reluctantly released the rotten door.

There was no source of light inside the old house, save for the sunlight that streamed in through the numerous cracks. Glancing up at the ceiling, the boy saw that the thatch was almost gone in places and that most of the beams were cracked and rotting. He wondered why the roof hadn't collapsed yet.

After confirming his surroundings, the boy closed his eyes.

"Has your sight returned?"

The boy nodded.

"Then why have you closed your eyes? Are you not happy?"

The boy shook his head.

"You are a strange child for choosing darkness over light," the old man said with a chuckle. The boy then heard the old man unsheathe his katana. "Ready?"

The boy nodded and unsheathed his katana.

The old man was the first to move. Normally he didn't make any sound, but this time Kazuki could hear a distinct *thunk* with each step as the old man rushed towards him. He could hear the old man's breathing too; it was slow and heavy. Something wasn't right.

Kazuki decided to end things as quickly as possible. In a flash of movement, the boy was gone. Opening his eyes slightly, the boy was now looking at the old man's back.

Perfect, now-

The old man turned, looked straight at him, and grinned. "You cannot fool me with those childish tricks of yours, Kazuki-kun."

The boy didn't have time to move, so his only option was to block. As their blades collided, the screeching metal echoed in the boy's ears. He hated that sound. The boy quickly pushed the old man away and jumped backwards, putting more space in between them. Sweat was pouring down the old man's face. His upper body was now moving in sync with his breathing.

Something really isn't right. Unable to concentrate, the boy lowered his blade. "Sensei, you–"

The old man charged. Kazuki barely raised his katana in time to block the old man's attack. "Concentrate on the fight, boy! Never let your guard down!"

Kazuki continued to block each strike from the old man's blade. Even in the old man's condition, it was hard for the boy to keep up.

I need more space. I can't move if he's this close.

When the old man attacked again, Kazuki put all of his weight into his blade and pushed the old man back. The old man stumbled a bit, but then caught himself and held his katana out in front of him.

"Good, Kazuki-kun, very good. You've improved greatly over the past few months. Even with these advanced techniques you've managed to keep up…I'm impressed. Not many adults can do that, much less children of your age."

Kazuki clenched his fists. *What's going on? He* never *praises me.*

Suddenly the old man started coughing violently. He dropped his katana and grabbed his throat. The boy sheathed his katana and went over to the old man, who was now collapsed on the floor, coughing up blood. Kazuki knelt and rolled the old man over onto his back. Using his legs as a pillow, the boy propped the old man's head up so that he could breathe a little easier.

The old man looked up at the boy and smiled. "Kazuki-kun…do you remember when we met? That day, when I found a near-dead little boy, clutching a katana in his left hand and a piece of cloth in his right hand…I brought him back to this place and somehow the boy survived."

The boy looked away from the old man.

"You were only eight years old at the time. You couldn't see and you wouldn't speak to me for the longest time. The only thing I was able to get out of you was your name…" The old man started to cough up more blood. The upper part of his kimono was now stained red. "Ah. Five years…you've grown so much, Kazuki-kun." The old man smiled as he wiped the blood from his mouth.

"Sensei…why didn't you tell me?" The boy still couldn't look at him. "I could have fought beside you–"

"It was my battle to fight, not yours," the old man snapped.

"But you're all I have left. I would have gladly helped you take revenge for the slaughter of your family."

"You are all that I have left too, Kazuki-kun. I did not want to lose you as well." The old man started to cough again. Blood splashed onto the boy's blue kinagashi. "I am sorry…"

The boy shook his head. He didn't want to look down. He didn't want to see the old man's face. He didn't even want to be in the room.

"People are not immortal, Kazuki-kun. They can never stay, no matter how much you want them to, when it is their time to go."

The boy knew that. He understood it best of all. But that didn't mean he had to like it.

The old man started to cough, and this time he couldn't stop. "…S…Sorry… Kazuki-kun. I knew that Ammon…would set up a trap…but I was too stubborn to…care…"

The boy tried to lift the old man's head higher to stop the coughing, but it was too late. For the second time in his life, the boy was going to watch a loved one die while covered in their blood.

"I have…one favor…to ask of you…"

The boy nodded.

"Please…whatever happens, do *not* seek revenge. It is an ugly thing…an obsession…that only leaves sadness in its wake. I want you to…have happiness, Kazuki-kun." The old man smiled at the boy. "Please…do not choose the darkness, my boy…you will not find happiness there."

Suddenly the old man stopped coughing. In fact, he stopped moving completely. His jaw went slack, his eyes rolled to the back of his head, his arms became limp and fell to the side. There was no heartbeat, no pulse.

Kazuki gently laid the old man's body to the side and stood up. It was as if the boy were in a trance. His eyes were dry and his heart beat steadily. Emotion had been ripped from his being long ago. Now there was nothing left, even for the old man who had been by his side for the past five years, raising and training him to use his katana. Kazuki was a hollow, empty shell.

The boy pulled out a piece of cloth that he kept in the folds of his kinagashi and laid it over the old man's face. The light pink fabric quickly darkened as it absorbed the sweat and blood. The cloth was the same color as cherry blossoms. It had been his mother's favorite.

He then picked up the old man's katana. The menuki under the black wrappings were both howling wolves, and the tsuba was a solid circle with a single circle etched in the upper corner – presumably it was the moon. Kazuki also noticed words carved into the metal, but the symbols were too faded to read.

As he sheathed the old man's katana, the boy watched the wave-like hamon slowly sink into the saya. Kazuki then carefully adjusted the old man's arms so that they hung at his sides, but with the left hand gripping the katana's tsuka. He couldn't remember exactly how the dead were supposed to be positioned, but he did his best trying to honor the old man.

While the boy searched the house for the flint, memories of the place flooded his mind. Waking to bird calls and the smell of hot rice, days filled with training and scolding, the occasional hike to the hot spring bath, listening to the old man tell stories and talk about the world…

Kazuki violently shook his head. He did not want to remember.

After finding the flint, the boy turned to the old man's corpse and hesitated. He then turned towards the open hearth in the center of the room and decided to light that instead. The boy added logs until the hearth was completely full before starting the blaze.

Kazuki stood outside of the house and watched the smoke waft, stream, and then bellow out of it. He convinced himself that the memories from this place would be destroyed along with it.

By the time the flames had engulfed the structure, the boy was gone.

There it is.

Shielding his eyes from the sun with his hand, the boy stared at the large, wooden castle on top of the hill. Even from a distance, he could tell that it was elaborately decorated with gilded roofs and was painted red with gold trim and accents. The boy wondered if all Hekigun bases were so…distinguished in design.

Tracing the lines of the tall stone walls up the hill with his eyes, the boy looked for any obvious traps or guard posts. He didn't see anything out of the ordinary, which made him even more cautious. The less guarded a place seems, the more guarded it is – especially if it's a Hekigun base.

Kazuki didn't know much about them, besides the fact that they were merciless killers that pretended to be bringers of peace. Their leader ruled over the country, and the members of the group were like the ruler's own personal army; the Hekigun would fully enforce any laws the ruler felt were 'necessary for the good of the people'.

Just thinking about them made the boy angry. They were all a bunch of liars…and liars need to be punished.

"Are you really going up there, Kid?" A voice asked from below.

The boy jumped down off of the roof, looked at the man standing before him, and nodded.

"But that's suicide! A kid like you would be killed in an instant!" The man, a local villager that he happened across, seemed to be concerned for the boy's life.

Kazuki didn't care. He started to make his way to the gate that led out of the man's garden and into the main street of the town. He was almost there when the man grabbed the boy's sleeve and pulled him back.

"Hold on, kid. I can't just let you go up there by yourself! I may have just given you all of that information about the base, but if you die up there I'll feel responsible and– Hey!"

Kazuki easily slipped loose from the man's hold and jumped back onto the roof of the man's house. The single-story house wasn't incredibly tall, but jumping up on top wasn't something your average villager could do.

"Get back here!" The man yelled at the boy from below.

Hmph. Loser. The boy turned to the castle on the hill and started to make his way towards it, running and jumping along the village roofs. Kazuki slipped a couple of times on the straw thatching, but each time he caught himself before he fell.

His heart began to race as he approached the bottom of the hill. He was excited. It had been one week since the old man's death, and the boy was finally going to get his revenge. Nothing was going to stop him now. Not even death.

Jumping down from the last roof, the boy crouched and surveyed the pathway of large, stone steps before him. As it wound itself up around the hill, there were plenty of curves and corners along the way that were perfectly suited for an ambush. There was, however, no ambush. In fact there were no guards or traps whatsoever. It didn't feel right.

The boy was cautious in his approach. He kept his right hand on the hilt of his katana, ready to unsheathe it at the first hint of danger.

His bare feet made no noise as they slowly took each step. His breath was steady and silent. As he reached the top step, the boy paused and looked around.

There was a large, flat section covered with grass, shielded on both sides by man-made stone slopes that were at least twenty feet high. In front loomed a golden gate that looked as if it had been built for giants. The shiny, undecorated, double doors were shut.

Suddenly, the boy heard the clinking of armored footsteps approaching. He turned and saw a group of five guards spread out on the steps behind him, each one armed with a sasumata.

Kazuki slowly backed up towards the golden gate. The guards slowly advanced.

Without warning, they all attacked him. Tightly gripping his katana, the boy immediately jumped into the air, avoiding the guards' frontal attacks. As soon as he landed on the ground, the guards sprung at him from different angles, trying to get the "U" shaped steel tip around the boy's torso and arms, hoping to force him down to the ground.

Closing his eyes, the boy concentrated on listening to the guards' movements. His left hand held the saya steady as he quickly drew his blade and moved accordingly as the sound waves registered in his brain. When the sounds ceased, the boy opened his eyes and found an almost perfect circle of red grass before him.

Flicking the blood from his blade, Kazuki grinned. He then sheathed his blade, carefully sliding it back into the saya, and walked away from the cluster of bodies.

The large, golden doors towered in front of him, but the boy managed to push one of them open, using all of the strength that he could muster.

Whoa.

Kazuki stared in awe at the inner courtyard that he had just walked into. It was probably large enough to fit his entire village. And there were countless buildings surrounding the main one; each of which was two stories tall. Though not as intricately decorated as the main building was, the side buildings were all painted the same bright red color and they looked a lot better than the richest homes in the village below.

Kazuki thought that the side buildings would be guard houses, but there was no one to be seen or heard anywhere. Had the villager given him false information? Was the main force away from the base?

The boy turned his attention to the main building in front of him. It was a four-story masterpiece with exterior walkways surrounding the entire building on each level. The castle was unlike anything Kazuki had ever seen. He couldn't help but stare.

A sharp pain in his left shoulder blade snapped the boy back to reality. He winced and reached his right hand around. The area around his shoulder blade was wet.

What the–

Before the boy could pull his hand back, a guard appeared before him. Three throwing knives were jutting out of both of the guard's hands.

Tch.

Kazuki quickly threw his left arm in front of him. With quick movements he was able to dodge most of the small silver blades, but two of them hit their target.

"Heh. Kid, you're not fast enough to dodge *all* of my attacks." The guard grinned as he watched the boy pull out two knives from his left arm.

Blood gushed from the openings as he yanked out the knives; the boy winced from the pain.

"I'll bet that hurts a lot, Kid. You should go cry to your mommy."

The boy straightened himself and stared at the guard. Tall and ugly were two words to describe the black-suited man. His black hair was tied up in a bun, and the only skin visible was from the neck up. The man wore a crooked grin and an angular scar marred the left side of his face.

Kazuki smiled. "You know, I would, but..." He charged foreword in the blink of an eye. The guard didn't have time to react. "She's dead."

The guard looked down at the boy, who was now standing next to him.

"Tell her I said 'Hi'."

With his right hand, Kazuki pulled his katana out of the guard's waist; it had penetrated his abdomen and was protruding from the other side. Blood spurted from the guard's body, staining the boy's kinagashi with more red. Kazuki slowly wiped the blood off of his face with his less-soiled sleeve.

"Gah!" The guard fell to the ground, landing in a pool of his own blood.

With a blank face, the boy stared down at the guard; he was barely alive and was beginning to convulse from blood loss. The guard screamed as the boy stepped on his head. Kazuki mercilessly ground his foot into the guard's skull, finishing him off in a slow and painful manner. When the guard finally lay motionless on the bloody stones, the boy flicked the blood off of his blade and returned it to his black lacquer saya.

As he walked towards the main building, Kazuki frowned. The wounds on his left arm were still bleeding, and they stung every time he moved his arm. Using his teeth and right hand, the boy tore off strips of cloth from his left sleeve and tied them around his wounds.

That should work for now.

Kazuki reached back and touched his shoulder blade. There was a small piece of metal lodged in his shoulder, and he couldn't reach it to pull it out. Blood was still trailing out of the wound, but there was nothing he could do about it.

Tch. The boy had been careless, and he knew it.

Kazuki walked through the front doors of the main building, which were unlocked and at least three times his height. He stepped into the entrance room, which seemed to take up the entire first floor, and the first thing he noticed was the small tree stuck in a plot of dirt in the middle of the room; its pale pink blossoms had just begun to open.

The boy turned away from it.

Decorated with brilliant, rich tones of gold and amber, the interior of the main building mirrored its exterior. Lavish red silk hung from the wooden rafters, shielding much of the room from the boy's gaze. Colossal columns rose from the floor at key structural points around the room, and they, too, were wrapped in red silk. The room seemed large because of the lack of furniture and the incredibly high ceiling; the second story must have been left open to the first. Towards the back of the room was a long staircase, which would presumably take him to the third floor, but Kazuki didn't move towards it.

No sunlight penetrated the room, save for the sliver that shone through the partially opened doorway behind the boy. Lit candles cast long shadows on the walls, making it seem as if everything in the room were alive and moving. One shadow in particular caught the boy's attention, making him uneasy.

Kazuki slunk back behind the cherry blossom tree and waited. There was no movement and no sound, but the boy was convinced that there was someone else in the room. Unsheathing his katana, the boy held the blade in front of him at eye-level. He could see the entire room through the reflection cast on the blade. Overwhelming silence enveloped the room; even the slow, steady breaths of the boy could not be heard.

Kazuki's heart skipped a beat when he felt that someone, or something, was moving closer to where he was hiding. He saw nothing, and no one, in the blade's reflection, but he knew that he couldn't trust his eyes alone. Closing his eyes, the boy concentrated on the silence of the room, searching for any sound waves.

A haughty voice suddenly entered the boy's ears, saying, "What's the matter, Kid? Can't see me, can ya?"

Kazuki quickly opened his eyes to find a tall and lean, but muscular man standing in front of him. He had one hand on the tree, while the other was on the tsuka of the boy's katana. His black hair was somewhat short and spiked in front, and he had three golden rings in his left ear and two in his right. He was wearing a loose, white shirt that opened at an angle and had little red loops and knots to keep it closed; although quite a few of the loops were undone, revealing a good portion of his muscular chest. There was a thick, red sash tied around the man's waist, on top of a pair of dark grey pants that looked like the kind sailors wore. The pants were tucked into a pair of calf-height red boots.

The boy also noticed a strange symbol on the man's forehead. It wasn't burned or carved into his light brown skin, but rather the skin had been dyed black in the shape of this symbol. Kazuki had never seen anything like it before and didn't know what the weird symbol meant, but he didn't have time to wonder.

The man stared at the boy, grinning, his green eyes flickering along with the candles. "What brings a little squirt like ya here?"

Kazuki noticed that the man's grip has loosened from his tsuka, so the boy quickly knocked the man's hand away and pointed the blade at his throat.

"I take it ya don't like bein' called 'little squirt', huh, little squirt?"

The man smiled as he dodged Kazuki's initial thrust. A second attack immediately followed, but the man caught the boy's katana between his fingers, stopping the blade inches from his chest.

"I'll tell ya what," the man grinned and yanked the katana away from the boy with his fingers, "if ya can manage to land one scratch on me, I'll stop calling ya little squirt."

Kazuki glared at the man.

"Ready?" The man reached for his sword, which hung loosely from the red cloth sash around his hips. The handle, which looked to be metal wrapped in sharkskin, had a golden ring on the end of it. The hand guard was painted red with gold accents, and was shaped like a dragon's head with the blade protruding from the dragon's mouth. It glistened spectacularly in the candlelight. The blade seemed to be one-sided, and, judging from its shape, was probably weighted at the end for powerful swings; the blade was widest near the tip, gradually shrinking as it neared the handle, and it was curved slightly, like the boy's katana. The blade itself had the image of a red dragon carved into it.

Kazuki had never seen anything so beautiful…and deadly.

"Go," the man said with a grin as he tossed the boy's katana back to him.

Before Kazuki had a chance to strike, the man disappeared into the shadows of the room.

He's fast.

The boy scanned the dim room for any sign of the illusory man. Out of the corner of his eye, Kazuki saw the man rushing towards him. The boy jumped up and grabbed a hold of the red drapery, avoiding the man's powerful swing. The man quickly vanished again into the darkness.

Well, if my eyes can't track him…

Kazuki closed his eyes. Like a bat, the boy could hear the vibrations and 'see' any movement without using his eyes. It was a hard trick to use in the heat of a battle, because it required his complete concentration, but the boy only needed to use it for a few seconds in order to find his opponent.

Found him.

Kazuki swung himself up into the wooden rafters, using the red drapery, and ran swiftly towards the man. With his eyes now open, Kazuki saw the man try to avoid his stealthy attack, but the katana was faster.

Kazuki grinned. "Looks like I landed a scratch."

A small trail of blood appeared on the man's cheek.

"Not too bad, Kid."

Lashing back, the man repeatedly swung his red dragon sword at the boy, but Kazuki blocked every attack. After a slight pause, the man came at Kazuki twice as fast as before. The boy had to concentrate solely on defending himself in order to keep up with the man's speed. In a split second, the red dragon sword struck Kazuki's cheek; the same red trail appeared.

"An eye for an eye," the man said, grinning, as he jumped down from the rafters. Kazuki followed closely behind.

The boy suddenly felt a strange pressure in his chest, but he had no time to wonder what had caused it, since the man immediately turned, raised his sword, and darted towards the boy. This time, for some reason, the man seemed to move at a very slow pace, even though he was running at full speed.

That's strange.

The boy easily stepped out of the man's way, and, as he passed, Kazuki kicked the sword out of the man's hand. Catching the red dragon sword before it hit the ground, the boy thrust the large blade at its master's throat. The man stood perfectly still, staring at Kazuki.

"How does it feel to be defeated by this 'little squirt'?"

The man grinned. "I haven't been defeated yet."

Wha–

The boy was caught off guard; he hadn't seen the red cloth that was wrapped around the red dragon's head. The man pulled the cloth and his sword came flying back to him. He caught it, and then dashed behind Kazuki, putting his arm around the boy's neck.

"Don't underestimate me, Kid."

"A…Are you…Ammon?" It was hard for the boy to breathe, let alone speak. He struggled to get free from the man's chokehold, but to no avail.

The man started to laugh. Kazuki wasn't sure what was so funny.

"Kid, ya think *I'm* Ammon?"

This guy is good. If he's just one of Ammon's bodyguards, then…

"Ooo that looks nasty. And painful."

Kazuki suddenly felt a sharp pain in his shoulder. Biting his lip to keep from screaming, the boy shook his shoulders back and forth, trying to free himself from the man's grip, which had loosened slightly. A small *clank* of metal sounded as something hit the floor in front of him. Kazuki glanced down, only to find the small metal shard that had been lodged in his shoulder blade lying on the floor.

What the…Why did he help me?

The man released him and Kazuki quickly jumped away.

"If you're not Ammon, then who are you? His bodyguard?" The boy asked as he aimed his katana at the man, hoping that the man would keep his distance.

The man shrugged. "Somethin' like that, I guess." He slipped his forefinger into the middle of the metal ring on the end of the handle and swung his sword around in a circle at his side. "Well, it's more like I *have* t' be his bodyguard."

"Why do you *have* to?"

The man looked at the boy and grinned. "Ya sure ask a lot of questions don't ya, Kid?"

Kazuki frowned. "Stop treating me like a kid."

"How old are ya?"

The boy paused for a minute before deciding that it was harmless to answer the question. "Thirteen."

The man laughed. "Ya *are* a kid!" He looked at the boy, who was still frowning. "But…" he said with a smile, "instead of 'Kid', I'll call ya by yer name if ya tell me what it is."

The boy shook his head.

The man stopped spinning his sword around and shrugged. "Oh well, I tried."

"Red Dragon, you flea infested dirt bag!" A loud, deep voice carried throughout the room.

The boy could tell that someone was approaching on his left, so he quickly turned his body and guarded himself from that direction. He didn't feel the need to watch the man with the red dragon sword as closely, because, if he had wanted to, the man could have killed the boy by now.

An extremely portly man came into view. He was wearing a yellow kimono with a black phoenix design sewn on the front. His black hakama strained against his wide belly. There were also a few crumbs and food stains left over on his kimono, presumably from past meals. His dark hair was tied up in a bun on top of his head, and his feet were bare.

"What the festering hole is taking so long?! Can't you take care of one lowly kid?!" he barked, saliva spewing from his lips.

The man with the dragon sword scratched his head and smiled awkwardly at the large man. "Eh…sorry 'bout that."

So his name is Red Dragon…

"You're worthless! I don't know why Commander Ammon

didn't just have you hung in the first place."

Wait, that man isn't Ammon either? Ugh. I don't have time for this anymore. "Hey fatso, where's Ammon?"

"FATSO?! You're dead, Kid!" The portly man waddled over to Kazuki and swung his fists at the boy. He missed every time. "Stay still, you little spawn of a demon!"

"You *really* think I'm going to stay still and let you hit me?"

The portly man became even more enraged and tried to head-butt the boy. Kazuki jumped into the air, grabbed hold of the red cloth, swung himself up, and landed on the rafter beams above.

He'll be dead in one strike.

Holding his katana vertically out in front of him, the boy set his sights on the portly man's fat head. Soundlessly, Kazuki jumped down from the rafters and, with all of his might, drove the blade tip first into the fat man's head. There was a strange symphony of bone cracking, wet flesh, and gargled screams.

The boy felt a strange sense of satisfaction as he held the blade in place. Blood spewed from the fat man's head, covering his large body's radius and more with the red liquid. Somehow none of it had managed to sully the boy's kinagashi. Seconds ticked by before Kazuki yanked his sword out of the tattered flesh and shattered bone medley. He stared at the now lifeless body, still stuck in its pre-death position, admiring his work.

"Huh." Red Dragon slid his sword through the red sash at his side and sauntered over to the bloody corpse. He cocked his head to the side, put his hands on his hips, and said, "I think he looks better this way. Don't ya?"

Kazuki frowned at Red Dragon.

"What?"

"Wasn't he your comrade?" The boy asked in a disapproving tone.

Still staring at the once human remains, Red Dragon folded his arms over his chest and shook his head. "Nope."

"But he was working for Ammon," the boy stated.

"Yer point is?"

Kazuki pointed the tip of his soiled sword towards Red Dragon. "You are too."

Red Dragon tugged on one of the three small golden rings in his left ear. "It's like I said before kid, I wouldn't be workin' for him if I didn't have to."

Suddenly there was a strange expression on Red Dragon's face. It was frightening the way his eyes seemed to darken and the edges of his lips curled upwards. He quickly made his way to the staircase that the portly man had entered from, but Kazuki stopped him before he could ascend.

"Where do you think you're going?" the boy asked in an accusatory tone.

The eerie expression vanished as Red Dragon turned towards him and pointed towards the ceiling. "Up," he said innocently.

"Are you trying to run away from me?" The boy's katana was almost touching Red Dragon's throat.

"I'm not tryin'," the man grinned and added, "*yet.*" He put the tip of his finger on the edge of the boy's katana and gently pushed it away. Before Kazuki could react, Red Dragon was gone.

Tch. I forgot how fast that guy is.

Heading for the staircase in front of him, the boy didn't bother to put his katana away. There were still bits of the fat man stuck on the blade that the boy would have to scrape and clean off, but now was not the time for that.

Kazuki looked down at his left arm. The wrappings he had fastened earlier were now loose and covered in blood. The throwing knives must have sunk in deeper than the boy had thought. His arm was almost useless at this point, because he could barely move it without intense amounts of pain. Tightening his grip on the katana with his right hand, Kazuki began his ascent. As battered as he was, the boy was determined to continue on. He would grant the old man's revenge, even if it killed him.

Reaching the third floor, Kazuki glanced around for more opponents, but all he found was a sea of corpses. Red Dragon was nowhere to be seen.

This doesn't feel right. These corpses are fresh, but I didn't hear anything downstairs...

There was a low murmur of sound coming from somewhere down the hallway in front of the boy. He slowly advanced down the corridor, stepping over the countless corpses strewn about the path. Each body was headless, or mostly headless. To any normal child, it would be a nightmarish scene.

Kazuki continued down the hallway. *It sounds like something is cracking...what is that?* The boy paused outside of the last door on the left. Something was happening inside, but he didn't want to barge in without knowing what was going on first. More cracking sounds, some rattling, and...whimpering. Someone was being tortured, and the boy hoped it wasn't–

"Ya comin' in or what, Kid?"

Kazuki jumped when he heard Red Dragon's voice from behind the door. He quickly swung the door open, only to find a very muscular man chained to the wall, with what looked like fresh abrasions on his face and bare chest. He had a piece of cloth stuffed in his mouth and a trail of tears down his cheeks.

The boy simply stared.

"Pure payback, Kid. It's only fair, ya know?"

With the next crack, Kazuki snapped back to attention. The thin bamboo pole in Red Dragon's hand was dripping with the blood of the muscular man. A new strip of flesh opened up on his chest and he cried out.

"They did this to you?" the boy asked as he watched Red Dragon work the whip.

"Every day."

"Why would they do that to one of their own–"

CRACK.

"Ya just don't listen do ya, Kid?"

More whimpering.

"I'm not one of 'em. I never was, and I never will be." Red Dragon's eyes had a fire raging within them.

Kazuki could only stare. He knew there were cruel people in the world, because he had experienced their work first hand, but this…this was just…***lovely***. Kazuki jumped at the word that had just entered his mind. It wasn't his, but someone else's grotesque opinion.

"Hey Kid, why do ya look so pale? Ya did worse downstairs ya know."

He's right…I did mutilate that fat guy back there. I could have killed him without running my katana through his head. But...why did I?

"Kid?" Kazuki snapped to attention as Red Dragon waved his hand in front of the boy's face. "What's with ya? Ya have some kinda disease or somethin' that makes ya space out like that?"

The boy frowned. "No. You got some kind of disease that makes it so you can't talk properly?"

Red Dragon threw his head back and laughed. "So ya do have a sense of humor after all!"

As Red Dragon continued laughing, Kazuki glanced back over at the bloody, recently deceased man hanging from the chains. It wasn't the amount of blood, but the ripped, jagged flesh hanging from the now visible bone and muscle that made him feel nauseous.

"Come on Kid, let's get outta here."

Kazuki stared at Red Dragon's outstretched hand. "I don't get you. One minute you're fighting me, and the next you're helping me? Whose side are you on anyways?"

Red Dragon grinned. "I'm on my own side, as always."

The boy didn't want to trust the man, but he couldn't help himself. And, at this point, an ally would be useful. Ammon wasn't going to be as easy to defeat with only one working arm.

"Where is he?"

"Who? Oh, right, Ammon." Red Dragon had, at some point, grabbed the boy's katana and was now wiping it clean with a torn piece of cloth from one of the dead henchmen's clothes. "Well, he's probably on the next floor, since it's the top n' all, but–"

Kazuki abruptly grabbed his katana from the man.

"Wait just a–"

He sheathed his sword and ran out of the room, heading towards the stairway leading upwards. He did not stop to wait for Red Dragon, because he knew that the man would come after him. *Plus, the guy's so fast that he'll–*

"I said wait! Kids these days never listen, do they?" Red Dragon sighed as he appeared next to Kazuki, effortlessly keeping up with the boy's speed. "He's not gonna be easy to defeat ya know." When the boy didn't stop, Red Dragon sighed again and asked, "Why are ya so determined t' kill him anyways?"

The boy was silent. He didn't say anything until they reached the top floor and were standing in front of two large sliding doors.

"Revenge."

"Huh?"

Kazuki looked up at Red Dragon. "I'm killing him to get revenge."

"Did he kill yer family or somethin'?"

The boy looked away from him. "Something like that."

Red Dragon grinned. "All right, Kid. Whatever your reason is, I've got a score t' settle with him myself, so let's go."

He slid open the door in front of them and stepped inside. Kazuki followed.

Dressed in a purple, silk kimono that was adorned with a white serpent design, and a white hakama, a tall, thin man stood at the back of the room, gazing out of the windows before him. His long, white hair, which almost reached his hakama, was neatly bound together at his shoulders by a thick purple ribbon.

"It seems the wild beast has finally been tamed…How interesting," the man said as he turned around and stared at Red

Dragon. His almost translucent skin was a stark contrast to his deep red lips, which widened and twisted into a sinister grin.

This is Ammon? The boy shivered from the thought as a glaring pair of pale blue orbs slowly shifted their focus towards him. Kazuki wasn't afraid of death, but something about this man terrified him. And it had nothing to do with his foreign complexion.

Two objects suddenly slid out of Ammon's sleeves and into his hands. Before the boy could see what they were, Ammon had vanished and Kazuki abruptly felt cold steel against the right side of his neck. In a split second the feeling was gone, and instead the boy felt something trickle downward.

Ammon reappeared in the same spot as before. He was holding what looked to be a pair of kama, one in each hand.

"Aren't those farming tools?" Kazuki couldn't help but ask aloud. He had never seen the rice harvesting sickles used as weapons.

"Yeah, but instead of crops, he reaps souls," Red Dragon responded in a low voice.

The boy looked up at Red Dragon and was astonished to see a small trail of blood trickling down his neck too. *If Ammon's speed can match or even top Red Dragon's, then I'm going to have a hard time taking him down.* Kazuki forced his heartbeat to remain steady. Being scared wasn't going to help him fight.

"Mmm…Red Dragon, I think I've found someone who tastes even better than you do."

The boy watched, horrified, as Ammon stood there, licking the blood off of the blade that had just been at the boy's throat.

What. The. Festering. Hole.

"Kid!"

Kazuki tried to focus back on Red Dragon, but he couldn't look away from the horrid scene.

"Get back!"

Even if he wanted to move, the boy was frozen in place.

"Kid, I told ya– Damn!"

Suddenly Kazuki was on his back. Something wet splattered across his face. *Huh?* The boy used his sleeve to wipe the liquid from his face. He looked down at it and found…*blood. Is it mine? No, wait…*

Kazuki looked up. Red Dragon was standing over him. A flash of metal came from one of Ammon's kama that had sliced through part of Red Dragon's right shoulder. Blood was dripping off of the blade, splashing into the red pool on the floor.

Kazuki watched as Red Dragon blocked Ammon's other kama with his sword in his left hand, and, before Ammon could strike again, Red Dragon kicked the terrifying man so hard that he slammed into the wall, leaving a dent.

"Arse's stench, that hurt," Red Dragon breathed as he pulled the kama out of his shoulder and tossed it to the floor.

"Red…Dragon…" Kazuki was shaking as he tried to stand up.

"I told ya t' move, Kid," Red Dragon said as he looked back at the boy.

Kazuki was shaking so badly that, once he stood up, he had a hard time keeping himself upright. Red Dragon quickly grabbed the boy and ran him to the other side of the room. As Kazuki looked back to where he had just been standing, he saw that Ammon was there with both kama once again in hand, ready to strike.

"Snap outta it, Kid!" Red Dragon slapped the boy hard across the face.

Kazuki looked up at Red Dragon. He was sweating profusely, *probably from the pain*, and looked rather pale, *probably from blood loss*.

"I can't fight him *and* protect ya." Red Dragon took the red sash from his waste and wrapped it tightly around his bloody shoulder. "Look, I can't last much longer like this." He looked down at the boy and said, "If ya need time t' get it together, I can buy ya some, but ya have t' be quick about it. I'll need ya t' back me up soon, Kid. Oh, and watch out for those kama. Ammon can do some serious damage with those things, if ya know what I mean." Red Dragon pointed to his wounded shoulder.

Kazuki nodded.

With that, Red Dragon launched himself at Ammon, who seemed more than ready to greet him.

Kazuki stood watching the battle between the two speed masters. They were both moving so fast that it was hard for Kazuki to track their movements with his eyes. Closing them, the boy 'watched' the battle. Even though he was injured, Red Dragon was holding his own against the pair of kama and their wielder. The boy thought that Red Dragon would be able to defeat Ammon, since he seemed the more skilled of the two, but, as the boy watched, it became more apparent that Red Dragon's shoulder injury was costing him dearly; he was no longer using his right shoulder or arm, and his right side seemed to be his dominant one.

I need to move, I need to fight! I need to get revenge! But no matter what Kazuki told himself, his body wouldn't budge. All of the training he had done was for nothing. In the end, he was still just a child haunted by bloody memories. He was ashamed of himself.

You will move.

The boy's eyes popped open. *What was that?*

You WILL move.

Kazuki jumped. *There it is again! That voice…where is it coming from?* Somehow the boy's fear began to melt away, leaving only the thirst for blood and carnage behind. *This…feeling…*

Fight! Tear your opponent to shreds. Let me hear his screams. Let me taste his flesh and drink his blood!

The boy lost himself in a sort of trance. It was as if he were watching himself from inside his own body.

Red Dragon and Ammon ceased fighting and stared at Kazuki, whose aura had suddenly changed.

"It looks like a more exciting opponent has appeared...so, Red Dragon, if you will excuse me."

Ammon began to make his way towards the boy, who was slowly walking towards him. Red Dragon made a move as if he were about to pursue Ammon, but he suddenly stopped.

"I am thrilled that you have decided to fight me. Your blood is so nice, I want to taste more of it," the terrifying man said as he licked his lips.

"I'm going to cut out that damned tongue of yours," Kazuki managed to reply as his right hand slowly unsheathed his katana. He wasn't sure what was happening with his body – he felt like he was and also wasn't in control at the same time. But if it helped him kill Ammon, he didn't care. That bastard needed to die.

Ammon, impatient for carnage as he was, made the first move.

Kazuki was unaware of the danger of fighting Ammon at close-range, since he had never encountered anyone who fought with a pair of kama. As Ammon arced his right kama at the boy, Kazuki blocked the attack with his katana, but that was exactly what Ammon wanted. With impossible speed, the terrifying man stepped in and slashed the boy's torso with his left kama.

"Agh!" Kazuki yelped.

He then felt his feet propel his body backwards as Ammon moved in for another strike. Whatever was controlling the boy's body seemed to know what was coming next. As Ammon suddenly disappeared from view, Kazuki felt himself jump up and back. When he landed some feet away from where he had been, the boy saw that Ammon was there, crouched on the floor; he had attempted a sweeping attack at the boy's legs.

Kazuki exhaled a breath of relief, but it was too soon to relax. In the blink of an eye, Ammon was up and running towards the boy with his kama at the ready. Kazuki swung his katana at the incoming target, but Ammon spun effortlessly out of the way. As the terrifying man whirled around, his blades lashed out. Kazuki's body reacted by turning his hips and making a horizontal cut with his katana, which parried the kama.

Using the momentum of his whirling body, Ammon kicked his leg out and tripped Kazuki. As the boy fell, Ammon brought his kama downwards in an attempt to puncture the boy's torso, but Kazuki nimbly grabbed hold of Ammon's left arm with one hand and, with mysterious strength and balance, thrust his katana into Ammon's side with the other. The pain diverted Ammon's attention – and kama – only for a split second, but it was enough time for

Kazuki to roll out of his fall, stand up, and be ready for Ammon's next attack.

During his subsequent assault, the terrifying man slashed downwards with his left and horizontally with his right, making it impossible for the boy to block both. Kazuki dropped his sword to his left side and then swung it up towards his right side. His katana made contact with the horizontal kama first, deflecting its blade, but the kama from above bit into the boy's hand. Kazuki would have yelped from the pain if he had been in control of his body.

Wounds heal.

But they still HURT! Swinging up, towards the oncoming blade, was stupid!

The boy felt himself grin. His right leg kicked out with tremendous speed and strength, knocking Ammon to the ground a few feet away from where he had been. A dull *thump* followed as the kama that had been in Ammon's right hand fell to the tatami floor. His other remained embedded in Kazuki's hand, leaving the terrifying man weaponless.

The corners of Ammon's mouth nearly reached his ears. "Marvelous," he cackled, "You must be the real thing."

"No. I'm nothing compared to the man you tormented and killed." As he spoke, the boy noticed that his voice sounded colder and deeper than usual, but the words were his own.

"Ah, so that's why your swordsmanship seems familiar," Ammon replied, never losing his sinister grin or icy glare. "In that case, let's find out who can use that old corpse's technique the best," he cackled before disappearing all together. A split second later,

Ammon's voice resonated softly in the boy's ear, "Or did you fail to learn it?"

Kazuki spun around but the terrifying man wasn't there. Nor was the kama that had fallen to the floor.

A disembodied, maniacal laugh filled the room. "What a pitiful student!"

How did he learn–

Concentrate! You are in the midst of battle! It is not the time for explanations.

But he–

Be silent and take your revenge!

That final word flipped a switch in Kazuki's brain. The endless stream of questions ceased, his mind went blank, and his heart regained a slow, rhythmic beat. He took a deep breath, exhaled, closed his eyes, and then sheathed his katana.

"Giving up already," the disembodied voice asked with disdain. "You bring shame upon that old corpse."

Wait.

"That brilliance from before faded all too quickly." The disembodied voice sighed, "You're just a failure."

Wait.

"I don't have time for your kind."

NOW!

Kazuki unsheathed his sword with unearthly speed. He felt no resistance to his blade. Had his timing been wrong? The boy opened his eyes. There was no one before him. But to his left and right, Kazuki noticed the scattered silver hairs and the ripped purple garment – the pieces of which were beginning to darken due to the red liquid they were slowly absorbing.

Red Dragon whistled in approval. "That sure was somethin', Kid." He walked over to Kazuki and smirked. "I dunno how ya did it with this thing stuck in ya."

"Huh–OUCH!" The boy yelped as Red Dragon pulled out the kama that had been stuck in Kazuki's hand. Somehow the boy had forgotten about it.

"So what was that all about, Kid?" Red Dragon stared down at the boy, his arms crossed. He wasn't mad and he wasn't surprised, he was simply curious.

Kazuki shook his head. "I have no idea. But at least Ammon is dead now."

For a few minutes Red Dragon was silent, and so was Kazuki. They were both lost in thought.

After reaching seemingly endless dead-ends to his many questions, the boy shrugged, flicked the blood from his blade, and slid his katana back into its black lacquer saya.

"What's next?" The man asked, unexpectantly.

The boy looked up at Red Dragon, puzzled.

"Well, ya killed Ammon – bisected him is more like it – but what now?"

Kazuki thought about it for a bit. He had never considered what to do after he had killed Ammon. "I don't know."

Red Dragon laughed. "Kid, ya've really got t' start plannin' more into the future."

The boy glared up at Red Dragon. "My name Kazuki. *Not* 'Kid'."

"Ha ha. All right, all right. Kazuki it is," the man laughed. "Then ya can call me Hasunuma."

The boy nodded in response.

"Well, Kazuki, since ya've got nothing else planned, why not come with me? I'm plannin' on taking down the entire Hekigun army."

"Why?"

"They're a corrupt bunch of cowards, and I've got business with their leader." Hasunuma grinned at the boy. "C'mon, Kazuki, what do ya say?"

Go with him.

Why? It's none of my business–

It is your business. Who do you think burnt down your village and killed your people?

Kazuki was dumbfounded. The village was ravaged by outlaws…wasn't it? And what was that voice in his head?

"…Fine. I'll go with you."

"Good. Then let's get going." Hasunuma began to walk away, but Kazuki stopped him.

"What about your wound? Don't we need to–"

Hasunuma laughed. "Worry 'bout yer own wounds, Kid." He then unwrapped the red sash from his shoulder. The boy stared in amazement when he saw that the flesh had rejoined and the wound was almost closed. "I'm just fine on my own."

Hasunuma patted Kazuki on the head. His hand was quickly swatted away. Hasunuma laughed and started walking again, this time he was closely followed by Kazuki.

The boy had so many questions about himself, about Hasunuma, and about what happened to his village that he didn't know where to start. He could only hope that he would find some answers by assisting Hasunuma in his slaughter of the Hekigun.

"Let's get ya t' a doctor, Kid."

"Don't call me that."

Hasunuma led the boy all the way down to the harbor. Kazuki wasn't sure what kind of ship he had expected to see there, waiting for Hasunuma, but he was shocked when there was no ship at all.

"Um. You *did* say that you commanded a ship, right?" the boy asked skeptically. Maybe it hadn't been such a good idea to trust this 'Red Dragon' guy.

Hasunuma smiled. "Yeah, and she's a real beauty," he said as he pointed to a spot on the horizon.

Kazuki stared out at the sea, but it was hard to focus with the sun as bright as it was. After a few minutes, he could make out a dark, boat-shape figure. He would have felt relieved, except that as the ship approached, he realized that it was a *pirate* ship. The red colored sails were a dead giveaway, since only registered, legal ships were given the yellow or white sails, depending on the type of vessel.

As the ship drew closer, it was hard not to notice the figurehead, which was a large, intricately carved dragon's head painted with red and gold; the stern was made to look like a dragon's tail.

I guess that's why those guys called him 'Red Dragon.' Kazuki looked over at Hasunuma. *That and he's got a red dragon sword.*

"Here she is," Hasunuma said with a grin, "my pride and joy, the Ryujin."

The ship had barely docked before two people jumped off and

ran towards Hasunuma.

"Cap'n!" A large, muscular man with a full, dark beard cried out. He was wearing nothing save a pair of black, loose-fitting, knee-length shorts with what looked like a blacksmith's apron that hung around his right hip, and his short, black hair was kept off of his forehead by a red head wrap. His ample exposed skin was proof enough that he worked in the sun; most Tsukigen natives had light to medium brown skin, but this man's skin was a darker hue and it resembled a leather hide.

He reached Hasunuma first and slapped him hard across the back. "Ain't ya a sight fer sore eyes," he exclaimed joyfully, a huge grin appearing on his face.

Hasunuma winced. "Glad t' see you too, Ginza."

Despite his modest height, it was clear that the man, Ginza, had enormous strength.

"We were getting worried," said a deep voice with a strong foreign accent.

This was the second person to approach Hasunuma, and, in Kazuki's opinion, this man was the very image of a giant from the fables he heard as a child. The man was impossibly tall, unbelievably muscular, and had completely different coloring from Tsukigen natives. Instead of having black hair and brown eyes, like Ginza, this giant had blue eyes and ample reddish-golden hair, which was tied together in a neat, braided cluster that spilled over his red head wrap and fell past his shoulders. He also had a full, wild beard of the same reddish-gold hue.

Another big clue to the man's foreign ancestry was his skin; most of it was hidden by his long-sleeved, dark blue top and full-length, black pants, but his face, fingers, and feet displayed a delicate, pale pink, freckled complexion. The giant also sported armor on his shoulders and across his chest that Kazuki had never seen before. It seemed to be made of metal, but it was hard to tell without touching it.

As the boy stood staring at the two muscular men, his attention moved from their appearance to what they were saying. He overheard them apologizing profusely to Hasunuma for falling into a trap set by the Hekigun. Apparently Hasunuma had given himself up in order to free them, and that's how he ended up in Ammon's…care.

"Don't worry about it, I'm fine," Hasunuma said with a hearty laugh. "I'm just glad they kept their word and that you both are alright."

The giant shook his head. "No, they tried to kill us after they took you away, but Rize arrived just in time and we turned the tables on them."

"Hanzo an' I made sure t' kill 'em all," Ginza said with a grin as he bumped his forearm against the giant's in a chivalrous gesture.

Another man approached the group and bowed slightly, offering his apologies too. This one had a normal height, weight, and muscle mass – not scrawny, but not intimidating either. He had the typical Tsukigen black hair and brown eyes, and had lighter brown skin, similar to Hasunuma's and Kazuki's, which meant that he probably hailed from a village in the mountains. His hair was pulled back in a loose, short ponytail and, like the other two men, he also wore a red head wrap. He was dressed in full-length black pants and what looked to be a hunter's vest made from some sort of animal hide.

There was a pocket in the upper right side of the vest that held a short knife.

Hasunuma waved his hand in dismissal. "As I was tellin' these two, there's nothing to be sorry for, Rize."

"But…they branded you," the man with the hunter's vest, Rize, said with concern.

Hasunuma rubbed the mark on his forehead. "Yeah, they tried to burn it, but since my skin healed, they tattooed it instead," he explained.

Rize untied his red head wrap and offered it to Hasunuma.

"Thanks," Hasunuma said with a smile as he took the red cloth and tied it around his head, concealing the mark. "But it's not all bad news. We can cross Ammon and another Hekigun base off the list!"

The men surrounding him cheered and raised their fists in the air triumphantly until a high-pitched whistle suddenly interrupted them. The boy turned to see where it came from and was surprised to find a young man, with a rather feminine looking face and extremely baggy clothes, standing on the deck of the ship. His short, choppy hair was a deep red color, and his medium brown skin radiated a golden glow in the sunlight.

Hasunuma looked at the young man on deck and smiled. "I promise, I'm fine, Kohaku. Can ya go get Jun? There's someone I need t' introduce."

All eyes immediately focused on Kazuki. His heart began pounding in his chest.

"Ah, well, I guess I can have him meet Jun later," Hasunuma said with a shrug. "This here is Kazuki," he said, pointing at the boy. "He took out Ammon and now he's gonna join the crew."

Wait, I never said I'd be a pirate! The boy thought, but couldn't bring himself to say it out loud.

Two of the men suddenly rushed towards him.

"Lookie 'ere," Ginza said excitedly. "It's a little oni!"

"But he's so tiny," the giant, Hanzo, remarked as he put his hand on the boy's head. "Did he really defeat Ammon?"

"Size isn't everything, Hanzo," the man with the hunter's vest, Rize, chimed in. "That's pretty impressive for a kid though," he said as he smiled at Kazuki.

"I'm not a kid," Kazuki mumbled as he pushed the giant's hand off of his head.

"What did you say, Lad?" Hanzo asked with a grin.

"Oi, 'is name's 'Little Oni'," Ginza protested.

"I thought the captain said it was 'Kazuki'," Rize interjected.

Ginza shook his head. "Nope."

"Um, excuse me, but my name *is* Kazuki," the boy corrected.

The two overly muscular pirates looked at Kazuki and then burst into laughter.

"Why's that funny?" The boy asked, very confused.

Rize came over and put his hand on the boy's shoulder. "Sorry, Little Oni. You've gotten yourself mixed up with an odd crew," he said with a grin.

"That he did," Hasunuma said from the deck; he must have boarded the ship at some point while the men were investigating Kazuki. "But ya won't find better," he added with a grin. "The one standin' next t' ya is Rize, my helmsman. The big, shirtless guy is Ginza, our incomparable blacksmith, and the giant muscle-head is Hanzo."

A man with medium brown skin and shoulder-length black hair, that was messily tied back, appeared on deck next to Hasunuma. He was wearing a strange looking blue shirt that was held closed on one side by a series of little black loops and knots. His black pants covered his knees, while his calves and feet were hidden inside tall black boots cinched tight with a series of buckles. He wore a belt that housed a katana on his left hip and a large knife on his right. The man wasn't as tall as Hasunuma, or as muscular, but there was something about him that made him seem scarier.

"I'm Jun," he said flatly. "And if I ever catch you in my galley, I'll gut you," he added before walking away.

Okay...I'm avoiding that guy at all costs.

The young man with the feminine face appeared on deck again. He punched Hasunuma in the arm and whistled.

"Right, sorry," Hasunuma laughed. "And this here is Kohaku. She's in charge of wound care and gathering information, among other things."

Did he just say 'she'? The boy wondered as he stared at the person next to Hasunuma.

Kohaku smiled warmly and waved at the boy. Her emerald eyes sparkled.

Yeah, that's a girl. But then...why is she dressed like that?

"Now that introductions are out of the way, let's get underway," Hasunuma said as he waved the others on board.

"Wait, this is your entire crew?" The boy asked skeptically. As far as he knew, it took at least ten men to man a fishing vessel, and this pirate ship was at least four times the size of one of those.

Hasunuma nodded.

The boy was stunned. "There's no way. This has to be some kind of joke, right?"

Hasunuma shook his head. "No joke. But once you see us in action, you'll understand. Now come on, men, we've got Hekigun bastards t' hunt!"

The men boarding all yelled, with plenty of enthusiasm, "Aye, Cap'n!"

Kazuki wasn't sure what to make of the situation. He was about to get onto a strange ship with strange people that were considered violent outlaws. The boy hadn't had any first-hand experiences with pirates, but he had heard plenty of stories about them. Although, he had to admit that, while very strange, the people he just met did not seem as evil as the stories depicted them to be. In fact, the Hekigun seemed much worse to him, but the boy hadn't seen much of the world outside of his village and the old man's place, so he couldn't be certain.

Well, I don't really have anywhere else to go, Kazuki thought as he slowly made his way up the gangplank and onto the ship.

"Come on, Little Oni! Cap'n wants me t' show ya the ropes," Ginza called out. He seemed rather excited.

"Alright, coming," Kazuki replied after letting out a huge sigh. *But if they can't get this ship going, I'm leaving,* he thought, still skeptical that such a small crew could work such a huge ship.

But within five minutes, the boy was proven wrong. He stood awestruck as the Ryujin sailed out into open water. Granted, the sails were still set since the ship never fully docked, but Ginza had told Kazuki that Kohaku usually loosened and set the sails herself. On top of that, the strength and speed of both Hanzo and Ginza was astounding; they weighed anchor and subsequently controlled the masts single-handedly.

The boy heard Hasunuma call out to him from the helm. "Pretty impressive, huh, Kid?"

Kazuki couldn't believe what he was seeing. "Who the festering hole are you people?"

"Ya really don't know?" Hasunuma asked with a laugh. "I'm the Pirate King," he grinned. "Welcome aboard my ship, Kid."

Main Story

It's been three years and the kid hasn't changed much, the Pirate King thought to himself as he stared out over the sea. *He seems normal enough, until we go into battle…and then it's like he becomes someone else entirely. In the heat of battle, he's almost violence personified. The carnage he creates is…not something a kid should be capable of.* Hasunuma closed his eyes. *If I can't open up his heart, I may have to re-think this whole thing…*

The Pirate King's mind wandered and he began to remember scenes he wished he could forget. "Agh," he groaned aloud in frustration.

"Hasunuma!" The Pirate King turned around to see a grumpy Kazuki staring him in the face.

"Well, if it isn't Little Oni!" Hasunuma patted the boy, now a young man, on the head. "What can I do for ya?"

Kazuki narrowed his eyes and smacked the Pirate King's hand away. "You always treat me like a child. I hate it. I'm sixteen now and–"

"And ya want some respect, huh?"

Kazuki nodded.

The Pirate King laughed and said, "Well ya gotta earn it, Little Oni."

Kazuki rolled his eyes. "And how, exactly, can I earn your respect?" He asked, not expecting a reasonable answer.

A smile spread across the Pirate King's face. "When ya've regained yer heart. That's when I'll give ya some respect."

Kazuki stared at the Pirate King.

Hasunuma laughed again and put his hand on the kid's shoulder. "Ya have no idea what I'm talkin' about, do ya?"

The kid shook his head, making the hairtail on the right side of his head dance. When the time finally came for Kohaku to cut his hair, the kid had grumbled about it so much that she left a long section on the side and tied it together with a red string. The kid seemed to like the new look just fine.

In the Pirate King's eyes, Kohaku treated Kazuki like a little brother, which was rather amusing for him. In fact, all of the crewmates treated the kid as some sort of family member.

So then why is he still...

Hasunuma smiled and squeezed the kid's shoulder. "It's all right, you'll learn one day."

Kazuki furrowed his brow, but didn't say anything in response.

The Pirate King released the kid's shoulder and stood up from the crate he had been sitting on. The kid had grown taller since their first encounter, and now the top of his head reached Hasunuma's chin. Kazuki hadn't become particularly muscular, but he was effective enough on the battlefield and pulled his own weight on the ship.

"Cap'n, sir! The shore's in sight," Hanzo suddenly called out.

"Good work. Tell Rize I'll meet him at the helm in a minute," the Pirate King shouted back.

"Aye!"

The Pirate King turned back to Kazuki and asked, "Ya still liking life on the Ryujin? I was surprised at how fast ya got yer sea legs. Usually it takes mountain folks awhile to adjust."

The kid shrugged. "It's fine. I actually came from a fishing village, so I kinda knew what I was getting into when I signed on."

"Oh, is that right?" Hasunuma replied with a raised eyebrow. The kid never talked about his past, so this was a rare reveal. "So ya've been on ships before?"

The kid shook his head. "No, I left before I was old enough to join the excursions." Suddenly Kazuki's eyes widened as if he'd realized he'd said something he shouldn't have. Quickly looking towards the prow, he said, "She's a beautiful ship though."

The Pirate King smiled. It was obvious the kid was trying to change the subject, but Hasunuma didn't feel like teasing him this time. And he liked it when others complimented his lady.

"She sure is something, isn't she? Ya won't find any other ship like her. I've had this beauty since the day I became a pirate."

Most pirate ships are commandeered military or transport ships, but not the Ryujin; the Pirate King and his crew built her from the keel up.

"How *did* you become a pirate, Hasunuma?" The kid asked. And it wasn't the first time either.

The Pirate King didn't answer and instead headed towards the helm. There were quite a few pieces of his past that he would never reveal, but he also didn't feel like making up a story and maintaining the lies, so he remained silent.

"Captain," Rize nodded in acknowledgement as the Pirate King joined him at the helm. "We're close to the section of shoreline you asked me to find."

"Good work, Rize. According to the girls, this is the best way to get in without being seen."

The helmsman gave Hasunuma a disapproving look.

"Is it *my* fault that they have the best intelligence?" The Pirate King retorted.

Rize sighed. "I think you just like incurring Kohaku's wrath," he mumbled.

"Huh?"

"We'll be near enough to row ashore soon," Rize said loudly.

"Got it," the Pirate King said as he turned to walk away. But before he took a step, he remembered something and asked, "By the way, have you heard from Douglas yet?"

"Not yet, Captain. I'll let you know as soon as Ami returns," the helmsman replied.

That's odd, I thought he would be done by now…then again, maybe he is and he just forgot to report back. The Pirate King smiled. *Probably got distracted by Nia again.* "Thanks," he said to Rize, before making his way back to the main deck.

Why won't he talk about his past? The young man brooded as he stared at the vast expanse of water before him. How infinite it seemed, stretching farther than the eye could see. He felt that the ocean was as wide as the distance between himself and Hasunuma. Had three whole years of living and working with the Pirate King not been enough to earn his trust?

In that time, Kazuki had grown accustomed to the other crewmates. At first, he had a hard time getting used to Hanzo and Ginza. To him, they were both like the giants from the tales of old: stronger than gods, but dimwitted to the core. And it didn't help that they loved to pick on him. But now, Hanzo and Ginza seemed more like weird uncles to him.

Kazuki had learned early on that Ginza was very helpful when it came to maintaining weapons, since he had been a blacksmith before he met Hasunuma. In fact, when Ginza first saw Kazuki's katana, he became so excited and had begged Kazuki to let him see the sword. After he examined it, Ginza's reverence to the blade left Kazuki wondering about his katana's origins, but neither he nor Ginza had any answers.

Hanzo was still sort of a mystery to the young man, because the giant never mentioned anything about his past, and Kazuki didn't have the courage to ask. Plus, he figured that if Hasunuma wouldn't tell him anything, then Hanzo certainly wouldn't, since the giant was much less talkative.

Rize was more like an older brother; since he wasn't as old as Hanzo and Ginza, he gave off a relaxed vibe, and actually taught Kazuki useful things. Thanks to Rize, the young man learned how to read and write, how to properly tie all sorts of knots, how to 'read' the weather and the waves, what edible plants to look out for while on the mainland, and much more. His abundant practical knowledge came from years of being a hunter in a remote village in the mountains. When Kazuki had asked him why he left the mountains for the sea, Rize smiled and replied that he wanted to see and learn more about the world. Kazuki immediately labeled him as a knowledge addict.

Kohaku, on the other hand, was a bit different. It was only hard to get to know her because she couldn't speak. Her actions were kind, and her smile was comforting, but Kazuki still didn't know much about her. Well, other than her skills in battle and as a healer; those he could attest to. Kohaku often made her own salves and medicines, which were more effective than anything the young man had used before, and she showed Kazuki the basics of dressing wounds with cloth wraps. Apparently, she was also good at stitching wounds, but Kazuki hadn't witnessed that himself; Ginza liked to tell a story about a big scar on his leg, and how it had required Kohaku's sewing skills, but that had happened before Kazuki joined the crew.

And Jun was…terrifying. That hadn't changed. Kazuki had quickly learned that going to the galley meant risking your life, so the Ryujin's cook persisted in the 'unascertainable' category.

The young man sighed and shook his head. The biggest mystery of all remained the Pirate King. Well, both he and the weird voice that Kazuki heard during battles. That was another anomaly that required research to figure out, and it was clear that Kazuki would have to do the investigating himself.

"Hey, Kid, ya ready t' hit the next Hekigun base?" Hasunuma asked as he returned to the main deck.

"Sure. Where are we headed?" The young man asked, knowing that he would get a reply this time.

"A small village that's inland a ways, called Yamaōgi. The townspeople there are being kept as slaves." The Pirate King grinned, "What d'ya say we bring them a breath of fresh air?"

"All right. How long 'til we land?" Kazuki couldn't wait to get off of the ship. It had been two weeks since they last landed anywhere and he hated those long stints on the sea.

"About fifteen minutes. Prepare yourself for reconnaissance first," the Pirate King said before heading to his quarters.

Kazuki nodded. Recon wasn't the hardest part of the missions, but it was the most gut wrenching. Seeing all that the Hekigun army had done – or were doing – to the villages and their people was hard to take in; especially when you weren't allowed to take action, no matter how bad the situation got. It wasn't his favorite task, but the Pirate King's orders were absolute.

"'Ey, Little Oni!"

Kazuki turned around and saw Ginza standing there. "What is it?" The young man asked with a sigh.

"Did I ever tell ya the story 'bout how the Cap'n became the Pirate King? Ya really should hear it!" The blacksmith smiled and placed his huge hand on the young man's shoulder.

"Ginza, look, I've got to–" Kazuki tried to prevent the blacksmith from continuing on, but it was no use. Once Ginza started on a story, he wouldn't stop until he had finished telling it.

Standing in front of the young man, as if to prevent him from leaving, the blacksmith began to tell the story: "The cap'n's always been the best pirate 'round! But 'cause 'e's so young compared t' the other pirate cap'ns, no one gave 'em any respect."

Ugh. Here we go…

"So one day the cap'n interrupts one a' the pirate meetin's that's only fer the top pirate cap'ns. They were all shocked t' see the cap'n there, 'cause the meetin' place was secret, an' the traps they laid out shoulda gone off when the cap'n went by. So they asked the cap'n why 'e's there, an' the cap'n just laughs. Then 'e says, 'I'm the new Pirate King, haven't ya heard?' An' the other cap'ns get all red in the face an' start yellin' at the cap'n, but Cap'n just stood there with a smile on 'is face. Finally, the old Pirate King gets off 'is fat arse 'n challenges our cap'n t' a duel. The cap'n accepts an' defeats 'em before 'e can even draw 'is sword!

"With the cap'n's sword at 'is throat, the old Pirate King weeps like a baby 'bout not wantin' t' die. The cap'n says, 'It's either yer life, or the life a' yer entire crew.' The old Pirate King quickly gave the order t' kill 'is crew, an' suddenly there's a big explosion. When the pirate cap'ns look t' the sea, the old Pirate King's ship's up in flames and sinkin' fast. The cap'n says, 'Their life, fer yers.'

"Then a few a' the other cap'ns turn t' the cap'n an' start yellin' at 'im fer killin' all those people. The cap'n holds his hand up t' silence them, an' says, 'All in favor a' havin' their lives spared in return fer the lives of their crew, say 'aye'.' The rest a' the cap'ns, except the ones complainin', said 'aye.' Cap'n then tells me an' Hanzo t' hold the complainin' cap'ns t' the side. We did that an' then the cap'n kills all the ones who said 'aye' b'fore we can blink! 'E then turns t' the old Pirate King an' says, 'We are the cap'ns, our task's t' look over our crew. Never should a cap'n value 'is life over that of 'is mates. Without them, we are nothin'. Remember that.'

An' then the cap'n cut the old Pirate King's head off!" Ginza exclaimed with glee.

"That's all very fascinating, but isn't Hasunuma just a hypocrite? I mean, he killed the old Pirate King's men," Kazuki scoffed.

"Ey! I'm tellin' the story! Shut up an' listen would ya?!"

The young man sighed, resigned to his fate.

Ginza nodded. "Right then. Now, the other pirate cap'ns were mad about that too. They said that the cap'n was all talk an' killed the crew in cold blood. But what they didn't know was that the cap'n had talked t' the old Pirate King's crew earlier, an' they agreed that the old Pirate King wasn't fit t' be in charge. 'E then appointed the first mate as the new cap'n of the crew and gave 'em a new ship. What exploded was only the old Pirate King's ship an' not 'is crew. The cap'n just wanted t' see what kind a' man the old Pirate King was with 'is own eyes. The others he killed 'cause they were also bad cap'ns, wantin' t' keep their lives in return fer those a' their crew. The first mates a' those crews also became new cap'ns. When the other pirate cap'ns realized what the cap'n did, they all took their hats off in recognition of the cap'n as the new Pirate King. An' that's how our cap'n became King a' 'em all!" Ginza was all smiles at the end, laughing largely and proudly.

Kazuki wasn't sure he fully believed that story, but he wasn't going to sit around and argue with the blacksmith. "How nice. Now can I please be left alone to prepare for the recon mission?"

"Fine, fine. Later, Little Oni!" Ginza lumbered back to his post. It was his turn to mop the deck, so any distraction he could find, he did.

Kazuki shook his head and sighed. Life on a pirate ship, let alone on the *Pirate King's* ship, was not an easy one. It was constant backbreaking work keeping the ship in top condition, not to mention all of the labor involved with battles against the Hekigun and their supply ships. Although, the young man *did* appreciate the fact that there was an unspoken rule to never fight on the sea; if there was a fight, the two ships would head to shore and battle it out there. Apparently, ships were too precious to risk losing in a battle on the sea.

Even with all the work, however, Kazuki had to admit that life on the Ryujin had its perks. They got three meals a day, their own rooms, and the crew wasn't all that bad – that is, as long as they didn't drink too much ale. Plus, they each got their fair share of whatever treasures they plundered from the Hekigun. Kazuki had his own stash of gold and jewels that he could use to trade with vendors when they went into the larger towns.

"Ahh!" Kazuki jumped. He had suddenly heard a high-pitched whistle in his ear. "Kohaku! How many times do I have to tell you not to do that to me?!" He scolded.

The sole female member of the Ryujin just smiled back at him. She pointed towards the helm, where Hasunuma was now standing, and then climbed back up the main mast to the crow's nest. She was often up there, on the lookout for other ships and distant shores.

I wonder what the view is like from up there…

Kazuki sighed and made his way to the helm. As he reached the top step, he asked, "Yes, Captain?" The young man hated addressing Hasunuma as such, but it was one of the ship's steadfast rules.

"We're dropping anchor. Make the final preparations," the Pirate King stated.

"Yes, Sir!" Kazuki acknowledged before heading straight for the supply room. He grabbed two satchels, one for him and one for Hasunuma, each with a week's supply of food, water, and some emergency medical equipment. The young man made it back to the deck as Hanzo was dropping the tender into the water below.

Hasunuma was already halfway down the rope ladder when Kazuki began to descend. "Ya ready for this, Little Oni? This one's going t' be tough," the Pirate King said as he stepped into the small boat.

"Yeah," Kazuki replied as he reached the tender. "Here," he said, handing one of the satchels he had grabbed to Hasunuma. Then the young man sat on the middle bench and grabbed one of the oars.

Hasunuma grinned and took a seat next to Kazuki. "Here we go," he exclaimed as he grabbed another oar and slid it into the water.

According to Rize's knowledgeable explanation, Yamaōgi is a small village on the Western side of the mainland. It's a fairly difficult village to get to, due to the fact that it's further inland and is surrounded on three sides by a large mountain range. The Hekigun army has apparently been running it like a slave colony for a while, and they've gotten away with it because of Yamaōgi's remote location.

Although the Hekigun are a bunch of liars and murderers, most people don't know that, because they keep their bloodiest and dirtiest operations out of the public eye. That, or they blame their misdeeds on the pirates. So it's difficult to find information when it comes to where the Hekigun are actually operating.

The only way Hasunuma finds out about these locations is

through his intelligence network. Which, in Kazuki's mind, consisted of either Kohaku or Hasunuma going into town, or mysterious messages brought onto the ship by Ami, Rize's falcon.

Well, he is the Pirate King, so there've got to be other pirates working under him...actually, now that I think about it, I haven't seen any other pirates since I joined his crew. Why is that?

When Kazuki and Hasunuma reached the shore, which was a pretty, sandy beach with dunes and reeds, they disembarked and pulled the tender away from the water. Since they didn't know how long they would be ashore, Kazuki got out a stake from his bag, drove it into the ground, and then tied one end of a rope around it – the other end was tied to the tender.

As soon as the small boat was secured, Hasunuma headed straight for the thick line of trees that edged the beach. The shade was much appreciated, but the summer air was hot and stagnant inside the dense forest. Kazuki had wanted to leave the ship, but now he longed for the cool sea breeze.

An army of cicadas called loudly from the trees, which the young man found oddly pleasant and annoying at the same time. Hasunuma hadn't spoken a word since they left the Ryujin, which wasn't completely unexpected, but it only made Kazuki more nervous; when Hasunuma was quiet, that meant there was something really bad going on.

In the shadows of the mountains, about five miles in from the beach, the Pirate King suddenly stopped. "Here's a good spot t' hide out," he said as he pointed to a small opening between some rocks nearby. "It's just big enough for us t' fit through, but it's not too noticeable from the outside."

Kazuki followed Hasunuma into the opening, a found himself in a cave that was bigger than it seemed from the outside. Not much light came through the opening, but Kazuki could sense how large the space was, and he could stand upright without hitting his head. There didn't seem to be any other openings, or at least none that could fit adult humans.

"If anything happens, we come back here," Hasunuma instructed. "Yamaōgi is only another mile or so in, and since we're right on the edge of the mountains, the terrain shouldn't be too hard t' navigate."

Before heading out, they took a quick water break and chewed on a few dried squid bits. Kazuki took the opportunity to ask Hasunuma a question.

"As the Pirate King, do you have command of all of the pirates in Tsukigen?"

Hasunuma laughed. "That's random, but yeah, technically I do."

"So then why don't you send some of them out to do this kinda stuff?" The young man asked in earnest. It didn't make sense to him that the King of pirates would be out doing this kind of work.

"Because I'm the *Pirate* King, not an Emperor or military leader. I command the pirate code – rules that pirates have t' obey – not an army," Hasunuma clarified. "And while there are some who fight the Hekigun with me, they do so because that's what they *choose* t' do."

"I guess that makes sense," the young man said slowly, "but then where are these pirates who want to help?"

"Off on assignments," Hasunuma replied. "There's a lot t' be done, Little Oni, which is why I've broken them off into groups and given them tasks t' complete. And speaking of, it's time t' get going," he added as he hastily shoved his water container back in his pack.

Kazuki followed suit and the two of them exited the hideout, leaving their packs behind. As they headed north, into the valley at the center of the crescent of mountains, they were very careful not to leave any trace of their movements behind them so that no one could locate their temporary base. The old man may have taught Kazuki how to fake invisibility, but Hasunuma had shown him how to make it real; the young man doubted that even expert ninja could follow the Pirate King's trail.

Suddenly Hasunuma stopped. "Someone's here," he whispered.

Kazuki looked around him, but he didn't see anyone. Closing his eyes, he heard a faint humming sound coming from the right.

"Heads!" Kazuki shouted as he pushed Hasunuma to the ground.

An oversized shuriken came whizzing through the trees. Hitting nothing, it flew off in an arc and disappeared.

Looking in the direction of the shuriken's origin, Kazuki took off to find the source. What he happened upon was not what he had expected; a mass grave of fresh bodies, all young men, hacked to pieces with what Kazuki could only assume was the oversized shuriken. The perpetrator was nowhere to be seen.

"Festering hole! It looks like we're too late," Hasunuma cursed as he caught up to Kazuki and saw the mess. "The village doesn't have much longer. This is one of the final steps the Hekigun take before they completely destroy a village."

"What do you mean 'one' of the final steps?"

Hasunuma's face darkened. "We need t' hurry. The women and

children are in grave danger."

Not wasting any more time, the two men raced towards the village.

"Remember, Little Oni, no matter what happens *do NOT* move unless I command it. Am I clear?"

Kazuki was speechless at Hasunuma's tone. He had never heard him sound so serious before. The Pirate King was always joking around and laughing, even in the face of danger, so why was he suddenly so serious?

"Kazuki!"

"Y-Yes!" The young man immediately answered.

"Good. Now hurry!" Hasunuma doubled his pace and Kazuki fell a ways behind. No matter how hard he trained, Kazuki could never match Hasunuma's speed.

It wasn't long before he caught sight of the Pirate King again, but Kazuki stopped dead in his tracks. Hasunuma was crouched behind a row of bushes, with his hand held out in back signaling Kazuki to stop. Slowly approaching the Pirate King, Kazuki crouched down and peered over the bushes.

"We made it just in time," the Pirate King whispered.

The village was small and quaint, only large enough for a few hundred people. From where Hasunuma and Kazuki were hiding, they could see the town square where the villagers would have their daily market. But not today. Instead, the women of the village were grouped together on one side and the children on the other. While the children screamed for their mothers, the women called back trying to calm the children down, telling them it would be all right.

The soldiers guarding the women started to cut at their clothes with their swords, calling them whores and worse while they went. The women held back tears as they tried to appear strong in front of their adversaries. One of the women spat at a soldier near her, and he grabbed her by her hair and threw her to the ground. He began tearing at her clothing, grabbing her while she screamed in protest.

Suddenly a small rock hit the soldier in the head. He angrily looked up to see who had thrown it. A small boy, who couldn't be more than six years old, stood with tears in his angry eyes and yelled, "Don't you touch my mommy, you monster!"

Kazuki's stomach dropped. The child reminded him of his past.

The angry soldier got up and headed towards the boy, his sword unsheathed. The boy stood, immobilized with terror, as the soldier loomed over him.

"You think that was brave, boy? Well you're *dead* wrong. I'm going to slice you up into little pieces and then I'll rape your mother until she dies from it." The soldier grinned and raised his sword. He swung down with all of his might and–

"No!" Kazuki yelled as he blocked the soldier's sword with his own.

Before the soldier could react, Kazuki swung his sword and sliced the soldier in half. Rage filling his mind, Kazuki cut down soldier after soldier. Unrelenting and ruthless, he sliced through each one, armed or not. The women screamed in terror and grabbed the children, running off into the forest. Just as he thought he killed the last one, Kazuki suddenly collapsed. There was a sharp pain in his back and he couldn't move.

"Hehehe. You're a little trouble maker aren't you?" A large, muscular man, resembling Ginza in form, approached Kazuki, grinning from ear to ear. "It seems you've killed all of my minions. Oh well, I can just make new ones at the next village."

"What are you, ugh, talking about?" Kazuki stood up slowly and grabbed onto the metal piece sticking out of his back. Using all of his strength, he managed to pull the piece out. It was extremely painful, and it took every ounce of willpower that Kazuki had to keep himself conscious. When he looked down at his hand, he found he was clasping an oversized shuriken that was dripping with his own blood.

"Oh, ho. You didn't know? All of those soldiers were men from this village that I made into my minions. And you slaughtered them all! Ahahaha!" The man laughed maniacally.

Kazuki froze. "But then, why did they…"

"Try and rape the women? Because I hypnotized them, of course! There's no way that they would work for me otherwise, you know." The man continued laughing.

"And the young men you massacred?"

"Oh, you saw that did you? Young men are much harder to control than older ones. Since they wouldn't listen, they died," the man said, as if it were a fact of life.

Kazuki shook with anger. "You've toyed with people long enough!" He threw the oversized shuriken to the ground and charged towards the large man, sword drawn. Just before his blade tasted flesh, it was stopped; an oversized shuriken blocked its path.

"What the – how did you get that back?" The young man asked, astonished.

The man laughed and replied, "Because that one isn't mine."

What?! Kazuki felt another sharp pain, this time in his leg.

"Agh!" As he fell to one knee, the young man drove his katana into the ground before him in order to steady himself.

"My shuriken has tasted your blood twice now, young one. It won't stop until it consumes the rest of you!" Another large man appeared from the shadows. He looked exactly like the other man that Kazuki had attacked. "Ha ha ha! You seem confused, young one! Well, you should be! We are the twin murderers, Yanchi and Yenchi," the man bellowed.

"Yanchi! I was going to finish him off!" The man standing in front of Kazuki angrily growled. "Go find your own prey!"

"But Brother, *I* want to kill him! He seems like fun," the other man replied.

As the two argued, Kazuki pulled the oversized shuriken out of his leg and limped away from the two brothers.

"Oh no you don't, young one!" Yanchi charged after Kazuki.

Off balance from his leg wound, Kazuki stumbled and fell over. Just as Yanchi was about to draw Kazuki's blood for the third time, a red dragon appeared and blocked the oversized shuriken.

"Hasunuma!" Kazuki yelled in surprise and relief. "Where have you–"

One look from the Pirate King and Kazuki fell silent. He was mad, *really* mad. Kazuki had never seen him like this before. It scared him.

"Oh, ho! Another play thing!" Yanchi exclaimed. "This one looks much more exciting! I'll take this one instead, Yenchi."

"No," Hasunuma growled, "I will fight you both."

Before more could be said, the Pirate King pushed Yanchi back with enough force to cause the man to stumble. He then raced forward and slashed at Yanchi, who barely stopped the red dragon from tasting his flesh.

"This one is made of tougher stuff!" Yanchi said as he struggled to defend himself against Hasunuma. The Pirate King mercilessly swung his sword at the man, over and over again. Without the protection of the oversized shuriken, Yanchi would have been hacked into hundreds of little pieces.

"Ha! If you can't do it yourself, I'll have to do it for you!" Yenchi exclaimed as he began running towards the duelers. He must have thought that a quick attack from a third party would knock the Pirate King off his feet, but he underestimated the Pirate King's strength and speed.

Yenchi's shuriken left his hand and sped towards Hasunuma's legs. An inch before the shuriken met its mark it was stopped in its tracks by the Pirate King's bare hand. The Pirate King now held the shuriken in his right hand, while still attacking Yanchi with the sword in his left. In an instant, Hasunuma flung the shuriken back at its owner.

"Fiery mountain gods!" Yenchi cursed, looking rather confused as he pulled his own shuriken out of his left shoulder.

"I told you he was stronger than that young boy, Brother," Yanchi laughed to himself. "Perhaps we should team up on this one?"

When Kazuki heard this, he pulled himself off the ground and tried to limp over to Hasunuma to help him, but the Pirate King wouldn't have it.

"You will stay right there, or I will make it so you can't move at all," he growled.

Kazuki got the message. He stumbled back a ways and sat down with his back against one of the village houses. The young man was so terrified of Hasunuma's anger that he didn't dare move again.

"He thinks he can handle us alone, Yanchi! Shall we prove him wrong?" Yenchi grinned with excitement.

"Let's!" Yanchi exclaimed and then jumped back from the Pirate King.

Hasunuma stood still. Kazuki couldn't believe that he was about to take on both of these men by himself. Yes, Hasunuma was a good fighter, but these guys were also very skilled.

"Bring it," the Pirate King growled.

Both brothers attacked Hasunuma simultaneously, slashing their oversized shuriken at him. The Pirate King blocked and dodged them with ease. The brothers were obviously becoming frustrated with the way the battle was going, and suddenly stopped their attacks. Yenchi looked at Yanchi and gave him a slight nod. Yanchi acknowledged his brother's signal and melted into a dark pool on the ground. Kazuki was so shocked that he couldn't speak, and instead watched helplessly as the dark pool merged into Hasunuma's shadow.

"All right, it looks like normal attacks won't work on you, so we'll play the hard way." Yenchi grumbled.

He resumed his attack on Hasunuma, his shuriken still failing to come in contact with the Pirate King. Hasunuma pushed back and began to force Yenchi into a defensive mode.

"You really are stronger than you look," Yenchi grunted, "but that won't help you for long!"

Just as Yenchi blocked the red dragon again, Yanchi re-appeared behind the Pirate King and grabbed him. His arms now forced still,

Hasunuma glared at the man in front of him.

"Ha ha ha! You see?! I told you we'd play the hard way!" Yenchi raised his shuriken to strike Hasunuma.

"Heh. You think your low-grade tactics will work against me?" Hasunuma grinned. Another Hasunuma suddenly appeared behind Yanchi and slashed his back with a duplicate red dragon sword. As Yanchi released Hasunuma from his grasp, the Pirate King leapt forward and sliced Yenchi across his stomach. "Think again, you idiots!"

Kazuki was as dumbfounded as the brothers. *TWO Hasunumas?!*

Without giving them time to register what was going on, both Pirate Kings attacked the brothers. With a deep cut in his back, Yanchi was now slower and could barely block all of Hasunuma's attacks. Falling to the ground, red lines appeared all over Yanchi's body.

"Yanchi!" Yenchi yelled, as he too fell to the ground with wounds all over his body. He glared at Hasunuma, now the only Hasunuma, and spat. "You may have defeated us, but the Hekigun will hunt you down and skin you alive for what you've done!"

Hasunuma grinned. "I'll be waiting for them." As the Pirate King sheathed his sword, the brothers fell to pieces.

Kazuki was stunned. In the three years of battling alongside Hasunuma, the young man had never seen him use that technique before. Then again, it's not like he was watching from the sidelines during those battles.

The Pirate King turned away from the mess he had made of the brothers and headed towards where Kazuki was sitting. He roughly grabbed the young man by his shirt and yanked him up off of the ground.

"By the gods, WHAT did I tell you?!" He yelled as he head-butted Kazuki hard. "I gave you strict orders *NOT* to move!" The Pirate King released the young man, who then fell to the ground, rubbing his forehead. "Do you ever stop and think before acting, Kazuki?!"

Hasunuma glared at the young man, who was now obviously shaking with fear. The Pirate King let out a huge sigh and squatted in front of Kazuki.

"Look, Kid, there's a reason why I told ya t' stay put. First ya gotta fully observe what's goin' on around ya. Otherwise ya get caught in a situation like this one where ya make a rash decision, regret it later, and then almost get killed fer not knowin' how many enemies there are."

Kazuki did his best to look Hasunuma in the eye. The Pirate King seemed to be back to his normal self, but the young man was still a bit fearful. "But…that boy was about to be killed, and those women were about to be ravaged by those soldiers," he mumbled.

Hasunuma nodded. "Yes, I know, and as much as it sucks sometimes ya gotta sit tight through some tough situations. I told ya this one wasn't goin' to be easy."

Kazuki was shocked. "You mean you would have watched that boy die, and let those women be-"

"No, that's not what I'm sayin'," Hasunuma sighed deeply again and scratched his head. "It's hard t' explain."

"Well explain it. I can't understand you at all!"

"Kid, I-"

"No! I can't believe that you would have let that boy die!"

"I said that's not what I would've done!"

"Then what *would* you have done?!" Kazuki's eyes were full of rage. He couldn't believe how cold Hasunuma was.

The Pirate King closed his eyes for a moment. When he opened them, they seemed much softer than before. "I probably would've sent out my doppelganger to save the boy, but not to attack the soldiers. Then I would've used the opportunity to talk to the soldiers and villagers to hear what was really going on. And then, if anything happened, my doppelganger would be the one in danger, not you or myself."

Kazuki's anger melted away, leaving only shame behind. How could he have doubted Hasunuma? After traveling and fighting with him for three years, he should know better than to think that Hasunuma would be cruel towards women or children.

"I'm…sorry. I dunno what came over me. I just get so angry sometimes and…yeah, I'm sorry."

The Pirate King reached over and ruffled the young man's hair. "It's all right, Kid. Ya don't have as much experience as I do when it comes t' this kinda stuff, so it's understandable that you'd be upset." He smiled, "Plus, yer still just a kid, and kids act irrationally and emotionally." Hasunuma then broke into laughter once he saw Kazuki's face react to that last comment.

"Yeah well at least I can speak normally without having to get angry to do it," Kazuki countered.

Hasunuma raised his eyebrow at the young man's comment.

"You spoke without that fake pirate accent when you were mad," the young man explained.

The Pirate King began to laugh again, "Hah! I can't hide anything from ya, Little Oni! So sharp and observant…if ya spent as much energy focusing on yer enemy as ya do on me, ya'd be a much better warrior! Ahaha!"

Kazuki opened his mouth to retort, but he was interrupted by a sudden high-pitched whistle. Before either man knew what was happening, there was a flash of light and burst of heat. A woman with short, red hair, wearing ill-fitting men's clothing, was now standing before them with her back facing them.

"Kohaku? Why are you here? And what was that?" The young man asked.

She didn't look back, but whistled a few short notes.

"Kohaku's always near, and she just shielded us from an attack." Hasunuma explained. "Someone else is here."

Before long a young man came into view. He looked to be about the same age as Kazuki, and had almost the same build, but his coloring was completely different. Instead of black hair he had white, instead of brown eyes he had blue, and instead of light brown skin his was as white as snow. And his aura was absolutely demonic.

"Shinigami-sama, I presume?" The strange young man asked in a monotone voice.

"Who are you?" Hasunuma replied.

"I wasn't talking to *you*." The strange young man hissed. He stared at Kazuki, who wore a confused expression. "Hmph. I guess I'm talking to the wrong side of you."

He began to walk towards the confused young man, when a kusarigama suddenly flew towards him and nicked his right ear. The strange young man paused and slowly felt his ear. When he pulled his hand away, there was some blood on it.

"That's odd. I haven't seen my own blood in a while. I'll have to congratulate you, girl."

Before Hasunuma or Kazuki could react, the strange young man had Kohaku in a chokehold with his unsheathed katana held high above her head, ready to strike.

"No!" Hasunuma yelled and quickly stabbed the strange young man's arm, freeing Kohaku. He grabbed her and carried her off a ways, putting some distance between them and the strange young man.

"More blood. Your speed is quite impressive for a human," the strange man nodded. "What is your name?"

"Isn't it customary t' give your own name first?" The Pirate King calmly replied.

"Ah, yes. Where are my manners? I am Eiri," the strange young man said.

"And I'm the Pirate King."

"Hmm. I've heard of you…some refer to you as the Red Dragon, am I correct?"

Hasunuma nodded.

"I see. Most impressive." Eiri turned his attention back to Kazuki. "Unfortunately, Red Dragon, I cannot play with you today. My mission lies elsewhere."

He began walking towards Kazuki again. This time, Hasunuma made a move to stop Eiri, but Kazuki held up his hand signaling him to stay put.

"Now, Shinigami-sama, if you won't appear on your own I'm going to have to damage your body until you do."

"What are you talking about?" Kazuki asked.

Eiri sighed. "Have it your way."

Faster than the eye could see, Eiri ran towards Kazuki. He held his katana low by his side and in both hands. Kazuki knew what that meant: an upward angle strike. Weakened and bleeding from his encounter with the brothers, Kazuki did his best to counter Eiri's attack.

When their katana met, Kazuki heard a familiar voice.

I know this sword. He he he. This will be entertaining!

Sparks flew from both katana as they met again and again. Kazuki was struggling. *I won't last much longer like this. Eiri is too fast and strong, I can't keep up!*

Suddenly Kazuki saw Eiri's katana coming at him in slow motion. The same thing had happened to him a few times before. He didn't know why everything suddenly slowed down, but it gave him the chance he needed. Kazuki's katana slashed across Eiri's chest. Blood, once again, had been drawn from the strange young man.

"Oh, are you finally awake Shinigami-sama?" Eiri asked with hint of excitement in his voice.

"Who is this 'Shinigami-sama'? I'm Kazuki."

The strange young man sighed. "Fine then, Kazuki, I will show you something interesting."

Eiri closed his eyes and was still. The air grew cold, the sky darkened, and Eiri's vast energy manifested around him, swirling like a cyclone. There was an uneasy feeling gathering in Kazuki's stomach. It was as if pure evil was about to appear before him. Suddenly the swirling energy disappeared, but the air was still cold as ice and the sky was as dark as a storm.

Eiri opened his eyes, his black eyes, and grinned. "Ah, I've found you at last, Shinigami-sama! Strange that your aura is quite calm…how unlike you."

Kazuki struggled to find his voice. This creature was not the same Eiri as before, and its presence chilled him to the bone. "I already told you, I'm *not* this 'Shinigami-sama'! I've never even heard of him," he reiterated.

The black eyed Eiri laughed a demonic laugh. "I figured you wouldn't come out so easily. Fine. Then maybe I'll explain a few details to your host?" He grinned.

Kazuki's body felt strange.

"Do you know what Shinigami-sama means? It means 'god of death'."

Images of blood and gore began flashing through Kazuki's mind; images of battles that he had fought in and people that he had brutally killed.

"Do you know who that title belongs to?"

Kazuki clutched his head. It felt like it was about to split open. He screamed from the pain and promptly fell unconscious.

Hasunuma was watching the whole thing happen from a short distance away. He wanted to run over and shield Kazuki, but he knew that would be a grave mistake. Kohaku was lying on the ground before him, unconscious; Eiri had nearly choked the life out of her. He couldn't leave Kohaku unprotected.

By the gods, what is going on? Hasunuma hadn't even felt Eiri's presence, let alone noticed the attack headed for him and Kazuki. And now the feeling coming from the strange kid was one of pure malice...This new enemy was trouble.

"Oh? Have I said too much?" Black-eyed Eiri grabbed Kazuki's hair and lifted his head from the ground. "Unconscious? That's not fair, Shinigami-sama, now I can't torture him to make you come out." He paused for a moment. "Hmm. Well I suppose I could just hack this body to pieces instead."

In an instant, black-eyed Eiri began doing just that. His movements were so fast that a normal person would simply see cuts appearing on Kazuki's body with no apparent source. Hasunuma's eyes were trained, so he saw each and every slice as it happened. The Pirate King couldn't stand to watch any longer. He got up and unsheathed his red dragon sword, but as he took one step towards Kazuki, his body froze.

"Stay out of this, Pirate."

Hasunuma's eyes widened. Kazuki's hand was around black-eyed Eiri's katana, stopping it in mid-air. The young man's eyes were staring straight at the Pirate King; they had turned black as well.

That's not Kazuki's voice. The voice Hasunuma heard was deeper and rougher than Kazuki's voice, but it was coming out of the kid's mouth.

"So you've finally shown yourself, Shinigami-sama! I'm so glad. Now I can kill you and take the title of Demon King for myself!" Black-eyed Eiri laughed maniacally.

Hasunuma was even more confused now. *Demon King? What the festering hole is he talking about?*

"I will explain everything later, Pirate, so stay back and shut up." The black-eyed Kazuki stood and turned his gaze to black-eyed Eiri. **"You wanted me, Second, so here I am."**

"I won't be named Second for much longer! I'll kill you and become number one, the King of all demons!"

Black-eyed Kazuki grinned a horrible grin. **"You are welcome to try!"** In an instant he was behind Second. His katana scraped Second's neck before black-eyed Eiri jumped away.

"As impatient as ever, Demon King," Second smiled, "but this is the first time you've fully awakened in your host body. You won't be able to keep control of it for long."

"You will be dead by the time that happens."

Hasunuma watched as the demons fought. Their speed and strength was far beyond anything he had ever seen, and their aura was frightening enough to make a grown man throw up. *They truly are demons.*

The Pirate King returned to Kohaku's side and sat down. After learning that the Demon King had been hiding out in Kazuki's body, the kid's actions made a lot more sense. All of the times that Kazuki brutally killed soldiers and rampaged through Hekigun fortresses – that was nothing a human could do. It was especially eerie, because it had never seemed like the young man was mentally present while he was slaughtering the soldiers. The Demon King must have been causing all of that to happen.

Hasunuma clenched his jaw and pounded the ground with his fist. There was nothing he could do to help Kazuki at this point, but he was determined to find a way to free the kid from the demon inside of him.

"Tired already, Second? I thought you were going to kill me and take my name?"

The Demon King smiled his wretched smile as he looked down at the demon lying on the ground in front of him. Blood gushed from many wounds on Second's – on black-eyed Eiri's body. He could barely breathe, let alone speak. Yet the wounds that had once covered Kazuki's body were beginning to close. How powerful was this Demon King?

"I see. In that case, you should DIE!" Just as the Demon King was about to deliver the final blow, his eyes widened and he stabbed his katana into the ground.

"Looks like…your time is…up…Demon…King." Second forced the words out of black-eyed Eiri's mouth. He somehow managed to pick himself up and slink away from the Demon King. "We will…meet…again."

In the blink of an eye, black-eyed Eiri vanished. But Hasunuma didn't have time to wonder where he went. Something strange was happening to Kazuki's body; it suddenly began shaking violently and something like steam began rising out of it.

"Damn, this thing is still hard to control." The Demon King looked at Hasunuma and yelled, **"Pirate! If you want me to answer your questions, go to the spot where Mizuya village used to be. I will tell you everything there."**

After a cry like a wounded animal escaped his lips, Kazuki's body slumped to the ground and didn't move.

Hasunuma ran over to Kazuki and called out to him. "Kazuki, Kazuki!" The Pirate King grabbed the kid's body and laid him on his back. "Kazuki!"

After a minute, the kid's eyelashes fluttered and he opened his eyes. His brown eyes. "Hasunuma?"

Thank goodness. The Pirate King smiled. "Glad t' have ya back, Little Oni."

Kazuki glanced around him. "What's going on? Where's Eiri?"

Hasunuma's expression darkened. "There's a lot goin' on, Kid, and I'm afraid I can't explain it all to ya." He paused for a moment before continuing, "But…I know where we can find the answers."

Kazuki looked suspicious. "Okay…then where are we going?"

"A village called, 'Mizuya'."

Kazuki, Hasunuma, and Kohaku made it back to their base in the hidden cave as the sun was cresting in the sky. Hasunuma wanted to get back to the Ryujin as fast as possible, but with Kazuki's leg injury they needed to take it slow and rest. Though many of his other wounds had closed while the Demon King was in control of his body, the kid's leg wound was one that had not fully healed.

Kohaku had left the cave to scout the area for enemies, while the Pirate King and Kazuki sat by the small fire she had built. Hasunuma remained silent, lost in thought, as there was much to think about. He wasn't sure how the arrival of demons would affect his plans of taking down the Hekigun, or how Kazuki would react if he knew about the Demon King inside of him.

"Um, Hasunuma?" Kazuki broke the silence.

Hasunuma looked at the kid and smiled. "What's up, Little Oni?"

"Well, it's just…I don't remember much of what happened back there. After Eiri arrived and we started fighting, my memory is oddly blank." The kid looked concerned. "Usually when I lose control of my body, I at least retain my memory, but this was different."

The Pirate King's smile faded.

"Hasunuma, what happened? You've been really quiet since I woke up."

The Pirate King scratched his head. "Honestly, Little Oni, I don't know what t' tell ya. I don't fully understand it myself, ya see, and I don't wanna lie to ya, so let's just wait and see what we find out in Mizuya, alright?"

Kazuki's eyes shifted to the stone floor of the cave. "Who told you that we would find the answers in that old, burned down village?"

Hasunuma stared at Kazuki. "You know the village, Kid?"

Kazuki nodded. "It's where I was born."

Hasunuma was shocked. He knew that the kid's village had been burned down, but he hadn't known the village's name. "Do you remember anything from when you lived in the village? Before it was burned down."

Kazuki nodded. "Of course. I lived there with my mother. She loved sitting beneath the cherry trees, reciting old legends to me. My father died at sea before I was born. He was a fisherman in the village; that's what all the men there were." Kazuki closed his eyes and sat there, unmoving and silent. It was a long time before he continued: "But one day everything was destroyed."

Hasunuma didn't dare ask more. Kazuki obviously did not want to talk about it or recall what had happened. "Sorry, Kid," he said softly.

More time passed before Kazuki opened his eyes and broke the silence again. "Hasunuma," he said.

"Yeah, Little Oni?"

"How did you do that doppelganger trick, and why haven't I seen you use it before?"

Hasunuma laughed. "Ha ha ha! Well, ya *have* seen me use it before ya just didn't know it. And *how* I did it is a secret."

Kazuki frowned. "What? That's not fair! I want to be able to do that too."

"Ha ha ha! Sorry, Kid. That's a trade secret," he grinned, although his heart ached terribly.

"Trade secret my arse. You're a pirate, not a ninja!"

"Well I was taught by a ninja, so technically I'm both." Hasunuma watched as Kazuki's jaw dropped. "Ha ha ha! I didn't think ya'd be that surprised, Little Oni! I mean if ya think about it, my speed and movement style is just like a ninja's."

"I guess…" Kazuki mumbled. He was still pouting because Hasunuma wouldn't tell him how to create a doppelganger. "Who taught you? Maybe I'll just go straight to your teacher and ask him to teach me too!"

Hasunuma's expression changed to a sad, longing one. "Ya can't do that, Little Oni. She's dead."

"Oh," Kazuki looked away, "Sorry."

An awkward silence filled the cave. Just as it was becoming unbearable, Kohaku returned. Kazuki was more than happy to see her.

"Oh, hey, Kohaku! Did you find anything out there?"

She shook her head before walking over to Hasunuma. She then knelt in front of him and placed her hand on his shoulder, looking concerned.

The Pirate King noticed and smiled at her.

Kohaku slowly nodded and then moved away from him.

Kazuki watched her and wondered if she, too, was trained by a ninja. She was always sneaking up on him on the ship and Hasunuma had mentioned before that she was always near, but Kazuki had never noticed her presence. Her fighting style was also fairly similar to Hasunuma's, as was her speed. While wielding her kusarigama, there weren't many who could best Kohaku.

As if she heard him thinking about her, Kohaku came over to Kazuki and crouched in front of him, staring into his eyes. Kazuki jumped a little, but recovered quickly and tried to hide his embarrassment.

"Is there more of that wrapping that you used on my leg earlier? I've managed to bleed through this set."

Kohaku looked down at Kazuki's bandaged leg. Blood had seeped through and stained the white cloth red. She nodded and pulled more wrapping out of the pack that Kazuki brought. After unwrapping the old bandages, Kohaku first inspected his wound. It was still soft and dripping, but the area around the open flesh was less swollen. She took some salve out of her pack and gently rubbed it on the wound. Then, skillfully and delicately, Kohaku re-wrapped Kazuki's leg.

"Thanks."

Kohaku nodded and dumped the dirty wrappings into the fire.

She leaned against the wall towards the cave opening and stared out, watching for enemies. Kazuki was convinced that Kohaku would be much prettier if she didn't have to wear men's clothing. From the little that he could see, the woman seemed to have nice, feminine curves. She also had a gentle face, complete with beautiful, emerald green eyes that seemed to reflect her fiery spirit.

"Somethin' catch your eye, Little Oni?" The Pirate King's low tone cut through the air.

Kazuki glared at Hasunuma. "No," he said, "I was just thinking that maybe Kohaku was also trained by a ninja."

"A very good observation, Little Oni." The Pirate King grinned, his voice now back to normal.

"Does that mean that she can do all the stuff that you can? Like the doppelganger trick?" The young man asked, hopeful.

Hasunuma paused for a moment before he nodded towards Kohaku and said, "Why don't ya ask her yerself? She'd probably tell ya if ya asked nicely."

"But…" Kazuki leaned towards the Pirate King and whispered, "she doesn't speak. How is she supposed to answer?"

Hasunuma laughed. "There are ways to communicate other than speech." He turned his head towards Kohaku. "Hey, Kohaku, come 'ere." He grinned, "Kazuki has some questions for ya."

"Damnit, Hasunuma! That's not what I–"

Kohaku was now standing before Kazuki. She was looking at him as if she were awaiting his questions.

"Um…" Kazuki wasn't sure what he was supposed to say. He felt comfortable asking Hasunuma anything and everything, but Kohaku was a different story. He didn't know her that well, and on top of that she was a woman. How was he supposed to talk to her?

Kohaku must have sensed that he was uncomfortable, because she sat down in front of him and smiled. It was so soothing. She then pulled something out of the pack at her side. It was a small ink jar, a brush, and a piece of paper.

Kazuki felt like an idiot. *She can write.*

"What did you want to ask me?" Kohaku wrote. Her handwriting was small but beautiful. Even after all of the lessons Rize had given him, Kazuki's handwriting was atrocious in comparison.

Kazuki gathered his courage and asked, "Are you a ninja, like Hasunuma?"

Kohaku giggled a little. *"Yes and no. We were taught by the same master, but Hasunuma knows far more techniques than I do."*

"Oh." Kazuki was a little disappointed. He had hoped that Kohaku could teach him the doppelganger trick.

"Was there anything else?"

Kohaku was far more willing to answer his questions than Kazuki thought. This gave him the courage to ask her what he had always wanted to ask: "Why can't you speak?"

Kohaku paused for a moment, then looked at Hasunuma. Kazuki could tell that she wasn't sure whether or not to tell him the story.

"I'm sorry," Kazuki said quickly, "I shouldn't have asked you something so personal."

"It's not that I don't want to tell you, Kazu, but more that it's a long story and I don't have enough paper with me to be able to write it all down for you." Kohaku's expression was so soft and warm that Kazuki had to believe her.

"But *I* can tell ya the story, if ya *really* want t' know," Hasunuma said with a grin; he was fully enjoying the moment.

Kazuki looked at Kohaku to make sure it was OK with her. When she nodded, Kazuki asked Hasunuma to tell him the story.

"Kohaku is from a village called, Hokuto, known for its ninjitsu school. People from all over the world used to travel to Hokuto to learn the secret ninja arts. But what they didn't know was that the school only accepted those that the master approved of. Many people were turned away, including the Hekigun boss, Hiiro Genji, himself. Needless to say, he was furious at being turned away, so he ordered his men to attack and destroy the village."

"Wait," Kazuki interrupted, "the master turned away tons of people, including Hiiro Genji. Why?"

The Pirate King shrugged, "I told ya, the master only accepted those she deemed worthy."

"And how exactly did she know if a person was worthy or not?" Kazuki wondered.

"Ya had t' go through a test. If you failed, then you were sent away," the Pirate King replied.

"But wasn't she asking for trouble when she sent Hiiro Genji away?" Kazuki stated, more than asked.

"Yeah, she knew that there would be trouble, but the master wasn't about t' set aside her morals and standards just so some sadistic bastard could get what he wanted."

"But she let *you* in."

Hasunuma glared at Kazuki.

Kazuki could see that Hasunuma was not in the mood for sarcasm, so he stopped interrupting.

"Anyways," the Pirate King continued, "That bastard ordered the destruction of the village and the massacre of its people. He sent his top two generals, and their armies, to get the job done. This was about…ten years ago?"

Kohaku nodded.

"Yeah, ten years ago. So, Kohaku was only fifteen at the time when they came to destroy her village. The Hekigun generals used the same sort of mind trick on the men of the village as they used today, so the villagers started killing each other. Those who weren't under their control were killed on the spot. Kohaku's mother saw what was happening and tried to hide her daughter, but it was too late. Kohaku's father was already under Hekigun control. Kohaku watched as her father battled her mother and won. Her own father killed his wife and then turned to his daughter, meaning to kill her too. Seeing her father covered in her mother's blood, Kohaku screamed. Her scream was so emotional, so animalistic, so ear shattering, that she damaged her vocal cords."

Kazuki didn't know how to react to the story. What Kohaku had gone through as a fifteen-year-old, was similar to what he had gone through as an eight-year-old. Kazuki turned to Kohaku and, though he was mildly afraid to, he asked, "What happened to your father?"

Kohaku's eyes were filled with sorrow as she wrote, *"I killed him."*

Hasunuma quickly added, "He was holding her up by her throat and was about to stab her. Kohaku was only protecting herself."

Kohaku shook her head and added, *"I didn't want to die. I knew that the man in front of me was no longer my father, so I dug my fingers into his chest and took out his heart. He then dropped to the ground and never got back up."*

Hasunuma sighed heavily and shook his head. "I arrived too late. By the time I got there, everyone was dead and the village was burning. I found Kohaku kneeling in front of two fresh graves, silently crying."

"Where was the ninja master? Didn't she fight for the village?"

Hasunuma nodded. "Yeah, she fought all right. But in the end, she knew it was too much for her to handle alone. She sent me an SOS message via falcon, but I didn't reach her in time. I was only able to grant my master her final wish – to take care of her daughter."

Wide-eyed, Kazuki finally understood. Kohaku was the master's daughter. The master knew that the village was beyond help, but she wanted her daughter to survive. She gave her life for Kohaku.

A mother always protects her children, no matter what. Kazuki thought he knew that best of all, but he was mistaken. "My mother also died protecting me."

Both Kohaku and Hasunuma stared at Kazuki. This was the first time he had ever mentioned his mother, or really anything about his past.

"Our village was also attacked – though by whom I'm not sure. They killed everyone, including my mother, and burned the village down. I don't remember much after my mother died, but I somehow escaped and was found by the old man. He raised me for five years, before dying in my arms after battling Ammon. Apparently, Ammon had killed his wife and children while the old man was away, so he sought revenge, but he couldn't kill Ammon in the end. That's why I went to kill Ammon. From there, you know the rest–"

Before Kazuki could finish, Kohaku wrapped her arms around him and held him tight. After a minute or two, she pulled away from him and gently patted his head. Kohaku gave Kazuki a warm smile and then pushed the edges of his mouth upward into an awkward, forced smile.

She giggled.

She understands my pain…but she's much stronger than I am.

"Hey, no fair hoggin' Kohaku all to yerself!" The Pirate King grabbed Kazuki and locked his head into his forearm. He playfully ground his fist into Kazuki's head and said, "This is what ya get for leavin' me out!"

"Agh! Hasunuma! Cut it out!"

Kazuki struggled to get away from the Pirate King. He could see that Kohaku was silently laughing at them. Kazuki felt warmth growing inside of him; something that he hadn't experienced in a long time, though he would never admit it. He was part of a family once again. It wasn't a perfect family, but, then again, no family is ever truly perfect.

Hasunuma finally let Kazuki go and said, "All right then, it's about time we headed back to the ship. Ya can walk now, can't ya Little Oni?"

Kazuki looked down at his leg. The bandages weren't soaked with blood, and the pain was significantly less than it was before.

"Thanks, Kohaku. Your medicine is seriously the best," he praised.

Proud of her handiwork, the ninja woman grinned.

"All right then, let's go!" Hasunuma yelled enthusiastically, and then led the way back to the ship.

Rize, Hanzo, and Ginza were waiting for them on deck when the three arrived back at the ship. Even the Ryujin's cook, Jun, was there; normally, he never came above deck unless Hasunuma summoned him himself.

"CAP'N! We're glad ya've returned safely!" They all shouted in some fashion. Well, all but Jun.

"Strange things were happening in the sky above the mountains," Rize explained, "so we got a bit worried."

The Pirate King laughed and said, "Thanks, and I'll explain later, but first we need t' move out fast. I've already got my sights on the next mission."

"The ship's ready to go whenever you're ready, Captain," Rize said with a grin.

"Good. I'll get ya the coordinates soon," the Pirate King responded before turning his attention to Ginza. "Hey can ya help the kid out? He got himself hurt and can't walk very well."

Ginza and the others stared at Kazuki, wide-eyed. It was rare for him to get injured, especially to this extent.

"Well dull m'blade an' call me a chicken! Little Oni, ya really messed up good this time," Ginza said as he helped support the young man.

"Ginza, take him t' his room, then lock him in there."

Kazuki looked at the Pirate King, as did the rest of the crew, unsure of what he meant.

"He disobeyed my direct orders. Until he remembers who's Captain, he is t' stay in his room. Is that clear?"

Everyone yelled 'YES CAP'N' and got to work setting sail, while Ginza helped Kazuki to his room.

"Sorry I gotta do this, Little Oni," Ginza said as he shut and locked the young man's door. "The cap'n's orders are law, and ya gotta obey 'em or else yer dead."

Kazuki heard the blacksmith walk away from the door, and then return.

"Ya know, Cap'n's only mad 'cause ya got hurt. Yer like a little brother t' 'im, so ya gotta be more careful."

Kazuki was silent. It was clear that Hasunuma cared for those around him, and Kazuki knew that he was wrong for disobeying a direct order from the captain, but the young man wasn't about to admit it.

"Be stubborn all ya want, Little Oni, but ya know I'm right."

Kazuki heard Ginza's footsteps gradually fade away. This time he didn't return.

"I know," Kazuki whispered to himself, "trust me, I know."

The Pirate King sat at his desk. In front of him was a map of Tsukigen. His eyes scanned the paper for Kazuki's old village. "I know it's somewhere up here…Aha! Found it." Hasunuma pointed to the upper left of the mainland. 'Mizuya' was written there in small letters. "It's right off the sea, but I don't remember a port town there…it must be up high, maybe even on the edge of a cliff."

It wasn't going to be easy to reach, but Hasunuma was determined to go there. He needed answers. For his and Kazuki's sake.

"Did you really have to lock him up?" Read the piece of paper

shoved in front of the Pirate King's face.

He looked at the woman standing before him; she had her hands on her hips and a cross expression on her face. "Yes, Kohaku, I *really* had to lock him up."

The woman didn't look convinced.

"First of all, the kid disobeyed my express orders and almost got himself killed because of it. And secondly, do you think I'd have him out there working with that leg of his? Not to mention the wound on his back; it may have closed up, but that one went deep – meaning he won't be able to do any heavy lifting for a while. And you know that the kid would push himself too hard and re-injure himself, or worse. I can't have him on deck until he heals properly."

Kohaku crossed her arms and grinned.

"Shut up." The Pirate King put his elbows on his desk and leaned forward, holding his head between his hands. "I don't know what to do with that kid. He could destroy everything I've worked for these twenty-one years, but I can't just abandon him."

Kohaku ran her fingers through Hasunuma's thick brown hair. She waited a moment before writing: *"He's family now. His fight is our fight."*

Hasunuma looked at Kohaku and smiled. "You're incredible, you know that?"

Kohaku smiled and nodded. Then she left the Captain's office.

Hasunuma watched her go and thought to himself, *She really is something else.*

Suddenly there was a knock on the door, and a voice called from the other side, "Captain, I have a message."

"Come in, Rize," the Pirate King responded.

When the helmsman entered the room, Hasunuma heard a familiar *screech*.

"Ami! Where've ya been, girl?" The Pirate King jokingly asked the falcon. When he held out his arm for her, Ami flew over and perched herself on his arm. The Pirate King gently stroked her chest. He was very relieved to see her.

"She brought this," Rize said as he placed a folded piece of paper on top of the desk in front of Hasunuma.

"Good girl," the Pirate King grinned. "Make sure she gets plenty of food and rest, Rize."

The helmsman nodded. "Of course, Captain." Then he whistled a short note and Ami flew back to perch on Rize's shoulder.

Once the two of them left, the Pirate King opened the note. As he read the message he grinned. "Well done, Douglas. That's twelve ships and nine bases off the list."

Kazuki was locked in his room for five days. He was given food and water, but being locked in a small room on a ship, in the stifling heat, with no window, was agonizing for the young man. When Ginza finally let him out, Kazuki raced to the ship's deck and deeply inhaled the fresh ocean breeze. He basked in the sunlight and drank in the scenery.

It looked like they were preparing to drop anchor; the shore wasn't too far off, but the water was too shallow for the ship to go any further in. And there weren't any docks in sight, so they'd be embarking on the tender again.

Kazuki stretched himself until he thought he would snap. His whole body was stiff and ached for movement. Unlike Hanzo and Ginza, Kazuki didn't spend his free time in his room working out; instead, he read old books that Rize had handed down to him. As the young man stretched, he ran his fingers over his leg. The injury had healed, but there remained a long, dark scar.

The power of the Demon King must have sped up my recovery, the young man thought to himself. *I don't remember my wounds healing like this before…either the Demon King's power is growing, or he's sharing more of it with me.*

"Get ready t' land, Little Oni. We're headin' t' Mizuya," the Pirate King commanded.

"Aye, Cap'n," Kazuki replied, devoid of enthusiasm.

From where the Ryujin had been docked for Yamaōgi, it should only have taken them three days maximum to reach the beach below Mizuya. What the crew had been doing for the other two days while Kazuki was locked in his room was a total mystery. All the young man knew was that he had been shut away for longer than was necessary and was bitter about it.

"What was that, Little Oni? Want t' stay in your room instead?"

Kazuki rolled his eyes and yelled with feigned enthusiasm, "Aye, Cap'n!"

"I suppose that'll do," The Pirate King grinned. "All right then, let's get movin'. Hanzo's gonna row us out this time since there's no place t' secure the tender ashore, and I don't want it bobbing around all those rocks."

Kazuki nodded and climbed the rope ladder down to the small

boat. He was shocked to find Kohaku sitting on one of the benches, across from Hanzo. "I thought we were just gathering information," the young man wondered aloud.

"We are," the Pirate King confirmed as he joined them in the tender. "Kohaku is coming with us to secure the perimeter, since we don't know if anyone is using the village or not."

The young man nodded. *That makes sense, though I'd be surprised if anyone is living in that harsh place.*

As Hanzo rowed them to shore, a grin began to spread across the giant's face. "You know, Lad, this coastline reminds me of my homeland. Instead of soft sand, our beaches are mostly covered in large, jagged stones. And we've got cliffs rising from the water with looming mountains behind them, like those right there," he explained as he pointed towards the shore.

Mizuya's coastline was different than the rest of the mainland. While some of the smaller islands had similar cliffs and rocky features, most of Tsukigen's beaches consisted of sand. Aboard the Ryujin, Kazuki had also noticed that the sea around the stony coasts tended to be darker and more murky than the clear blue water that lapped at the sandy shore.

"What's the water like there?" Kazuki asked with interest.

Hanzo smiled. "It's cold, but crystal clear. Absolutely beautiful if ya ask me."

Kazuki nodded in agreement. Although he grew up looking down at the cold, dark depths, the young man preferred the warm, brilliant blue sea.

"It's been nine years since I last saw home," the giant muttered, looking forlornly at the landscape before him.

Just as Kazuki was about to ask more about Hanzo's mysterious homeland, the tender gently bumped into a rocky outcropping.

"We'll disembark here," Hasunuma directed as he jumped out of the boat and onto the jagged rocks.

Kazuki turned around to offer a helping hand to Kohaku, but she was already gone. Instead, he waved 'bye' to Hanzo and followed Hasunuma onto the rocks slick with seawater.

As the young man stumbled over the wet stones, he noticed some old wooden chests strewn about; weathered and broken, their contents were long gone. A few rotten boards here and there were all that remained of the long, angled docks that once stood above the stony beach, stretching from the tree line into the water. The young man had scant memories of running supplies down to the docks as a child and watching the men of the village repair any broken boards.

All of that work, and nothing remains…

"Hurry up, Little Oni," Hasunuma called out from the tree line.

Kazuki scampered over the rocks, making his way to Hasunuma as quickly as he could. He slipped once, but caught himself. With his face inches from the side of a rock, Kazuki noticed something shining in the crevice. He dug his fingers in and managed to pull the object out. The young man stared at the golden crest in his hand. A single serpent twirled around the sun; the symbol of the Hekigun. It was what the Hekigun officers pinned to their belts.

"So the Hekigun *were* here…" Kazuki mumbled to himself.

Did you think that I would lie?

I don't know you, so how can I trust you?

You will know me soon. And then you will have no choice but to trust me.

"Hey, Little Oni! Stop daydreamin' and help me find the path t' yer old village," Hasunuma called out again, this time sounding annoyed.

Kazuki slipped the crest into his pocket and hastened to the Pirate King's side.

"We should see a dirt pathway that starts about halfway up the slope." Kazuki said, hoping that the path had not changed too much in the eight years of his absence. Just as the docks had disappeared with time, a mountain path not traveled would surely vanish behind walls of green. But if it hadn't become *too* overgrown, Kazuki was sure he could find the path and lead them to the village.

As a boy, he traveled the path multiple times a day. In Mizuya, the children were put to work as runners for the adults; they traversed the sloping path, delivering messages, supplies, and food. Some were even sent off on foraging errands that would take all day to complete. Since Mizuya was remote, and located high up on a cliff, the villagers had to work hard to survive. No one could afford to shirk their duties, not even the smallest of children.

The only fond memories Kazuki had of his life in Mizuya were the ones with his mother. He was a quiet child who didn't have many friends and was terrified of angering the village men. Kazuki shivered when he remembered their cold, glaring eyes and their hardened, frowning faces. His mother's smile was the only one he could remember seeing, and it had always made him feel at ease.

Because of its remote location, the only visitors the village received were the occasional traveling merchant, medicine peddler, or fisherman from the Chiumi Islands – a cluster of small islands off shore, situated between the mainland and the second largest island,

Rurin. Whenever there was a visitor, one of the children had to lead them from the docks to the village. Otherwise they would lose their way and become lost in the vast mountain range that surrounded Mizuya.

A dark thought suddenly occurred to the young man: *If only the villagers knew about the path, then how did the Hekigun find it?* Kazuki made a fist and pounded the nearest tree trunk as he passed. *Someone betrayed the village.*

Correct.

Kazuki busied himself with the search for the path, wanting to ignore his thoughts. "It should be…here! Hasunuma!"

The Pirate King joined Kazuki. In front of them was a small dirt path that was more of an animal trail than a human one; there were branches, roots, and fallen trees in the middle of the path, and it veered left and right randomly as it climbed the ridge. While most of the obstructions had come with years of disuse, even cleared, the path seemed impractically difficult. But Kazuki knew that the forest was vast, the mountain slopes were treacherous, and the path that had been carved before them offered the safest route to the village on the cliff.

As they climbed, Kazuki's legs began to tire and his breathing became shallow. Hasunuma, on the other hand, seemed to be fine.

"Come on, Little Oni! Isn't this where ya used t' live?" The Pirate King teased.

It had been a long time since Kazuki had last walked up the path to Mizuya, and on top of that he had just gotten out of his room that he had been locked in for a whole week.

Stop making excuses and ask the pirate to train you already.

I don't need it. Kazuki stubbornly denied. He then pushed himself and caught up just at Hasunuma came to a sudden halt.

"Shinigami-sama, Shinigami-sama…I'm here for your head!" A shrill voice sang.

Kazuki didn't remember much from his fight with Eiri, but he did remember that Eiri had referred to him as 'Shinigami-sama.'

"Who are you?" Kazuki asked as he stepped out from behind Hasunuma and stood beside him.

The shrill voice belonged to a man who looked like a rogue samurai. He was wearing a dirty, grey kimono with a brown hakama, and he held his unsheathed katana at his side with no sign of its' saya anywhere. His hair was tied back in a loose and messy knot, and his face was strangely sunken in, as if he hadn't eaten in weeks.

"Who am I?" The shrill voice replied. "I am Twelve, soon to be the Demon King!"

"What are you talking about?" Kazuki stepped forward, but Hasunuma stopped him from going further.

"Don't worry about it now. We'll find out what he means once we reach Mizuya," Hasunuma said calmly as he put himself between Twelve and Kazuki. Just as he reached for his sword, a high-pitched whistle came from above and Kohaku appeared in front of them.

She smiled and gave them a 'go on ahead, I'll take care of this guy' look.

"All right," Hasunuma replied, "but be careful. He's not human."

Kohaku nodded and changed her stance from offensive to defensive.

"Wait!" Kazuki yelled as Hasunuma dragged him away. "We can't leave her to fight that guy alone! What if she dies?!"

The Pirate King laughed aloud and kept moving forward at full speed. "Trust me, Kid, someone's going to die, but it won't be Kohaku."

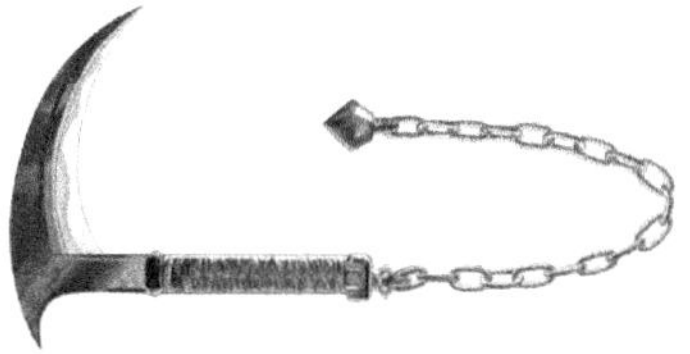

When she was sure that Hasu and Kazu were far enough away, Kohaku gave a short whistle and motioned to the rogue samurai to attack her.

"You aren't Shinigami-sama," he groaned, "but since you are keeping me from him, I'll have to kill you first!" Twelve cried as he lunged at Kohaku.

Stepping out of the way, she easily avoided his katana and threw a handful of poison needles at his back. He whirled around and deflected them all with his katana.

He's fast, Kohaku grinned, *but not fast enough!*

Kicking off of the ground, Kohaku launched herself high into the air and unleashed a volley of poisoned needles on Twelve. The rogue samurai managed to either block or dodge all of the needles, but that was what Kohaku had expected him to do. With lightning speed, she appeared behind Twelve. He screamed as Kohaku ran her kusarigama across his back.

*I thought this would be more fun...*Kohaku sighed as she jumped away from the now extremely angry Twelve who was wildly slashing at her.

"You bitch!" Twelve yelled as steam began rising from his body.

"I was saving my strength for Shinigami-sama," his eyes turned black, "but now I'm going to use it to rip you apart!" Twelve's speed doubled, as did his strength, and Kohaku struggled to keep him at bay.

Oops. I guess I made him mad.

After she sidestepped another slash, Kohaku considered her options for victory. She blocked Twelve's katana again and saw the rage building in his black eyes. Twelve's anger would be his downfall, she decided.

First, Kohaku had to make him so blind with rage that he wouldn't be able to think. So, jumping backwards, she threw a few shuriken at Twelve. Then, the ninja woman disappeared from his sight. The rogue samurai turned this way and that, trying to find her. Kohaku watched from above as he grew more and more angry.

"Where are you, ninja whore?!"

Oh, I'm a whore now, am I?

Kohaku began phase two: another shower of poisoned needles. This time Twelve easily blocked them all. He was also ready for Kohaku's sneak attack from behind, but it didn't happen.

"What the–"

Boo!

Kohaku tapped Twelve on his forehead and, just as she had predicted, he looked up. Kohaku was standing upside-down on a large tree branch, looking down at Twelve. Before he could react, Kohaku drove a poisoned needle through each of his black eyes. Twelve's scream echoed through the valley.

That's what you get for calling me nasty names.

Kazuki stopped walking. He had just heard a blood-curdling scream from somewhere below. "Hasunuma…you don't think–"

"Do you know what ninja are best at?" The Pirate King suddenly asked.

The young man thought about it for a minute, and then replied, "Stealth."

"Well, yeah, they're good at that, but why do you think they often win battles even when outnumbered?"

Kazuki tried to come up with a good answer, but he couldn't. He shrugged.

"Ninja are amazing tacticians," Hasunuma said as he continued up the path. "They're trained t' think on their feet and quickly analyze their enemy's weakness." He turned back to Kazuki and grinned. "Basically, they defeat their enemies by outsmarting them."

"So, Kohaku is–"

"I told ya not t' worry about her, didn't I? Now come on."

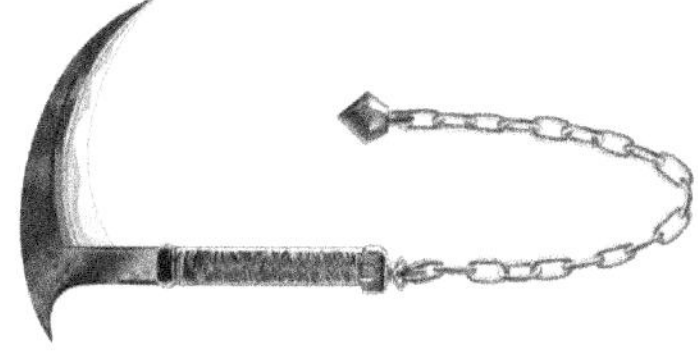

Twelve's skin was beginning to rot off of his body. The poison worked quickly.

"My host's flesh may be rotting off and my eyes may be gone, but if you think that this is enough to kill me, you're dead wrong."

The now horrific looking Twelve resumed his attack on Kohaku, slashing at her from every angle, trying to cut her up. He was still seething with rage, but he was more in control of himself now.

Hasunuma was right. This guy isn't human.

Kohaku held out her kusarigama and changed her stance from defense to offense. Holding tightly onto the sickle end, Kohaku twirled the chain above her head and then launched it at Twelve. The weight on the end of the chain struck Twelve hard, breaking off his half-decomposed left arm.

"So you can do more than run, you sly bitch." Twelve grinned eerily. "Strange that you haven't said one word, even though I'm sure you're just dying to retort. Maybe you got your tongue cut out, like most whores? Hehehe. I'll bet you moaned the wrong name and paid the price!"

Kohaku smiled. It wasn't the smile that she showed Hasu and Kazu, it was a different smile: a smile that, coming from a woman, would have scared any man away.

Twelve was cornered and he knew it. Kohaku wasn't about to fall for his petty last-minute attempts at making her angry. Before Twelve could say anything more, Kohaku swung the chain of her kusarigama and wrapped it around his neck. She yanked the chain towards her, intending to cause Twelve to fall to his knees so she could deliver the final blow, but, instead, his poison corroded neck broke off.

Kohaku stared down at Twelve's decapitated head. *One step less than I had planned, but that's OK.* She was about to leave when she noticed a strange scent in the air. It was like burning, rotting flesh.

Anyone else would have thought that the smell was coming from the rotting corpse of Twelve, but Kohaku knew better. *There's a demon here.*

A dark shadow rose from Twelve's corpse. It had no features, but the smoke-like wisps exuded a demonic aura.

"Hear me, human," Twelve's voice hissed, "you may have defeated me this time, but I *will* be back." The strange smoke then disappeared, as if it were evaporating. The atmosphere felt lighter and the sounds of the forest returned.

*Demons...*Kohaku thought about what Twelve had said, but it didn't make any sense. He hadn't given her enough information. Determined to find answers, Kohaku made her way up the mountain trail towards Mizuya. *Hasu had better tell me what's going on.*

There wasn't much left of Mizuya. The entire village had been burned to the ground eight years ago, and, since then, nature had run its course. The burnt wood had frozen and thawed many times, furthering its decay, while the numerous cherry blossom trees lining the streets stood withered and barren. All that remained of the houses were their stone bases, which were cracked and crumbling.

Kazuki stared at what used to be his home. He had never considered what it would feel like to return to the place where he and his mother used to live, only to see it in ruin. He wished he hadn't come back.

Do not be such a coward. You must face your past before

moving forward.

The young man didn't like the tone of the voice he heard. *How about you explain a few things first? Like who you are.*

Very well.

Kazuki suddenly felt very strange. It was as if something were tearing him in half from the inside out. He groaned and clutched his head. Hasunuma came over and asked if he was all right, but Kazuki couldn't answer; he had no control over his body.

"Greetings, Pirate," came a voice from Kazuki's mouth. It was deep, rough, and full of malice.

Kazuki watched as Hasunuma slowly backed away from him. "We meet again, Shinigami-sama. Or should I call you 'Demon King'?"

"My enemies refer to me as the 'Demon King,' while those who fear and respect me address me as 'Shinigami-sama'."

"Demon King it is," Hasunuma said with a grin, but his eyes were cold. Kazuki never saw Hasunuma show fear, but he could sense the Pirate King's hesitation with this new entity.

Kazuki could feel himself grinning. **"You interest me, Pirate. You have some abilities that humans do not."**

"Thanks," Hasunuma said flatly, "but if ya don't mind, how about explainin' t' me what you're doin' in the kid's body."

"Ah, yes. As I promised, I will tell you."

Though the voice was coming from his own throat, Kazuki felt like he was eavesdropping on a conversation he shouldn't hear.

"I am in this body for two reasons: One reason being that it is time for the demon games once more, and the other being that I liked this child's innate thirst for revenge."

Hasunuma furrowed his brow. "What do you mean 'it's time for the demon games once more'?"

"Every hundred years, the demon games are held to decide who rules on high as King of all demons."

"What exactly do these games involve?" Hasunuma asked warily.

"The Demon King, in this case myself, and the top nineteen demons descend upon the Human Realm. We each choose a host for the games, and then the battle begins. Traditionally, the demons would battle each other before confronting the Demon King, but, as I have ruled for the past three hundred years, they ignore each other and focus solely on killing me."

"Why involve humans in your demon battles? You consider us weaker, right?"

"Yes, and that is precisely the point. It is much more fun with a handicap."

Hasunuma frowned. "That can't be the only reason."

"You are correct. The truth is that we demons cannot die in the Demon Realm. No matter how much we fight, a true winner cannot be decided upon, because none of us can be killed. In the Human Realm, however, we can experience death. Or something close to it."

Kazuki could see that Hasunuma was finding it difficult to take all of this new information in. He didn't blame the Pirate King. Kazuki had just as much, if not more trouble believing it all.

If you're the Demon King, then why did you choose me? Why not pick someone stronger, like Hasunuma?

"Why did I choose you?" Kazuki felt himself laugh. **"I always**

choose hosts like you. My first, Masamune, proved correct my theory about the incredible strength and determination that young humans possess. That is why I have won three games in a row."

Hasunuma must have figured that Kazuki had somehow asked the question, because he blurted out, "Wait a minute, is Kazuki still there?"

"When I fully take over, my host enters a state of unconsciousness. I purposefully allowed him to stay alert this time so that he could understand the situation."

Hasunuma looked both pained and relieved. "So that's why he doesn't remember anything..." the Pirate King shook his head and continued, "I still don't understand why you choose kids."

"Young humans are the most impressionable and honest. For instance, if someone were to hurt their loved ones, their first instinct is to hurt that person back. More often than not, they seek and exact their revenge."

There was something familiar about what the Demon King said. Kazuki thought back to the old man's death. He had exacted revenge upon Ammon although the old man told him not to. And what about his mother? He had exacted her revenge too.

Kazuki remembered that terrible night: he was eating dinner when he suddenly heard the screams of the villagers. He had opened the door to look outside, when a strange man attacked him with a sword. Kazuki had tried to shut the door, but the strange man kicked his way in. As the strange man raised his arm to strike again, Kazuki's mother jumped in front of him, trying to protect him. The strange man brought down his sword and slashed through Kazuki's mother; the tip of it had protruded just enough to simultaneously slice open the boy's chest.

Kazuki's eight-year-old body had moved before it could think or register pain; he grabbed the short sword from his belt, lunged at the strange man, and stabbed him through the crotch.

I remember slicing his thigh open as I pulled the sword out. There was so much blood...And then I fell to the floor. I think I watched the strange man scream and struggle for a bit before he died...but after that it's all a blur.

"I was there, though not in flesh yet, and I saw what happened to you and your mother. I watched as you exacted your revenge with your last breath. You were smiling as you watched the man slowly die before you. That smile is what made me choose you."

Wait...you're making it sound like I died that night. I didn't die.

"Yes, you did. How else would you have become a candidate host for us demons? We can only inhabit the body of a dead human."

Kazuki's stomach dropped. Or it would have if it could respond to his feelings. He was dead...dead and playing host to the King of demons.

Hasunuma said what Kazuki couldn't: "You've got to be joking. Kazuki's alive and well. Who else have I spent the last three years with?"

"My host may be alive now, but that is because I am inhabiting his body. It takes a while for the soul to leave once a human dies. In that span of time many things could happen to the soul or to the body. If a demon inhabits a newly dead body,

the soul of that human becomes trapped inside. Most demons prefer to inhabit the older dead, but I find that a newly dead host can still grow once inhabited by a demon. How or why that happens, I am not sure, but that is the reason that my host has been given a second chance as it were; living the life it never would have otherwise."

"So you're saying…that once you're gone, Kazuki goes back to being dead," Hasunuma said slowly. He then charged the Demon King, grabbed his shirt, and pulled him close. Hasunuma's red dragon sword now rested on the Demon King's throat. "I should kill you right now and end this madness," he growled, his eyes filled with rage.

"Oh?" Kazuki felt his mouth curl up into a crude smile. **"You would end your friend's life to get rid of me?"**

Kazuki wasn't sure how to feel about this new development. *Hasunuma can't be serious...he wouldn't actually kill me, would he?*

"You can't fool me, demon," Hasunuma replied while pushing the red dragon closer to the Demon King's neck. "The kid may have gained a life, but what kinda horse pile life did he get? The top nineteen demons will be trying to kill him every chance they get, and even if he does somehow manage to defeat them all, he'll die when you leave his body. So why shouldn't I just kill him now and end his suffering?"

Laughter came bellowing out of Kazuki's mouth. **"You truly are the most interesting human I have met in a long time."** Kazuki's arm moved and knocked Hasunuma's hand away from his shirt. He then grabbed the Pirate King's sword hand and forcefully pushed the blade away from his neck. **"For amusing me, I will reward you with this bit of knowledge: if I win the game, my host gets to live."**

Kazuki's body suddenly began to shake. Instead of feeling like he was being pulled apart, this new sensation was that of being squished together. Unable to withstand the pressure, Kazuki's knees buckled and he collapsed to the ground.

After a minute or so, when he felt more in control of his body, Kazuki lifted his head and looked at Hasunuma. "It's just me now." *I think.*

Hasunuma sheathed his sword and helped Kazuki get up. He seemed glad that Kazuki was back to normal, but anger and confusion lingered on his face.

"Let's find some place t' sit down awhile." The Pirate King said flatly as he began walking towards the edge of the village. He chose a spot on the outer rim, where the earth dropped off into the sea far below. "There's a lot we have t' think about."

What. The. Festering. Hole. Were the words that repeated over and over again in Hasunuma's mind. The Pirate King wasn't sure how to handle this newfound situation. Finding out that the King of demons was inside Kazuki, who had actually died eight years ago, and that nineteen of the highest ranked demons would be chasing after them from now on, was beyond what the Pirate King had initially suspected. He was trying to decide whether or not the new information would help or hinder his personal plans when Kazuki came over and sat on beside him on the cliff's edge. They stared silently out at the dark sea below them.

It seemed like hours passed before Kazuki broke the silence. "Hasunuma…" he began, but trailed off.

The Pirate King knew that this revelation was far more difficult for the kid than it was for him, so he let Kazuki speak at his own pace without interruption.

"The only words that I can think of to say right now are: trust me," the young man said.

The Pirate King continued to stare at the water below. The waves crashed onto the rocks, spewing foam into the air. However, the two were so high above the ocean that the salty spray could never reach them, no matter how hard the water seemed to try.

"I know I've got the Demon King inside of me, and I know he can take over my body whenever he wants to, but…I know that even if he did take over, I wouldn't harm you or any of the crew."

The Pirate King closed his eyes. The roar of the waves below resounded in his ears.

"There's not really any way that I can prove that to you, but please believe me when I say that I won't betray you," the kid's voice was strong, without a hint of uncertainty, when he spoke.

Kazuki's pleading was making Hasunuma's decision all the more difficult. If the Pirate King were to let the kid stay with him, then not only would he be in constant danger, but his crew would be as well. But, if he left Kazuki by himself, the kid would either die or turn into a real death god, and neither of those alternatives sat well with the Pirate King.

With no response from the Pirate King, Kazuki continued trying to convince him. "So far, all we know is that the Demon King is inside of me, nineteen other demons that are inhabiting human corpses are after me, and if I don't kill them all then I will die…Again." He took a deep breath and added, "I don't know what your ultimate goals are, besides annihilating the Hekigun, but I can't see how my having demonic powers would be a bad thing."

Hasunuma sighed and opened his eyes. "It's much more complicated than that, Little Oni." He stood up, continuing to stare at the sea, and drew his red dragon sword. "I swore an oath to kill Hiiro Genji, and to protect my shipmates. With all of those demons chasing after you, it would put the crew in danger and possibly interfere with my plans."

He then turned, looked at Kazuki, and continued, "Have you thought about what would happen if the demons were Hekigun members? Or if they attacked the ship while we were away? Also," Hasunuma pointed his sword at Kazuki, "how can I trust that you could stop the Demon King if he decided to kill me and my crew? Every time he takes over, you go to sleep."

"Well this last time–"

"He *allowed* you to stay conscious this last time. I don't think he'll make a habit of keeping you awake. Especially if he knows you're going to interfere," the Pirate King pointed out.

The kid stared at the blade in front of him. He stood quietly for a few minutes before saying, "I don't know how to convince you, Hasunuma. If you don't believe me, then kill me. But I swear to you that I won't harm you or your crew."

The Pirate King quickly grabbed Kazuki's left hand. He ran his sword along the kid's palm, making a large gash. After drawing the blade across his own palm, the Pirate King locked hands with Kazuki.

"Now we have a blood oath. If you don't keep your word, I will kill you." Hasunuma watched as Kazuki stared at him in disbelief. The Pirate King grinned and added, "We're in this together, Little Oni. I'll protect you as your captain, your friend, and your brother. In return, I ask that you do the same for me and my crew."

The Pirate King watched as a smile crept across Kazuki's face. It wasn't the usual smirk or grin that he had seen before. It was a real smile, which reflected the kid's soul. "Aye, Cap'n!"

Hasunuma let go of Kazuki's hand. "Well now that the fun's over, let's talk strategy." The Pirate King was about to go on, but stopped and stared at Kazuki. "Can he…hear us?"

The young man finished bandaging his wounded hand and then crossed his arms. "I was wondering that myself. I mean, he's been in my body for eight years now, and I only started to hear him a few years ago, during that Ammon incident."

"It's almost as if he were lying in wait or something…have you tried asking him?" The Pirate King wondered.

"No." The kid paused for a moment. "But since he hasn't said anything yet, I guess he's not listening."

I think something else is going on…

Hasunuma sat back down on the rocks and tried to come up with an explanation. It wouldn't make sense for the Demon King to always be alert, because otherwise he would have helped Kazuki out when those twin brutes were attacking him. The demon would want to protect its host, right? Also, there's those five years to consider, when the kid was completely unaware of the demon inside of him. There's such a vast difference in power between humans and demons, so it must be difficult for a demon to–

"That's it!"

Kazuki jumped from Hasunuma's sudden exclamation.

"It takes time for a demon to get used to a human body, so demons must have to rest or recuperate in-between possessions in order to regain their power."

Kazuki gave Hasunuma a strange look.

"What, not following me?" The Pirate King asked.

"No, I'm following, I just don't agree," the kid said.

"How would you explain it then?"

Kazuki sat down next to Hasunuma and explained his theory. The kid's idea was that the demons feed off of evil energy, so they can only be active when evil is nearby. And that was why the Demon King wanted him to go with the Pirate King, in order for the Demon King to gain more power by having the kid fight the Hekigun.

"That's a nice theory Little Oni, but that doesn't explain why the Demon King didn't show up when you were fighting those dumb twins. Or why he didn't come out when that demon showed up in that dead ronin's body."

Kazuki frowned. "Maybe he just didn't feel like it."

The Pirate King laughed, "Right, Kid. I'm sure that the King of demons acts solely on his feelings."

"He's the Demon King, he can do whatever he–"

"Ouch!" Both men yelped as someone smacked them on the back of their heads.

"What was that for, Kohaku?" Hasunuma whined as he turned

and looked at the ninja woman.

"Yeah, what he said," echoed Kazuki as he gently rubbed his head.

She took out her paper and ink and scribbled, *"Stop arguing like children, you two! We need to think this through together or we'll never find an answer."*

Kazuki and Hasunuma stared, mouths wide open, at Kohaku. The Pirate King was shocked that even *he* hadn't sensed her presence.

"Yes, I heard it all, I'm sorry. I didn't mean to spy on you this time, I promise."

"This time? What do you mean *this* time?" Kazuki glared at Kohaku, who just sighed.

"It doesn't matter. What matters is how we can help you win this demon tournament so that you can live again." The ninja woman wrote.

"Leave it to a woman to set a man straight," Hasunuma laughed.

Rolling his eyes at the Pirate King's last remark, the kid said, "All I need to do to win is kill all of the other demons. How hard can that be?"

The Pirate King and Kohaku both stared at Kazuki.

"What?" The kid skeptically asked.

"Do you recall the time you got your arse whooped by Eiri or should I say, Second?" The Pirate King reminded him.

Kazuki frowned.

"I take that as a 'yes'. Which means that you need more training before you can take on the rest of the demons."

Kohaku suddenly nudged Hasunuma's shoulder and wrote something down. She purposefully hid the contents from Kazuki.

"Hasu, you forgot about your accent!"

"Oh. Oops." The Pirate King burst into laughter. "I guess I got too comfortable around him."

Kazuki looked very confused.

"It's about my accent," the Pirate King clarified.

"Oh, that. Yeah, why do you try to fake it?" the kid casually asked.

Kohaku scribbled something down. This time it was meant for Kazuki's eyes. *"Hasu wasn't trying to deceive you or anything, he just didn't want anyone to know that he's educated. There's no such thing as an educated pirate, is there?"*

"I'd still call that deceiving, but I can understand why he'd try to hide that from people," the kid nodded as he spoke.

"Good. Now let's get back to the topic of your training, Little Oni." Hasunuma grinned as Kazuki scowled. "Kohaku and I could teach you basic movement and speed, but neither of us uses a katana." He paused for a moment before adding, "If I remember correctly, there was an old master swordsman somewhere near the town of Aiichi, where Ammon's fortress was."

"His name is Jisai," Kohaku scribbled.

"Alright, so we need to find old man Jisai and get him to teach you some sword techniques," the Pirate King said.

Kazuki looked down and replied, almost in a whisper, "He's dead."

Hasunuma and Kohaku exchanged glances. They both seemed to remember the old man in Kazuki's story.

Putting two and two together, the Pirate King said, "Sorry about that, Little Oni," as patted the kid's head. "Well, that explains why you can fight so well. He must have been a great teacher," he added with a smile. "I guess Kohaku and I will have to suffice for your secondary training then."

Kohaku tapped Hasunuma's shoulder. *"What about Jun?"*

"I doubt Jun would be willing to teach him," the Pirate King shrugged, "but it wouldn't hurt to ask."

"Wait," Kazuki interrupted, "are you talking about Jun, *the cook*?"

Kohaku nodded.

The kid broke into laughter, "You've got to be kidding me! What would a cook know about fighting with a katana?"

Hasunuma grabbed Kazuki's collar and glared at him. "Don't talk about my crew like that." He let go of the kid and said, "Plus you don't know anything about Jun, so shut your mouth."

Kazuki mumbled "Sorry," and then kept his mouth shut for a while.

"Alright, now let's get back to the ship. I need to update the crew on the situation." Hasunuma stood up and walked towards the head of the trail that lead down to the sea. He paused and looked back to Kazuki who hadn't moved. "Ya comin' or what?"

The kid rolled his eyes and got up to follow the Pirate King, his arms crossed.

Hasunuma laughed, "Ya may have an old demon inside of ya, but ya still act like a stubborn kid."

"Whatever, accent faker," Kazuki mumbled.

"And ya just proved my point," Hasunuma laughed to himself as he, Kohaku, and grumpy Kazuki headed back down the path to the sea.

Hanzo was waiting for them when they arrived at the rocky shore. The giant waved them over, and while the Pirate King and Kohaku easily traversed the slick rocks, Kazuki struggled to keep his balance.

"Yeah, he definitely needs more training," the Pirate King mumbled to himself as he waited for the kid to join them on the tender.

The giant must have heard Hasunuma, because he then laughed and said, "We could all use some training, Cap'n."

"Ya think so?" The Pirate King inquired with a grin.

Hanzo nodded. "Of course. We've been on the Ryujin for far too long this stint, and it's affecting our bodies. At least, I can feel it," the giant added as he flexed his abundant arm muscles.

"And here I was just thinkin' about settin' up a little training camp soon," Hasunuma laughed. "What good timing."

After arriving back at the Ryujin, Hasunuma gathered everyone on deck. Rize and Ginza hustled over, while Jun appeared minutes later, covered in blood splatter, and still holding his well-used chef's knife. Kohaku and Hanzo joined the line of shipmates standing in front of their captain, but Kazuki stood further back. He was afraid of what would happen once the others knew about his…situation.

"I have somethin' important to tell ya, so listen up!" The Pirate King boomed.

Kazuki's heart leapt in his chest.

"At Mizuya, we found out about Kazuki's past. He was killed there eight years ago by the Hekigun army."

Hanzo and Ginza started to protest that remark, but they were immediately silenced by one look from their captain.

"The reason why he's here now is 'cause a demon took over his body. And not just any demon, but the King of demons himself."

The crew began muttering amongst themselves.

"And that's not all," the Pirate King continued, "there's a demon game goin' on where the top nineteen demons try t' take on the Demon King. Since he's in Kazuki's body, they'll all be comin' after him. And since Kazuki's part of our crew, that means they'll be comin' after us too."

Silence overtook the ship.

"The only way t' win is for Kazuki to defeat all nineteen demons. If he does that, he can have his life back." The Pirate King stared at his crew. "I know this isn't gonna be easy. By the gods, we may even die 'cause of this. But I say we give the Little Oni a chance. What say you?"

Kazuki stood there, eyes shut tight, with fingernails digging into his palms. The silence was a dull knife pushing into his stomach. *There's no way these guys are going to agree to risk their lives for mine. I might as well do them all a favor and jump ship right now.*

Time seemed to stretch on forever until Kazuki heard an unexpected noise from the crew.

"AHAHAHAHAHA!" All of the crew, except for Kohaku and Jun, burst into roaring laughter.

Kazuki couldn't understand what was going through their minds.

Even the Pirate King looked slightly confused at their reaction. The young man felt so unsure of himself that he blurted out, "Why are you laughing?! It's not a joke!"

The crew turned and looked at him, tears in their eyes from laughing so hard.

Ginza was the first to answer: "We know the cap'n's not jokin', but we can't help it! It's just too funny!"

When Ginza broke into laughter again, Rize took over the explanation: "'Cause your name is 'Little Oni,' and it turns out you actually *are* a little oni!"

The crew continued to laugh at what they thought was an extremely funny coincidence.

"It explains a lot about you, Lad," Hanzo added, "There were times we were battling the Hekigun and you were tearin' through bodies like a demon. Now it all makes sense."

"I take it that's *his* sword then?" Jun asked as he eyed the katana at Kazuki's side.

Kazuki's left hand found his katana as he avoided Jun's gaze. "I never really thought about it before…but I guess you're right. I've had it since the day I died." The young man stared down at the katana. *So this is yours, huh?*

Kazuki almost jumped out of his skin when he suddenly felt a large hand on his shoulder. "That explains the high-level a' craftsmanship. They say demon weapons 're forged in the Demon Realm usin' some kinda magic," the blacksmith explained enthusiastically. "An' they're supposed t' be unbreakable."

"I'd like to test its abilities," Jun murmured.

"But don't ya worry, Little Oni! We got ya covered!" Ginza said with a hearty laugh as he squeezed Kazuki's shoulder.

The young man knew what they were trying to do for him, but he only felt worse. "You don't understand!" He yelled as he swatted away Ginza's hand.

Everyone grew silent.

"These demons will *kill* you! They want to kill the Demon King so badly that they will do whatever it takes!"

The crew stared hard at Kazuki.

Realizing the strangeness of the situation, the young man quickly averted his gaze. He then added, "I-I don't want any of you to die for my sake."

Hasunuma was the first to respond this time: "Kid, if you think my crew is so weak that they can't take on a couple 'a demons, then yer dumber than ya look."

The crew laughed heartily.

"Cap'n's right! We ain't gonna roll over fer a buncha wussy demons!" Ginza said.

"Yeah! They don't stand a chance against the likes of us!" Hanzo added.

"I'd like to see them try to get past my steel arrows!" Rize boasted.

"Hmph. Yer steel arrows ain't nothin' compared t' my naginata. I forged it so nobody but me can use it–"

"Yeah, yeah, we *all* know about your super heavy, thick-bladed naginata, Gin," Hanzo butted in, "But I'm gonna kill the most demons with my steel knuckles!"

"Ya can't kill demons with those puny things. An' I outta know since I made 'em fer ya," Ginza retorted.

"You wanna test 'em out, Gin?!" Hanzo bellowed.

"Enough!" Hasunuma demanded.

The crew fell silent.

"I'm sure that Kazuki gets what ya mean without ya havin' t' fight about it," the Pirate King reprimanded while giving Hanzo and Ginza a look that dared them to continue arguing. Then he turned to Kazuki and grinned. "See, Little Oni? We're all in agreement."

Kazuki looked away.

"Got a problem with that, Kid?" The Pirate King asked in a serious tone.

"No…" Kazuki hesitated to continue, "I just…Thanks." The young man's cheeks grew hot and he quickly turned away from the rest of the crew.

"Ahaha! Look at 'im, 'es blushin' like a girl!" The blacksmith teased.

"Shut it, Ginza!" Kazuki glared.

"Ya wanna fight, Little Oni?" Ginza asked as he approached Kazuki and tried to lock the young man's head in his large arm. Kazuki quickly avoided the blacksmith's arms, but he bumped into Hanzo and was trapped.

"Heh. Looks like you're ours now, Lad!" Hanzo grinned. He grabbed Kazuki's shoulders and pushed him down to the deck.

While the young man struggled to get up, Ginza lifted a large bucket over his head. Kazuki frantically looked for Hasunuma to stop them, but he had already left the deck.

"Think ya can beat us, Little Oni?" Ginza grinned as he dumped the contents of the bucket over Kazuki.

"Think again, Lad!" Hanzo said, while he and Ginza burst into laughter at the sight of grumpy Kazuki covered in fish guts.

"I hope the demons come after you first," Kazuki grumbled.

"Me too, Lad! Then I'll kill them all before you wet yourself in fear." The giant continued to laugh as he went back to his duties on deck.

Ginza joined him a moment later after saying, "Glad t' have ya 'round, Little Oni," to the still angry Kazuki.

Mumbling unpleasant phrases, Kazuki went below deck to wash up. As he passed by the kitchen he noticed that the door was slightly cracked. He thought it was odd, because Jun insisted that the door be kept shut. Kazuki was about to close the door when he heard Hasunuma and Jun inside. Tension seeped out of the room like a clogged toilet.

"I heard what you said, *Captain*, but I'm not teaching that kid anything unless it's food related."

"And I'm saying, *Jun*, that ya need t' do what I say and teach the kid some technique."

"I told you, that's not my job," the cook growled.

"He already knows the basics, he just needs t' refine his skill. It won't be hard," the Pirate King tried to assure the cook.

"Says you," the cook scoffed.

Hasunuma sighed. "Look, I wasn't gonna bring this up if I didn't have to, but the kid was taught by Jisai."

The atmosphere suddenly changed completely. Kazuki peered through the crack in the door. What did the old man have to do with Jun? Kazuki watched as Jun threw his deba knife across the kitchen. It lodged itself in the back wall as Jun grabbed Hasunuma's shirt.

"You're telling me that my *father* taught that kid?!" Jun spat.

Kazuki's eyes bulged as he held back a gasp.

"My father wouldn't even teach his own son how to fight!"

"We've been over this, Jun," the Pirate King growled as he forcibly removed Jun's hands from his shirt. "Your father thought you'd been killed fourteen years ago and you never went back to set him straight. How could he teach a dead son how to fight?"

"I wasn't dead to him my whole life!"

"He lost you when you were ten years old! You don't teach kids that young t' use a sword that's bigger than them."

"Well he didn't think twice about teaching Kazuki, now did he?" Jun fumed.

"By the gods, Jun! It's your own damn fault for not going back to see him before he died trying to get revenge for a son who wasn't actually dead," the Pirate King retorted.

Jun's fist flew towards Hasunuma's face, but the Pirate King was faster. He grabbed Jun's arm and threw him into the wall. The wood cracked from the impact. Hasunuma didn't waste a moment as he grabbed Jun by the neck and whispered something in his ear. The Pirate King then let go of Jun and waited for the cook to nod before turning to leave the room. Kazuki saw him coming and quickly ran down the hallway to the shower stall.

Steam began filling the room as Kazuki thoroughly scrubbed off the fish remains. He had to pick a lot of it out of his hair, which normally would have made him think of all sorts of ways to get even with Hanzo and Ginza, but not today. Kazuki couldn't get the fight between Hasunuma and Jun off of his mind. If Jun was truly the old man's son, then the old man had no idea his son was still alive. How could Jun not go and tell his father? The old man wouldn't have gone on a suicide mission for revenge if he had known about his son.

The young man pulled more fish guts out of his hair and watched as they swirled down the drain. Hasunuma had acted strangely too. Why was he so harsh on Jun? Yeah, he's the captain of the ship, but that doesn't give him the right to be such a–

"Little Oni, ya in 'ere?"

Kazuki twitched. "What do you want, Ginza?"

The blacksmith chuckled and said, "Ya washin' off all those tasty fish guts, Little Oni?"

"Shut up and tell me what you want," the young man grumbled.

"Not me, Cap'n wants t' see ya in 'is quarters."

Kazuki's stomach dropped.

Ginza began to leave, but he turned back towards the young man and added, "And I'd hurry if I were ya. Cap'n's in a foul mood."

Kazuki nodded in response and Ginza left the room. He ran his fingers through his hair one last time and then shut off the water.

While Kazuki was drying himself off, Ginza came back into the room and asked if Kazuki had seen Jun. The young man fervently shook his head and Ginza remarked that it was odd for Jun not to be in the kitchen, and, if Kazuki sees him, to tell Jun to start making lunch. Once again Kazuki nodded and Ginza left the room.

After getting dressed as quickly as he could, Kazuki made his way to the Captain's Quarters.

There was a knock on the cabin door followed by, "You wanted to see me, Captain?"

Hasunuma didn't bother to look up from the map as he replied, "Yeah, come in."

Kazuki entered the room and closed the door behind him. He stood awkwardly by the door for a while before Hasunuma impatiently beckoned him to sit down.

"I'm not in the best mood as it is, so I'm going to make this quick: The conversation between Jun and myself was a private one. I don't appreciate eavesdroppers."

"But I–"

"Kid, don't even try. Not only am I a trained ninja, but I could smell you a mile away."

Kazuki's mouth dropped.

I guess he hadn't thought about that. "I assume it was Hanzo and Ginza again." Hasunuma sighed, "Whatever. Jun was too worked up to sense you, so let's keep your spying a secret, shall we?"

The kid slowly nodded.

"And no, I am not answering any of your questions regarding the conversation you overheard, so get that look off of your face."

The Pirate King returned his focus to the map in front of him. He was trying to figure out where they should go next in order to gather more information. They could try Minoku, the port town closer to the Capital, but that would be risky since the Hekigun had recently established a large base there. The other option was Giyosan, another port town, which didn't host a Hekigun base and was further away from the Capital. Although it seemed like an easy decision, the problem with Giyosan was that the only way to gather information there was through the red-light district. And while the Pirate King had no problems with gathering the information himself, he knew that the kid wasn't going to agree with him.

"Did you need me for something else, or can I leave?" Kazuki asked, sounding mildly annoyed.

Hasunuma looked up from the map and grinned at the kid. *Decision made.* "I need ya t' come with me on a mission."

It took four days to reach Giyosan from Mizuya. When the Ryujin was docked in the harbor, all of the crew, except for Hanzo and Jun, descended the gangplank to the docks below.

Giyosan was one of the largest port towns on the mainland. Half a day's boat ride from the nefarious Northeastern cluster of islands off of the mainland, Giyosan was quite popular with the more…devious citizens. It made perfect sense seeing that the gambling and pleasure town, O-kane, laid claim to the largest of the three cluster islands, while the two smaller islands were known pirate domains. The Pirate King exclusively owned the West Island, so the other pirates had to keep to the East Island.

Either way, the Hekigun had less control over that part of the country, so it was the perfect place for people, like the King of pirates, to gather information and restock supplies.

Kohaku, Rize and Ginza were given the restocking task, while Hasunuma and Kazuki gathered information on the Hekigun. Hanzo remained on the ship in order to guard it from thieves, since the

Ryujin was a popular and well-known ship; it was the Pirate King's ship after all, and everyone knew its name and iconic, fearsome, red dragon figurehead. Jun hardly ever left the galley, but, even when he was on board, he rarely accepted guard duty.

However, the main reason Hanzo wasn't allowed to leave the ship was because he stood out too much. It wasn't his size alone; the giant's fair skin and blue eyes shouted 'foreigner,' and that was unacceptable, even in Giyosan.

Ever since Hiiro Genji took power, he cut off trade routes with other countries and persecuted foreigners. The Pirate King's guess was that Hiiro Genji had been afraid that other countries would come to aid the Tsukigen people in ousting the Hekigun, but the move had been more brutal than expected; Tsukigen's economy and development were crushed by the move. Hiiro Genji had brought a dark age upon them, and the Pirate King was determined to give his last breath to end it.

The grim expression on Hasunuma's face suddenly changed when he realized they were nearing the largest red-light district on the mainland. He couldn't wait to see the kid's reaction. *I'd bet the Ryujin that the kid'll flip out and refuse to go inside.* Which worked perfectly for the Pirate King; he didn't want an audience.

"Why are there so many women out here? Is there a big market today?" Kazuki asked as he scanned the crowded streets.

Hasunuma couldn't help but laugh at him.

"What's so funny?" The kid asked, glaring at the Pirate King.

"Nothin', nothin' at all, Little Oni." The Pirate King stopped laughing, but a huge grin shone on his face. "These ladies aren't looking t' buy somethin', they're looking t' *sell* somethin'."

"Oh, like clothes, hairpins, and jewelry, I guess," the kid said. Seeming satisfied with this answer, he continued to follow Hasunuma.

The Pirate King, on the other hand, tried desperately to keep his mouth shut. *This is too good.*

To everyone but innocents like Kazuki, it was pretty clear what the multitudes of women wandering this area were up to. Not only were they painted and dressed up splendidly, but even their movements and facial gestures were calculated. Unlike on O-kane, the women here weren't allowed to call out to or grab passersby in order to entice them, so over the years they had developed many subtle techniques for acquiring business.

When Hasunuma and Kazuki turned the corner, the two passed through the large gold and red gateway into the red-light district; which was named as such, because, according to the law, all of the 'pleasure shops' had to have a red lantern lit outside of the establishment in order to designate it as such. That way there could be no mistaking any visitor's intentions. In Giyosan, they had also built a large gateway to call attention to the special part of town, which, in turn, made it more of a feature than a blemish.

"What's with the gaudy arch?" Kazuki asked as he looked back at the gateway.

"It's lettin' us know where we are."

"And where is that?"

Hasunuma didn't want to ruin the surprise just yet, so he replied, "The information district."

Kazuki furrowed his brow and began scanning the crowd again. A few moments later, the two of them stopped in front of the largest building on the street. Instead of two floors, it had three, and the building was the width of four regular shops. Protruding from the second floor were small wooden balconies, each connecting to a single room. The third floor was special; it was only about the size of two regular shops, and it was split in half so that there were only two rooms, each the size of one regular shop. Each room had access to a rooftop terrace that was concealed from the street by large camellia bushes. The third floor was for VIPs only, and Hasunuma always stayed in one of those rooms when he visited.

Money always talks, especially here.

The Pirate King grinned, and, before the kid could say anything, a large woman with an equally large smile on her face emerged from the building.

"Well, if it isn't Red Dragon! It's *so* good to see you again! Please come inside. I'll have the usual girls meet you in the suite upstairs. Oh!" The woman finally took notice of Kazuki. "And who is this young charmer?"

"This is the youngest member of my crew," the Pirate King answered.

The woman grinned, "Oh, so is this a special occasion?"

The Pirate King laughed, "No, no, nothin' like that. In fact, I don't think he'll be joinin' us." Hasunuma glanced at Kazuki who was not only crimson red, but was slowly backing away from the doorway.

"Is this–" the kid almost asked, but he was interrupted by three painted women that dashed out of the building and threw themselves at Hasunuma.

"Red Dragon, I've missed you so much!" The first painted

woman shouted as she wrapped herself around Hasunuma's left arm.

"Where have you been, handsome?" The second painted woman cooed as she pulled Hasunuma's right arm into her ample chest.

"I've been so lonely without you!" The third painted woman moaned as she hugged his waist.

This wasn't anything new to the Pirate King. In fact, it happened each and every time he returned. His usual response was: "Take it easy ladies! There's more than enough of me t' go around." Then he would tell them all to go inside and wait for him, and every time they did just that. Including this time.

Before the Pirate King entered the building he looked back at Kazuki. The kid's mixed expression of shock, disgust, and betrayal was hilarious to Hasunuma. He grinned and tossed Kazuki a small sack full of coins.

"Kid, I'm gonna be a while so go buy yerself some candy or somethin'." Hasunuma laughed and entered the building, leaving Kazuki alone on the street.

Kazuki stood in the street, staring at the door to the repulsive building. He couldn't believe what had just happened. This was no 'information gathering' mission; Hasunuma just wanted an excuse to spend time with those painted women. Kazuki was disappointed and disgusted.

"Why the long face, handsome? Can't afford that place, can you?" A painted woman asked as she crossed the street and approached Kazuki. "Not many can. The prices there are outrageous!" She then grabbed his hand and said, "But if you come with me, I'll show you a nice time at half the cost."

Kazuki jerked his hand free and growled, "Don't touch me." He then quickly walked away from the painted woman and made his way back through the gaudy gateway.

As he stepped back onto the main street, Kazuki did his best to avoid eye contact with any of the painted women. He stared down at the gravel and sand road, walking as quickly as he could in order to get out of that area.

"OUCH!" Someone exclaimed as Kazuki felt his head bump into something. When he looked up, there was a big, rough looking man standing in front of him. The man's arms were crossed and he had an evil look in his eye as he glared at Kazuki.

"Sorry," the young man said with a quick bow.

"That ain't good enough," the man growled. "Give me yer coins an' I'll ferget about yer horse pile attitude."

Yeah right, Kazuki thought, but he said, "I have nothing to give you, unless," he added with a grin, "you want me to show you my sword." The young man grabbed his saya with his left hand and pushed up the tsuba with his thumb, slightly disengaging the katana from its sheath.

The man bared his teeth like a wild animal. "Yer askin' fer it!"

But before the man could do anything, a whistle was blown by a town guard who appeared beside Kazuki. He was just as large as the rough looking man, but he was dressed in the garb of the guards: a triangle shaped straw hat, a black hakama, and a white, side fastened top with elbow-length sleeves. The top had the emblem of the guards painted on it: a sasumata with the sun in the center of the weapon's "U" shaped metal tip.

"I suggest that you walk away," the guard said, his voice deep and solemn.

The young man nodded, released his left hand, and began to back away as the guard had instructed. He knew it would be suicide to mess with a town guard. Not only were they extremely well trained in combat arts, but if a person messed with one of the guards, then the whole squad would hunt that person down; there was no escape from the guards. Truly they were more fearsome than mid-ranked Hekigun officers.

According to Rize, the guards were a remnant force from the time before Hiiro Genji. When the Emperor was in power, he elected special troops to keep the peace in larger towns. Unlike soldiers, the special troops were stationed there and could even have families while enlisted. Being chosen for a guard's position was a coveted prize since the job was both honorable and well-paid. Even now, without the Emperor, the guards continued their duties with respect to the ruler who had personally chosen them.

Kazuki thought it was a good thing that the guards decided to continue on, because the Hekigun hadn't done anything in regards to keeping towns safe from lawlessness. Sure, there was less violence and theft in towns where there was a Hekigun base, but in order to receive any proactive protection, the towns people have to give offerings of valuables, coins, women, and more to the Hekigun. Most towns resented the Hekigun's demands and started their own peacekeeping forces, but the best ones were those that were leftover from the Emperor's reign; and the guards in Giyosan were some of them.

With poor judgement, the rough looking man that Kazuki had bumped into decided to continue his fight. He unsheathed his sword and raised it high above his head for a powerful straight cut, but this was another mistake. The guard quickly jabbed the "U" of his sasumata around the man's throat and effortlessly lifted the man off the ground. The rough looking man's feet kicked in the air as he struggled to breathe; his windpipe was pressed against the sasumata. Before the man became irrevocably injured, the guard dropped him to the ground. As the rough looking man lie coughing and sputtering, the guard tied the man's arms together behind his back and then began to drag him away, presumably to his guard post.

The onlookers applauded the guard and spat on the rough looking man as he was dragged by. A few dared to kick the man, but after a glare from the guard, no one else touched the man.

Kazuki shook his head and walked away in the opposite direction. *It's a good thing he came before I drew my sword,* the young man thought, *otherwise, I'd have been dragged away too.*

Rize had warned Kazuki to abide by the town's laws in order to stay out of trouble with the guards, but the young man had almost broken one of the main laws: do not brandish any weapons in the streets.

I've got to be more careful.

Kazuki glanced at the stores as he passed. The shops in Giyosan were mixed instead of organized by type, which is what the other large towns did. There was a butcher next to a jeweler next to a craftsman next to a fishmonger. It seemed a bit odd to the young man, but, honestly, he didn't care either way.

Kazuki didn't like going into any towns, organized or not. They were too loud, too crowded, and he felt uncomfortable and paranoid, as if everyone he passed was judging him or thinking of ways to deceive him. The young man realized that that probably wasn't the case, but he couldn't help but feel that way. In the end, he usually decided that staying aboard the Ryujin was best. Which is where he would be if it weren't for Hasunuma.

Kazuki furrowed his brow. *Seriously, what is wrong with him?!*

Thinking about Hasunuma made the young man angry, so he tried to distract himself by scanning faces in the crowded street. Some were young and some were old, some were fairly attractive and some were definitely not. A few seemed capable of fighting, though most were regular people, and there was a good amount of countryfolk amongst the 'better-bred' townsfolk. But everyone there seemed to have a purpose, whether it was buying, selling, or simply going about their daily business. And although a variety of people walked the streets of Giyosan, everyone looked to be a Tsukigen native.

Come to think of it, I've never seen anyone else who looks like Hanzo. Eiri might be the closest, but, even though his coloring is different, for some reason it seems like he's actually a Tsukigen native...Hmm, I guess Ammon was pretty pale too, so maybe they're natives from somewhere I haven't been yet.

Suddenly the young man saw a familiar, pretty face in the crowd on the other side of the street. He crossed over and noticed that Kohaku was standing in line for a store labeled 'Seasonings', though she was carrying a lot of boxes that looked quite heavy.

"Do you want me to carry those for you, Kohaku?" Kazuki asked, relieved to no longer be alone in the unfamiliar city.

The ninja woman smiled and handed the boxes to Kazuki. They *were* extremely heavy, but the young man would never let it show.

"What do you need in here?" Kazuki asked, trying to gauge how long he'd have to stand there, holding the boxes for.

A short, shrill whistle came from Kohaku's lips.

The young man had memorized most of Kohaku's whistle responses, so he knew that this one meant, "Jun." *She must be getting something for him then.*

She then whistled two notes, one high, one low.

"Oh, he left me and went into one of *those* places." Kazuki replied as he rolled his eyes.

Kohaku's eyes seemed to search the street for Hasunuma.

"No, not here," Kazuki clarified. "He went into the biggest building in that section past that gaudy red and gold arch," the young man said indifferently.

Kohaku turned to Kazuki and smiled. It wasn't a pleasant smile, like the one she gave him earlier; hiding behind this smile was a sea of rage. Kazuki could feel her wrath emanating from every inch of her body. Without another exchange, Kohaku took off towards the gaudy gateway, leaving Kazuki, once again, alone in the city.

As the young man wondered if he should stay or head back, he heard a familiar voice called out from the crowd.

"Hey, Little Oni!"

A moment later, Rize appeared next to Kazuki. He was also carrying large, heavy looking boxes.

"Have you seen Kohaku? We were just about done gathering supplies when we got separated."

"Not surprising with this many people around. And yeah, I saw her," Kazuki said as he nodded towards the boxes she had placed in his arms.

"Where'd she go? We have to get these loaded on the ship," Rize said, looking a bit worried.

Kazuki sighed. "She ran off as soon as I told her that the captain left me and went into one of *those* buildings. You know, the ones past the gaudy red and gold arch."

Rize stared at Kazuki, his mouth wide open.

"What?"

"You told Kohaku that the captain went to the red-light district?" Rize asked, wide-eyed.

"Yeah. What's wrong with that?" The young man asked, unsure of the reason for Rize's reaction.

Rize began laughing and set the boxes down beside him. "What's wrong with that? Hah! The captain's gonna be angry when he finds out that you told Kohaku where he was."

Kazuki still couldn't figure out what he did wrong. "Why will he be mad?"

"You really are just a kid aren't you?" Rize declared as he laughed even harder. When he finally calmed down enough to speak again, he added, "Think about it, Little Oni. Why would the captain not want *Kohaku* to know he was in the red-light district?"

Kazuki thought about it for a moment and replied, "Because it's embarrassing?"

Rize slapped the young man on the back and continued to laugh at him. "Sometimes I wonder how you can be so innocent when it comes to women. I mean, you're old enough to know and yet you're clueless."

Kazuki turned bright red. "Well, the only women I've known are my mother and Kohaku, so how the festering hole am I supposed to know anything!"

Rize patted Kazuki on the shoulder and apologized. "Sorry Little Oni, I sometimes forget that you haven't seen much of this world." He picked his boxes back up and said, "If you help me carry all this stuff back to the ship, I'll find you a good woman to turn you into a man."

Kazuki frowned. "I'll help you, but I don't need you to find me a woman."

"Oh, so you've already found one?" Rize joked. "Remember, you can't have Kohaku 'cause she already belongs to the captain."

Kazuki understood what Rize meant, but he didn't understand how that was possible. "What are you talking about?"

In lieu of a response, Rize started walking towards the ship with the boxes. Kazuki followed the helmsman, his question left unanswered until they arrived back at the Ryujin.

"Have you ever wondered why Kohaku dresses like a man?" Rize suddenly asked as he set the boxes down on the deck.

"I thought that was so no one would know she was a woman?" Kazuki offered. As he offloaded his boxes next to Rize's, the young man sighed with relief; his arms had been screaming the whole way back to the ship.

Rize laughed. "You should know by now that no amount of baggy men's clothing is gonna hide those big breasts of hers."

Kazuki face began to flush. He *had* noticed.

"The captain doesn't want other men looking at his woman. If Kohaku were dressed normally, every man would be drooling and fighting over her." Rize sighed and added, "If you still don't believe me, you should watch the way the captain and Kohaku act around each other."

"Ok…" Kazuki still wasn't sure about what Rize was telling him, but he would be paying more attention to Kohaku and Hasunuma's interactions from now on. "But then why would he go see those painted women if he has Kohaku?" The young man asked, thinking more about it.

Rize shook his head. "Honestly, we all agree that the captain's an idiot when it comes to women, but, in this case, he does have a valid reason for seeming like a two-timing horse's arse." The helmsman then smiled and said, "Thanks for helping me bring these boxes back, Little Oni. If you want, you can explore the city while we wait for the captain to return."

Kazuki almost said 'no' to Rize's offer, but then he thought about gathering information: the original reason for he and Hasunuma to go into town. "Yeah, I'm gonna go look around for a while."

"Alright. I'll send Ami for you when the captain returns."

Kazuki nodded and left the Ryujin. This time he headed for the opposite end of town, hoping he could find more there than painted women and rough looking men.

"Oh, Red Dragon! Not there, it tickles!" The first painted woman giggled in delight. Her name was Sakura, and she was beautifully proportioned from head to toe.

"No fair! I want a turn!" The second painted woman whined as she watched the Pirate King kiss and caress Sakura. Her name was Renge, and her red-orange hair was as unique as her sensual dancing.

"Why don't we all join in?" The third painted woman whispered with a grin. Her name was Sumire, and she was a beauty who required a man with a mature palate.

The three women were sisters. Not triplets, but sisters. The eldest, Sakura, was always first. She also was always dressed to look like her namesake; her medium brown skin acting as the bark of the tree, she draped herself in sheer, light pink cloth that had delicate white petals painted on it. And her dark hair was always pulled back and ornamented with cherry blossom themed pins.

The middle sister, Renge, could never wait for her turn without a fuss. She was a talented dancer whose performances always won her a standing ovation, but she had a childish side to her that sometimes showed.

And the youngest, Sumire, was wild and passionate – always wanting to try something new. Not just any man would do for this woman, but, when she found a suitable guest, the desire to see her again would grip the man so intently that he'd end up spending a fortune and, usually, find himself drowning in debt.

Though all three women were the most beautiful in town, the Pirate King chose them for their wonderful memories, not their luscious bodies. When it came to getting information on the Hekigun, Hasunuma would have paid to see an old hag if necessary. But it wouldn't be as enjoyable as the current situation he was in.

"Now ladies, ya know the rules. I need information from ya in order t' continue…" Hasunuma baited.

The sisters complied like starving animals.

"One of the top Hekigun generals started traveling here last month just to see me." Renge bragged. "He said that he's been given charge of a base on Rurin."

The Pirate King grinned. Pulling Renge close to him, he began to slowly kiss her neck. Renge moaned and ran her fingers through Hasunuma's hair.

"What else did he tell ya?" Hasunuma whispered in Renge's ear.

Through her moans Renge managed to say, "He's got at least two-hundred men in the camp, including five high ranking and very talented officers."

"Very good," the Pirate King said as he continued to kiss and caress her.

"That's nothing!" Sumire squealed. "I've got quite a few fans in the Hekigun, and they've all been telling me how their generals have gotten much stronger in a short amount of time."

Hasunuma left Renge and grabbed Sumire. He began untying her kimono, but, to Sumire's great displeasure, Sakura interfered.

The eldest pulled the Pirate King away from her little sister and embraced him. Running her fingers down his back, Sakura said, "I've saved the best for last." She kissed him deeply before telling him, "Hiiro Genji is back in Chuushin."

Hasunuma's eyes blazed with interest. He began to kiss Sakura's neck and shoulder while pulling at the sheer fabric draped around her body.

She giggled with pleasure and added, "He won't be leaving anytime soon. Apparently, there's something going on at his castle…people are saying it's some kind of test or experiment."

The Pirate King froze for a moment, but then continued to undress the eldest sister. He didn't want the sisters to suspect anything. Just when he had gotten Sakura ready, a shuriken came flying through the air, aimed for Hasunuma's head. The Pirate King reached up and grabbed it, stopping the shuriken before it made its mark.

He grinned. "Nice try Kohaku, but if yer goin' t' kill me, don't be so obvious about it. I sensed yer anger before ya even got here."

The ninja woman was crouched in one of the open windows that led to the rooftop terrace. The look on her face was priceless; although she was clearly fuming, it made Hasunuma happy knowing that she was jealous.

Two more shuriken came flying at the Pirate King. He let go of Sakura and stopped both metal stars. The sisters didn't panic or move – they were used to this sort of thing happening.

"Kohaku, if ya want t' bed me so badly then why don't ya join us? Ya could learn a thing or two from these wo-"

A whole fleet of shuriken came flying towards the Pirate King, who now had to use his sword to deflect all of the metal stars.

"Sorry ladies, it looks like this time I'll have t' cut our information session short." Hasunuma's smile melted the painted sisters' hearts. They begged and pleaded for him to stay, but Kohaku kept sending shuriken into the room, so they soon gave up and let the Pirate King leave.

He made his way down to the main entrance, where the Pirate King made sure to pay the large woman in charge. He couldn't risk angering her since those sisters were the best source of information in town. A few extra coins were given to her for any damage Kohaku may have caused. The large woman thanked the Pirate King and told him to come back soon. Hasunuma winked and told her that she would see him again.

As Hasunuma made his way out of the red-light district, Kohaku appeared behind him. "Why do ya always interrupt me durin' the best part?" Hasunuma teased.

Kohaku launched a few shuriken at the Pirate King's back, but he was able to stop them all. He laughed and suddenly turned around to face Kohaku. She stopped walking, but was now only inches from Hasunuma's face.

"It's cute when you get jealous," the Pirate King whispered.

Kohaku's cheeks flushed and she raised her hand to slap the Pirate King.

Hasunuma stopped her hand mid swing and grinned. "I'll reward ya for bein' so adorable, Kohaku." Whispering in her ear, Hasunuma said, "In my quarters on the Ryujin there's an ornate golden box. Inside of that box is something your mother left for you."

Kohaku gave the Pirate King a look that read 'why didn't you tell me about it earlier?!'

Hasunuma pulled away from Kohaku and gently released her hand. "Let's just say it isn't something I would give to *my* daughter."

Without a sound, the ninja woman disappeared before his eyes. Well, she would have if Hasunuma wasn't so highly trained. He actually saw her run off at an impressive speed, and then watched as she jumped on top of the nearest shop and used the town rooftops as her own personal road back to the Ryujin.

The Pirate King headed back to the ship as well, but at a much slower pace on the regular streets. A smile appeared on his face. *At first, I never wanted you to have it, but now…now I can't wait to see you wear it.*

The Pirate King let his mind wander on the subject and his smile quickly disappeared. He remembered that he wasn't the only male that would appreciate Kohaku's mother's gift. Hasunuma immediately regretted telling Kohaku about the box.

The Pirate King then sighed and said to himself, "Oh well, I'll just have to kill any man that looks at her."

No matter where he went, Kazuki saw painted women. There weren't as many as there had been around the gaudy arch, but he hadn't been on a single street where there wasn't at least one painted woman. Thankfully, none approached him, but the young man still found them irritating. Maybe it was because of what Hasunuma had done, or maybe it was because they weren't what Kazuki thought of or wanted when it came to women, but, either way, their presence was bothersome.

Why do they put all of that stuff on their faces anyways? It makes them look like actors from a masked troupe. I'm sure they'd all look better without it.

The young man may not have known that many women, but he still had his own preferences. He liked women who were naturally beautiful, had a calming aura, and were strong enough so that, if something happened, they could at least defend themselves long enough for Kazuki to come to their rescue. Otherwise, he wasn't interested.

Kohaku was a fine example of the young man's type, but her downside was that she couldn't speak. Since Kazuki's hearing was his prime sense, he wanted a woman with a sweet voice that he could listen to all day long. And, unlike Hasunuma, Kazuki didn't have a preference for a specific body type. It would be nice if the woman had something to grab onto, but-

"AIYEE!"

The young man heard the scream, but he seemed to be the only one; none of the townspeople around him reacted. It was high-pitched, so it must have been a woman, and the sound came from somewhere to Kazuki's right. There was nothing to be seen in the immediate area, so the young man took off running down the first alleyway to his right. The alley opened up onto another busy street.

As Kazuki searched the crowd, he noticed a 'Wanted' board posted on one of the shop walls. He approached the sign and found sketches of criminal after criminal, including Hasunuma and his entire crew. There was a sign for Kazuki too, but the sketch of him wasn't at all accurate - probably because anyone who had seen Kazuki in action was dead. The young man was about to walk away when a different poster caught his eye. There was no image, just,

'Shinigami-sama,' written in bold, red strokes and what looked like map coordinates written underneath.

"AIYEE!"

Kazuki heard the woman's scream again and this time he knew exactly where to go. After ripping the poster off of the wall and shoving it into his pocket, Kazuki ran down the street and took the second alleyway to his right. He then took the first left and then another right before arriving at the scene of the crime.

In the middle of the alleyway, a fairly large and muscular man was on top of a woman on the ground. Kazuki couldn't see the woman's face, but the way that her feet were squirming under the man told Kazuki that she did not want to be there. The man had the woman pinned to the ground with one hand, while the other began climbing up her leg.

"Get off of me, you big oaf!" The woman yelled, but the man showed no signs of giving up.

The man didn't look like he would be hard to defeat, but Kazuki wasn't going to take any chances. First, he glanced around to make sure there was no one else nearby; he didn't want anyone to call for the guards. Next, he called out to the man in order to get his attention; Kazuki had to lure the man away from the woman, so that the young man could defeat him without restraint.

"Hey, loser. Can't ya hear the lady? No means no." Kazuki winced as soon as the words left his mouth. He had imitated one of Hasunuma's lines, hoping he would sound cool, but it was forced and weird coming from him.

I'm never trying that again.

Although he may not have sounded cool, Kazuki definitely got the man's attention. He stopped fondling the woman and turned his head towards Kazuki.

"You say somethin' t' me, Kid?!" The man growled as he stood up, keeping the woman's neck in his grasp.

The woman was much shorter than her attacker, so, when the man stood up, the woman's feet didn't touch the ground. It looked like she was now struggling to breathe.

"I'll kill you once I'm done with this bitch!" The man howled.

Not gonna let go, huh?

Kazuki dashed towards the man. Unsheathing his katana with incredible speed and precision, Kazuki sliced off the man's arm that was clutching the woman's throat. The woman fell to the ground with the man's arm dangling from her neck. Kazuki quickly flicked the blood off of the blade and re-sheathed his katana.

"AGH!" The man yelled as he clutched his bloody stump. "You little bastard! You'll pay fer that!" The man charged recklessly at Kazuki, who stepped aside and watched the man run past him.

"Leave now or your arm won't be the only thing I take from you," the young man warned.

The man only grew more furious, unleashing a slew of curses. Kazuki drew his katana and took an offensive stance. When the man charged Kazuki again, the young man easily side stepped once more, but this time, as the man passed, Kazuki bisected him using a horizontal slash. The man's upper and lower halves hit the ground with a wet *thud.* As streams of blood flowed out, the sand beneath the gravel drank deeply, turning a purplish hue.

The fight had not been a challenge, but Kazuki had given the man a chance to run. It was what the Ryujin crew had taught him;

during a fight, even against a guy who deserves a good beating, if you're stronger, you need to give your opponent a chance to surrender. That was apparently the 'proper' way to handle smaller conflicts, which seemed silly to Kazuki since they were all considered a bunch of 'lawless' pirates anyways. Did it really matter how many horrible, wicked men they killed? And wouldn't sparing their lives invite more atrocities in the end?

Kazuki shook his head. *Evil men should never get a second chance.*

As the young man returned to reality, he saw the woman that he had saved peeling the dead man's hand off of her neck.

"Gross!" She exclaimed as she flung the hand away from her. The woman took one look at Kazuki and then jumped up and threw her arms around his neck. "Thank you *so* much for saving me! I would have been super unlucky if it weren't for you!"

Kazuki wasn't sure how to react. Not only did a strange woman have her arms around him, but her beauty was dumbfounding. She had pale pink skin, golden yellow hair, and vibrant, emerald green eyes. Her face was clean, except for a little paint on top of her eyes and on her lips, and she looked as though she might be close to Kazuki's age. From what Kazuki could feel on his chest, the beauty was significantly less buxom than Kohaku – but he didn't mind. She also smelled sweet, like honeysuckle.

Before the young man could find the words to speak, the beautiful young woman unlocked her arms from around him and began to walk away; her narrow hips swaying as she went. Accentuating her delicate frame, the soft green kimono she wore had a white flower pattern on it that resembled cherry blossoms.

"Wait," was all that Kazuki could muster.

The enchanting young woman turned around and blew a kiss at the young man, "Don't you worry, Shinigami-sama, I will see you again soon. Ta-ta!" And in the blink of an eye, the she was gone.

Kazuki stood there in a trance, staring at the spot where the beauty had been. Had he imagined the whole thing? No, her attacker's halves were still lying on the ground.

Wait…did she say 'Shinigami-sama'?

A sudden sensation on the young man's shoulder snapped him out of his daze.

"Ow," he groaned. "Hey, Ami."

The grey-blue falcon screeched and stared into Kazuki's eyes. Her razor sharp beak was only an inch or two away from the young man's face, while her equally sharp talons gripped his shoulder. As formidable a predator as Ami was, Kazuki didn't feel he was in danger; he knew that Rize had trained her well, and that Ami would never attack a friend.

"Right, I guess it's time for me to return to the ship." The young man nodded and then took one last look around the alleyway before making his way back to the Ryujin.

As he walked, Kazuki played the scene over and over again in his head. He thought that there must be some detail that he missed, but nothing stood out. Aside from the young woman, that is.

"I wonder if I'll see her again," the young man muttered to himself.

Ami screeched cheerfully as she rode on Kazuki's shoulder. Usually, she flew back to the ship on her own, but this time she decided to accompany the young man.

Kazuki smiled and gently rubbed the falcon's chest. There was a calming quality about Ami that he appreciated.

"In Mizuya we had messenger birds, but they were doves, not falcons. You're the first raptor I've seen hanging around humans."

Scree-scree!

"You must really like Rize," the young man said with a smile. "I can understand that."

Screeee-scree-scree-scree!

Kazuki laughed. "Yeah, Kohaku's nice too. You're a lucky–"

"Excuse me, Sir," a man suddenly called out as he approached them, "is that a peregrine falcon you have there?"

The young man's smile vanished. He stopped walking and turned to the man. "What of it?" He responded coldly.

"Well, the bird would fetch a handsome price," the man, a merchant, explained as he rubbed his hands together. "I could help you sell it for a forty percent cut."

Kazuki glared at the merchant.

"Eee! I meant, thirty percent," the man squealed.

Kazuki took a few steps towards the merchant and got right in his face. Although they were around the same height, Kazuki's aura made him very intimidating to the merchant.

"Lose interest now or lose your life," the young man snarled.

"Yes, yes! So sorry to bother you," the merchant squeaked as he ran back to his shop.

"Arse's stench, that guy's such a weasel," Kazuki grumbled as he continued walking back to the ship.

Screee!

"I'm not gonna tell Rize about it."

Scree-screee!

"As much as he'd love to skin a weasel, Rize's bounty is high enough. If you want to risk his life, then *you* tell him," Kazuki retorted.

Ami playfully nibbled the young man's hair.

"…Why don't I feel like a crazy person for talking to you, Ami?"

The falcon cocked her head and looked him in the eye.

Kazuki chuckled. "I'm sure it's my imagination, but sometimes I feel like we're actually having a conversation."

Screee!

When they reached the docks, Ami flapped her wings as if she were about to take flight.

"We're almost there," Kazuki reassured her.

As the two boarded the Ryujin, Ami snapped her beak at Kazuki, gave a shrill screech, and then flew up to the crow's nest – presumably looking for Rize.

Kazuki made his way to the Captain's Quarters. He had to tell Hasunuma what happened in the alleyway – maybe the Pirate King could make some sense of it all. The young man knocked on the cabin door. There was a soft whistle from inside the room.

"Kohaku? It's Kazuki. Is Hasunuma in there? I've got something important to tell him."

The lock clicked and the door opened. Kazuki stepped inside of the cabin, only to freeze when he saw Kohaku.

She was wearing some sort of sleeveless short dress, or long top, that was a deep shade of purple with a barely distinguishable floral pattern on it. The bottom half had slits running up both sides that would have revealed too much flesh if Kohaku hadn't been wearing tight black shorts underneath. Her thigh-high boots, or whatever, were also tight and black; between the tops of those and the bottom of the shorts was a short strip of exposed skin that was very enticing. As was the amount of cleavage seen from the 'V' line of her top.

By the gods...I now fully understand why Hasunuma made her wear men's clothing.

Kohaku's arms were covered from her biceps to her palms in the same sort of tight black material, and she had a thick black belt around her waist that had lots of pouches attached to it.

I guess those are for her medical supplies and small weapons that she always carries around.

"Kid, if you stare at her any longer, I'll gouge your eyes out."

Kazuki turned around to find Hasunuma standing behind him in the doorway. The look on his face told Kazuki that he wasn't joking. The young man then remembered what Rize had mentioned earlier.

The Pirate King pushed his way around Kazuki and took a seat at his desk.

Someone tapped Kazuki on the shoulder.

When he turned, he saw Kohaku and shut his eyes. The female ninja gave a light whistle, letting the young man know that it was all right to open his eyes. She held out a piece of paper for him to read.

"Kazu, don't pay any attention to what Hasu says. He's just a grumpy old man. My mother had made this outfit for me before she died. It was supposed to be my coming-of-age present, but Hasu only told me about it today. What a jerk!"

Kazuki couldn't help but smile as he nodded in understanding. "Well, I'm sure she'd be happy with how it turned out. You look stunning."

Kohaku smiled and gave Kazuki a pat on the head before she left the cabin.

It was now just Hasunuma and the young man. Tension filled the air, but Kazuki wasn't going to let the Pirate King intimidate him.

"Hasunuma, how can you be so overly protective of Kohaku when you're the one going to the red-light district?"

"Because her mother left her in *my* care." Hasunuma got up from his chair and approached Kazuki. "I won't let any man touch her."

Kazuki stood his ground. "I don't think you're protecting her for her mother's sake. I think you're jealous."

"Yeah right," Hasunuma scoffed, "why the festering hole would the King of Pirates be jealous? I can get any woman I want."

"Except for Kohaku apparently."

Hasunuma grabbed Kazuki by the collar. "Did you come in here just to piss me off, or is there something else you wanted to say?"

Kazuki grabbed the Pirate King's wrist and pulled himself free. "Actually, I had something I needed to talk to you about," the young man said as he placed the crumpled wanted poster on Hasunuma's desk, "but I think I'll wait until you cool down."

Kazuki then pulled open the cabin door and left Hasunuma standing there, full of fury.

The Pirate King dug his nails into his palms. Small red streams began trickling through his fingers. He deeply inhaled and exhaled for a few minutes before relaxing his hands and sitting down at his desk.

"That kid sure knows how to provoke a beast."

He wiped the blood off of his hands and watched as the crescent shaped cavities quickly disappeared.

Hasunuma frowned. "More experiments, huh?"

He leaned back in his chair and closed his eyes. Distant memories flashed by as colored images; a boy writhing in pain, evil eyes glowing in the darkness, flames engulfing an underground lab, and a sole survivor crawling from the wreckage. Hasunuma opened his eyes, dismissing the pictures from the past.

"I guess I didn't destroy enough of his lab…" the Pirate King gripped the hilt of his red dragon sword, "but I won't make the same mistake twice."

A crumpled piece of paper on the desk caught Hasunuma's eye. He grabbed it and flattened it out as best he could. On it, in big red letters, read: 'Shinigami-sama'. This must have been what the kid wanted to talk about. Below the name were small numbers. At first Hasunuma assumed they were coordinates, but when he tried to find the location on the map, it led him to the middle of the sea.

What else could these numbers be?

The Pirate King tried decoding it in a number of ways, but every time he thought he had solved it, the answer made no sense. Then another idea came to him. He quickly got up and left the room.

When he walked out on deck, Rize called out to him from behind the helm. "Captain! Are we ready to leave port yet?"

"No, not yet. I need t' solve somethin' first." He looked around, but didn't see Kazuki anywhere. "Hey, Rize, where's Little Oni?"

"Not sure, Captain. I don't think he left the ship though. Want me to look for him?"

"No. I'll get Ginza t' bring him t' me. He has a knack for findin' the kid." The Pirate King then called Ginza over and ordered him to find Kazuki.

A few minutes after Hasunuma returned to his cabin there was a knock on the door. The Pirate King granted entry, and Kazuki walked in.

"Have you cooled down yet?" The kid asked.

"What?" Hasunuma had forgotten all about the earlier incident. "Oh. Yeah, sure." He held up the poster and asked, "Any idea what these numbers at the bottom mean?"

Kazuki frowned. Either he didn't know the answer, or he was disappointed at the lack of reaction from Hasunuma. "I thought they were coordinates."

"No, they're not. I tried decoding them in every way that I know how, but nothing worked."

"So, we have nothing?"

"No," Hasunuma grinned, "we have *something*. I think that these numbers could be understood by a demon."

Kazuki frowned again and sat down in the chair opposite of the Pirate King.

"Think about it this way: the poster is public, but the message is private. What better way to ensure that the right person gets the message than to code it in a unique way?" The Pirate King mused.

"And that way is through some sort of demon code?" The kid seemed skeptical, as per usual.

"Exactly."

Kazuki crossed his arms. "How are we supposed to translate it if it's meant for demons?"

Hasunuma stared at the kid. Did he really not understand what the Pirate King meant? "Well, one of us has the King of demons inside of him…and I was thinking that he could help us out."

"Oh." Kazuki said, unfolding his arms and scratching his head. It was obvious that he hadn't realized the answer until now. "Well, I guess I could try to ask him." The kid closed his eyes and sat there motionless.

Quite some time had passed before Hasunuma heard a familiar, **"Yes?"**

The Pirate King was amazed that the kid was able to summon the Demon King. This brought up many new questions about how the link between the two worked, but Hasunuma decided that now was not the time to ask.

"The kid found this poster in town," Hasunuma pointed at the paper on his desk, "It's got your name on it and some numbers below."

The Demon King stared at the paper. **"I take it you want me to solve this for you?"**

"Well, I've tried all the *human* ways to solve it. I figured you could give me a demon's perspective on the matter."

The Demon King grinned. **"You are clever, Pirate. Too clever."** He continued to stare at the paper for a while before saying, **"It is a demon code as you suspected. The numbers on the left indicate the location, while the numbers on the right indicate who sent the message."**

"So who are we meeting and where?"

"Thirteen through Nineteen are waiting at Tenrou Shrine in the mountains. Do you know this place?"

The Pirate King grinned. "Yeah, I know the place. It's the perfect spot for a demon battle."

The Demon King's black eyes locked onto Hasunuma. **"Seven demons are a lot for one child to battle on his own."**

"Who the festering hole said he'd be fighting them alone?"

The Demon King grinned. **"Good. Train him well, Pirate. Not only are the abilities of a demon beyond that of a human, but most can manipulate the elements as well. The child cannot defeat the others as he is now."**

The Pirate King's grin widened as he cocked his head to the side. "What, the King of demons is going to let a child fight for him?"

The Demon King smiled. **"Where is the fun in a slaughter?"**

Right…

"Do we have a time-limit on this meeting?" Hasunuma asked, hoping that there would be time to properly train the kid and his men before heading to the shrine.

"Yes, demons are surprisingly patient when using this method to call me out. They do not know when I have received the message, so I would say that you have about a month or so before they become restless and leave the shrine to seek me out." The Demon King then stared meaningfully at Hasunuma before he added, **"I will be watching you, Pirate. Remember that."**

"Thanks for the warning," the Pirate King shot back, unafraid.

Then, without another word from the Demon King, Kazuki's body slumped onto the desk – with steam rising from it.

As the steam disappeared, the kid's body sat up. "Did it work?" Kazuki asked, back in control of his body.

"Yeah, Kid, it worked." Hasunuma patted the kid's head. "Sorry I asked you to do that. I know it's not fun."

Kazuki grinned. "I can handle it."

Hasunuma laughed. "Tryin' to be an adult now, are ya?"

"Why are you talking like that?"

"What'd ya mean, Little Oni? I always talk like this." Hasunuma turned towards the cabin door. "Isn't that right, men?"

There was a long silence before they heard, "Sorry, Captain. We didn't mean to eavesdrop." That was Rize.

"Yeah, we heard a funny sound and wanted to make sure you were OK." That was Hanzo.

"*Is* e'vry thin' OK, Cap'n?" That was Ginza.

"Yes, yes, we're all fine. Just a quick visit from the Demon King," the Pirate King said casually.

Suddenly the door busted open and all three pirates stormed the cabin. "Where is 'e? I'll kill 'em!" They all shouted in one manner or another.

The Pirate King laughed. "He's gone now. Ya can rest easy." He paused for a moment and then corrected himself, "Actually ya can't rest. We've got demons to hunt." There was a loud cheer from all three pirates.

"He solved the puzzle?" Kazuki asked, eager to hear the answer.

"Sure did, Little Oni. Seven demons are waitin' for us at Tenrou Shrine."

With an enormous sigh, Kazuki fell onto his bed. It had nearly been a month since he began training and his body was continuously exhausted. In a few days the crew would head to Tenrou Shrine to battle the seven demons that waited there. Hasunuma had required everyone to train for a month before leaving, because 'battling demons wasn't the same as battling humans'; in other words, the Pirate King was worried about how his crew would fare since very few humans have the strength or abilities to battle a demon one-on-one.

At first, Kazuki was against the training. He didn't need any extra help since he had the Demon King inside of him, but Hasunuma refused to listen to the young man's excuses. He told Kazuki that 'a real man relies on his own strength, and not on the power of others'. Rolling his eyes, Kazuki had agreed to the training and accompanied the crew to the Pirate King's personal island.

Of the two medium-sized islands south of O-kane – the large gambling island northeast of the mainland – the western island belonged to the Pirate King. Hasunuma had said that the island was established as such when the first Pirate King came into existence. Tales of buried treasure and rooms of solid gold sparked the interest of many sailors, but few dared to set foot on the island. Some say it's cursed and some tell of ghostly guardians that kill any who approach it. Kazuki asked Hasunuma many times about the tales, but he could never get a definite answer from the Pirate King. The Ryujin crew didn't know the truth either.

Living on the island for almost a month now, Kazuki hadn't seen or experienced anything out of the ordinary. He was convinced that the tales were made up in order to scare people away, but, at the same time, he did wonder about what had happened the people who had actually disappeared after landing on the island. Perhaps the pirate kings of the past had killed the intruders themselves? Although the tales say that no one was on the island at the time of each group's disappearance.

Maybe there really are ghosts…

Kazuki shivered. He could deal with demons, but ghosts were different.

Someone suddenly pounded on the door to Kazuki's room. "Hey, Kid, it's almost time. Hurry it up!"

It was Jun. The worst part of the day was training with Jun. He could handle stealth and agility training with Kohaku at the crack of dawn, and speed and endurance training with Hasunuma afterwards. He could even handle practical lessons with Rize and strength training with Hanzo and Ginza – although Kazuki certainly wasn't lifting boulders like they were. But swordsmanship with Jun at the end of the day was the *worst*.

Jun wasn't the easiest person to get along with in general; he had a bad attitude about everything and was only happy when he was alone in the kitchen. Or at least that's what everyone thought. No one really knew how Jun was on his own. Except for maybe Kohaku, since she was the only person he was remotely nice to.

On the first day, Jun had told Kazuki that he wouldn't teach him unless Kazuki could land a single hit on Jun. To the young man's surprise, it took him one week to hit the Ryujin's cook. After that, the lessons were more of a 'watch and learn' than an instruction. It wasn't easy for Kazuki to learn the techniques that Jun taught, but he was slowly making progress.

Jun didn't talk much during the lessons, but that's not why Kazuki felt awkward around him. Because of the conversation he had overheard on the Ryujin, Kazuki wanted so badly to ask Jun about his father and why the old man said his family was all dead when Jun was still alive, but he didn't have the courage to ask. He was afraid that Jun would kill him for mentioning his father.

Kazuki continued to lie on his bed, trying to find the willpower to get up and go to his lesson, when he heard another familiar voice.

Do you want to live?

Kazuki frowned. "Of course I want to live. Why else am I going through all of this training?"

You do not seem very passionate about it. People who strive to live work hard every day to achieve their goals. You do not work hard, and, therefore, do not have the will to live.

Kazuki closed his eyes. "I *do* want to live. It's all just…a little overwhelming." The young man sat up and stared down at his open hands. "I'm just a kid. I don't have as much knowledge or worldly experience as Hasunuma, or as much strength as Ginza and Hanzo, or as much skill and dedication as Kohaku and Rize. I don't have anything to protect or a dream to fulfil." Kazuki brought his fingers to his palms and made two fists. "You chose the wrong human, Demon King."

There was a deep roar within Kazuki that shook him to the core. ***A helpless child with nothing to live for – is that all you think you are? I have lived for hundreds of years and have known many*** *humans. All of them had dreams for the future, all of them wanted to live, and all of them had something to protect. You cannot fool me, human. I have seen what resides in your heart.*

Kazuki sighed and relaxed his hands. "Then you know that they would be better off if I were dead."

Who would be better off?

"The crew. Kohaku. Hasunuma."

Why?

"The demons might kill them in order to get to me."

And why do you care about what happens to the crew, the female ninja, and the pirate?

"Because they're the only family I've got!" Kazuki's eyes widened once the words left his mouth, and he felt his heart ache for the first time in many years.

Now you understand what you fight for – what you need to protect. They are your reason for living.

A burning sensation filled Kazuki's body. He felt a new source of power within him, one that was not the Demon King. He grinned and covered his eyes with his hands. "I'm such an idiot."

Hasunuma chugged the mug full of ale. He sighed as he put it down on the counter in front of him, only to have the mug refilled again by Kohaku. It had been another long day of training, and he was itching to get back to his beloved ship. He looked around the room that was an exact replica of the bar on the Ryujin. Everyone was there, drinking their exhaustion away, except for Jun and Kazuki. Hasunuma wondered if the two of them would ever get along. He hoped that Jun would at least teach Kazuki a few proper sword techniques. The kid needed all the help he could get when it came to using that katana. Not that he hadn't killed plenty of Hekigun soldiers with it beforehand, but the kid never practiced – which is a crucial part of properly and effectively wielding a sword.

"Hey, Cap'n!"

Hasunuma faced back towards the bar and took a swig from his mug. "What'd ya want, Ginza?"

The blacksmith approached the Pirate King and sat beside him. "Want me t' sharpen yer blade? I've already finished with the others."

The Pirate King took out his red dragon sword and looked it over. "Yeah, she's gettin' a bit dull. You sure ya don't mind?"

The blacksmith's face lit up. "Not at all, Cap'n! Forgin' may not be m' job anymore, but I still love workin' on weapons."

"Then she's all yours," the Pirate King said with a smile as he handed over his beloved sword.

As he watched the blacksmith examine the weapon, the Pirate King wondered if Ginza ever regretted joining his crew. Even when he first met Ginza, Hasunuma could tell that the blacksmith loved his job. And, by the gods, he was good at it too. The red dragon sword wasn't an easy piece to make, and it had turned out better than the Pirate King had ever imagined. Once he joined, Ginza had made weapons for the other crewmates too. Except for Rize and Kohaku – theirs were passed down to them and they wouldn't give them up for anything. But Ginza was great at keeping all of the weapons in top killing condition, even if he hadn't originally forged them.

Maybe running his family's ironworks by himself was too painful.

"Hey, Cap'n," the blacksmith said as he slammed his now-empty mug down. "Ya think we can defeat the demons waitin' fer us at that shrine?"

Hasunuma took a swig from his own mug.

"Not that I don't think we can, Cap'n. I just dunno what'll be waitin' fer us."

After another swig, the mug was empty again. "It's definitely a trap, Ginza. But I'm not about to send that kid out there alone."

"I know, Cap'n. An' we're gonna protect 'im 'til the end! Ain't that right, guys?" Ginza boomed.

As mugs were raised high, a loud and enthusiastic "YEAH!" filled the room.

Hasunuma grinned and joined his mug with the others.

After another round, when Hanzo and Rize were busy discussing the particulars of Hanzo's homeland and Kohaku was busy refilling their drinks, the Pirate King quietly asked Ginza something that he'd wondered about for a while: "Is Little Oni similar to your brother?"

The blacksmith stopped mid-drink. He slowly put his mug down on the counter before answering, "Sorta."

"Sorry, I know you don't like talking about the past," Hasunuma said apologetically.

Ginza shook his head. "Nah. It's been s' long it shouldn't hurt anymore."

"Just because it shouldn't, doesn't mean it won't," the Pirate King gently countered.

"M' little brother was a good kid," the blacksmith slowly began.

"'E was never mean t' anyone, and always did what was asked of 'im." The corners of his lips rose slightly. "Unlike Little Oni."

Hasunuma grinned. "'Ain't that right?"

"But 'e was small like Little Oni," Ginza continued. "So 'e wasn't cut out fer bein' a blacksmith. In fact, 'e was really smart an' made up all sorts a' really good poems," the blacksmith boasted.

"You don't happen t' remember any of them do ya?"

Ginza shook his head. "Nah. Ya know m' brain can't keep that kinda stuff, Cap'n."

"That's too bad," Hasunuma noted before downing the rest of his mug.

"If it weren't fer those Hekigun bastards, I'm sure m' brother would've become a famous poet," Ginza lamented.

"When we first met, and you told me about what they did to your family, I added your pain to the countless others that have suffered the Hekigun's cruelty; and that is what fuels my vengeful wrath. We will not stop until the Hekigun have been purged from Tsukigen, Ginza. I promise you that," the Pirate King declared as he stared into the blacksmith's moist eyes.

"I know yer a man a' yer word, Cap'n," Ginza replied. "Which is why I'm gonna do everything in m' power t' help."

The Pirate King nodded. "Then I'm adding the kid to yer responsibilities."

The blacksmith's eyes widened.

"I can't always look after him, and you've got a knack for it." Hasunuma said with a smile as he patted Ginza's thick back. "So, I'm countin' on ya," he added as he held his other hand out towards the blacksmith.

Ginza blinked a few times and then grabbed the Pirate King's hand. With a firm grip and a voice full of confidence, he replied, "I ain't gonna lose anyone else."

Walking along the winding path that encircled the compound, Kazuki made his way to the training grounds. The Pirate King's home was not made of solid gold like the stories said, but of bamboo, straw, and other native island materials. It was a gorgeous building nonetheless, and the way that the single-storied structure incorporated and blended in with its surroundings was any nature lover's paradise. When they had first landed on the island, Kazuki saw no sign of civilization and was afraid that they would be living in a cave for the whole month. But when he saw the house suddenly appear before him in the midst of the tropical forest, Kazuki almost fell to his knees in relief and disbelief.

Hasunuma had told him that he and the rest of the Ryujin crew had built this place on the island. Previous pirate kings built their own homes too, but they were burnt down upon the arrival of each new pirate king – in accordance with the customs established by the first pirate king. Though, truthfully, the burning of each house probably had more to do with looking for hidden treasures than any ritual.

If it hadn't belonged to the Pirate King, the island would have been a nice place for a small village. There were plenty of fruit trees, edible plants, mushrooms, and some wild animals worth hunting for meat. And there was an abundance of fish, of course, that could be caught from the beach, by small boat, or even by diving. Fresh drinking water wasn't an issue either, because there were numerous springs inland.

I guess the worst part would be the storms, Kazuki thought as he tried to think of the downsides to the island. But in his month-long stay, there had only been a handful of storms, and none of them had been that bad. Granted, the Pirate King's house was near the center of the island, surrounded by dense jungle, so they wouldn't bear the brunt of the storms there anyways.

Snakes, he then decided were the worst thing about the island. They were large and hung around in the trees, which was more than unsettling. Kazuki had become a little paranoid about snakes hanging above him ever since their second day there, when he experienced one slither onto his shoulder during stealth training.

Spiders weren't great either, but their bites didn't kill humans, so Kazuki determined them to be merely a nuisance in comparison. It only took him a few days to get used to running through invisible webs, and afterwards he didn't even bother trying to wipe them away.

Hunting had also been part of his training, and it was by far the most enjoyable part. Going out with Rize either before dawn or around dusk, finding a spot to hide, and then waiting for their prey was alright, but it was the thrill of the actual hunt that excited Kazuki. There had been a few times where they chased rabbits or boars through the jungle, and the feeling Kazuki got from spearing one and then eating it later – after Rize taught him how to field dress, prepare, and cook it – was amazing. It felt like the effort he had spent was worth it, which he couldn't say about the rest of his training. Sure, the young man was improving, but the progression was slow and there weren't tangible results. Maybe in his next real battle he would get some satisfaction from his training, but there wasn't anything enjoyable about it now.

Kazuki suddenly looked up at the sky. He thought he heard a familiar *screech*, and, as he suspected, Ami was soaring high above him. Twice, Rize had shown Kazuki how to hunt with Ami, but, unfortunately, she had been sent out with another message and had been gone for about a week.

I'm glad she's back.

Kazuki always felt anxious when Ami left, as if she would never return. Rize seemed to get a bit lonely without her, but he told Kazuki once before that he trusted Ami to return to him, which is why he didn't get anxious. The young man wasn't sure how the others felt. Jun probably didn't care, Hanzo and Ginza were likely only concerned for Ami's safety on behalf of Rize, and Hasunuma might have cared, but he also might simply be interested in getting his messages – it was hard to tell with him sometimes.

Kohaku obviously cherished Ami though. If the falcon wasn't with Rize, she was with Kohaku. Admittedly, Kazuki was a little jealous of how close those two were to Ami, but it couldn't be helped since Rize had found Ami as a wounded fledgling, and Kohaku had helped him tend to her wounds. So, in Ami's eyes, Rize and Kohaku were her parents.

Finally arriving at the grassy field known as 'the training ground', the young man was met by a frowning Jun, standing with his arms crossed.

"You're late, Kid. I don't like my time being wasted," the cook grumbled.

"I know. Sorry."

"Sorry, what?"

"…Sorry, Sensei," Kazuki said, gritting his teeth, as he picked up his practice sword from the ground. Jun had made some out of bamboo for them to use, since he said he couldn't guarantee the kid's safety otherwise. The practice swords may not have been lethal, but they still hurt like the wrath of the gods. Kazuki had many bruises from missed blocks and sloppy footwork.

"You always seem to forget that I'm the teacher and you're the student," Jun griped as he slowly raised the bamboo sword at his side, "let me help you remember who's in charge."

Jun launched himself at Kazuki. The young man dodged the practice sword and swung his at an upward angle for a counterattack. A loud *crack* resounded as the two bamboo swords collided. Using all of his strength, Kazuki pushed Jun back and made ready for another attack.

Jun's philosophy of fighting was: keep attacking and you'll eventually hit something. While Kazuki may not have shared this theory, it had worked for Jun every time thus far. Most of the time Kazuki became too worn out to defend himself, which gave Jun the automatic win. But not this time; the young man was determined to defeat Jun in order to show him how much he had improved over the past month.

"Something about you is different, Kid. You've got fire in your eyes," the cook remarked before jumping into the air and aiming a downward blow at Kazuki's head.

The young man blocked Jun's practice sword as he came down and pushed the cook away. Before Jun could reset for another attack, Kazuki disappeared.

"Heh. So you *were* paying attention." Jun grinned and followed Kazuki's lead.

Kazuki had thought that the old man's vanishing technique was about speed – moving too fast for the eye to track. But in sparing with Jun, the young man realized that the technique was more about *how* one moves. Using misdirection techniques and taking advantage of certain situations – or temperaments – were key factors to unlocking the true vanishing technique that the old man had mastered.

Normally, it would have been impossible to track Jun; he was way too good at the technique. Kazuki, however, had mastered the one skill that could render the technique null: 'seeing' without using his eyes. After finally realizing the trick, the young man was able to track every movement that the cook made.

Jun moved at a rapid pace, but, as the results from his other training sessions bore fruit, Kazuki was now just as fast. Each time their bamboo swords collided, Jun was on the defensive. He barely got his blocks up in time, and Kazuki was relentless in his attacks. The young man thoroughly enjoyed the cook's struggle, since he held a grudge from previous training days.

"You can see pretty damn well with your eyes shut, Kid," Jun grumbled as he strained to block a side attack from the young man.

"I had five years of solid practice," Kazuki replied with a smirk.

Any untrained humans who happened to pass by the training ground at this point would run away terrified. Neither Kazuki nor

Jun could be seen or heard; all that was left was the hollow *crack* of the bamboo swords colliding. It was an eerie sound that would make anyone double-check their surroundings – especially with the haunting stories about the island.

Suddenly there was a loud *thump,* and Jun's body appeared on the ground. He lay there motionless for a time, before slowly getting to his feet. He staggered, almost falling back down, but caught himself using his bamboo sword as a cane.

"You sure knocked the wind out of me, Kid." Jun coughed a few times, clearing his throat. "I hate to admit it, but you won that round. You should thank the others for training you."

Kazuki stood in front of the cook and replied, "I will."

Jun straightened up and held the practice sword aside in his left hand. "You know," he began awkwardly as he scratched his head, "my father taught you pretty well too."

Kazuki's eyes widened. He hadn't expected Jun to bring up the topic of his father.

"He never taught me anything. Everything I learned was from watching him practice…He was such a stubborn old crab," Jun added with a rough smile.

"Can I ask what happened?" Kazuki blurted out.

Jun glared at the young man.

"He told me that all of his family was killed by Ammon, but you're still alive."

Jun turned his back to Kazuki. He began to walk away, but stopped suddenly. "His family *was* killed by Ammon. All but me anyways." Jun turned around and locked eyes with Kazuki. "Why do you care what happened?"

Kazuki stared right back at Jun. "Because he was like a father to me."

Jun stared at Kazuki for a few more minutes before relaxing his face. "Fine. I'll tell you." He sat down on the wooden bench close by. "My father was a master swordsman. He had a few pupils, but he was so damn picky about who he taught that not many people met his high standards. Even those that did would quit because of his attitude, and, after a while, no one was left."

Kazuki listened to Jun intently. The old man he knew wasn't like Jun what had described. Maybe there was some mistake?

"My old man got bored without pupils and started challenging random warriors to battle. He won every time because of that technique of his. By the time I was ten, he was pretty famous around town and the villagers would ask him to help fight off bandits and such. Before long, the Hekigun showed up." Jun's face darkened. "The villagers secretly begged my father for help in getting rid of the Hekigun that had taken over our village."

*I think I know where this is going...*Kazuki thought. He wasn't sure he wanted to hear the rest.

"My father, being the proud, stubborn old man he was, agreed to fight the Hekigun. He left in the middle of the night to go fight them. I snuck out of the house and followed my father. All I cared about was watching him fight so I could steal more of his techniques." Jun closed his eyes and took a deep breath. "What I didn't think of was how dangerous the enemy could be. I watched as my father killed many soldiers. It looked like he would win, until Ammon appeared. He creepily grinned at my father and the dead soldiers surrounding him and said, 'Crimson looks good on you. I'll have to reward you for this bloodshed.' He then held up what was in his hands for my father to see. It was my mother's and my three sisters' decapitated heads."

Kazuki put his hand to his mouth. The gruesome image plastered in his mind.

"They had gone to our home while my father was at the camp and butchered my family. If I hadn't followed my father that night, my head would have been dangling at Ammon's side too," Jun said as he shook his head.

"But," Kazuki spoke cautiously, "how did Ammon know about your father's plan?"

Jun opened his eyes and looked up at the sky. "The villagers ratted him out for gold."

Kazuki couldn't believe Jun's story. There was no way that the villagers would ask the old man to save them, only to turn around and betray him for gold.

"I'm not lying, Kid." Jun stared at Kazuki, reading his face. "I was right there when Ammon told my father what had happened. My father freaked out and tried to kill Ammon right then and there, but he was too angry to be able to use his technique properly and was beaten. The only reason Ammon didn't kill my father right then was because he wanted to watch my father suffer more."

"But what happened to you? The old man must've seen you or known that you weren't killed."

"I ran away." Jun's eyes shifted to the ground. "I'm not proud of it, but I ran away that night. I was only a kid, and I was terrified beyond belief. My father, the best swordsman I knew, had been beaten by a psycho who murdered the rest of my family."

Kazuki's stomach dropped. The old man must have returned home to find Jun missing as well. He probably thought that he was also killed, even though his son was alive this whole time.

"You…you never went back?" Kazuki quietly asked.

Jun shook his head. "After a few years I returned, but that man wasn't my father anymore. When I told him who I was and what had happened, he punched me and told me that all of his children were dead, and to never show my face to him again." Jun raised his head back to the sky. "That man chose revenge over happiness."

Kazuki didn't know what to say.

Jun stood up from the bench and approached Kazuki. The young man hung his head and wouldn't look at Jun.

The cook placed his hand on Kazuki's shoulder and, in a strangely soft tone, said, "I'm glad that he didn't die alone after all." He then walked away, leaving Kazuki standing in the middle of the practice field.

As he watched water droplets hit the grass beneath him, the young man grieved anew.

If it weren't for the Hekigun, these tragedies wouldn't happen.

Oh, but they would. Death is inevitable, after all.

Natural deaths are one thing, murder is another.

Is it so different? Either way a person dies and those who care lament their loss.

Kazuki wiped his eyes. *A demon wouldn't understand.*

Suddenly, the young man felt a strange sensation well up inside of him and then quickly vanish. Had it been sorrow or anger? He wasn't sure.

How wrong you are.

After the Demon King's curt response, Kazuki felt an emptiness inside of him that meant the Demon King had retreated and was no longer present. The young man hadn't thought it possible, but perhaps the Demon King could feel human emotions after all.

As the Ryujin settled into the most remote section of Giyosan's port, Hasunuma inhaled the air that smelt of salt and fresh baked bread. He had chosen to dock there because he didn't want to draw a lot of attention; everyone in his crew was a wanted criminal, and although the guards would never bother them, the prices on the crew mates' heads made them active targets of less respectable or desperate men.

After restocking their supplies, all of the crew, except for Jun, headed for Tenrou Shrine. It was about a two-day journey on foot from the port town to the shrine. Over seven hundred years ago the shrine was built in a remote area, surrounded by old forests and mountains. It was not an easy place to get to, but that's probably what made it so desirable for the demons.

Never having been there himself, the Pirate King had to rely on verbal directions from the locals in Giyosan, paired with a combination of his innate sense of direction and Rize's tracking skills. Thankfully, there was somewhat of a trail to follow, since there were people who visited the shrine to worship the gods there. But, at some point, the trail veered from the common cart path that rural villagers used to get to Giyosan, and the less-traveled portion wasn't as easy to distinguish from the forest floor.

"Hey, Hasunuma? I think we need to take a break," the kid suggested.

The Pirate King turned around and saw everyone breathing heavily and drenched in sweat. It was the second day of their journey and the crew had been climbing a steep slope in the forest for a while now. Though the dense trees blocked most of the sunlight, it was still hot and humid. There was no sea breeze to help cool them off either. As much as Hasunuma wanted to let his crew take a break, he knew that they had to keep going in order to get to the shrine by nightfall.

"Come on ya lazy dogs! Was all that trainin' fer nothin'?!" Hasunuma yelled as he turned to the front and continued walking at his break-neck pace. He heard the crew groan behind him as they tried to keep up. *Sorry guys.*

"Seriously? Not only are we not taking a break, but we're supposed to keep up with your crazy-fast pace?" Kazuki remarked as he walked up next to the Pirate King.

"We need to get to the shrine by nightfall," Hasunuma replied.

"Why? If we keep going like this, the guys will be too exhausted to fight by the time we get there anyways."

"I'm glad you're using your brain, Little Oni, but I don't think you're grasping the entirety of this situation." Hasunuma looked behind him to make sure no one else was close enough to hear him before he added, "There are *other* things lurking in this forest besides gods."

Kazuki went pale. Hasunuma knew that the kid was scared of ghosts, though the kid would never admit it. However, in all actuality it wasn't the ghosts in the forest that the Pirate King was worried about; it was the demons.

According to Tsukigen mythology, demons are made from human souls that cannot find peace after death. Instead of moving towards the path of reincarnation, the souls wander the lands until they become corrupt and transform into demons. Granted, as the Demon King himself had mentioned, demons can't be in the Human Realm unless they possess a corpse, but death is all too common in the world; whether it be human or animal, demons find their hosts readily available. And once they find a host, the demons stalk the land, leaving carnage and destruction in their wake – according to the myths.

The Pirate King wasn't sure how much of the mythology he believed, but, supposedly, demons are both drawn to and repelled by strong spiritual power; while they desire the power for themselves, they are often destroyed by it when they fail to kill or possess the wielder of such power. The reason why Hasunuma wanted to get to the shrine by nightfall was so that the shrine could provide them with spiritual protection from the demons lurking in the surrounding forests.

He couldn't see them, but he could feel their presence. There were other things too – things that Hasunuma couldn't identify – and while some posed no threat, there were others that radiated danger. As long as the Demon King resided in the kid's body, Kazuki would be a spiritual power magnet. Not to mention the ever-present threat from the demons partaking in the demon games.

"We're definitely on the right track. How much further d'ya think?" The Pirate King asked aloud as he heard something rustle the leaves in the tree above him.

"Maybe three miles," Rize responded as he swung himself down from the tree. "This place feels wrong…there aren't any signs of life in this lush forest."

The Pirate King nodded. "That's because the creatures here are smart. They've fled the area around us because it's filled with a demonic aura."

"Is it the Demon King?" The helmsman asked as he looked back at the kid, who was still struggling to keep up.

Hasunuma shook his head. "Not this time."

Ghosts…they don't really *exist, do they?* Kazuki wondered as he scanned the forest. His constantly moving head caught the attention of the two pirates behind him.

"Ya hear somethin', Lad?" Hanzo shouted.

The loud noise caught Kazuki off guard and he jumped.

"Woah. What's got you all spooked?" The giant asked.

Kazuki turned around. "There aren't *really* ghosts…are there?" He asked, almost whispering.

Hanzo and Ginza looked and each other and grinned, simultaneously saying, "Ya scared?"

Kazuki frowned and turned back around. "I'm not scared! I was just wondering."

"If you're not scared, Little Oni, you should be," Rize said flatly as he suddenly appeared in front of the young man. The helmsman was impossible to track in the wilderness.

Kazuki glared at him for teasing him too, but Rize wasn't grinning. "This forest around the shrine attracts spirits of the dead. They feel the energy from the shrine and cling to it, hoping to find a way to the next life," the helmsman explained.

Now Hanzo and Ginza were scanning the forest along with Kazuki.

"Thankfully, the shrine should have at least one powerful maiden, called a 'Miko', who protects it from evil spirits with spells and barriers," Rize continued.

Ah, so that's why we need to hurry to the shrine.

"I think I heard a story once about this place," Hanzo began with a grin, "something about a young girl getting lost out here."

"Oh, yeah," Ginza continued, with an equally devious grin on his face, "She was lookin' fer 'er mommy an' went in t' the forest."

"…What happened to her?" Kazuki asked, but he wasn't sure that he wanted to hear the answer.

"They say she got eaten by a demon," Hanzo replied in an eerie voice. "And now she wanders the forest looking for other little kids to eat!"

Kazuki yelped as he felt something grab his arm. He whipped around, only to find Ginza with his hand covering his mouth, trying to hold back his laughter.

"To the Demon Realm with you both!" Kazuki yelled, his face flush with embarrassment. He yanked his arm away from Ginza and began walking away from the two laughing pirates. The young man had almost caught up with Hasunuma when he saw something out of the corner of his eye. He stopped and slowly turned his head to the left.

A good distance away from where he was, there was someone standing in the forest. The person was fairly small, but it was hard to see much detail as the person seemed to be shrouded in shadows.

Kazuki was about to call out to the person when it suddenly smiled. A wide, inhuman smile that chilled Kazuki to the bone. As the shadowy figure crept closer, Kazuki saw that its eyes were empty sockets and its legs vanished beneath the knees. The figure stopped no more than twenty feet from the young man and then vanished. Kazuki swore he had heard it laugh.

"Ey, Little Oni, why'd ya stop?" Ginza had caught up with the young man. "Ya look pale, like ya've seen a *ghost*." Ginza began to laugh again, but when he put his arm around Kazuki's neck, the blacksmith froze too.

"I saw her," Kazuki whispered.

Both of them stood there, staring at the spot where the shadowy figure had been, until they were brought back to reality by Hasunuma's harsh tone.

"I thought I told ya NO BREAKS!" The Pirate King shouted.

"But, Cap'n!" Ginza tried to tell Hasunuma what had happened, but the Pirate King didn't seem to care.

"If we don't get t' the shrine by nightfall, you'll see more than just ghosts. Now hurry up!"

Hasunuma's threat was enough to energize the crew. They were almost fighting to get up the hill, closer to the shrine. No one wanted to be the last one in line.

Kazuki decided to stay next to Hasunuma the rest of the way, and he kept his gaze straight ahead.

When they arrived at Tenrou Shrine, the sky was awash with hues of pink and purple. Carved into the mountainside, the shrine sat at the top of a four-hundred-step stairway. Kazuki remembered Hasunuma telling the crew about the stairway; how it was also carved into the mountain, winding back and forth among the rocks, and how dangerous it would be to climb. If the demons were to ambush them there, the pirates would be at a huge disadvantage. The young man looked towards the shrine. It was so high up that he could barely see it and, as large as it seemed from below, Kazuki could only imagine its enormity.

Hasunuma walked up the first five steps and paused. There were no sounds besides the wind in the trees and Ami shrieking overhead. She had been following them above the canopy, but she hadn't been visible until they arrived at the clearing around the mountainside where the shrine sat.

Hasunuma took a deep breath and then slowly exhaled. "All right, let's climb this thing," he said with determination.

Kazuki followed behind the Pirate King and the crew filed in behind Kazuki. The only person that wasn't there was Kohaku – and Jun, of course, since he was guarding the Ryujin. The ninja woman had taken another approach to the shrine; one that only someone as skilled as her could take. It wouldn't have been smart to have them all clustered together in case of an ambush.

As they climbed the stairs, Kazuki noticed a change in the air. It wasn't just that the air was becoming thinner, but there was a strange feel to it; almost like there were invisible walls pushing against him.

With each step, the feeling worsened.

"You feeling alright, Lad?" Hanzo asked with a concerned expression. He was walking behind Kazuki and must have noticed the young man's sudden unsteady footing.

"Y-Yeah. I'm fine." Kazuki replied as he leaned against the rocks. His breathing was ragged and his knees were shaking.

Without saying a word, Hasunuma turned around and picked him up. The Pirate King threw Kazuki over his shoulder and continued to climb the stairs. The young man tried to protest, but the words wouldn't come out. He was steadily losing consciousness. Why was no one else affected by the strange atmosphere?

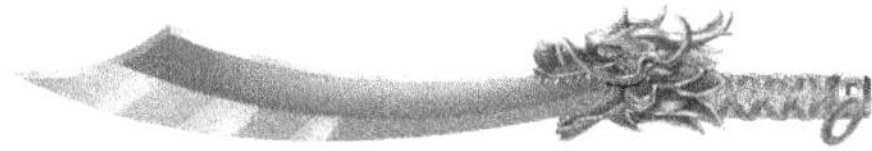

The poor kid had passed out before they reached the top. Hanzo and Ginza had both volunteered to carry Kazuki, but Hasunuma assured them that he was fine carrying the kid. If the demons attacked, they would probably aim for Kazuki first, and the Pirate King wasn't about to put his crew in any more danger than necessary.

At the top of the stairway, there was a group of seven men waiting for them. From their earthen colored garb and their shaves heads, it was clear that they were priests of the shrine. They seemed to be unarmed, but they could have had a knife or two tucked into their robes, so the pirates stood still and waited for the priests to make the first move.

A man dressed in fancier robes – wearing a brown hakama and

green kimono with a blue haori overcoat – stepped forward and addressed the pirates. "Welcome to Tenrou Shrine, dear travelers. I am the head priest. What is it that brings you here?"

The Pirate King stepped forward and replied, "We got lost in the forest and our friend here is ill," he gestured towards Kazuki who was still unconscious and hanging over the Pirate King's shoulder. "Could we rest here for a bit?"

The head priest smiled. "Why, of course you may rest here. We will prepare a room for you immediately." He turned around and headed into the large building to the right of the sacred temple.

"Come, follow us," the other priests beckoned to the pirates as they followed the head priest into the building.

The Pirate King followed, his crew behind him. When they entered the hall, the priests tried to take Kazuki to another room to rest, but Hasunuma politely declined their offer, saying that he didn't want to leave the kid alone. The priests smiled and nodded and showed the pirates to a large, open room.

"Please wait here and we will bring you some food," one of the priests said before they all bowed and left the room.

"Cap'n somethin' ain't right here." Ginza whispered as he cautiously looked around the room.

The Pirate King gently laid Kazuki down on the floor next to him. He checked to make sure he was fine before he answered Ginza. "Whaddya mean?" Hasunuma grinned, "They're bein' really generous."

"Why would priests be generous to pirates?" Rize interjected.

"'Cause they have to be. They're priests after all." The crew still looked anxious, so the Pirate King added, "If they see ya lookin' all scared they're gonna be offended and kick us out. We have t' let Little Oni rest, so behave."

The crew slowly nodded just as the priests returned with food.

"Please eat as much as you'd like," one priest offered with a smile as he gestured towards the copious amounts of food they had brought in.

There were all sorts of dishes: bowls filled with rice and soup, plates filled with meat and fish, and cups filled with ale. The crew sat there, practically drooling over the feast before them. They were about to grab plates when the door to the room opened. The head priest entered with a smile. There was a beautiful woman behind him, which he introduced as the miko, or shrine maiden. She was wearing a striking red kimono with gold patterns sewn in it. Her breasts were ample and almost spilling out of the partially opened kimono, while her long legs peeked through the opening in the front. The pirates immediately forgot about the food and stared at the woman with the same drooling faces.

"I will leave you in her care then," the head priest said as he bowed and left the room. The other priests followed, leaving the pirates alone with the shrine maiden.

"May I dance for you?" The woman smiled. After hearing all of the pirates shout 'yeah' with enthusiasm, the miko giggled. "Watch closely, dear guests."

Taking a fan from her kimono belt, the shrine maiden began to dance for the pirates. Her elegant and gentle movements were as lovely as she was, but her smile and dance were not that of an innocent, virginal miko. There was something erotic about the way the woman moved her hips, and she often leaned forward, revealing her glistening breasts. The pirates were, of course, enthralled with her performance. Nothing could break their concentration, except for their captain.

Hasunuma stood up and approached the miko.

She stopped mid-dance and stared at the Pirate King.

"Yer very beautiful, Miko," Hasunuma said as he smiled and grabbed the woman by her waist. "Yer dancing has captivated me and my men."

"Oh," the woman giggled, "I'm glad you enjoyed it, dear guest."

"Call me Red Dragon," Hasunuma whispered in the maiden's ear.

"Red Dragon," She moaned with pleasure.

"No fair, Cap'n!" The crew yelled at once. They wanted the miko to moan for them too.

"Oh, so you're the captain," the shrine maiden smiled, "then I *must* make sure that you're well taken care of." She giggled again as she wrapped her arms around Hasunuma's neck.

Kazuki awoke to the sound of a woman giggling. His head still felt foggy as he slowly pushed himself up to a sitting position. He didn't know where he was, but he looked to his right and saw Hanzo, Ginza, and Rize. Glad to see familiar faces, Kazuki was about to call out to them when he noticed something was wrong. They all looked agitated, almost angry, as they glared at something to the young man's left. Kazuki turned his attention to his left and saw exactly what was angering the pirates.

Hasunuma, yet again, had some woman giggling in his arms. She had long dark hair and was wearing a red and gold kimono. Her chest was almost fully exposed, as were her legs. The woman was charming, but something didn't feel right. Kazuki was about to say something to Hasunuma when he froze. The young man couldn't believe what he was seeing. He closed his eyes and opened them again, only to find the same image before him: Hasunuma's hand shoved *through* the woman's chest.

The other pirates exclaimed different curses as they got up to approach Hasunuma, but he ordered them to stay back.

"W-why?" The woman managed to breathe.

The Pirate King grinned and pulled his hand out as he answered, "Because yer a demon."

The woman's eyes widened. "H-how did you kn-know?" She was struggling with every word. Blood was gushing out of the hole in her chest.

"A real miko wouldn't dress and act like a whore."

The woman grinned wickedly and said with a deep voice, "You're too smart, Pirate." The woman then screamed as a black shadow came out of her chest. Her body suddenly became limp and she fell to the ground. "I may not have been able to kill you, but my brothers will!" The black shadow angrily hissed before it vanished, leaving behind the scent of smoke.

There was a long silence. Hasunuma wiped the blood off of his hand as the crew stared at the lifeless body of the woman before them.

Kazuki broke the silence and asked, "What's going on? Where

are we?"

The pirates looked at Kazuki.

"What?"

Hanzo and Ginza ran over to the young man and asked if he was feeling all right. When he assured them that he was fine, Rize smiled and said that they were glad to see Kazuki awake. The young man looked away in embarrassment and saw the feast on the floor before him. Suddenly there was a large, deep growl. Everyone stared at Kazuki, who was now bright red.

"H-Hey can I eat some of that?" Kazuki asked as he reached for a bowl of rice.

"If you want to get poisoned, then go ahead." Hasunuma said.

"Poisoned?" Kazuki and the other pirates groaned as they stared at all of the good-looking food.

"Yeah. Poisoned. Now get ready, 'cause those 'priests' will be here any minute."

The young man regrettably dropped the bowl of rice. He had been keeping his hunger at bay, but with this feast in front of him he couldn't control his stomach any longer. Kazuki sat on the floor, arms and legs crossed, trying to will his stomach out of growling. With no luck, he sighed heavily and fell back onto the tatami floor. Before long he hallucinated a rice ball floating in front of his face. He tried to ignore that too, for fear of being laughed at even more by the rest of the crew.

"Are you gonna eat this or not?"

Kazuki blinked a few times. The rice ball was real. He snatched it from the air and wolfed it down. Once the rice ball was gone, the young man's stomach finally quit growling.

"You're welcome," Rize sighed as he stood staring down at Kazuki. "It's tough when Hanzo and Ginza eat all the food Jun sends with us, right? I mean, just 'cause we're smaller, doesn't mean we don't need as much food."

Kazuki laughed. "You're right, Rize."

"Sadly, that's all I had left…so hopefully that'll be enough to last ya through the fight."

The young man gave the helmsman a thumbs up and said, "Yeah, thanks."

A minute later, as Hasunuma predicted, a group of five priests came running into the room. They saw the body of the shrine maiden lying on the ground and growled.

"How *dare* you kill our shrine maiden?! You will pay for this!" One of the priests shouted as he lunged forward with a dagger in hand. Unlucky for him, he aimed for Rize. Before the priest reached the ground, he had an arrow through each eye and one through the heart. Rize may have been the smallest of the pirate men, but his speed was more deadly than having layers of muscle mass.

Without a moment's pause, the remaining four came rushing at the pirates. Hasunuma moved in front of Rize and sliced the attacking priest's stomach open with his red dragon sword. Kazuki, Hanzo, and Ginza took on the other three.

Hanzo smashed through a torso with his 'knuckles'; which were basically modified brass knuckles, made of iron, with sharp spikes protruding from each knuckle. Ginza sliced a priest in half with his ridiculously heavy, thick-bladed naginata. And the young man took out the last assailant with a quick draw of his katana. The priest's neck was slit before he came within two feet of Kazuki.

The bodies of all five priests were strewn about the room, but the hair on the back of the young man's neck was still standing. Something wasn't right.

"Hasunuma," he stated more than asked, "Something's wrong."

The Pirate King frowned at the corpses. "Agreed."

Kazuki's senses were screaming, but he saw nothing. He looked from body to body, trying to figure out what was wrong, when he suddenly heard a sound. *Tinkle, tinkle…Tinkle, tinkle.* It was a bell, a small bell, like the type used during ceremonies to pacify spirits. But where was it coming from?

Before the young man had a chance to figure out the mystery, the room shook violently. Ginza shouted 'earthquake,' and everyone scrambled towards the door. Hasunuma and Rize were the closest, and mere seconds after they exited, the doorway collapsed. Kazuki, Hanzo, and Ginza were left trapped in the room. As the young man frantically looked around for another exit, he noticed that the bodies of the priests were suddenly missing.

Hasunuma tried to go back, but Rize dragged him along the corridor towards the outer courtyard.

"We can't go back," he kept shouting, "they'll find another way out!"

The Pirate King knew that his helmsman was right, but he was worried about the others. What if more demons showed up? There was nothing he could do about the earthquake, but–

Hasunuma and Rize stood still. The world had become quiet once again.

"The earthquake…it just…stopped," Rize said slowly as he let go of Hasunuma's arm and looked around them.

The trembling rocks and buildings sat still, as if the previous minute had never happened. Only the building from which they came had been damaged, while the rest of the shrine grounds were left untouched. The Pirate King stood amazed for a minute or so before his frown returned. He remembered something that the Demon King had mentioned: *Demons can control the elements.*

"Rize, we have to go back. NOW." Hasunuma turned around, only to find one of the priests standing in front of him. The Pirate King jumped back and brandished his red dragon sword. "I guess I miscounted," he smirked.

"No, you didn't," the helmsman retorted, his tone serious. "That one's got a hole in his gut. Hanzo's work, no doubt."

Rize was right. This was one of the priests that they had killed earlier. So why was he standing there in front of them? *These demons can't be* that *kill-resistant…can they?*

Hasunuma decided that it was better to find out now than later. He sliced away at the priest, creating large gashes all over his body. However, no matter how deep the wound, there was no blood to be seen. The priest also showed no signs of pain or fatigue. He kept swinging his daggers at the Pirate King, almost mindlessly. Hasunuma kicked the priest hard in the chest and sent him flying back into the wall of the shrine.

"Rize. Pin him down."

The helmsman responded, "Aye, Captain," and shot a total of four arrows at the priest; one in each shoulder and one above each knee. The arrows penetrated the priest's flesh and buried themselves deep within the wooden wall behind him. Still, there was no reaction from the priest.

"This guy's either really tough or really crazy," Rize remarked as he readied another arrow.

"Neither," Hasunuma replied, "He's a puppet."

Suddenly someone began clapping. The pirates whirled around to find the head priest standing there with a wide, eerie grin. "How marvelous! I've never met a human as clever as you, my dear pirate." He stopped clapping. "What was it that gave away my dolls?"

"It's easy to tell when there's no soul present, Demon."

"Ah. Yes. Unfortunately, even with fresh dolls, the souls don't last very long. Oh well, I suppose there's no more need for this rouse." The demon snapped his fingers and the priest's body went slack. "How about we play another game instead?"

"Did you kill all of the priests and use their bodies to make your dolls?" Rize growled.

"Why, of course I did. It was awfully *boring* waiting for Shinigami-sama to arrive, so I decided to have a little fun with the priests. I told them that they could each have a turn playing with the shrine maiden if they agreed to do me a favor in return. They all readily agreed. Poor, pretty, little thing. She was quite devastated when her trusted fellow priests tore off her clothes and–"

An arrow flew into the head priest's mouth and exited out of the back of his head.

"I don't wanna hear anything else from you!" Spit flew from Rize's mouth as he spoke. He always had a quick temper when it came to violence towards women and children. And Rize wasn't the only one who felt that way. The entire Ryujin crew was very clear about their feelings towards that sort of cruelty.

"Oh my!" The head priest's tongue still flapped around inside of his mouth. "And here I was going to explain the rules of the new game. Such a pity."

"What's a pity is that I missed your tongue, Demon." Rize readied another arrow. He pulled back the bowstring until it was taught and then released the tension. But his arrow didn't fly.

The head priest chuckled. "As I thought. She's yours, yes?" Held out in front of him was Kohaku. Long, bony fingers tightly gripped her neck. Her eyes were closed and her body seemed limp.

"What have you done to her?!" The helmsman shook with anger.

"Why, nothing," the head priest grinned, "yet." He cackled and added, "Splendid, splendid! Now, shall we begin the game?"

"Why, you–" Rize took a step forward, but was blocked by Hasunuma's arm. The helmsman looked sideways at the Pirate King. He must have seen the confidence in Hasunuma's eyes, because Rize immediately backed down and stood quietly. His anger subsided.

"Demon, do ya *really* think that I would be so foolish as t' have a weak and helpless woman by my side?"

The head priest furrowed his brow and cocked his head to the side like a confused child.

Hasunuma stood firm. "Hey, Kohaku, how long are ya gonna play the maiden in distress?" He grinned. "If ya don't do somethin' soon, I'll have to wake you with a kiss…"

Instantly, Kohaku's eyes popped open and she cut off the head priest's hand with her kusarigama.

"Arrgh!" The head priest shrieked as he held his bloody stump with his remaining hand.

Kohaku jumped away and settled herself between Hasunuma and Rize. Holding her kusarigama in front of her, the ninja woman whistled, letting her companions know that she was ready for battle.

"You will pay for that limb you took! Dolls, attack!" The Head Priest retreated behind a wall of bodies. Four of them were the priests from earlier, while there were another four that they hadn't seen before. By the way they were dressed, Hasunuma guessed that the others had been unlucky visitors to the shrine.

Hacking and slashing their way through the bodies, Hasunuma and Kohaku made their way to the Head Priest. Knowing that the dolls were difficult to kill, Hasunuma instructed Kohaku to cut off the dolls' limbs. Once all of the dolls and their parts were strewn about the shrine courtyard, the Pirate King and the ninja woman faced the demon.

A huge grin appeared on the Head Priest's face. Hasunuma was about to ask the demon what found so entertaining, when suddenly he heard an arrow whizzing through the air behind him.

The room had stopped shaking and the earth became quiet once again, yet not everything was all right. All of the bodies of the priests, save the one that had arrows in it, had disappeared from the room. Kazuki stood towards the center of the room with Hanzo and Ginza on either side of him. None of them moved or dared to breathe. There was a presence in the room that brought a heavy atmosphere with it.

"I know you're there, demon," Kazuki said in a low voice.

High-pitched laughter reverberated around the room, and a man suddenly appeared before the pirates.

"So it *is* you, Shinigami-sama!"

The man looked like a side-street performer. He had spikey red hair, a half red and half white painted face, and was wearing a white suit with red diamonds on one half – the half opposite his red face.

"But you see, I know you're not truly Shinigami-sama right now. If you were, you'd have realized that there isn't just me in this room."

Another man suddenly appeared before them. He stood next to the white and red demon and crossed his arms. "Seventeen," he growled, "I told you to stay hidden."

"Why should we, Sixteen?" The redhead scoffed. "Shinigami-sama is right here!"

The demon called 'Sixteen' shook his head. He looked like the ringleader of a side-street performance; he wore a white suit with a white shirt and tie and white shoes, and his dark hair was slicked back beneath his tall, white hat. For whatever reason, side-street performers in Tsukigen always dressed in foreign attire.

Kazuki had only ever seen one side-street performance, but the performers' talent with illusions had amazed him. If these demons were in the bodies of such performers, this battle wasn't going to be easy. Kazuki had to get Hanzo and Ginza out of the room as quickly as possible.

"Hanzo, Ginza, you two go and find the captain. I'll stay here and take care of these demons," Kazuki said as he took a step towards the side-street performers, his right hand grabbing the tsuka of his katana while his left steadied the saya.

"No chance, Lad!" Hanzo said as he put his large hand on Kazuki's head. "We're under orders to protect you."

"And we ain't scared a' some weird lookin' demons!" Ginza added.

"But–"

"Unlike you, Lad, we follow the Cap'n's orders," Hanzo said with a grin.

"An' we'd never leave a mate behind," Ginza added as he patted Kazuki on the back. The blacksmith then hoisted his large and heavy blade up in front of them.

"You protect, while I attack. Got it, Gin?" Hanzo directed as he brought his fists up and assumed an offensive stance.

"Oh? It looks like those humans want to fight, Sixteen. May I?"

"You can't have all of the fun, Seventeen. I get Shinigami-sama to myself then," The demon ringleader said as he pulled out a stack of cards from his pocket and began to shuffle them.

"Fine, fine," Seventeen said before pulling a long, thin sword from his throat. "I'll kill the pale giant first."

Hanzo and Seventeen slowly approached each other. They stopped about six feet from one another and stood there, grinning. The demon was the first to move. He ran forward and slashed at the giant, who caught the demon's sword between his steel knuckles.

"Good catch, Giant. But now your weapons are useless–" Seventeen was cut short when the giant's right foot collided with the demon's stomach, sending him flying across the room.

"Don't get distracted," Hanzo reprimanded. "You might be a demon, but I know you felt that one," he added with a grin.

The giant's true weapon was his strength, not the spiked knuckles that Ginza had forged for him; those were just for show. Kazuki had seen Hanzo's bare fists and feet knock down full-grown trees and fragment boulders.

Seventeen shakily stood up. His body had hit the wall so hard that there was now a body shaped dent in it. The demon straightened his suit and brushed the dust off of it.

"For a human, that was impressive. And I will reward you with a trick." Seventeen said flatly as his sword suddenly caught on fire. "Watch closely now." His blade burned so hot that steel turned red. With a quick flick of the sword the fire was extinguished, but the blade kept its red glow. "You'd better watch out. It's hot."

Seventeen grinned and leapt towards Hanzo, his sword high above his head. When the demon brought his sword down, the giant blocked it with his steel knuckles, but then he quickly pushed the sword away; the spikes of Hanzo's knuckles had begun to melt.

The giant released his grip and shook the steel knuckles off of his hands. They made a dull *thud* as they hit the ground.

"Tsk Tsk. I *told* you it was hot," the demon taunted.

Hanzo glared at the demon and attacked him with his bare fists. His punches were rather fast, but the demon dodged them all. Seventeen kept laughing, which only made Hanzo angrier. His speed increased slightly, but the demon continued to dodge. Just when it seemed as if Hanzo would never make contact, Seventeen went flying across the room.

Kazuki blinked. "What just happened?"

"'E kicked 'im again," Ginza replied, but he didn't seem happy. "Hanzo, switch with me," he called out.

Kazuki expected the stubborn giant to refuse Ginza's command, but instead Hanzo simply nodded and took the blacksmith's place next to the young man. Kazuki almost protested for him, but then he finally noticed how worn-out Hanzo really was. His breathing was ragged and sweat was pouring down his body. Not only that, but there were burn marks on his metal armguards.

"How the festering hole did that happen?!" Kazuki blurted out. He hadn't seen the demon move his sword at all while Hanzo was attacking.

"Something's weird about that guy, Lad. It's like his sword isn't the only thing that's burning," Hanzo said as he stared at the demon with a furrowed his brow. "We have to watch closely to see what his trick is."

Hasunuma turned around to find an arrow aimed towards him. "Rize! What are you–"

Another arrow went flying and hit its target. The Pirate King stumbled backwards as an arm suddenly fell to the ground in front of him. Arms, legs, and torsos with heads began dancing around Hasunuma and Kohaku. A volley of arrows flew around them, and the animated parts twitched as they became pinned to the ground.

"They can't attack you if they can't move," Rize said as he released more arrows. Before long, there wasn't a single doll piece left un-pierced.

"Thanks, Rize." The Pirate King relaxed his shoulders slightly. "Now, without further interruption," Hasunuma began as he started walking towards the Head Priest with his sword unsheathed, "we'll deal with *you*." He pointed the tip of the red dragon sword at the sweating demon.

"W-wait, wait! I was only meant to distract you!"

"Only meant to distract me? From what?" Hasunuma kept his sword trained on its target as he moved closer to the demon.

The High Priest tried to back away from the Pirate King, but he tripped on his robes and fell backwards. "Eek! Please don't kill me!"

Hasunuma stood in front of the High Priest and held the red dragon an inch from his face. "Distract me from *what*?"

Terror was written all over the demon's face, which the Pirate King thought was rather strange. Why would a demon, who can't die, be so terrified of death? A demon vanquished in the human realm simply goes back to the demon realm…right?

"I-I can't tell you."

The tip of the red dragon began digging into the High Priest's flesh.

"Ahh! No, truly I can't tell you! He'll kill me!" The demon pleaded.

"There's someone pulling your strings, eh?" The Pirate King grinned.

But before the High Priest could say anymore, a bolt of lightning struck his body; nothing but ashes and a charred spot on the ground remained.

"That's quite enough from *him*," spoke a deep and cold voice.

The Pirate King shivered. He remembered the voice well. "Eiri."

Ginza thrust his heavy blade forward again and again. Seventeen dodged each attack, but not without great effort. Besides its ridiculous weight, Ginza's weapon's most surprising characteristic was its range of mobility. One would assume that a weapon that large and heavy couldn't move quickly; but that wasn't the case. In fact, Ginza could wield that thing so proficiently that it looked like he was playing with a bamboo stick.

The unique naginata's blade swung towards the demon's stomach, then, suddenly, the blade changed directions and cut upwards towards the demon's head. Again and again, the direction would change, and the blade cut towards the demon's legs, or shoulders, or wherever. Sure, this kind of movement was normal for a smaller, lighter weight weapon, but any opponent would be caught off guard by such quick movements from such a long, heavy weapon. And, most of the time, that was the key to Ginza's success.

"I'm watching the demon, Lad, but I can't figure it out," Hanzo grumbled as he stood beside the young man, his fists clenched. "How's he burning without touching anything?"

Kazuki shook his head. No matter how closely he watched Seventeen, he could only see defensive movements. Neither the young man nor the giant could figure out how the demon kept burning Ginza without ever touching him.

"Can't you use your oni eyes or something, Lad? Maybe a demon can see what we humans can't," the giant suggested.

Kazuki furrowed his brow. "It's not like that, Hanzo. My body may be housing a demon, but that doesn't mean I can use its powers."

"Come on, Lad! I've seen you fight a hundred times. I know what you can do." He gave the young man a nudge with his elbow. "Don't think that the Demon King is just sitting in there on his arse. Surely there's a way to use that power of his."

Kazuki stared wide-eyed at the giant. Why hadn't he thought of that before? There was an infinite source of power within him and all he had to do was figure out how to tap into it.

…What is it?

I…I need your power.

Need or want? I do not think you need me at all for this battle.

You've been watching haven't you? This demon is using some sort of fire trick that keeps burning-

Burning? I do not see anything burning.

Kazuki looked from Seventeen to Hanzo's armguards. The scorched gold-plated metal was perfectly intact, as if no burn had been there in the first place.

Do not bother me again with such nonsense.

The young man's mind began working in a new direction. "Hanzo! Hanzo look at your armguards."

The giant looked at Kazuki strangely, but did as the young man asked. When he saw the unblemished metal, Hanzo's eyes widened.

"Do you see what I see?"

"Yeah…" The giant took a few steps to his right and grabbed his knuckles off of the floor. They, too, were in perfect condition. "By Thor's might! What's going on?"

There was no time for explanations. Ginza was tiring and needed backup fast. "Hanzo, go help Ginza take down that demon. And don't worry about getting burned, he's just playing mind games with us."

Hanzo didn't fully understand what the young man meant, but he followed Kazuki's lead. The giant put his knuckles back on and lunged towards Seventeen, who had been forced towards the giant by Ginza's attack. The demon didn't have time to react and took a direct hit to his back. There was a loud crack and the demon began gasping for air. He coughed hard a few times and blood came spilling out onto the floor.

"Two against one isn't fair," he breathed.

The pirates grinned at each other and replied, "We're pirates. We don't do 'fair'."

The demon wiped his mouth and laughed. "In that case, I suppose demons don't play fair either." He snapped his fingers and his whole body became engulfed in a red flame.

Ginza backed away a few feet, but Hanzo stayed where he was. He stared hard at the demon. Kazuki wasn't sure of what was going through the giant's head, but he hoped that Hanzo's brain had finally registered the situation. The giant's right arm shot forward and grabbed the demon by the neck. Flames surrounded Hanzo's hand and burned through his flesh, but the giant did not release Seventeen.

"Hanzo! Let go ya fool, before yer hand's gone!" Ginza yelled.

He then watched as the giant struck the demon several times in the head with his other knuckled fist before throwing Seventeen to the floor.

"Gin," Hanzo said with grin, "this demon's been playing us for fools!" He raised his hand to show the blacksmith that there were no burns.

Ginza frowned and walked over to inspect Hanzo's hand more closely. After a second or two, the blacksmith closed his eyes and crossed his arms; he was thinking.

"You haven't forgotten about me, have you?" Seventeen hissed as he charged the two pirates.

Only opening his eyes slightly, Ginza moved his arms so quickly that the demon didn't have time to react. There was a scream, and an arm went flying through the air. Seventeen flopped around on the floor, moaning and caressing his bloody stump.

"So yer tellin' me that this ain't real," Ginza said slowly as he looked at Hanzo and then to Kazuki. "It's all just a trick?"

Kazuki and Hanzo nodded.

"That *is* what street performers do for a living, Ginza," The young man explained. He then looked over to the demon, who was no longer writhing on the floor, but standing with his sword ready for battle. "Looks like you two aren't finished yet."

The two pirates looked over their shoulders at Seventeen. The demon was clearly about to lose and was not happy about it. His eyes were now black and his body secreted smoke, along with a burning smell. He charged the two pirates with the last of his strength, hoping to take at least one of them down with him. Unfortunately for him, Seventeen would die disappointed. When he landed on the floor between the two pirates, he was missing his left arm and side of his torso, and his face was twisted all the way around to the back.

"Nice teamwork," Kazuki said with a grin.

Hanzo and Ginza exchanged their 'oh yeah' sign to each other. They always did that after a battle. Kazuki could never figure out where it came from or what it meant, but he had more important things to focus on. The two pirates may have defeated one of the demons, but there was still another left and they didn't have the strength to fight. Sweat poured down both of their faces and necks, and their breathing was rather heavy. While the fighting hadn't lasted all that long, the toll of keeping up with a demon was pricey for a human. One fight was all they could commit to; and in this instance they had fought together.

"Well, that wasn't what I had expected," an unamused voice said, "but it's my turn now and I won't be losing to a couple of humans."

"That's right," Kazuki said as he stood in front of the two pirates, his sword unsheathed, "you'll be losing to one: me."

Hanzo and Ginza tried to protest, but the young man told them to back off. There was something in the tone of his voice that persuaded the two pirates to obey the young man's orders.

"Correction: you are *not* human, Shinigami-sama, but I will defeat you nonetheless." Sixteen reached for the sword at his side. He drew, but there was nothing there except for the hilt in the demon's hand.

Ginza and Hanzo burst into laughter. They called Sixteen some unsavory names and ridiculed him for having a useless weapon. The demon just stood there holding his sword hilt.

"If this is supposed to be another trick, demon, we won't fall for it," Hanzo declared with a grin.

Sixteen swung his arm as if he were aiming to cut the giant.

Tinkle, tinkle…

Kazuki heard the bell again as the invisible sword was swung. His senses were screaming. Before he knew what he was doing, the young man shoved Hanzo aside. The giant lost his balance and fell to the floor.

"Ow! What *was* that?!" Hanzo exclaimed as he held his foot.

Ginza and Kazuki both looked at the giant's foot; there was a fresh wound on the side of it.

"But…there's nothin' there," Ginza murmured.

"I told you these side-street performers are tricky," Kazuki said, glancing over at Sixteen.

"If you were merely a human, that giant would have died," Sixteen said in his unchanging, monotone voice.

"If you're trying to provoke me into bringing out the Demon King, it won't work. I can defeat you on my own." The young man readied his sword to attack.

"So you say," the demon said blankly.

Kazuki lunged forward with a horizontal slash, but Sixteen jumped backwards and avoided it. The young man followed with an upwards diagonal cut, a downwards diagonal cut, and another upwards diagonal cut, but the demon avoided them all. Kazuki tried thrusting, slashing horizontally and vertically, and any other cut he could think of, but Sixteen kept avoiding each one. The young man got close to hitting the demon once when he faked a cut to the head and thrust for the demon's stomach instead, but Sixteen was somehow still able to avoid it. Kazuki jumped backwards to make space between them.

"Is it my turn now?"

Sixteen raised his invisible sword up and sliced straight down. The young man dodged to the side, and immediately the demon sliced towards him again. Kazuki moved to block the invisible blade, but he had forgotten about the remaining priest's body and tripped over it.

Tinkle, tinkle…

Blood ran down the fresh wound on the side of Kazuki's leg. He grimaced from the pain, but managed to stand up and resume a defensive stance.

Kazuki could hear Hanzo and Ginza talking behind him. They were concerned for the young man and wondered if they should fight too.

He tried to reassure the two pirates by saying, "I was just a bit careless. It won't happen again."

Sixteen swung at the young man over and over. Kazuki managed to dodge the attacks, but he was so focused on figuring out the invisible sword's trick that it seemed as though the demon had the upper hand.

"Are you sure you don't want to call upon Shinigami-sama?" Sixteen asked as he continued his attack.

Kazuki didn't respond. He was sure that he was close to figuring out the trick.

The young man put more than ten feet of distance between himself and the demon. He stood there with his sword at his side, completely calm. Sixteen shrugged his shoulders and, without moving forward, swung his invisible sword vertically at Kazuki. The young man closed his eyes and leaned his head ever so slightly forwards.

Tinkle, tinkle…

The sword caught the edge of his chin, but the wound was nothing more than a small scratch. Before anyone could react, Kazuki dashed forwards and cut towards the demon's neck. Sixteen panicked and raised his sword in a last second attempt to block the attack, but what Kazuki's katana collided with wasn't another blade; it was a hilt.

The young man grinned and jumped back from the demon. "I've figured out your trick, demon."

Sixteen, who had seemed emotionally dead, was now wearing a distinct frown on his face. "That is impossible, as there is no trick being performed."

"Lad, let us fight," Hanzo called out. He was probably getting annoyed at having to watch and not participate in the fight.

"We can back ya up," Ginza added, also clearly wanting a piece of the action.

"No. This will be over in two moves," the young man grinned. He stood with his legs about shoulder-width apart. Both hands held the katana's tsuka, while the blade's tip was aimed towards the floor. Kazuki knew that his stance thoroughly confused everyone in the room, which made him grin even more.

Closing his eyes, the young man told Sixteen to attack him. The demon, having no idea what was in store for him, readily obliged Kazuki and slashed towards him.

Tinkle, tinkle…

As soon as Kazuki heard the bell he thrust his katana hard into the tatami floor. He then pulled the blade out and slashed horizontally at Sixteen.

Kazuki flicked the blood from his blade and returned it to the saya at his side. The floor was now stained red by two demons. Their hazy shadows appeared: one from the halved corpse of Sixteen and one from beneath the floor. They abruptly vanished without a sound; only the smell of smoke remained.

"Little Oni, could ya tell us what the festering hole's goin' on?!" Ginza shouted. Both he and Hanzo were confused as to what had happened in those final two moves.

"It's simple, really. The 'invisible sword' wasn't actually invisible; the blade never existed in the first place. There was a demon beneath the floor that was attacking me. So, while it seemed like Sixteen was hitting me with his ridiculous sword, it was all an act to cover for the demon hiding below us."

"But how in Loki's mind did you figure that out?" Hanzo asked.

"Well, I think the demon beneath the floor had a bell or something like it, because every time the demon moved I heard the tinkling of a bell. Also, when the attack hit me, I could tell that it was coming from below and not from above." Kazuki pointed to the small cut on his chin, "'Cause otherwise this would be on top of my head and not the bottom of my chin, right?"

The two pirates stared at the young man.

"And if his sword had been real, Sixteen wouldn't have used his hilt to block my attack that time."

Kazuki could see that the wheels were slowly beginning to turn in the pirates' heads. He chuckled to himself and then reminded the two pirates that they needed to regroup with the captain and Rize. Hanzo and Ginza followed after the young man; their minds still working through the events and what Kazuki had told them.

When they arrived in the shrine's courtyard, the shipmates found themselves surrounded by corpse pieces writhing on the ground, pinned by a sea of arrows.

"Looks like Rize's been busy," Hanzo grinned.

Ginza elbowed the giant and said, "An' he ain't the only one."

The two pirates, along with the young man, stared at the scene before them: Kohaku was chasing a very acrobatic female in a yellow and black striped, skin-tight outfit, while Rize took aim at a smaller woman wearing a white kimono.

Kazuki was ready to jump into the fray, but Ginza held him back. "Let 'em handle this, Little Oni. We already had our fight," the blacksmith grinned. "An' anyways, watchin' Kohaku battle another woman's pretty excitin', wouldn't ya say?" Ginza laughed heartily and heavy-handedly patted the young man on the back.

Ouch! Spawn of a demon...Ginza, you're too strong! Kazuki thought as he pretended he hadn't felt anything. The blacksmith had been right though: it would be a good opportunity to watch Kohaku fight. *But not for* that *reason...*

The young man shook his head and watched as the ninja woman caught up to her prey. She already had her kusarigama out, which meant that the battle hadn't just begun, but the other woman was so limber that she could easily bend herself out of the way of Kohaku's attacks. Luckily, the acrobatic woman didn't seem to have any offensive skills as she, too, found it difficult to hit her target.

They were hard to see, but Kazuki noticed that the acrobatic woman was throwing long, thin needles at Kohaku. Thinking that they were most likely coated with poison, the young man became worried when one grazed Kohaku's shoulder, creating a small trail of blood. He wanted so badly to charge in and help the ninja woman, but Kazuki knew that this was not his battle.

Since joining the Ryujin crew, the young man had learned that there were a lot of unspoken rules for combat. The most important of which was: 'never interfere in another's fight.' There were specific moments or instances where it would be acceptable to intervene in a fight, but that sort of moment had not come yet. So the young man waited, but not patiently. His anxiety rose when a needle penetrated Kohaku's left shoulder. She had moved a half a second too slow. Kazuki watched intently, looking for any signs of poisoning. What he witnessed was Kohaku's left arm suddenly go limp.

The acrobatic woman cackled, "Finally, a hit! This fight has just been decided, little girl. There's no way that you can wield that weapon of yours without two–Ahh!" The woman shrieked as the metal weight at the end of the kusarigama chain smacked her right in the chest. She was knocked backwards by the impact and began coughing up blood soon after.

Kohaku was grinning. She wouldn't be the deadly ninja woman she was without having trained to use her weapon one-handed. It wasn't an easy feat, but Kohaku was able to swing the chain around using her neck, torso, and legs. Only someone with immense skill could pull it off.

Kazuki smiled. "She sure is something."

"What's this?" Ginza exclaimed dramatically. "Does Little Oni fancy the cap'n's woman?" He was teasing Kazuki, but deep down the young man knew that Ginza was closer to the truth than anyone would ever know.

"Shut it," Kazuki replied.

"I see that you're no ordinary human," the limber woman spat as she wiped her mouth with the back of her hand. "But no matter how well-trained you are, you can't defeat a demon!"

Launching herself at Kohaku, the demon woman unleashed dozens of needles at once. The female ninja placed the kusarigama handle in her mouth and used her right hand to swing the chain around in front of her, deflecting all of the incoming needles.

"Tch. Not enough?" The acrobatic woman grumbled. "Fine then," she said as she jumped high into the air, "I'll just–Ugh!"

Faster than anyone could see, Kohaku had switched the weighted end with the bladed one and threw it towards the demon woman's stomach. It tore through flesh as it settled into the demon's core, before ripping through one side as the ninja woman pulled the chain hard towards her. The acrobatic woman seemed to be in shock as she was yanked towards the ground. She slammed into the dirt with such force that Kazuki could hear her bones crack. Without so much as a scream from the demon woman, the pirates watched as black smoke rose from her broken body and then quickly disappeared.

Kazuki breathed a sigh of relief.

"I'd say that was a pretty good fight, wouldn't you?" Hanzo commented.

"Not 'er best, but fine enough," Ginza replied.

Kazuki shook his head as the two pirates smirked at each other.

When he glanced back towards Kohaku, she was gone. Puzzled and slightly worried, the young man took a step towards where he had last seen the ninja woman, but was stopped in his tracks by a stray arrow. Kazuki immediately turned his attention towards where the helmsman was fighting. It was extremely rare for Rize's arrows to miss their intended target.

The woman in the white kimono was not moving. She stood perfectly still as she stared at Rize, paying no attention to the arrows whizzing past her. She bore no expression on her face and she did not speak.

"How come Rize ain't hittin' 'er?" Ginza wondered aloud. His attention had also been drawn to the helmsman's battle by the stray arrow.

Kazuki watched intently as Rize fired another arrow towards the woman in white. As he followed the arrow's path, the young man's face suddenly paled.

"What's wrong Little Oni?" the blacksmith asked.

Kazuki slowly turned his face towards Ginza and said, "S-she's a…ghost!"

The blacksmith froze.

"Hahaha! Very funny, Lad," Hanzo laughed as he approached them. "He's just getting us back for earlier," he said as he heartily smacked Ginza across the back. When neither Ginza nor Kazuki laughed, Hanzo's smile faded. "You *were* joking…right, Lad?"

Kazuki slowly shook his head back and forth. He had seen Rize's arrow hit the woman square in the chest and then fly right through her body, leaving no visible damage behind. The helmsman's arrows weren't passing by her…they were passing *through* her.

"I thought there was a difference between ghosts and demons," Hanzo whispered.

"Maybe they're in league t'gether," Ginza whispered back.

"…Or maybe it's just a trick like with the other two demons that we fought," Kazuki suggested, not wanting to believe that there was a ghost standing before him.

Both pirates stared at the young man. Disbelief showed in their expressions.

"I'm not sure yet, but we had better figure it out before Rize runs out of arrows," Kazuki said. *Or before that thing starts attacking him.*

It wasn't long after the pirates began watching before Kazuki's fears came true: the woman in white, who had previously been as still as stone, began to move towards the helmsman. Reaching into her mouth, she pulled out a sickle that looked to be covered in blood and raised it over her head.

Rize saw what was happening and quickly jumped back a few feet. Though his intent had been to create more space between himself and the ghostly woman, the helmsman watched in horror as the woman in white continued gliding towards him at an incredible speed. Rize shouldered his bow and drew a medium-sized dagger from the holster on the right side of his chest. He thrust the blade in front of him as the ghostly woman's sickle was brought down, but instead of metal hitting metal, the sound was that of flesh being torn.

"Ahh!" The helmsman cried out. He quickly jumped away from the ghostly woman and put his hand to the wound on his left arm. It wasn't deep enough to render his arm useless, but it was undoubtedly painful.

"Towering horse pile," Ginza spat. "This doesn't look good."

"You figure anything out yet, Lad?" Hanzo asked with great interest.

Kazuki shook his head. He couldn't figure out what the woman in white's trick was no matter how hard he tried. The young man was about to unsheathe his sword to assist the helmsman when suddenly he heard a shrill screech. It sounded like Ami, and it was coming from a cluster of rocks high above the shrine.

Rize must have heard it too, because he suddenly looked towards the same cluster of rocks and quickly fired an arrow in their direction. After the arrow flew off, the helmsman winced and grabbed his left arm. He didn't see the ghostly woman raising her weapon behind him.

"Rize! Look out!" Kazuki shouted.

The helmsman turned his head to see the bloody sickle heading towards him, but instead of moving out of the way, Rize grinned at his attacker. Right before the tip of the sickle pierced the helmsman's eye, the ghostly woman vanished.

Kazuki, Hanzo, and Ginza let out a huge collective sigh. They ran over to Rize and helped him bandage his wound.

"What the festering hole were ya thinkin'?!" Ginza yelled. "Don't ever gamble with yer life again, ya hear me!"

"Yeah, yeah," Rize chuckled. "Sorry I worried you."

"But what happened to that ghost lady?" Hanzo asked as he glanced around the temple grounds.

"I finally shot her real body," Rize replied. "I think the one I was fighting was just an illusion or something. Though I never would've found her out if Ami hadn't helped me." The helmsman smiled as he held out his right arm for the falcon to gracefully land on.

As Ami ruffled her feathers, Kazuki smelled a faint trace of smoke. "Well, that's one more demon down," the young man said with a grin, "nice work, Rize."

The helmsman nodded and then looked around. "Where's Kohaku and the captain?"

"Kohaku was 'ere a second ago…" Ginza said as he, too, began looking around.

"But we haven't seen the cap'n since we came out here," Hanzo added.

"I've got a real bad feelin'," Ginza groaned.

Suddenly there was a huge explosion inside of the main temple. The building broke apart into thousands of wooden shards that flew off in all directions. The pirates did their best to shield themselves from the fragments that flew their way. As the debris settled, the pirates looked back towards the main temple. Smoke covered the remains of the structure, but a shadowy human figure could be seen emerging from the wreckage. As it neared them, the pirates gasped. The figure was Kohaku, and she was dragging an unconscious Hasunuma behind her; a trail of blood ran down the back of his head and neck.

The pirate men all ran towards the ninja woman and assisted her in carrying the Pirate King to a safer location. They sat him against the large, sacred tree that towered over what had presumably been the priest's quarters, and waited breathlessly for the Pirate King to awaken.

"That man is more powerful than I thought," a cold voice said, cutting through the silence. Kazuki turned around and came face-to-face with black-eyed Eiri. "I shall have to kill him, I think," Second said as his lips curled into a demonic smile.

"You won't touch him," Kazuki announced as he unsheathed his katana.

"We won't let ya kill our cap'n," Ginza said as he purposefully blocked Second's view of Hasunuma.

"Not like you could anyways," Hanzo added as he stood next to Rize and crossed his arms. Rize and Kohaku were silent as they, too, stood in front of the still-unconscious Pirate King.

"And which of you lowly humans is going to stop me?" Second laughed, "Or should I ask, 'which of you wishes to be slaughtered first?' If I had my choice, I would start with the woman," he grinned as he pointed towards Kohaku.

There was a flash of light and suddenly Second's outstretched hand fell to the ground.

"You will kill no one," Kazuki growled, thrusting his katana towards Second's face.

"Oh my," Second calmly said as he reached down and picked up his severed hand. "Is it already time to play, Shinigami-sama?"

Kazuki watched as Second placed his detached hand to his wrist, and within seconds it was as if his hand had never been cut off, let alone scratched.

"I told you before, I don't need to become a demon to fight you," Kazuki replied, though he wasn't so sure of himself anymore after what he had just seen.

Second sighed, "Still a foolish child, I see. Well, no matter," he began as he raised his sword to meet Kazuki's, "this time I will beat the lesson into you so that you never forget it."

Kohaku wasn't sure if any of the pirate men could see Second and Kazu's fight; their speed and power far surpassed what any human could hope to achieve. Sparks flew each time the two katana collided, creating beautiful golden bursts in the air around them. By the time the sparks became visible, the two combatants had already moved on from that space, creating more spectacles elsewhere. It was as if someone were lighting small golden fireworks around the temple grounds.

Kazu's training has served him well, but I doubt that he's fighting solely with his own abilities…whether he realizes it or not.

In terms of purely human abilities, Kohaku estimated that Kazu ranked somewhere between Hanzo and Rize. And since it seemed that even Hasu couldn't beat Second, Kazu didn't stand a chance. Yet Kohaku stood watching in amazement as the young man fought on par with Second. She could think of no other explanation than that of the Demon King sharing his power with Kazu.

So this is the power of the two greatest demons. The ninja woman surveyed the men around her and shook her head. *Humans don't stand a chance against them.*

Realizing the gravity of the situation, Kohaku whistled to the pirate men.

"You don't have to tell us, Sis," Hanzo said with a serious expression. "We're well-aware of our uselessness in this battle."

"Thunderin' sea snakes, we can't even see 'em!" Ginza added, frustration showing clearly on his face.

"And I doubt Ami could help me find the target this time," Rize said as he watched the falcon circling high above them. After a moment, he shook his head and sighed, "Which means our best option is to get out of the way."

The ninja woman nodded. In order to win the fight, Kohaku knew that Kazu couldn't afford any distractions. If the pirates were to stay nearby, there was a high probability that Second would use them to his advantage.

Under her silent command, the ninja woman and the pirate men began carrying the Pirate King away from the demonic battle. They were only able to get a short distance away before a powerful wind knocked them to the ground.

"And just where do you insolent creatures think you're going?"

Kohaku immediately threw a shuriken towards the demon standing before them, but it was pushed aside by another powerful gust of wind.

"I let my guard down in front of you on our first meeting," Second said as he stared emotionlessly at the ninja woman, "which was a mistake that I will not replicate."

As the demon took a step towards Kohaku, an arrow suddenly lodged itself in Second's shoulder. Before he could react, Second had his torso sliced open and his head twisted around by none other than Ginza and Hanzo. The pirate men smiled with the success of their joint attack, but their joy was short lived; their faces paled with horror as they watched Second's torso mend together, his head snap back into place, and the barbed arrow be effortlessly pulled from the demon's shoulder, leaving behind no trace of injury.

"Now do you understand the futility of your attacks?" Second sighed, "Be grateful that I allowed you a sliver of hope before crushing you all."

With a sweep of his hand, Second unleashed a massive blast of energy. Kohaku instinctively shielded Hasu and held him to the ground with the aid of her kusarigama. Ginza tried to steady himself by thrusting the blade of his weapon into the ground, but the blast was too strong and he was thrown back about fifteen feet; Hanzo and Rize suffered similar fates.

I can't let him get to Hasu! The ninja woman told herself as she grabbed a small packet of powder from her belt and threw it at the demon. Second attempted to brush it aside with a wave of his hand, but when the blast of energy hit the packet, it exploded. Kohaku began dragging Hasu away as quickly as she could, knowing that her distraction would not buy her much time. *Come on, Kazu, we need you! Where are you?*

Suddenly the ninja woman felt a sharp pain in her legs and she silently screamed. Unable to bear Hasu's weight any longer, Kohaku collapsed to the ground. She looked down at her legs and saw blood seeping from a horizontal slash across both of her calves.

Second approached her, his sword glistening with fresh blood. "You seem to have a lot of tricks in your arsenal, woman. I applaud you for your efforts to keep me from my prey, but it's over." Second raised his sword above him.

Kohaku frantically searched her belt for something else to throw, but there was nothing there. Her kusarigama lay stuck in the ground a few yards away, as she had left it behind in order to drag Hasu to safety.

Second's blade began to fall towards the Pirate King's head.

Kohaku desperately reached for him. She felt something well up inside of her as she silently cried out, *Hasu! Hasu! HASU!*

Kazuki lay on the ground with a broken leg and some broken ribs. His wounds were the result of his own foolish decision. Second had set up a trap, and Kazuki had taken the bait without a second thought.

I warned you, did I not?

Shut it. Kazuki grimaced as he rolled onto his side.

You are not going anywhere with those injuries.

Kazuki tried to move his leg, but was paralyzed by the excruciating pain that radiated through his body.

See?

Shut. Up. The young man turned onto his stomach and pushed himself up with his arms. He began to cough and noticed droplets of blood dispersing onto the dirt beneath him. Kazuki dug his nails into the soil and shouted, "Dammit! I can't stop now, I have to save them!"

As I said before, you can save them if you let me take over.

"And risk you killing my friends in the process? No way."

But you were asking for my assistance earlier…And what benefit would their deaths have for me, might I ask? I am solely interested in fighting Second.

"You really think I'd believe that? I've felt your urge to fight Hasunuma."

He he he. Well, I cannot deny that he intrigues me. But I swear to you that I will not harm any of your companions. This battle is between myself and Second only.

Kazuki wasn't sure if he should believe the Demon King or not. He knew that if the Demon King took over his body, Kazuki would be unable to stop him if the demon changed his mind. The young man also wasn't particularly happy with the fact that he needed a demon's help in order to protect his friends.

"HASU!" A voice suddenly cried out in the distance. It wasn't familiar and sounded rather odd…like it came from someone who hadn't spoken in a–

Kohaku!

Kazuki frantically searched around him for the source of the voice, but Second had placed a barrier around the young man; all he could see around him was an endless sea of haze.

Your companions are in trouble.

"Fine! You can take over my body on one condition: don't shut me out."

…That will mean that some of my power is restrained…but if that is your condition, then I accept.

"And you'd better not go back on your word, Demon King. I'll be watching you."

Kazuki felt himself laugh. **"I may be a demon, but I *am* a King. I will hold to my promise, human child."**

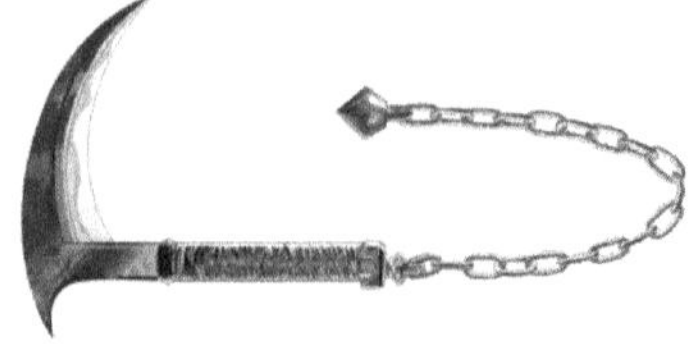

Kohaku felt tears run down her cheeks. She had to blink multiple times to drive the water from her eyes so that she could see clearly. What she thought she had seen…was it real? The scene before her was unbelievable: Second's katana hovered inches away from Hasu's face as the Pirate King held the blade between his palms. Not only had he managed to regain consciousness in time, but Hasu was, somehow, also able to react at lighting speed in order to stop the katana before it cut him.

"That's quite the wake-up method ya've got there, Eiri," Hasu said with a grin. "However, I'd refrain from using it again if I were you, because it upsets the ladies," he added as he nodded towards Kohaku.

When Second turned his gaze towards the ninja woman, Hasu kicked the demon as hard as he could, sending him back a few feet. Hasu then stood up, still holding onto Second's katana, and added, "And if you're a gentleman at all, then you'd never make a woman cry."

The Pirate King launched the katana blade-first towards its master. Unfortunately, the sword seemed to possess a will of its own as it slowed its approach and rotated itself so that Second could easily grab hold of the tsuka.

Second frowned. "You puzzle me, human. How is it that you are so powerful and have such advanced healing abilities?"

Hasu shook his head and said "I don't think you should be worrying about me right now." He pointed towards Second and grinned. "Your opponent is right behind ya."

The person standing behind the demon was Kazu – or it at least looked like Kazu. There was a dark shadow surrounding the young man's body, and his eyes had turned completely black. Second only turned his head slightly before he was knocked a good twenty feet away to the left. One swift backhand from the young man's body was all it took to send the demon flying.

"Even in the kid's body, the Demon King has that much power…pretty terrifying, don't ya think?" Hasu said as he squatted down next to Kohaku.

The Pirate King was right; just how much power did the Demon King possess? It seemed as though he could easily rule the world if he wished. Was there something that kept the demons at bay? Some sort of demon law perhaps that kept them in the shadows…

BOOM!

The ninja woman shielded herself as a gust of dirt and debris blew over her. She looked to Hasu once the dust settled and saw him watching the two demons battling. The Pirate King was grinning and it seemed to Kokahu that he was itching to join in the fight.

She shook her head and sighed. *Men.*

The ninja woman skillfully bandaged her leg wounds with the medicinal wrappings that she kept tucked inside of her belt. She then tried to stand up, but found it impossible in her condition.

Suddenly Hasu's smiling face was in front of hers. "Might I be of service, Milady?"

Kohaku gave the Pirate King 'the look'.

He laughed and said, "I mean no offense, Milady. I simply wish to offer you my assistance."

Before Kohaku could protest, she felt herself being lifted off of the ground by a pair of strong arms. The Pirate King cradled her like a princess, which made the ninja woman rather annoyed – and slightly happy. While she was no delicate flower, Kohaku certainly had a romantic side to her that she kept hidden from everyone else. In her world, there was no time or place for the sort of dramatic and elaborate scenes that she secretly dreamt of. After all, she was a ninja: a tireless assassin soaked in blood.

The Pirate King's grip around the ninja woman tightened for a brief moment as he whispered in her ear, "You really saved me back there, Kohaku. I was out cold until I heard your voice…if you hadn't called my name, I'd be dead right now."

The ninja woman's cheeks grew warm. *Hasu…I need you here with me…so you're not allowed to die. I won't let you.*

The Pirate King smiled as he added, "Although, your voice wasn't exactly angelic. You might want to work on–Ouch!"

Kohaku punched Hasu's chest with force. The Pirate King laughed as he carried the embarrassed ninja woman further away from the demonic battle.

Kazuki watched intently as the Demon King fought Second. He was amazed at how effortlessly the Demon King blocked each of Second's attacks. Sparks flew each time the demons' katana collided. The swords themselves seemed to be flowing with power of their own, causing Kazuki to wonder if somehow they, too, were demons.

The young man felt himself grin, **"You are very observant, human child. A demon's weapon is indeed imbued with power, but it is the power of its master that flows through it."**

Are you trying to tell me that even though I'm able to wield your katana, I can't unleash its true power?

As Second's sword met with the Demon King's once more, Kazuki felt a sort of burst of energy between the two katana.

"Did you feel it that time? My power radiating through the sword."

The Demon King sent his strength through his katana and pushed Second a few yards away. He then swung his katana downward, unleashing a massive amount of energy that shot towards the other demon. As Second tried to block the attack, a crater appeared in the earth around him and he was forced to kneel under the pressure. What looked like tiny bolts of purple lightning began appearing in the bowl of the crater and seconds later there was a fierce explosion.

The Demon King raised his katana so that Kazuki's black eyes reflected in the blade. **"In other hands, this sword would simply be a sharp piece of metal. It only resonates with its master."**

"Don't tell me that you're talking to your host, Shinigami-sama," Second stated as his silhouette appeared within the dust clouds. "It makes me very angry that you think you can defeat me when you aren't using your full strength," he said as he patted away dirt from his hair and clothes.

Kazuki felt himself laugh. **"And yet it seems to be more than**

enough to win this battle." The Demon King pointed the tip of his katana at the demon before him. **"Are you truly trying to defeat me, Second?"**

Suddenly Kazuki felt the air around Second change, and a violent blast of wind shot towards the Demon King. It was filled with an intense hatred that had a paralyzing affect. The Demon King, however, seemed unaffected as he charged towards his opponent. The speed with which he attacked his foe was almost incomprehensible, and yet Second somehow managed to parry all of the Demon King's strikes.

Kazuki heard bellowing laughter erupt from his mouth. **"Yes, excellent! This is how our battle should be!"**

Had Second not been fighting seriously beforehand? The thought made Kazuki nauseous. These demons were beyond powerful; no human could ever hope to defeat them. So why were they hidden away like ghosts, relegated to some special demon world, when they could easily control or destroy this world? Kazuki waited for the Demon King to respond to his queries, but he received no answer. The Demon King was fully concentrating on the battle before him, as it seemed as if the tides had begun to turn in Second's favor.

"What's this? Tired already, *Your Highness*?" Second goaded.

At first, the young man thought that the demon was merely attempting to provoke the Demon King, but, to his surprise, Second was simply stating a fact. Kazuki could feel the demonic energy within him dissipating.

What's going on? I thought you were the strongest demon.

The Demon King grinned as his breathing became heavy and steam began rising from Kazuki's body. **"I told you...that keeping**

you awake…would be costly."

Yeah, but this is beyond a little restriction. Why is your energy suddenly leaving my body?

"Heh…You will find out…shortly."

The Demon King looked to the sky. Kazuki noticed that dark grey clouds now swirled above them. Refocusing on Second, the Demon King readied himself. The young man had no idea what the clouds meant, or what the Demon King was planning to do, but he decided to watch silently as the battle neared its end.

Launching himself at Second, the Demon King released his left hand from his katana and reached for Second's neck. When the lesser demon realized what the Demon King was trying to do, fear flickered through his eyes momentarily. Reacting faster than any human could, Second jumped away from the Demon King's grasp only to suddenly find himself impaled through the stomach by the Demon King's katana.

Without a moment's pause, the Demon King raised his katana above him – with Second still attached – and said, **"You seem to forget with whom you are battling…so let me remind you!"**

Before he could say anything more, a huge bolt of lighting came crashing down from the clouds above and struck Second. The charge continued downward, enveloping the Demon King in its warm, white glow. Kazuki felt a strange sensation within him before he lost consciousness.

The Pirate King had just reached the rest of the crew when the bolt of lighting struck.

"What the– I'm hopin' that was from Little Oni," Ginza said as he stared at the large, white beam funneling down from the dark sky above.

Seconds later it vanished, and the Pirate King had to blink a few times to readjust his vision. Lying on the ground was Kazuki – something like steam was rising from his body, and the kid wasn't moving. Second was nowhere to be seen.

"Little Oni!" Ginza yelled as he hurried over to the kid. The blacksmith reached down, but quickly pulled his hands away. "Fiery mountain gods, 'es too hot t' touch!"

"Don't worry," Rize said as he made his way towards Ginza and the kid, "if that bolt of lighting was what I think it was, then Little Oni should be fine…eventually."

"*Eventually?*" Ginza repeated with a skeptic tone.

"Well, I've only heard about it, so–"

Rize was suddenly cut off by a lighthearted giggle.

"No need to thank me, gentleman! Just doing my job!"

A young girl appeared before them. She looked to be around Kazuki's age and was dressed in the robes of a miko. Her long golden hair, held loosely back by a red knot, danced softly in the wind while her emerald green eyes seemed to glisten in the dim light.

"Um. What's with the long faces?" She asked when she finally noticed the looks she was receiving from the pirate crew.

"Who in Asgard are you?" Hanzo questioned as he made his way towards the kid. The giant was carrying Kohaku on his back, presumably bringing her closer to Kazuki so she could examine him.

"An' what've ya done t' our brother?!" Ginza bellowed as he stood up. The girl was about half of his height.

"Your brother…?" The girl peeked around the blacksmith and saw Kazuki lying on the ground. "Oh my gosh!" She shouted as she threw her hands up above her head. Immediately she ran over to the kid and knelt down beside him. "I am so, so sorry! I had no idea my sealing spell would harm a human!"

"So it *was* a sealing spell," Rize said in amazement, "I'm glad I finally got to see one in person."

Ginza shot the helmsman a look that could kill.

"Er, but I wish Little Oni hadn't been hit by it," Rize quickly added.

"Little Oni?" The girl raised an eyebrow, "What kind of a name is that?"

Rize and Ginza turned their heads towards the Pirate King with a pleading look on their faces.

Hasunuma had to laugh to himself. *Of all of the things to happen at such a crucial moment…* "Alright, alright," he said as he joined the group surrounding the kid, "I'll explain it to ya. But first," he grinned, "introductions are in order. That there's Kohaku, and that giant next to her is Hanzo. The angry guy is Ginza, and the stary-eyed guy is Rize."

"Hey!" The helmsman blurted out in protest while Hanzo and Ginza attempted to stifle their laughter.

"And who are *you*?" The girl asked in a strange tone, accompanied by a not-so innocent smile.

The Pirate King leaned down and put his face very close to the girl's. With a smile he replied, "Someone who isn't interested in flat-chested girls."

Seeing at how red her face turned, Hasunuma drew his face back before the girl had a chance to slap him. He laughed heartily and the other male crewmates joined in. Kohaku simply shook her head and sighed.

"Hmph, with your level of rudeness, I'd say you all are thieves or ronin," the girl pouted.

"Somethin' like that," Hasunuma grinned. "You can call me 'Red Dragon' if you want, but others simply call me–"

"The Pirate King!" The girl gasped.

"That's our cap'n," Ginza said with his chest puffed out.

Hanzo and Rize agreed with a hearty cheer.

"You're a bunch of pirates then," the girl stared wide-eyed, "even *you*?" She added when her eyes met Kohaku's.

The ninja woman nodded.

The girl's eyes shifted down slightly. Her face flushed when she noticed Kohaku's ample chest and the girl quickly averted her gaze. "S-So I guess this guy is also a pirate…" she trailed off as she gently brushed Kazuki's hair away from his eyes.

"He's our youngest crewmate," the Pirate King clarified. "And ya almost killed him," he added as he drew his red dragon sword and aimed the blade towards the girl's throat.

"It's not like I *meant* to," the girl protested. "Demon sealing spells aren't supposed to work on humans."

"How did you know that guy was a demon?" Rize asked.

She showed him a smile and sassily replied, "Because I'm a miko – in case my attire didn't already give me away. I was born with spiritual powers that make me sensitive to non-human entities."

Rize crossed his arms and said, "I got that part." He then mumbled, "But I guess your aim is as bad as your personality."

"Is this your shrine?" Hanzo asked.

The miko shook her head slowly. "No, but," she bit her lip and forced herself to continue, "my shrine shared a similar fate not too long ago."

None of the pirate men knew how to respond to the girl's statement. They all looked away and scratched their heads, hoping someone else would say something comforting. The Pirate King was about to fulfill that role when he noticed Kohaku reaching across Kazuki's body to grab hold of the miko's hand. The girl jumped a little at the sudden contact, but then her emotions took over and she began to sob aloud. Kohaku simply held the girl's hand and smiled warmly at her.

"Um. I'm not dead yet, so please stop crying," a voice suddenly said.

All eyes shot to Kazuki, who was now attempting to sit up.

"Little Oni!" Ginza cried out.

"Welcome back, Lad," Hanzo added with a smile.

"You had us pretty worried," Rize said with a sigh.

The kid sat up and smiled apologetically, "Sorry about that. The Demon King took control and I couldn't do any–"

"WHAT?!" The girl suddenly yelled, startling those around her, "You've got the *Demon King* inside of you?!"

"Uh, yeah," Kazuki nervously replied.

The miko let out an enormous sigh, "Well that explains why my sealing spell worked on you too."

"Wait a minute," Kazuki said, staring at the girl, "I know you…you're the girl I rescued in Giyosan!"

"Who, me?" the girl pointed to herself.

Kazuki nodded.

"Sorry, but I think you have the wrong girl," the miko said, a look of genuine confusion shone on her face.

"But I know it was you," Kazuki said confidently, "I could never forget such a…a uniquely featured woman."

The kid's face had turned so red that Hasunuma couldn't hold back his laughter. "Ha ha ha! Is that the best ya got, Kid?" *I'll bet he was about to say that he could never forget such a 'beautiful woman'.*

Kazuki glared at the Pirate King.

"I appreciate the, er, compliment," the girl interrupted, "but I promise, I've never met you before today." And then she seemed to suddenly think of something and added, "Unless you met me when it wasn't me."

A chorus of 'huh' and 'what's that mean' came from the male crewmates.

"Care t' explain, little lady?" The Pirate King asked, his sword still unsheathed and aimed in the girl's direction.

"Hey, she's not our enemy, so put your sword down," Kazuki demanded.

"I beg pardon, but *who* is captain here?" The Pirate King replied, his voice sounded lighthearted, but his expression was deadly serious.

Kazuki frowned. "You are," he grumbled.

"Oh, it's alright," the girl said energetically, "it's not like I trust you all either. Anyways," she continued, "I suppose I should at least explain my actions, since I ended up hurting you – though it really was an accident."

The miko then made eyes at Kazuki, and Hasunuma could see that the kid wasn't going to have anything negative to say about the girl either way. *This is exactly why a kid like him isn't in charge.* The Pirate King grinned slightly. *Although this could be a fun little development…*

"As I mentioned before, I am a miko from another shrine – though I will not tell you which one, so that you cannot go and loot it," she glared at the men around her, except for Kazuki. After a moment her expression softened and she continued on, "I had just returned from a purifying ritual when I discovered that my shrine had been attacked by demons. Unfortunately," she took a deep breath and then exhaled, "I was too late, and everyone had already perished."

Pushing through her emotions, the miko continued her story, "After performing funeral rights, I decided to visit nearby shrines to assess whether or not it had been a focused attack or the start of a demonic invasion. Tenrou Shrine is the fourth that I have visited, and, thankfully, it is the only one besides my own that has been decimated. However," she glanced at the kid, "now knowing that the Demon King Himself is present in our realm, I have concluded that there is, in fact, a demonic invasion of sorts."

"Actually, I can explain that," Kazuki interrupted.

"Later, Little Oni," Rize interjected, "let the miko finish speaking first." The helmsman was more accustomed to questioning possible enemies than the kid was, and he was subtly trying to teach the kid how it was done.

"When I arrived at Tenrou Shrine," the miko continued, "I felt the presence of multiple demons. Before I could fully assess the situation, two men came running out of one of the buildings while part of it collapsed behind them. I hid, not knowing who the men were, and ended up watching them battle multiple demons. I realize that I should have come out and helped sooner, but," the girl paused for a moment before admitting, "I was scared."

"Well, you must've found the courage to fight, 'cause you ended up casting that sealing spell," Hanzo commended.

"Yes," the girl nodded, "when that last demon seemed to be too powerful to defeat, I mustered my courage to use the spell. I *was* successful," she said pointedly to the Pirate King, "since the other demon was sent away. I just didn't expect to harm this guy in the process," the miko said, gesturing towards Kazuki.

"But you were there almost the entire time, so how come ya didn't know the kid had a demon in him?" The Pirate King retorted.

"First of all," the girl began in a defensive tone, "I was too far away to hear most of your conversations. Secondly, I can't always pinpoint the exact location of the demonic entity, so I thought that the presence I felt was only coming from the white-haired guy who was attacking you. And thirdly," the girl's tone was now accusatory, "you don't seem to want to trust me no matter what I say, so you should just leave me here and go back to your ship already!"

"We can't do that yet," the Pirate King began, "because if you're a threat, we can't let ya live now that ya know the kid's secret."

"B-but I–" the girl stammered as the Pirate King raised his sword.

"Knock. It. OFF!" Kazuki shouted. He sprung up from the ground and stood in front of the girl. "I don't care if she's a threat, I won't let you kill her!"

Hasunuma stared at the kid; he was completely serious and would most likely attack the Pirate King if he moved his sword any closer to the miko.

Unable to hold back any longer, Ginza, Rize, and Hanzo all burst into uncontrollable laughter. Kazuki looked around at them, thoroughly confused.

"Haven't ya learned *anythin'* 'bout the cap'n yet?" Ginza said as he continued to laugh.

"You know the captain would never hurt a woman or a kid," Rize explained as he, too, continued to laugh.

The Pirate King began to laugh as he slid his sword back into his sash and patted Kazuki roughly on the head. "Yer always so serious, Kid! Relax a little and trust me," he said with a grin. "Don't worry, little lady, we won't harm ya. In fact, why don't ya come along with us? Yer powers will be useful since we're also hunting down demons."

"What? Are you serious?" The girl replied. "Why would I go anywhere with a bunch of dirty, lawless pirates?"

"I could give ya a handful of reasons, but I think just this one will do: stick with us, and this kid will protect ya with his life," he put his arm around Kazuki's neck and added, "ain't that right, Kid."

Kazuki pushed the Pirate King away and looked at the miko. "Ignore him," he said, "but…I really will protect you if you come with us. Just like I did – well, you don't remember that time, but I swear I won't let anything happen to you."

Both of the kids blushed and they quickly turned away from each other.

"Well, I…I suppose I could travel with you for a little while," the girl said with a slight smile. "As long as you tell me what's going on with all of these demons," the miko added, attempting to hide her embarrassment.

"Of course," Kazuki said, a little too enthusiastically.

"This'll be great!" Rize exclaimed.

"Now we might be able to defeat that super powerful demon!" Hanzo joined in.

"Yeah, that guy's trouble," Ginza added, "I mean, 'e even exploded that buildin'!"

"It must have been some powerful elemental magic," the miko added. "The stronger ones can do that sort of thing, you know."

"Um…" the Pirate King interrupted, "actually, that was me."

Everyone stared at him.

"I was trying out a new technique and sort of overdid it. Ha ha… ha?"

Only Kazuki could muster a response, "You're absolutely ridiculous. Are you even human?"

"That's funny comin' from you, Kid," the Pirate King retorted. "Ow!" He suddenly yelled as Kohaku punched his shin. "Did I really deserve that?"

The look on Kohaku's face was easy to read: 'For making us worry like that? YES.'

Kazuki shook his head as he watched Hasunuma get berated by his crew, yet again, for his reckless behavior. *And he says that I don't learn my lesson after getting into trouble. Some role model he is.*

Despite his negative thoughts, the corners of the young man's lips rose. There was something about Hasunuma's ridiculous behavior that always seemed to cheer everyone up. It was almost as if the Pirate King was reckless just to get a few laughs from his crew in the end. Kazuki was sure that it wasn't always true, but he had to admit that the Pirate King definitely knew how to dispel tense situations and bring people back from the brink of despair.

"Ah, I'm sorry, but I didn't quite catch your name," a voice like a lark timidly spoke.

The young man turned his attention to the girl at his side. She was just as beautiful as he had remembered – though she was more stunning in the green kimono than in her miko garb.

"It's Kazuki," he replied. "And what should I call you?"

"Oh! My name's Reika," the girl smiled. "I'm sorry that I don't remember you from before, Kazuki, but," her voice suddenly shrunk to a whisper, "I-I really appreciate you saving me." The miko's cheeks flushed pink and the young man found himself wanting to grab the girl and hold her tightly in his arms.

"Hey, if you two keep flirting we're gonna leave ya behind," a voice called out, shattering the moment.

"W-We're not flirting!" the two of them yelled perfectly in sync, which only served to make them more embarrassed.

"Yeah, yeah, just hurry up, will ya?"

Step in a horse pile, Hasunuma! "Sorry, Reika," Kazuki sighed, "he's kind of a pain, but he's a good guy deep down." *I think…*

"Don't worry," the girl giggled, "I've dealt with his kind before."

Kazuki wasn't sure what she meant by that, but he didn't have time to think about it; the Pirate King had told them to catch up and the young man knew better than to keep him waiting. The last thing Kazuki wanted was to be lectured like a child in front of Reika.

As they made their way down the winding stone stairway, Kazuki remembered how awful he had felt on the way up. With Reika descending in front of him, the young man hoped that he wouldn't pass out again. But the more Kazuki thought about it, the more he realized that he felt completely normal; the strange atmosphere no longer seemed to affect him.

"I'm impressed that you were able to make it all the way to the shrine, Kazuki," the miko chimed. "Even with the priests gone, the spiritual barrier is no joke."

Ah. That explains why I was the only one affected.

"Well, 'e had some help," a voice from below corrected, "the cap'n had t' carry 'im when–"

"Thanks, Ginza," Kazuki shouted, "but I really don't think she needs to know all of the details!" The young man heard hearty laughter from below as well as a few giggles from the girl before him. *I seriously hate him sometimes.*

"I guess one good thing came from my mistake then," the girl said happily.

"What's that?" Kazuki asked.

"Well," the girl stopped on the steps and turned to look at the young man, "the Demon King has been sealed inside of you, yeah? So that means you won't be affected by spiritual barriers and the like."

Kazuki's eyes widened.

"Hee hee," the miko giggled, "you're welcome!" She began humming to herself as she turned away and continued descending the treacherous stairway.

The young man, however, was not grateful for the girl's blunder. How was he supposed to defeat the other demons without the Demon King's powers?

After traveling as far as they could through the forest before dusk, the pirate crew chose a clearing near a stream and set up camp. While Ginza and Hanzo gathered firewood, Rize and Ami hunted and foraged for food. That left the kid, the miko, the ninja woman, and the Pirate King back at camp. It was unbearably awkward.

"Do I have to teach the kid everything? I mean, come on. Talking to a woman is no grueling task," Hasunuma whispered to Kohaku as he crouched next to her.

The ninja woman was sitting on the ground with her legs stretched out before her, her back resting against a large tree trunk. Her legs would likely take a few weeks to mend, even with her special medicinal ointment applied to the wounds.

The ninja woman elbowed him in the ribs, "Maybe for *you* it isn't," she whispered back, "but to an innocent young man, it seems nearly impossible."

"I would hardly call that kid innocent," Hasunuma retorted. "Hey, you two," he called out to the kids, "why don't ya go fetch some water from the stream – and maybe a fish or two while yer at it."

Kohaku whistled to the Pirate King in protest.

"What? I'm sure they'll be fine," Hasunuma said nonchalantly.

The Pirate King watched as the two embarrassed youths grabbed some water skins and headed away from the camp. They were walking parallel to each other, but keeping a sizeable distance in-between them.

Hasunuma shook his head and sighed, "And I thought this would be entertaining."

"You shouldn't tease him so much," Kohaku scolded, "he's got enough to worry about."

"But that's precisely why the kid needs to be teased," Hasunuma countered. "If Kazuki doesn't lighten up a little, he won't be able to keep the Demon King from possessing him."

Kohaku may not have noticed a change in Kazuki, but the Pirate King did; he had always kept a close eye on the kid, especially during battles. Early on, it just seemed like Kazuki would switch into battle mode and end up going a little too far with his kills, so the Pirate King had dismissed the kid's behavior as a result of him being young and emotionally scarred. But after it was discovered that the Demon King was inside of the kid, Hasunuma reexamined Kazuki's previous battle performances. Although the kid had never admitted it, the Pirate King knew that Kazuki didn't always remember the entire battle. In fact, the kid never seemed to remember the bloodiest and most violent parts.

Hasunuma felt as though the Demon King was merely pretending to be subdued, all the while plotting and biding his time for the one moment where he could take advantage of Kazuki's darkened heart and take control of the kid for good. From the start, the Pirate King had made it part of his mission to rehabilitate the kid by healing his damaged heart. And now, more than ever, it was vital that he succeed.

"I'm worried about that girl, Hasu," Kohaku began, "something about her doesn't feel right."

"I know, I don't trust her either," Hasunuma replied, "but if we play our cards right, I think she could do more good than harm."

The ninja woman slowly nodded. It was pretty cute how worried she was about the kid. If she ever had the chance, she would probably make a good mother…

The Pirate King clapped his hands together loudly and said, "Anyways," aloud, trying to stop his own thoughts from progressing any further.

Kohaku gave him a strange look. "Are you feeling alright?" she asked.

"Fine, fine, now that I can hear your lovely voice again," the Pirate King grinned. "It almost sounds normal now – Ouch! It's against the code to hit your captain, you know."

The ninja woman suddenly yanked the Pirate King's arm, knocking him off balance and onto the ground. As he lay on his side, facing her, the ninja woman smiled seductively and said, "And what exactly do you plan to do about it, *Captain*?"

Hasunuma was momentarily stunned. He was well used to women playfully teasing him, but Kohaku was a different story. It had been many years since he had felt this kind of tension with her; back when she was a playful girl, living happily with everyone in Hokuto. But things had changed.

"What's this?" The ninja woman cooed as she reached out to the Pirate King, her left hand slowly crawling up his chest, "Have I rendered the great Red Dragon speechless?" As her hand reached his collar, she gently slid her forefinger up the center of his neck and raised his chin so that the Pirate King's eyes met hers. Although she seemed to be teasing him, the look in her eye was genuine.

Hasunuma grinned, "Oh no, Milady, we are simply beyond words at this point." He pulled the ninja woman into him with one arm and outstretched the other for her head to rest on. The Pirate King almost wrapped one leg around her, but thought it better to keep things simple…for now.

Kohaku's face had turned bright red, and the Pirate King could tell that she was panicking inside.

She's adorable. Hasunuma leaned his head closer to hers and whispered into the ninja woman's ear, "As much as I would love to continue this," he paused for effect, "we're about to have company."

Kohaku quickly pushed herself free of the Pirate King's grasp and sat back against the tree. She then turned her head away from Hasunuma and crossed her arms.

Hah! I'll bet that if her legs worked, she would have taken off into the forest just now.

"Hey Cap'n!" Hanzo said, announcing his return. "Huh?" He

looked around the campsite, "Where are the lad and little lady?"

"I sent 'em off on an errand," the Pirate King said as he stood up. "Now help me get the fire going." He grinned as he added, "Kohaku's looking rather flushed an' I'd hate for her t' get sick from this chilly night air." Hasunuma waited for a reaction from the ninja woman, but she remained silent; her head still turned away from him. *She's too embarrassed to face me or even retort with a whistle. Now* that's *interesting...*

"Aye, Cap'n!" Hanzo said as he immediately began constructing the fire's base with the wood he collected.

Ginza appeared a few minutes later and began aiding Hanzo in getting the fire started. Although the two pirates were not exactly quiet in their task, Hasunuma ignored their usual bickering; his attention was focused solely on the woman who was desperately trying to avoid him.

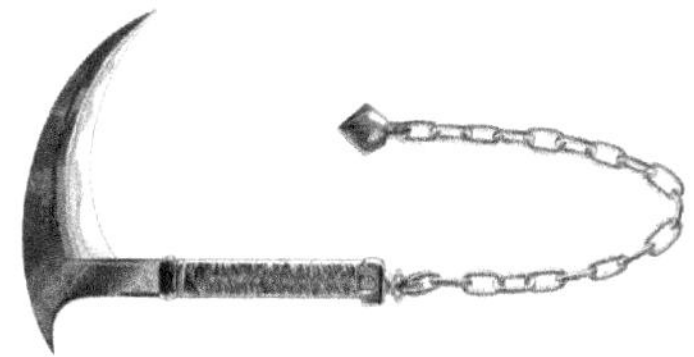

Kohaku felt Hasu's gaze upon her. Her heart pounded in her chest and she could barely breathe. *Stupid, stupid, that was so stupid, Kohaku!* She mentally berated herself. *Did you honestly think that you could beat Hasu at his own game? Especially when you can't get away!*

The ninja woman had tried to act reserved around the Pirate King, but recently she felt herself becoming more desperate for his attention. It was similar to the way she felt when they were growing up together in Hokuto, but now, as a woman, that sort of innocent affection no longer reigned in her heart; Hasu was a strong, handsome, intelligent, and caring man, and Kohaku didn't want him with any woman but her.

Ever since she changed into the outfit her mother left her, the ninja woman reveled in the way that Hasu looked at her. There was now a welcome sort of tension between the two of them that seemed to grow stronger each day. A new yearning began building up inside of her, and Kohaku was eager to see whether or not she could capture the Pirate King completely.

While Kohaku was not as experienced in the art of seduction as the Pirate King, she was a fast learner. Observing people was one of the many jobs that ninja were often given and, throughout the years, she found herself learning many things from people who never even knew she was there. Sometimes, she awkwardly found herself watching lovers during secret trysts – for blackmailing purposes – or following them as they tried to escape their families.

As a ninja, there was also physical training for missions that required a certain level of charm. Before a ninja-in-training came of age, he or she would learn seduction techniques from a more experienced ninja of the same sex. Then, as part of the trainee's coming-of-age ceremony, he or she would thoroughly experience physical pleasure from a superior of the opposite sex – often someone of his or her own choosing.

Unfortunately for Kohaku, the village was destroyed a few months before her coming-of-age ceremony. So while she understood the art of seduction in theory and basic practice, she was a total novice when it came to following through. And it was hard to think straight while close to Hasu's face, or wrapped in his arms…

"'Ey, Rize," Ginza enthusiastically announced, "good timin'! I got the fire goin' fer ya, an' it should be hot enough soon."

"You mean *we* got the fire going," Hanzo corrected.

"What'd ya find, Rize?" Hasu interjected, presumably trying to head off the ensuing fight between Hanzo and Ginza.

"I found some ferns, bamboo sprouts, and mushrooms," the helmsman replied. "As for meat, Ami got us two rabbits an' I snagged a small boar." He paused for a moment before adding, "But, even though we searched a wide area, I didn't hear any birds or see many animals…just like before, the forest is eerily quiet."

Silence swiftly overwhelmed the camp. The pirates were now on high alert, and no one dared to even breathe, lest it drown out any foreign sound. To them, there was only one possible explanation, and it weighed heavily on their minds.

"Well," the Pirate King began, breaking the tense atmosphere, "animals *are* better at sensing the presence of other creatures."

…That's not exactly comforting, Hasu.

Rize shook his head and unloaded the carcasses from his back. As he began to prepare the meat for the fire, he glanced around and asked, "Where'd the kids go?"

"I sent 'em to get fresh water and some fish, so they'll be awhile," Hasu said nonchalantly as he grabbed a spare knife from his pack and helped Rize process the boar.

"I'll bet the fish won't be the only slippery thing they find," Ginza snickered.

Hanzo laughed. "The lad might be too green for any of that."

"I offered to buy him a crash course back in Giyosan, but he turned me down," Rize admitted.

"Too bad fer 'im," Ginza shrugged, "those Giyosan women're some a' the best in Tsukigen."

Hanzo shook his head. "Can't say I know, since I've only experienced what O-kane has to offer."

"They're good too, 'specially since some a' them're foreign," Ginza explained. "But once this arse's stench 'bout no foreigners on the mainland clears up, I'll take ya t' m' favorite place," the blacksmith added with a grin as he slapped Hanzo's shoulder.

"Looking forward to it," the giant grinned back.

Ugh. Men.

Being the only woman on board a ship meant that Kohaku had heard, seen, and smelled it all; there was no longer anything about men that could shock or surprise her. And while there were plenty of things, in her opinion, that were unpleasant, she understood that men were fundamentally different than women, and there was no changing them.

But all in all, the men of the Ryujin weren't that bad. Kohaku never had to worry about her safety or privacy, and the men usually remembered to – at the very least – wear a loincloth when walking around anywhere on the ship, besides the bathroom. Sometimes they even refrained from lude talk around her, and they mostly bathed enough to not reek too badly.

Things would be totally different in Khepria, the ninja woman thought wistfully.

Khepria was the country her best friend Nia was from, and, according to Nia, it sounded like a woman's paradise. The men were all warriors who spent their days training and sparring, while the women ran the country. There wasn't one ruler, but a group of important women who lead some sort of council that dictated the laws and other political matters. And women were the ones to inherit land, titles, and businesses.

When Kohaku had first met Nia, the ninja woman was astonished that her friend owned a foreign trading business. Not only that, but she had a side job as an assassin, and was married to one of the most notable warriors on Khepria. And Nia had only been seventeen years old when Kohaku first met her.

Life for a Tsukigenese woman was a different story. While Kohaku could have inherited the position as Head of Hokuto from her mother, it would have been Kohaku's husband that would have actually been in charge. In Tsukigen, women were supposed to support their men, raise their kids, and take care of aging extended family, all while never vocalizing their own opinions or desires. And, in general, any woman who tried to work in a "man's profession" faced a slew of challenges. For instance, if Kohaku had become a pirate with any other crew, she would have had to endure endless sexual harassment. Truly it would have been worse than becoming a prostitute.

Kohaku was lucky to have been born in Hokuto – the rules there were different to some degree – but there were still some traditions that reflected the patriarchal Tsukigen mindset. While women in Hokuto were more free to speak their minds, there was still a rank hierarchy that had to be followed. Also, women were often pressured into resigning from their ninja duties once they gave birth. Not all complied, but most felt obligated to tend to the home.

But not in Khepria, where the women ruled and the men were basically devoted, high-quality pleasure figurines. The responsibilities of housework, child rearing, and elderly care were all equally divided between a husband and wife. In fact, Nia had said that some Kheprian men *preferred* to do what the Tsukigenese would consider "women's work."

Now that *would be ideal,* the ninja woman thought with a grin.

Her gaze found Hasu and she began fantasizing about what their life would have been like if they had been born in Khepria. Although surely even Kheprian women had their grievances, life seemed to be much more pleasant for them and their families.

Family…I wonder if Hasu would ever…

Kohaku shook her head. She knew the Pirate King better than anyone, and therefore knew the answer to her silly question, but part of her still wondered about it.

"How're yer legs?" Enquired a robust voice.

Kohaku shifted her eyes to the burly man squatting beside her. "Useless," she replied with a wry smile, "but there's not much pain thanks to the medicine."

Ginza punched the ground, making a fist-sized hole in the dirt. "I'm sorry we weren't much help," he muttered.

The ninja woman shook her head. "There's no need to apologize. The fact that you stood with me to protect him is what counts," she said with a nod towards Hasu.

"Hmph," Ginza grunted, "I can fight humans all day long, but demons… demons're stronger than I thought they'd be."

Kohaku nodded. "Yes, even in human bodies, they're extremely powerful. I don't understand why we haven't seen this sort of demonic activity before now. There must be something keeping them in check."

The blacksmith shrugged, "Yer guess's as good as mine. All I can tell ya is that I've only seen two demonic weapons so far, and that's a huge relief."

Kohaku tilted her head to the side. "What do you mean?"

"I've examined Little Oni's katana a few times, an' I've seen it in action. That sword's as bloodthirsty as its owner," Ginza replied with a furrowed brow. "M' dad used t' tell me stories 'bout divine and demonic weapons. I thought they were all a' buncha rubbish made up t' get kids interested in forgin', but seein' the weapons in person… gives me the shivers." The blacksmith shook his head. "If there's any truth 'bout those things in the stories I've heard, we've got more t' worry 'bout."

"Ginza! Get over here and help us with the rack," Hasu barked.

Kohaku turned her attention to the commotion by the fire and did her best not to laugh aloud. The impromptu rack that Hasu and Hanzo had fastened to hold the meat over the fire had collapsed and the two men were desperately trying to prevent their dinner from falling into the flames below.

The blacksmith grinned at Kohaku. "Before 'e said 'e didn't need m' help."

"Sounds about right," the ninja woman said with a smirk.

Kazuki wouldn't have been able to catch a fish, even if his life depended on it. He was so nervous he couldn't concentrate, let alone keep still long enough to fool the fish.

"That looks like fun! Can I try too?" a lark-like voice chirped.

To the young man's horror, the lovely young woman slipped out of her sandals and began pulling off her knee-high socks, revealing delicate legs with slim ankles, all encased in glistening pink skin. His heartbeat quickened.

"You shouldn't come in. The water's really cold," Kazuki said flatly. The young man found himself trapped in a foreign situation and desperately tried to keep himself calm. Weren't women – especially miko – supposed to keep themselves covered?

"Oh, I don't mind! Almost all of the purifying rituals involve bathing in frigid water, so I'm used to it," the lovely young woman stated as she pulled back her long sleeves and tied them up.

Well I *mind!*

Kazuki's heart raced even faster as he watched Reika step into the stream and wade towards him. "Watch your step. The rocks are slippery." His voice didn't sound familiar. Though normally it wasn't overtly emotional, his usual cadence certainly wasn't as listless as it now sounded.

"You're such a worrier!" She giggled.

Reika was now within arms reach of Kazuki. He was terrified that if she got too close, she'd hear his heart beating frantically within his chest.

"So how does this work?" She asked as she stared down into the cold, dark water.

"Normally, this is done in the early morning," the young man explained, "so I'm not sure that we'll be very successful…and the moon's only half-full." Kazuki could see a few shadows in the water, but he was mostly relying on his overly developed sense of hearing to locate the fish. There was no way Reika could find them.

The young man glanced at the girl next to him. Her golden hair and pink skin seemed to glow vibrantly in the dim moonlight, as the reflection from the gently rippling water below illuminated her. She was a rare beauty, indeed, and as the young man studied her delicate features, he felt new sensations grow within him. Although he harbored feelings for Kohaku, this felt different. He wanted to know what this young woman thought of him and how she would feel wrapped up in his arms. He wanted to understand her completely and protect her from any possible harm – or another man.

Great, now I'm starting to think like Hasunuma.

Suddenly Reika's gaze met his and Kazuki quickly turned away and resumed his explanation of the task at hand.

"A-Anyways," the young man cleared his throat, "the trick is to be perfectly still so that the fish become accustomed to your presence. Then, when one swims close enough, you grab it."

"With your bare hands?" Reika asked, looking skeptical.

"Unless you've got some sort of spear or something to stab it with."

The lovely young woman turned her gaze back to the water below and sighed. "Alright then. Let's give it a try!"

Kazuki watched as Reika stood as still as a stone, intensely staring at the dark water surrounding her legs. Her facial expression was rather amusing, but the young man didn't dare laugh. He turned his attention back to the fish near his own feet, when suddenly there was a large *SPLASH!*

"Oh darn!" Reika said as she pulled her empty hands out of the water. "They're really fast."

"Or maybe you're just really slow," Kazuki countered. His eyes immediately widened in surprise at his own words.

Reika shot him a look that resembled a scowl and said, "Well I don't see *you* doing any better."

Fine. "Watch me," he retorted.

Kazuki closed his eyes and concentrated on the vibrations from the fish below. His hands slowly approached the water. His fingertips gently penetrated the surface and continued to gradually submerge into the dark, frigid stream. The young man ceased moving and held his breath. After a few moments pause, he abruptly yanked his hands out of the water. Within them was a wriggling, sizeable fish.

"No. Way." The young woman breathed. "How did you do that?!" She demanded.

Kazuki grinned and said, "I told you, you've gotta be quick to catch a fish."

"Yeah, right," Reika pouted, "I'll bet you used some sort of demon magic to call it to you."

"Except that you sealed the Demon King away, so I can't use any of those powers," Kazuki said pointedly. "And anyways, what kind of demon would need a fish-summoning power?"

There was a moment's pause before laughter filled the night air. "Can you imagine?" Reika laughed, "A big, scary demon standing in water saying, 'Come here fishy!' Hahaha!" She continued laughing, saying, "I'm sorry. I don't know why I find it so funny, but it just is!"

Kazuki hadn't meant to make a joke, but he was glad that Reika didn't seem to be mad at him anymore. Not to mention, her smiling face was much more pleasant to look at than her angry one. Perhaps the best way to interact with women was to make them laugh?

The young man looked down at the unhappy creature in his hands. "Would you like to hold it?" Kazuki asked as he awkwardly shoved the fish towards Reika.

"Sure!" She said brightly as she finally stopped laughing. The young woman reached towards Kazuki's outstretched hands. "Come here, fishy," she giggled as she grabbed onto the wriggling fish.

"Be careful," the young man warned, "it's pretty slippery and still has a lot of fight left."

"Oh, I think I can – Ah!" Reika shrieked as the fish leapt from her hands. She tried to catch it mid-air, but slipped and fell forward instead.

Reacting faster than the eye could see, Kazuki caught the lovely young woman in his arms before she hit the water. "I *told* you to be careful," he teased.

The young man expected a snippy remark in return, but only silence prevailed. He looked down to see Reika's reaction, and only then did Kazuki fully realize the situation.

The young woman's chest was pressed against his stomach and her head lay against his chest. Her face, though partially obstructed from his view, was clearly red from embarrassment. Kazuki's arms held Reika tightly as a precaution against her falling, and now that the danger was over, he was supposed to release her – but he didn't.

She's so small and delicate…

Kazuki closed his eyes for a moment to relish the feeling, but it didn't last long.

"Um. I think I'm all right now, so…could you please let go?" the lark-like voice chimed.

"Oh, uh," the young man eyes popped open as he awkwardly pushed Reika away from him. She almost fell back from the force of his shove, but she regained her balance in time. "Sorry about that," Kazuki mumbled as he scratched his head and looked away from her.

"It's fine," Reika giggled, "I guess that's twice now that you've saved me."

Once again, the babbling of the stream and the nighttime call of the bugs dominated the air; the young man had no idea what to say or do now, so he silently stood in the cold water.

Reika finally made a comment about how the water was getting pretty cold and began to make her way towards the shore. Kazuki merely watched her go.

"Um. Aren't you coming too?" She asked as she looked back towards him. "I think Red Dragon will get mad at us if we stay away from camp for too long."

At the mention of Hasunuma, Kazuki snapped back to reality. Angering the Pirate King off was a terrifying proposition. Wading through the water, the young man felt disappointed that he didn't have a fish to show off to the crew. He might have tried once more to catch one, but Reika was already on the shore, ready to leave.

"Sorry I let your fish go," the lovely young woman said as Kazuki joined her.

"It's fine. We at least got the skins filled with fresh water," the young man's voice sounded stiff again.

Kazuki led the way through the dimly lit forest, since Reika couldn't see very well. The two were quiet, but after they heard a branch snap nearby, Reika grabbed hold of the back of Kazuki's shirt and began to hum a tune to herself. While Kazuki listened to her lovely voice, his thoughts kept returning to the moment he held Reika in his arms. It was such a pleasant feeling, holding her close like that. He wondered if it would ever happen again.

Maybe if I save her from something again…wait a minute. "Hey, Reika, what did you mean when you said that the person I rescued in Giyosan was you, but not you," Kazuki suddenly asked.

He couldn't see the young woman's expression, since she was walking behind him, but she stopped humming and made a sound as if she were trying to remember.

"Oh! That." She said with an awkward half-laugh. "Well, I've got amazing spiritual powers, but…the thing is, it attracts a lot of spirits and demons and the like. So, sometimes I get possessed by them."

"What?!" Kazuki exclaimed.

Reika jumped a bit at his sudden volume. "W-what's wrong?"

Kazuki whirled around. "You mean to tell me that you randomly get possessed by demons, and that doesn't seem like important enough information to share with a group of people being hunted by demons?!" The young man fumed.

His yelling caused Reika to back away from him until she found herself against the trunk of a tree.

"How stupid can you be?!" He shouted. "What if a demon possessed you and made you attack us? Or better yet, what if you were actually a spy for the demons, letting them know our exact movements–"

WHACK. Reika slapped Kazuki hard across his face. She had tears in her eyes and she was shaking uncontrollably. "How *dare* you accuse me of working with them! They…they killed my family!"

Oh. I forgot about that...

Kazuki suddenly felt like throwing up.

"And I am in total control of my body, thank you very much," she chided. "Demons and spirits only possess me if I *let* them, and I only do that if there is a *very* good reason." Reika sniffled and began wiping her tears away, only to have more fall. "This is all your fault," she sobbed.

Kazuki wasn't sure what to do. His only reference point for how to stop a woman from crying was from watching Hasunuma, and anything the Pirate King did with a woman was probably inappropriate. But, without any other ideas to choose from, Kazuki sighed and gently grabbed Reika's chin. He reached out with his other hand and softly held her cheek, wiping away her tears with his thumb as they fell.

"I'm sorry," he said. "I-I haven't been around girls much, so I don't know how to act around you. I didn't mean to scare you or make you cry." It was embarrassing to admit all of that, but Kazuki didn't know what else to tell her.

Please just stop crying.

"Your hands are warm," Reika suddenly said through her sniffles. She had placed her left hand on top of Kazuki's hand – the one that rested on her cheek. "I imagined them to be cold, because of the demon inside of you, but you're actually quite warm," she smiled and looked up into Kazuki's eyes.

The young man felt his cheeks flush and was thankful for the dim lighting. He quickly pulled his hands away from the young woman and said, "W-well if you're cold, we should hurry back to camp. They should have a fire going by now."

Kazuki had turned and begun to walk away when he suddenly felt someone grab his hand. His pulse quickened, but he didn't pull his hand away. Without looking back, and without another word, he continued walking towards camp. All he heard were a few giggles behind him as the warmth of his hand spread to Reika's.

The Pirate King and his crew had just begun enjoying the roasted meat when the kid and the miko came strolling back. It did not go unnoticed that the two were holding hands.

"'Ey! Little Oni!" Ginza said with a mouthful. "What took ya so long?"

"Yeah," Hanzo added with a grin, "what were you doing all this time with the little lady?"

"I don't see any fish," the Pirate King added, happily adding fuel to the fire.

Immediately, Kazuki pulled his hand free from the miko's grasp. The kid's face was bright red as he denied any wrongdoing. "We just filled up the skins like you asked!"

"He actually did catch a fish," the miko added, "but when I tried to hold it, it was really slippery, so–"

"I'll bet it was!" Ginza interjected, and the pirate men all burst into roaring laughter.

The Pirate King watched as Kazuki rolled his eyes and sat himself as far away from the laughing men as possible. The miko followed him, which only seemed to make the kid even more annoyed and embarrassed. He got up and walked away from her, but the miko didn't seem to get the hint and she followed him again. Not knowing what to do, the kid sat down next to Kohaku and grabbed a piece of roasting meat. The miko seemed to be a bit resentful of his seating choice and moved to a spot next to the Pirate King.

Now we're getting somewhere! Hasunuma thought as he smiled and welcomed the miko. "Ya've chosen the best seat here," he said enthusiastically. "Feel free t' eat as much as you'd like," he added as he put his arm around her and reached towards the fire for some meat. He pulled a sizable chunk off and handed it to the miko.

She looked at it with a face that read: 'You seriously expect me to take that with my bare hands and eat it like an animal?'

The Pirate King smiled and shoved it into her hands. "Go on! Eat up!"

Glancing out of the corner of his eye, Hasunuma checked to see the kid's reaction. Kazuki was positively glaring at him, which only encouraged the Pirate King more.

"Hey, as a miko ya gotta know some shrine dances, right?" Hasunuma asked, his arm still around the girl.

"Of course, but–" the miko began, but was swiftly cut off by cheers from the pirate men.

"Woohoo!" Shouted Ginza.

"Yeah, dance for us, Lass!" Encouraged Hanzo.

"It's been a long while since I've seen one," admitted Rize, "so I'd be happy to watch one of yours."

Before the miko could protest, the Pirate King ushered her to an open spot by the fire and flashed her a handsome smile. "It would please us all greatly to watch you dance," he said gently as he leaned in closer to her.

The miko's face turned bright red and she put her hands out to stop Hasunuma's advance, saying, "Alright, ALL RIGHT!" She looked around at the excited crew and said very clearly, "But just ONE." Mumbling under her breath, she added, "I don't think the spirits will like me entertaining pirates with one of their sacred dances, but…" she glanced towards the kid and sighed.

The Pirate King sat back down and watched as the miko took a deep breath and then began to dance. Her movements were graceful and flowed like water. Hasunuma was surprised that a girl her age could have such mastery of her body.

Then again, Kohaku was more agile than her at that age.

While he continued to feign interest in the miko's dance, the Pirate King shifted his attention to the kid, checking to see his reaction. Kazuki was completely captivated by her. It was plain to see. Hasunuma then made eye contact with Kohaku and grinned. She made a face that showed she was unimpressed with his tactics, but the ninja woman eventually nodded in agreement.

We can definitely use this girl.

Kazuki felt enchanted, as if some spirit magic had taken him over. He could not take his eyes off of the lovely dancing woman before him. His heart raced and his body felt as if it were on fire as he watched all of Reika's movements. Her graceful fingers flitted through the air, followed by her delicate limbs and flowing golden hair. The light from the fire caused her pink skin to glow in a similar golden hue that made her seem like a divine goddess.

As her body slowed to a stop, the young woman ended the performance in a beautiful pose; the image of which was forever burned into Kazuki's mind. When Reika relaxed her body, the young man could have sworn that she looked right at him with those gorgeous emerald eyes of hers. But the moment was quickly broken as a roar of applause startled the young woman. The crew stood up and approached Reika, all of them shouting words of praise.

The young woman's face was flushed as she responded with, "Oh no, I'm not that good," and, "Thank you, but really I'm quite clumsy."

Kazuki thought to approach her himself when the Pirate King made his move.

"Absolutely wonderful!" Hasunuma announced as he pulled Reika into him. "You move with such grace for a girl your age," he added as he flashed her a winning smile.

Reika seemed not to know whether to push him away or just grin and bear his attention, but Kazuki knew what needed to be done. The young man pushed through the crowd surrounding her and pulled the young woman away from the Pirate King.

"She's a miko," Kazuki said as flatly as he could manage, "so I don't think you should be touching her so freely, *Captain*." He addressed the Pirate King pointedly.

Hasunuma laughed heartily and slapped Kazuki on the back. "Alright, Alright, I get yer point, Kid."

The rest of the crew grinned and winked at the young man before joining their captain around the fire once more.

Kazuki felt like he had missed something, but he quickly dismissed the feeling and turned around to face the lovely young woman behind him. "Sorry about that."

"It's fine," she said with a smile, "I'm glad they all enjoyed my dancing. I haven't performed in a long while, so I felt a bit rusty."

"Oh, but you were great! The way you danced was truly spectacular," Kazuki replied without much thought. It took him a second to realize what he had actually said when he noticed Reika's face turn bright red. His heart thumped loudly in his chest as the young man desperately thought of a way out of the situation.

Hasunuma, of course, provided it for him. "Hey Kid! Why don't ya explain the whole demon games thing t' the miko? Maybe she can give us a hint as t' where the next demon might be."

Kazuki heard the rest of the crew snicker behind him. *Easy for them to laugh*, the young man thought to himself as he tried not to let their teasing get to him. "Let's sit down then," he calmly suggested to Reika, "It's kind of a long story."

For a while the crew was respectfully quiet as Kazuki explained the entire demon games objective. The young woman was shocked to hear about Kazuki's childhood tragedy, but was even more surprised to learn about the details of the games themselves.

"So this has been going on for centuries?" She asked, wide-eyed.

"Apparently so," Kazuki replied.

"Well why hasn't anyone found out about them before?"

The young man shrugged, "Probably because all the humans involved end up dead in the end." He crossed his arms and added, "Well, except for the winner supposedly. But that could be a lie."

"I certainly hope it's not," Reika exclaimed. "How awful would it be if you went through the trouble of winning the games only to die anyways? It would be so horribly cruel for your friends, who are desperate to help you." For a moment, the young woman looked rather forlorn, but she suddenly shook her head and added, "Ugh! That wicked Demon King better not be lying to you!"

Kazuki was unsure how to react to the young woman's strong feelings. He hadn't really given his possible end a second thought before, because he didn't particularly care about his own life. All he wanted to do was protect the people around him. It hadn't occurred to him that there were people who would be upset if he died.

"That's what *we're* 'ere fer," Ginza proudly proclaimed.

"That's right! We won't let the lad die," Hanzo promised.

"You can count on us!" Rize added with an enthusiastic smile.

The young man felt himself start to smile, but he swiftly hid his reaction. Instead, he simply nodded.

Hasunuma leaned forward and said, "Now that you see why we fight the demons, could you honestly say that helping us would be a waste of your time and talents?"

Reika bit her lip and averted her eyes from the Pirate King. She had only told the pirates a piece of her story, and Kazuki could tell that there was something important missing from the equation. Whatever it was, it would be the determining factor in the young woman's decision. "I…I…" she hesitated.

"Let her think on it a little more, Captain," Kazuki suggested. "We just gave her a lot of new information, none of it pleasant, and our path is extremely dangerous…so maybe we can wait for her answer until we get back to the ship?"

The young man hoped he wasn't over-stepping too much. Hasunuma was fairly relaxed with him, but Kazuki knew that, in the end, Hasunuma was still the captain of the ship and the leader of the group; *he* would be the one to make the final decision.

The Pirate King grinned. "How very mature of ya, Kid. I'm impressed." He stood up and announced, "Alright, we'll honor Little Oni's wishes and let the miko decide once we return to the Ryujin. For now, let's get some shut-eye. We'll need to pick up the pace tomorrow in order t' reach the docks by sundown."

The crew all shouted, "Aye, Cap'n!" before finding their own spots by the fire to settle down in.

As there was only enough rope and blankets in their packs to make one small makeshift tent, it was immediately given to the two females. Hasunuma leaned himself up against one of the large trees used to make the tent – probably to keep an eye on Reika – while Kazuki shifted closer to the fire. There was an odd chill to the night air that sank into his very bones.

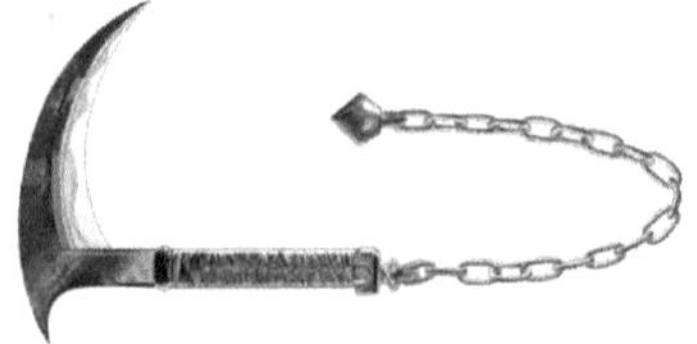

Kohaku's eyes popped open. She could hear something lurking in the woods, surrounding the camp. It was no bird or animal, and though it seemed human, she couldn't be certain. Swiftly, but quietly, she whistled a few short notes.

"I hear them," the man outside of the tent responded. "Care to place a bet with me? Drunk or dead?"

The ninja woman sighed. *Why can't he ever be serious in these sorts of situations?* She whistled one short note. And then added three more after a slight pause.

"No, let them sleep. There's only about four or five of them from what I can tell, and I can easily–"

Before Hasu could finish his sentence, the world took on a purple glow. Beneath the blanket beside her, Reika suddenly sat straight up and began chanting something in an odd language. The young miko's eyes were open, but they were empty.

White runes appeared in the air around the camp, creating what seemed to be a barrier of some sort. All sounds were muted save the steady drumming of the ninja woman's heartbeat. She watched, breathless, as the silhouettes of the walking dead slowly approached the barrier. Once they came into contact with the runes, the dead instantly vanished. All that remained was a bluish sort of haze that lingered for a moment before it, too, disappeared.

When all of the intruders were gone, the runes faded away and the world was normal once more. Kohaku could once again hear the wind in the trees and the chorus of loud snores emanating from around the smoldering remnants of the campfire.

The ninja woman looked back to see the miko lying down, fast asleep, as if nothing had happened. Kohaku had felt all along that something wasn't right about the girl, and now she knew why. The miko had a mysterious power inside of her, and the ninja woman wasn't sure of how much control the girl had over it.

"Was that the work of our little miko?" Hasu whispered.

Kohaku replied with a hushed, "Yes."

"Very interesting. I wonder if that power works against demons as well…"

The ninja woman had also considered that possibility, but if the miko couldn't control her power, then it could easily backfire on them. Granted, it would probably only affect Kazu, but still, the question remained whether or not it was worth the risk. Despite the possibility of her betraying them, Kohaku was beginning to agree with Hasu that more good than harm could come from the miko's presence. After watching the girl interact with Kazu, Kohaku hoped that the girl would choose to stay with them – if only for Kazu's sake.

As the morning light broke through the trees, the crew woke and began to eat whatever remained from last night's meal. Though they were thoughtful enough to save a few scraps for the two ladies,

Kazuki wasn't as fortunate; he ended up with only a single mushroom for breakfast. The young man's stomach grumbled as he helped Ginza pack away the makeshift tent. All he could do was look forward to the grand meal that Jun would prepare for them upon their return.

Unfortunately for the young man, hunger wasn't the only thing on his mind that morning. The moment he saw Reika, Kazuki was reminded of the fact that she would surely part with them once they arrived at the docks. As much as he wanted her to stay, Kazuki wasn't confident that he could protect her properly. There was still no sign of the Demon King's presence, and if they ran into Eiri again...

"Good morning, ladies," Hasunuma announced with a smile. "I hope you slept well."

Kohaku, who was riding on Hanzo's back, chose to ignore the Pirate King. She pointed Hanzo in the opposite direction of Hasunuma and didn't bother looking back.

Kazuki thought Kohaku's stubbornness was cute and found himself grinning at her defiance.

Reika, on the other hand, responded sleepily, "The ground is no place for a lady to sleep." She covered her mouth as she yawned. "I can't wait to get back to civilization."

"Oh? In a hurry t' make your decision are ya?" Hasunuma asked, grinning.

"Ugh," Reika heavily sighed, "Don't bother me with your fake accent first thing in the morning. I haven't the patience for it."

The crew immediately halted whatever they were doing and stared at the miko. She had just called to attention something that was meant to remain unnoticed.

"I mean really," she continued, unaware of her mistake, "why do you talk like that anyways? Your real cadence is much more…" Reika broke off as she finally noticed that everyone was staring at her. "What?"

The Pirate King burst into laughter. "Whatever are ya talkin' about? I always–"

"Hasu," Kohaku said, cutting the Pirate King off. She shook her head and said, "Everyone knows, so you don't have to worry about it anymore."

The crew all scratched their heads and sheepishly looked at each other.

"Wait. So *all* of you knew?" The Pirate King asked as he surveyed his crew. Seeing them all nod without making eye-contact, Hasunuma shook his head and laughed. "By the gods! Why didn't anyone say something before?"

"Well," Hanzo started after getting a prod from Kohaku, "we thought you might be angry with us."

"Yeah, an' we figured there was a good reason fer it, so we didn't want t' ruin it fer ya," Ginza added.

"Honestly, we've known for years," Rize said guiltily. "But don't let our knowing stop you if you want to keep speaking that way."

Hasunuma laughed even harder. "Are you kidding me? I hated talking like that! I just thought you guys would appreciate a more rough and uneducated-sounding captain."

The crew erupted in laughter and denied needing a captain with a fake accent. Reika apologized for bringing the whole thing up, but Hasunuma quickly pardoned her for her mistake.

Kazuki was glad that the issue was now resolved – since he also hated Hasunuma's fake accent – but he was curious to know the real reason for why Hasunuma thought it necessary to speak that way in the first place. The young man had often wondered if the Pirate King was perhaps trying to mask his origin. After all, most pirates were uneducated men who gave up work in the field for life on the sea, so it would have been very odd for a highborn, educated man to give up his position for the life of a criminal. And Hasunuma was definitely educated. Kazuki couldn't be sure about the highborn part though.

I'm sure I'll figure it out one day, Kazuki thought to himself as he grabbed the remaining water skin. The crew had begun to move out and the young man followed behind them.

While he was wondering whether or not to make his way through the crew towards where Reika was, the lovely young girl suddenly appeared next to him.

"Hey there," she chimed.

"Hi," the young man mumbled in reply.

"Is something wrong?" Reika asked as she leaned in closer to Kazuki.

"Not really," the young man said as he took a small side step away from her.

"Oh," the young woman replied, her cheerfulness gone.

For a while the two of them simply followed the pirates in silence. They could hear Hanzo and Ginza arguing with each other about this and that, and every once in a while they caught snippets of Rize and Hasunuma's conversation about coordinates. It seemed that the Pirate King already had an idea of where to head next.

Kohaku was silent as she rode on Hanzo's back, but every so often she would look back at Kazuki, smile, and nod towards the miko. He guessed that this was her way of encouraging him to talk to Reika. While the young man appreciated the support, it didn't make the prospective task any easier.

Kazuki walked a few paces ahead of the miko, but he was constantly glancing over his should to check on her location. When Reika finally seemed to notice what the young man was doing, a small grin appeared on her face and she quickened her pace so she could better match Kazuki's. Now that they were side-by-side once more, the young man felt compelled to say something to the miko.

"Nice day, huh," was all that he could muster.

The girl giggled and replied, "Yes, it is a rather lovely day."

"You know, I really don't think you should come with us," the young man said flatly.

Reika immediately stopped walking. "*Excuse me?*"

Kazuki noticed Kohaku shaking her head at him and realized that he should explain himself better to the miko.

He stopped walking and turned to face the angry young woman. "What I mean is that it's dangerous to travel with us, and you'll probably get hurt if you stay."

The miko seemed to lighten up at his words.

"It's not that I don't want you to join us," Kazuki added, "I'm just worried about you." As soon as those words left his lips, the young man realized that they were much more embarrassing to say out loud than he had imagined.

A smile finally surfaced on Reika's lovely face, and she moved closer to Kazuki as she asked, "Why are you worried about me?"

The conversation was now headed down a path that the young man was completely unprepared for. "B-because…" he stuttered, "not only are we fighting the Hekigun, but we're fighting a bunch of demons too."

"I'm well aware of that, Kazuki," Reika sighed, twirling her hair around her finger, "but you seem to forget the powers that I possess. To me, humans are more scary than demons."

"Powers or not, coming with us would be extremely dangerous," Kazuki retorted. "We pretty much make enemies of everyone we meet." Well, that wasn't exactly true, but facts aren't always helpful when trying to prove a point.

"Truly? These days it seems as if very few people actually support the Hekigun. More information about their terrible deeds finds its way into the cities every day. And, of course, no one would freely support those fiends for what they've done."

I guess she's less of a shrine recluse than I thought.

"That may be true, but pirates are still considered to be scum no matter what."

"And rightly so," Reika said with a firm nod. "Your fancy little group may be different, but most pirates are just as bad as the Hekigun."

Although he'd never come across a group of pirates that didn't adhere to the Pirate King's code, Kazuki knew they existed. A few times the crew had docked at a port that had recently been attacked by rogue pirates. The aftermath was awful: burnt buildings, dead villagers, as well as stolen women, children, and goods. Hasunuma always made sure to help out however he could, but, more often than not, his efforts went unappreciated. And while Kazuki understood the villager's rage, it always made him angry when they hurled stones and insults at the Pirate King. Hasunuma seemed used to it though, as he would simply laugh it off and order the crew to set sail, after leaving behind a fair amount of gold behind to help with reconstruction.

"Anyways," Reika chimed, breaking Kazuki's train of thought, "my powers are sufficient enough to protect me from demons. As for humans," she smiled sweetly, "that's why I have *you*."

The young man couldn't argue with her about that. He would certainly protect her with his life if necessary, but that wasn't the issue. "Yeah, I'll protect you, but–"

"See? Then I'll be fine," the lovely young woman chimed.

A few remarks cycled through Kazuki's head before he replied with, "How is it that you are so confident in your abilities?" *I'm a better fighter than you, but I certainly don't have that level of confidence. Even with the Demon King...*The thought suddenly prompted another question: "Where does your power come from anyways?"

Reika gave the young man a look that read 'you don't know?' But she smiled away her initial reaction and explained, "Miko are gifted with divine spiritual powers. Our purity and connection with the gods is what gives us our abilities. Well, that and lots of training." The young woman sighed as she added, "We have to memorize tons of old texts and chants in order to be effective. It's kind of a pain."

"So…you think that gods exist, and that they have given you this special power because you worship them," Kazuki said skeptically.

"Of course they exist, silly," Reika corrected, "I mean, the evidence is all around you."

"What, you mean the trees and sky and such?"

"Yes. The rocks and trees, plants and animals, air and water, you and me…everything! The world is made from the gods, and so everything in it is sacred; everything contains a piece of the gods."

"Okay…" Kazuki said, rolling his eyes, "then what about demons?"

"Even demons," she replied. "They are made from distorted human souls and, therefore, are partially divine." The miko tilted her head to the side, as if a thought had just occurred to her. "Perhaps that's why demons have powers? Somehow they must be able to unlock the divine spirit within and call forth the natural elements."

Kazuki laughed. "You're joking, right? I mean, didn't you say that a miko's purity is what allows them to access the gods' divine power? Demons aren't even remotely pure. And if we're all partially divine, then anyone should be able to access the gods' powers, not just specially trained shrine worshipers." The young man continued his rebuttal without pausing to allow Reika to respond. "And why is it that we only experience *demons* interfering in human lives? If gods existed, wouldn't they be inclined to help us out? It seems odd that only the darker half of the spiritual world would have any influence over or interaction with the Human Realm."

"Goodness, you're totally ignorant, aren't you! I wish the head priest were still around so he could set you straight." Reika suddenly grimaced, as if she were remembering what had befallen those at her shrine. "Well," she heavily sighed and shook her head, "I'll do my best in his stead." She locked eyes with Kazuki and began, "In response to your first remark, it's probably due to the fact that so few humans are pure. Once tainted, the spiritual powers that a person may possess become unstable. The gods aren't so foolish as to allow their powers to be used by the corrupt."

"But demons–"

"As for your second remark," Reika continued over Kazuki, "the gods cannot interact with normal humans. Only those who are pure, or those who were born with an uncommonly high amount of spiritual power, can see or hear them."

"That seems rather convenient," Kazuki mumbled.

Reika ignored his comment and continued her explanation. "And while the gods have assisted humans many times, there are few that would attribute their sudden good fortune to the gods' divine powers. For instance: when it finally rains after a long drought, or when there is a bountiful harvest, or when a ship survives a storm at sea; all of these things happen because of the gods' intervention."

"Then explain to me why there are droughts in the first place, or why diseases spread and kill thousands, or why demons are so free to walk among us," the young man scoffed. "Even if the gods exist, they don't seem to care enough about their creations to bother helping them. That or they never had that sort of power in the first place."

"Well, Kazuki, it seems to me that no matter what I say, you won't believe that they exist," the miko said as she tossed her hair.

"Of course not. Seeing is believing; and with all of the demons I've seen, there hasn't been a single god around to stop them."

"You're assuming that it's the gods' duty to stop demons or to make sure that no one suffers," the miko pointed out. "Just because they created us, doesn't mean that they are bound to protect and watch over us. The gods are divine beings. What could we humans possibly hope to understand about them? Good and evil are human concepts that don't apply to gods. They are what they are, and they will act however they please. Some may help humans while others may ignore them, but it's not our place to judge their divine thoughts or actions."

Kazuki shook his head. "Look, for now I think we'll just have to agree to disagree about the status of gods." He then pointed towards the empty trail in front of them and said, "We've got to catch back up with the others."

The lovely young woman nodded and joined Kazuki as he ran down the forest path. Thankfully, it wasn't long before they saw the rest of the pirate crew; they had stopped to rest a short ways ahead.

"The lovebirds're back," Ginza announced as Reika and Kazuki approached.

"Good, then we can keep moving," Hazunuma replied. He shot Kazuki a look that warned him not to fall behind again.

Reika giggled and whispered in Kazuki's ear, "He really cares about you, doesn't he?"

"I dunno about that," the young man said quickly as he felt a warm sensation growing in his chest.

The miko giggled again and said, "Boys are never true to their feelings." She then called out to the Pirate King, causing everyone to pause. "Red Dragon, I realize it's a bit early, but I've made my decision."

"Oh?" Hasunuma grinned, "And what does the miko say?"

"She will temporarily join your crew in order to eradicate the demons. Err, that is, if you'll have me," she added awkwardly.

Kazuki wasn't sure if Reika was trying to be polite or if she was slightly embarrassed by her declaration.

Hasunuma laughed and replied, "Of course we'll accept you! We need all the help we can get," the Pirate King grinned at Kazuki and added, "isn't that right, Kid?"

The young man averted his eyes and subtly nodded in agreement.

"Having a miko with us is gonna be great," Hanzo asserted.

"Yeah, and I can't wait to see what other spells she can use," Rize added.

"Maybe she can zap 'em all an' we'll be done with 'em before ya know it!" Ginza suggested with a laugh.

This, of course, sparked a new conversation between the three of them about what sorts of powers would be awesome for the miko to have. Kazuki shook his head, but the corners of his mouth rose slightly nonetheless as he listened to the pirates' suggestions the entire rest of the way to Giyosan.

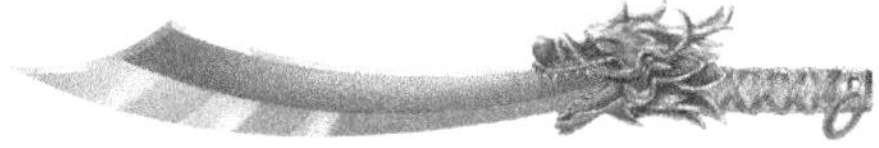

When they reached the remote section of the port, it was immediately evident that something was wrong. Townspeople crowded the docks while some members of the local peacekeeping force tried to keep them in control. These men were not part of the guard force that served the Emperor; they were a group of men who only trusted themselves to keep the peace in their area of town. And, while they wouldn't necessarily cause the crew any physical harm, these self-appointed peacekeepers were proficient at spreading gossip and lies.

The Pirate King walked right up to the man in charge and said, "What's all the commotion about, Tarou?"

The man, who was much older than Hasunuma, shook his head. "It's about damn time you showed up, Red Dragon. Care to explain this mess?" He pointed towards the dock that housed the Ryujin. There were bodies of men strewn about the walkway, as well as some floating in the water around the ship.

As the crew took in the sight, there was movement on the deck as another corpse rolled off the side and splashed into the water. A familiar, sour face peered over the rail at them.

"Sorry about the mess, Captain! I'm almost done cleaning up, so hold on a minute would ya?"

The Pirate King let out a bellowing laugh. "It looks like my cook just dealt with some unsavory guests. And that's not against the law, Tarou."

The crowd around them began to mutter in agreement.

The older man frowned and grabbed Hasunuma's shirt. He tried to pull the Pirate King down towards his face, but Hasunuma didn't move an inch even though Tarou was using all of his strength.

Frustrated, the older man yelled, "Gods be damned, Red Dragon! You expect me to believe that horse pile? There's no way that one man, let alone some measly cook, could have taken out that many ruffians by himself. You were here, weren't you?!"

The Pirate King shrugged. "I really wasn't here, Tarou," he said calmly as he unclenched the older man's hand from his shirt. "I just returned from Tenrou Shrine."

Hasunuma looked behind him and signaled for the miko to come to him. She slowly made her way forward, blushing bright red as the crowd stared at her.

When she arrived next to Hasunuma, he put a hand on her shoulder and said, "We are under orders to protect this here miko until she reaches her destination."

Tarou looked at Hasunuma skeptically. "You really expect me to believe that you're protecting this girl? She's probably some poor villager that you stole and plan to sell!"

"I would never do that to a woman," the Pirate King retorted, his voice remaining calm.

There were a few giggles from the crowd when a woman clearly said, "Well *that's* true."

Ignoring the masses, the older man snorted as he said, "Then why in all the Demon Realm would the Pirate King do something so nice and selfless?"

"He's not, really," the miko chimed in.

Both men stared at her.

She'd better not–

"What I mean to say is, I'm paying these pirates to escort me. They are doing this for gold, not out of kindness."

The Pirate King smiled and patted the miko lightly on her head. *Good thinking.*

"Listen here, girl, I–"

"And besides," the miko said over the protesting older man, "aren't all those dead guys a bunch of criminals? So, in a way, his cook did you a favor."

Hasunuma had to cover his mouth to hold back a laugh.

Tarou spit on the ground and glared at the miko. "You shut your mouth, girl!"

The crowd of townspeople suddenly began shouting at the peacekeeping force leader.

"Hey, she's right!"

"They deserved to die!"

"And Red Dragon obviously just walked in from the western woods."

"We all saw him."

"It's not like you're ever going to catch him anyways, Tarou."

"Give up."

"Yeah, stop tryin' to show off, Tarou Tard!"

The crowd laughed aloud after the last remark, and the older man's face grew red."You may have gotten off this time, Red Dragon, but one day I'll get you. Count on it!"

Not on your life, Tarou.

The older man then called out to his men and they left the docks, presumably heading back to their base on the outskirts of town. The crowd dispersed with them, though some of the women seemed interested in lingering a while longer. Hasunuma would have happily given them the time of day, but duty called; he had to find out the story behind the dead bodies all over his ship.

"I owe you one, little miko," Hasunuma whispered in the miko's ear.

She brushed him away and said haughtily, "And don't you forget it." She turned and looked him right in the eyes. "I *will* collect on that later."

The miko's smile suddenly changed from devious to sweet as Kazuki approached them.

Heh. So that's how it is…

Before the kid could say anything, the miko took his hand and asked him to take her to the ship. He nodded stiffly in response and began to walk towards the Ryujin.

Hasunuma then signaled the rest of the crew to follow the kids to the ship. As he made his way towards his ship, the Pirate King noticed something familiar about the bodies he passed.

Now why would his *men try to board my ship?*

Rize seemed to have noticed too, because he suddenly bent down to one of the bodies and said, "Captain, this medallion…aren't these Silver's men?"

The Pirate King nodded.

"But why would he–"

"I'm not sure, Rize. We need more information. Let's hope Jun got something from at least one of them before killing them all."

The helmsman shook his head, "Knowing him, I doubt it."

As the Pirate King reached the deck of his ship, he laughed heartily at the sight before him; Kazuki wore a huge frown on his face as Jun handed him the mop and pointed to the bloody spots on the deck. The miko timidly offered to help, but Jun ignored her and instead made his way towards Hasunuma.

"It looks like we missed quite the show," the Pirate King mused. "Too bad. It's been a while since I've watched you work."

"Did that idiot Tarou leave?" Jun asked, ignoring Hasunuma's comment.

"He did," the Pirate King said with a nod. "Thanks for calling down to me."

"Yeah, well that guy wouldn't leave us alone otherwise," Jun grumbled. "Ever since you stole his thunder by protecting this area of town from those rogue pirates however many years ago, he's had it out for you."

Hasunuma shrugged. "He should just be happy that this section of town still exists. Those rogue pirates were ready to set it ablaze before we stepped in."

Jun stared pointedly at the Pirate King as he replied, "Yeah, well *some* men can't take being shown up."

Before Hasunuma could reply, Rize interrupted with a loud, shrill whistle. Seconds later, Ami came soaring down from above and gently landed on the helmsman's shoulder. He gently stroked her chest and then turned to Jun, asking, "Were those really Silver's men?"

The cook nodded. "We've got a tricky situation on our hands," he said with his usual gruffness.

"What else is new," Hanzo commented as he stepped onto the deck.

Ginza was right behind him, and when he saw Jun glance over, the blacksmith pointed to the injured ninja woman riding on the giant's back.

Jun immediately went over to Kohaku and helped her dismount. He carried her to a large wooden crate and sat her down gently. Though the cook was rude and standoffish to just about everyone, Kohaku was different. Normally, Hasunuma would have greatly minded that sort of special attention towards Kohaku, but what Jun felt for the ninja woman wasn't lust; it was a familial sort of affection, like a brother would have for his sister. As long as it remained that way, the cook was allowed to live.

"Thank you, Jun," Kohaku said with a smile. "I was careless…but my salve is working well, so it's not as bad as it looks. But the wounds are deep, so it will take them a while to fully heal."

Jun's jaw dropped and his eyes widened.

"What? Oh. Yeah, I got my voice back," the ninja woman said with a nervous laugh.

A small smile appeared on the cook's face as he patted Kohaku on her head. "Glad you made it back." The rare sight quickly vanished as Jun turned to Hasunuma and said, "But it's too bad she's out, 'cause I think we'll need some spying done for this next mission."

"Why's that?" Rize asked.

The cook continued to look directly at the Pirate King as he responded, "They've got your second-in-command locked up at Masayoshi Island and they're going to execute him in four days."

Seriously? Why me? Kazuki lamented as he mopped up Jun's bloody mess.

"Sorry Kazuki," Reika chimed, "it's because you were first on board wasn't it? I shouldn't have rushed you…"

"It's not that," the young man replied, "so don't worry about it." *I think he still hates me.*

"Is there another mop? I can help you."

No way am I letting a girl clean this *up.*

"No. Thanks though," Kazuki replied as he shook his head. The young man then pointed towards a bunch of barrels that were tied together with rope and said, "You can sit on those until the deck is clear."

Reika nodded and walked over to the spot where the young man had pointed. She lifted herself onto one of the barrels and sat there, her gaze flitting around the ship. The young woman's legs hung freely down the front, unable to reach the ground below, and she began to kick them slightly as she quietly hummed another unfamiliar tune. The smile on her face told the young man that Reika was looking forward to a new adventure, but Kazuki was still worried about her safety. Was it really the right decision to let her join them?

"What happens when we die?"

Reika stopped humming and raised an eyebrow at the young man.

"I mean, according to your beliefs," Kazuki clarified. He was slightly embarrassed, since his question seemed random, but he needed to know the answer.

"Well," the young woman slowly began, "after your soul departs your body, you become one with the gods, as you were in the beginning. And your body becomes one with nature as it was in the beginning." Reika shrugged and added, "That's what I was taught anyways."

"What about ghosts and demons? Aren't they supposed to be lost souls or something?"

"Pretty much. I mean, if your soul has been corrupted in some way or if you have a lingering attachment to this world, then you become a wandering ghost. And if a ghost isn't saved in time, it'll become a demon." Reika explained. "Which is why miko like me are super helpful, because we have the power to purify the soul and send it back to the gods. Some priests can too, but they usually aren't as powerful," she added, sounding rather snooty in Kazuki's opinion.

"So, you're saying that the gods won't take your soul back if it's not to their liking?" Kazuki scoffed.

"Hey, as I said before: who are we to question the will of the gods?" The young woman sighed and shook her head. "Why do people assume that every aspect of a religion has to be likeable, or make perfect sense, in order for it to be real? Having a belief or faith in something is like having a strong bond of trust – even though you can't always see or know what's going on, you have to trust that things will work out. So yeah, maybe it's hard to accept that gods exist when life is tough, but life isn't always bad. People tend to forget the good and focus on the bad. That's just our nature it seems. And it takes real effort to recognize that human flaw, but once we do that, we can redirect it into something positive."

Kazuki listened to what the young woman said, but he couldn't agree with her. "Then how exactly would you put a positive spin on playing host to the Demon King?"

Reika seemed to think about it for a moment before her face suddenly flushed. "Well, um," she twirled her hair as she spoke, "you wouldn't have met these pirates…or me for that matter."

*That's true…but is that truly worth all of the lives lost in the process? Including mine...*Kazuki shook his head. He couldn't believe that some invisible entities were controlling his life in such a ridiculous way. If there were any gods, they abandoned humans long ago.

"Hey, Kid," Hasunuma called out as he walked over to them, accompanied by the rest of the crew. "You think you can go on a mission without me and not screw it up?"

There were many things the young man wanted to say in response, but he kept them all inside and simply replied, "Yes, Captain."

"Good," the Pirate King said with a grin. "Oh, and you're also in charge of the miko while she's with us."

Now I know *he's messing with me.*

"Are you serious?" The young man heard Jun ask in a skeptical tone. "You *really* think the kid can handle this one alone?"

"I never said he would be going alone," the Pirate King replied with a smile. "*You* will be accompanying them."

"Them?"

"Yeah, the miko is going too."

"WHAT?!" Jun yelled. He looked like he was ready to punch Hasunuma.

Ginza burst into laughter. "That's great! Good thinkin' Cap'n!"

Hanzo tried not to laugh, but his shoulders were noticeably shaking.

"But Jun, I thought you *liked* going to O-kane," Rize teased.

"Oh, ha-ha," the cook grumbled. "Laugh all you want now, 'cause you won't be once something happens to the kid and his little girlfriend."

"Yet nothing *will* happen to either of them," the Pirate King said with a deadly serious tone. "Isn't that right, *Jun*?"

The crew grew quiet and Jun simply mumbled a 'Yes, Captain,' in response before storming back to the galley.

"Now then, Rize get to the helm, Hanzo and Ginza prepare for departure, Kid finish cleaning up and then help them ready the ship, Kohaku…you just sit tight, and same goes for you, little Miko," the Pirate King commanded.

The crew responded with a loud, collective, 'Aye, Cap'n,' before starting their designated tasks. Hasunuma nodded in response and then made his way towards the helm.

"So where exactly are we going?" The young woman asked Kazuki after the rest of the crew had left.

"Rize mentioned some place called, 'O-kane'," the young man replied nonchalantly. He was only half paying attention to her at this point, since he was concentrating on getting the deck cleaned quickly so that he could help Hanzo and Ginza with the ship preparations.

"Really?!" Reika gasped. "I've only read about it and heard stories, but–"

"Lad, we need you to run up and loose the sails!"

"Got it!" Kazuki yelled back to Hanzo. He tossed the mop aside and ran for the ropes. Normally, Kohaku would do the untying, but now her job fell to Kazuki to complete; the other two were far too large to climb the ropes, and Rize was at the helm.

As the ship finally pulled out into open water, Kazuki took a deep breath and wiped his brow. It was work enough with just four people, but with three it was nearly impossible. The sun had begun to set, and the young man paused a moment to take in the oranges, yellows, pinks, and purples that were painted across the sky.

"Wow. It's beautiful," Reika chimed.

Kazuki kept his eyes on the slowly deepening hues and simply replied, "Mmhm."

After a minute or two the young woman spoke up again. "You know, it takes a lot of work to get a ship going. I never realized that until watching you three just now."

"Yeah, I think we're a bit understaffed here," the young man groaned.

The young woman nodded thoughtfully. "I would have figured that the Pirate King would have loads of men aboard his ship, but I guess there's only six of you, including him. Why is that?"

Good question.

Kazuki shook his head. "I have no idea. Since I'm a fairly new addition to the crew I don't know the whole story, but I also thought it was weird when I first joined. Any other ship you'd find out here has at least twenty men." The young man then noticed the mop in the young woman's lovely hands and said, "Oh, thanks, I almost forgot to finish washing the deck."

"Actually," Reika said with a smile, "I took care of that for you."

Kazuki stared at her for a moment before taking in the sight of the blood-free deck. "Oh. Well thanks, but…I mean…were you alright with that?"

"If you're referring to cleaning up human blood, then my answer is 'no, not in the least'. But I wanted to help you out in some way since I'm temporarily part of this crew, so I felt inclined to finish cleaning while you helped with the sails and all."

The young man stared at Reika in disbelief, which made her giggle.

"Once I convinced myself it was spilled wine and fish blood, it wasn't so bad," she said with a smile.

That only makes me feel worse.

Kazuki took the mop from Reika and set it aside, leaning it against one of the barrels. He then gave her a brief pointing tour of the main deck before leading her below. After showing her the bathroom and the location of his room, Kazuki opened the door to the room next to his.

"This is the extra room where you'll be staying. If you have any questions or problems, come see me. And whatever you do, *don't* go into any of the other rooms. Pirates are very protective of their stuff."

Reika smiled and nodded in agreement. "What about the kitchen?"

"You mean the galley," Kazuki said as he shook his head fervently. "NEVER go in there. Jun hates it when other people enter his space. You might even get a knife thrown at you."

At this, the young woman laughed out loud. "Truly? This I *must* see! Let's go," she said as she tugged on Kazuki's arm and led him towards Jun's domain. It wasn't a hard place to find, seeing as all one had to do was follow their nose.

As soon as they crossed the doorway, a metal twang rang in their ears.

"Kid, you know damn well not to come in here," the cook growled.

"Sorry, Jun, but–"

"Oh, that's my fault," Reika chimed, "I asked him to show me the kitch– I mean the *galley*."

The cook continued to glare at Kazuki, ignoring the young woman.

"Wow! It's really nice in here!"

Both men turned to see the young woman freely walking around the space.

"It's so clean and organized…quite the opposite of what I imagined," she said with genuine awe.

Kazuki thought his heart would stop. Unknowingly, Reika was only a few steps away from certain death. The young man quickly looked to Jun, who was now watching Reika with a keen interest.

"You even have the latest cookware and an impressive store room! It's no wonder you don't let any of those brutes in here – I mean, *crewmates*," Reika quickly corrected herself.

A grin spread across Jun's face. "You really know your stuff."

"Of course. I helped prepare meals for the entire shrine every day," she boasted.

"Well then," the cook said with what looked somewhat like a smile, "you feel like helping out in here?"

Kazuki's jaw dropped. Never had he heard of, or witnessed, Jun inviting someone into his kitchen, let alone asking them to help him cook.

The young woman's eyes lit up. "Certainly! Just tell me what you want done and I'll do it."

Jun nodded. "Alright then," he said. "And you can leave now, Kid," the cook added as he pointed the tip of a large knife towards Kazuki.

The young man didn't need to be told twice. He left the galley quickly, though he wished Reika was still accompanying him, and sought out the Pirate King for more information about his next mission.

"Are you sure that's wise?"

The Pirate King looked up from his desk and smiled at the ninja woman. "They'll be fine."

"But I don't think Kazu can use the Demon King's powers, since he got sealed by the miko. What if Second shows up? Or what if Silver has a strong demon with him?"

"Are you his mother?" The Pirate King laughed. "Even without the Demon King's help, the kid knows how to fight."

Kohaku didn't look convinced.

"Hey, I'm sending Jun with them," Hasunuma added, trying another approach, "and you trust in *his* skills."

"Battle skills, yes. Support skills, no," she said frankly. "You know very well that he's the lone wolf type. In fact, the last time he was on the battlefield with us, Jun was so focused on his own fight that we almost lost Rize!"

"True," Hasunuma replied as he recalled the incident. "But he won't let anything happen to the kid."

"How can you be so certain?" Kohaku asked with a raised brow.

The Pirate King grinned. "I think he likes 'im."

Kohaku frowned. "Are you blind? Haven't you seen the way he treats Kazu? How can you say he–"

There was a knock at the door, silencing the room. After a

moments pause, Hasunuma told the person to enter. It was no surprise to him when the kid walked into the room.

"Is this a bad time?" the kid asked as he looked back and forth between Kohaku and Hasunuma.

"No, no," the Pirate King assured him with a smile. "What's on your mind, Little Oni?"

"I was hoping to get more information about my next mission," he said.

"Oh? And here I thought you were coming to me for seduction advice," the Pirate King smirked. "Let me give you a few suggestions–"

A shuriken suddenly flew across the room and lodged itself in the wall next to Hasunuma's head.

"On second thought, let's just stick to the mission at hand," the Pirate King said as he pulled the metal star out.

The kid looked back at Kohaku and gave her a nod of thanks.

They were both so easy to provoke, it was hard for the Pirate King to resist the temptation. But with two against one, Hasunuma decided to play nice.

"I'm sending you, Jun, and the miko to O-kane. I have business with someone there, but, alas, there is a more pressing matter elsewhere that requires my attention. So I need you to take care of this person in my stead."

The kid raised an eyebrow. "When you say 'take care of,' do you mean 'kill'?"

"Perhaps," the Pirate King shrugged. "That will be up to you to decide, Little Oni." He thought about it for a moment before adding, "Or Jun. Depending on who finds him first I suppose."

"What has this person done, and who is he?" the kid asked.

"What he has done is attempt to invade my ship," the Pirate King said, his voice revealing only a fraction of the wrath he felt towards the man. "As for who he is, the man goes by the name 'Silver'."

"Sil-ver?" the kid repeated awkwardly.

"As in the foreign currency," Kohaku explained. "The man fell in love with it at first sight and now he calls himself by the same name."

"OK…so how do I find this weirdo?" the kid asked.

"That should be easy enough," the Pirate King replied. "Jun will know where to go, so just follow him."

The kid nodded, but looked as if he had something else he wanted to say. After a few moments of indecision, he finally asked, "Is it *really* necessary that Jun come with us?"

"What, you think this mission will be too easy?" The Pirate King retorted. He knew full well what the kid was actually referring to, but he couldn't help but tease him a little.

"No, I just…well, I think…I mean…" The kid mumbled; he was clearly unsure of how to express his true feelings on the matter.

"Look, Little Oni, Jun's personality may be a bit undesirable, but his ability to fight is what will keep you alive. I don't know what Silver has planned, but you need to be prepared for anything."

"O-kane is a town built on greed and lust," Kohaku added. "It's the ideal place for demons to hide."

The kid finally seemed to get the hint. He nodded and said, "Don't worry, even without the Demon King I can defeat lesser demons. And Reika's power should be useful too." The kid paused for a second before adding, "*If* she can control it properly."

Hasunuma laughed. "Ha! You'll have to report back to us on that, Little Oni. We'll reach O-kane's main port by morning."

The kid nodded and left the Pirate King's cabin.

"I wish I could follow them," Kohaku sighed.

"Me too," the Pirate King admitted, "but with those injuries, you won't be going anywhere for a while."

"So, what are you going to do about D?" The ninja woman asked.

The Pirate King grinned. "Oh don't you worry, I've got something special planned for him."

It had never entered Kazuki's mind that there could be a red-light district that encompassed an entire island, but that's exactly what O-kane was. Or, at least, that was half of it. Along with gambling and illegal trade. The other half was basically a foreign trade port, but the young man wasn't lucky enough to be on that side. If Hasunuma had told him more about the island beforehand, Kazuki wouldn't have left the ship. Mission or not, this island was an entirely alien and repulsive place to the young man, and he wished to be as far from it as possible.

With every step he took, more and more painted women approached him, trying to entice him into their gaudy buildings. The women surrounded Jun too, but all it took was one look from him and they silently turned away in search of another victim. Thankfully, Reika suddenly seized Kazuki's arm and clung to him, which somehow sent all of the painted women away in a huff and prevented them from approaching. The young man wasn't sure exactly why it worked, but he was grateful regardless.

"Thanks," he said with a huge sigh of relief.

"You're not so great with women are you?" Reika giggled.

Kazuki turned his face away in embarrassment.

"But that's totally fine," the young woman added softly as she squeezed his arm.

"Stop flirting and hurry up," an annoyed voice said. "I want to get to Silver before he sends out a search party."

Jun continued his break-neck walking pace, causing Kazuki and Reika to jog in order to keep up with him. It was a difficult feat to perform on O-kane's overly crowded streets. Although they had long since left the main road, the traffic hadn't lessened.

It seemed to Kazuki that no matter where you walked, there were tons of people flooding the pathways. Some were painted women while others were brightly dressed purveyors of gambling dens, both of whom were vying for customers amongst the drunken men and women who staggered about, searching for the next bar. But all who walked the streets were clearly comfortable with the shady atmosphere of O-kane; pirates, ruffians, thieves, slavers, drug pushers, and most likely murderers moved freely about in the lawless town. Apparently, it was the one place where the Hekigun couldn't enforce their rule. It didn't matter how awful you were or what crimes you committed – you were welcome on O-kane.

According to Jun, however, there was one exception to the rule: any crime committed on the island was punishable by their special peacekeeping force. They were nicknamed the 'Shadow Knights,' and, although they enforced the mayor of O-kane's laws, they seemed to be well respected, unlike a lot of other peacekeeping forces that Kazuki had encountered on the mainland. The young man supposed it was because the people knew that the Shadow Knights wouldn't interfere with their business unless they either killed someone or angered the mayor in some way. It seemed odd to Kazuki that a lawless town would have a mayor, but, then again, it was probably the only way to keep things from getting too unruly.

"What's this Silver guy like?" Reika suddenly asked.

Kazuki didn't answer, since he had never met the man before, and Jun seemed like he was ignoring the young woman, until a few minutes later, when the cook mumbled something about 'a weirdo with a serious need for attention.' Kazuki and Reika looked at each other curiously, unsure of what Jun's comment meant, but they decided that they'd find out soon anyways, so they dropped the issue.

As they made their way further inland, Kazuki noticed that the style of the buildings began to change. Instead of the typical wood and paper buildings, like those on the mainland, there were taller structures made of different materials. Some seemed to be constructed of various types of stone while others looked almost to be built out of hardened clay. And some of the roofs had metal or ceramic squares stacked on them instead of layers of thatch.

It must be because of all of the foreigners here, the young man thought. As far as the Hekigun were concerned, anything foreign was illegal. That must have been why O-kane was rife with foreigners; it was the only place in Tsukigen where they were allowed to live and work.

"Wow, some of these outfits are spectacular!" The young man

heard Reika exclaim as she pointed to a woman wearing an exceedingly long kimono that had gemstones sewn into the fabric in a striking pattern.

Kazuki hadn't paid much attention to their clothes before, but now the young man gazed at the people around him with interest. Some men wore what looked like a traditional kinagashi or a kimono with hakama, but the colors and patterns were bold and vibrant, unlike those on the mainland. Other men wore foreign-style suits that were also rather flashy. The women's clothes seemed less gaudy and more extravagant, but they were also heavily influenced by foreign styles. There were even some outfits that immediately made the young man blush. For instance, Kazuki saw a woman who was wearing a dress that seemed to be made of fish netting; while the outline of the dress was visible, there was no real fabric hiding the woman's skin or underwear beneath it.

"I might have to come back here just to shop for clothes," the young woman innocently said. She clearly hadn't seen the net dress.

How can she be so carefree in this lawless place?

Maybe Reika hadn't noticed, but there had been more than a few looks thrown her way – all by men with ill-intentions written all over their faces. Kazuki had done his best to stare them down, but his presence didn't seem to deter the men one bit. In fact, some of them had even given *him* a look over in response.

"We're here," Jun said as he stopped in front of a large building that looked as if it had been encased in silver.

I guess this guy's not afraid of being found, Kazuki thought as he glanced at the shining walls of the building; with the sun beating down overhead, it was almost impossible to look at.

As they made their way inside, it was clear that everything was either covered in, or made to look like it was covered in, silver.

'Obsessed' was putting it lightly.

"I was wondering when Red Dragon would return my call," a shrill voice rang out as the three of them approached a large double staircase. A short, round man appeared at the top. The styled white hair on his head was clearly a wig, and he was wearing a sparkling silver two-piece foreign-style suit. He looked like a pompous jerk.

Reika glanced at Kazuki and giggled.

"What's this?" The man gasped. "Why is Red Dragon not here? Where is he?!" The strange man seemed more than a little upset at Hasunuma's absence.

"If you think that sending a few henchmen would cause the captain to come running, you're more of an idiot than I thought, Silver," the cook said plainly as he shook his head. "Not to mention, thanks to said henchmen, the captain has more pressing business elsewhere."

Kazuki didn't sense any fear from Jun as he stood between them and Silver. Granted, Silver didn't seem all that threatening to begin with.

"Hmph. So those idiots talked, did they?" Silver spat. "In which case, Red Dragon deigned to send his dogs after me, I see," he scoffed. "Normally he only sends you into town to gamble, Jun."

"Yes, well, this time is a little different," the cook replied.

"Babysitting duty by the looks of it," Silver cackled. "Shall I have my sitters take care of them for you? I promise they'll be extra sweet," the strange man grinned creepily as he looked at Reika.

"Especially to that little lamb of yours," he added as he licked his lips. "She'd bring in quite the price you know."

"She's not for sale," Kazuki shouted as he blocked Silver's view of Reika.

"What a yappy pup," Silver frowned. "Perhaps he needs to be taught a lesson."

The strange man then clapped his hands together and two women appeared next to him. They were clad in what Kazuki could only describe as fancy silver underwear, and not much else. Their white hair was cut short, like a man's, but their faces were delicate and beautiful. Both women stood a good three heads taller than the strange man, and there was nothing round about them.

"Ladies, that boy down there needs to be disciplined," Silver said as he pointed to Kazuki, "but be careful not to harm the little lamb. We don't want to have to lower her price due to a few bruises or scars, now do we?" He grinned.

"As you command, Master," the two women said in unison as they bowed to Silver.

"Be on your guard, Kid," Jun cautioned. "They may look like women, but I'd bet my chef's knife that they're demons."

Kazuki agreed with the cook. Even without the Demon King active inside him, the young man could feel the inhuman aura of the two women who were now descending the staircase towards him. Swiftly, he ushered Reika aside and stood ready for their attack.

"I'll take the demoness on the left. You focus on the other one," Jun commanded.

The young man nodded and turned his attention towards the last step of the right staircase.

The silver women descended slowly. Like lionesses stalking prey, their eyes never left their target as they moved in closer for the kill. The silver woman on the left seemed slightly confused when she reached the bottom and Jun was standing there blocking her path. The silver woman on the right, however, remained focused on Kazuki.

As she reached the last step, she smiled a devious smile and said, "Such a naughty little boy." She took a step towards Kazuki. "It's time for you to get punished."

Without warning, the silver woman's fist came flying towards Kazuki's face at lightning speed. The young man barely dodged in time, only to suddenly feel the silver woman's foot collide with his stomach. Spit flew from his mouth as Kazuki stumbled backwards and gasped for air. But the silver woman didn't give him time to catch his breath. She kicked Kazuki again from behind and the young man fell forward with a *thud*.

"Oh dear," she pouted, "this boy is much too little to be any fun."

"Stop messing around, Kid," Kazuki heard Jun shout from somewhere else in the room. "You're making your sensei look bad."

Kazuki rolled his eyes and pushed himself up off of the floor. "Understood," he replied unenthusiastically.

"Does the little boy want another spanking?" The silver woman teased as she readied herself in an offensive position.

"You can beat her, Kazuki!" Reika's enthusiastic voice chimed from behind.

The young man didn't dare turn around or respond; he knew that taking his eyes off his enemy could mean death, but he was also extremely embarrassed by the young woman's cheers. Instead, he did his best to focus on the silver woman in front of him. It wasn't just her speed that was troublesome; as slight as her build was, the silver woman had tremendous strength. Without the Demon King's healing abilities or power to tap into, the young man knew it was going to be a tough win. He took a deep breath, closed his eyes, and unsheathed his katana.

"Dear sister," the silver woman giggled, "I believe the little boy is trying to fight me with his eyes closed."

"Oh my," the other women responded from across the room. "I wish I could play with him too! This guy may be hot, but his grumpy attitude totally ruins his face," she said in a huff.

Kazuki grinned as he heard Jun unsheathe his katana.

I guess he's getting serious too.

O-kane's main port was more crowded than usual. Most of the time, there was plenty of room to stroll along the docks and one could easily hop in and out of the many shops along the way. But today, there were incredibly long lines for the fishermen's stalls, and the rice, sake, and clothing shops; and that usually meant that there was a festival going on.

If it's like this on the normal side of the port, I can only imagine how crowded it is on the other side, the Pirate King thought as he squeezed his way through the throngs of people.

The 'other side' of the port referred to the side that housed less savory activities – where Jun, Kazuki and Reika were. Foreigners called O-kane "Half Moon Island," because while one side was 'light', with normal shops and trading posts for foreigners to use, the other side was 'dark', housing the black market, gambling joints, and red-light venues.

Making his way further down the pier, the Pirate King stopped when he reached a rather unique-looking shop. Unlike the others, which were made of wood, this shop had been constructed of colorful stone that was smooth and polished. No goods were arranged out front, there were no windows into the back area, and there seemed to be no one around to assist customers.

The Pirate King approached the counter and called out, "Hey, Nia, you in?"

A pretty, dark brown face popped out from the curtained doorway behind the counter. "That you, Red Dragon?"

"For the love of gold, Nia, you *know* it's me," the Pirate King sighed. He didn't have time to play her games today.

"Impatient as always," she said with a laugh. "Come on back so you can tell me what you need *this time*."

Hasunuma jumped over the counter, ducked behind the curtain, and ventured into the back area of the shop. There was very little light inside, but neither the Pirate King nor Nia had any problems navigating the dark, tight space.

"Sit down, sit down," she beckoned.

The Pirate King situated himself on a pile of rugs while Nia sat across from him on a stack of boxes. Even in the dim light, Hasunuma could see the woman's dark and delicate form. Her slender arms were folded gracefully in her lap while her legs remained fully covered beneath her floor-length skirt. Her long black hair was neatly braided, and numerous golden rings hung from her ears, matching the many thin golden bracelets around her fragile-looking wrists.

"You look well, Nia," the Pirate King said with a smile.

"So do you, Hasu," she replied. "How's Ko?"

The Pirate King momentarily hesitated before answering, "Oh, she's fine."

"Don't lie to me," Nia snapped.

Nothing gets past her, as usual.

"Actually, she got injured and won't be able to walk for a while," Hasunuma explained with a sigh. "That's part of why I'm here."

"I'm no healer," she replied, "so how exactly do you expect me to help?"

"Well," the Pirate King began, "I thought you two might like to spend some quality girl-time together. On my ship. While I'm away. With the rest of the crew."

"Ah," the delicate woman smiled, "yes, I see. It'd be wonderful to spend some leisure time with Ko again."

"But no wandering off this time," the Pirate King warned.

Nia laughed. "That was a special occasion. And anyways, you said Ko can't move, so you've got nothing to worry about."

When the two of you are together, I have plenty *to worry about.*

"So long as I have your word," he replied skeptically.

"Now what's the other reason for your visit?" Nia asked.

The Pirate King grinned. "I need to borrow the Sphynx."

The delicate woman let out a surprisingly robust sigh. "My man's in trouble again, isn't he?"

Kazuki's blade arced through the air and met its target, but the silver woman's flesh wasn't cut. When he opened his eyes, the young man was shocked to discover that his katana had instead sliced into a thick layer of ice that now surrounded the silver woman's arm.

"That was quite the disappearing act, little boy," the silver woman teased. "Too bad all that effort was wasted. You can't cut me," she said as she wagged her finger in front of the young man.

Kazuki ignored the silver woman's taunt. He yanked his blade free and aimed his second strike at the top of her head. But just as before, right when his blade made contact with her skin, a layer of ice appeared and prevented any damage.

"I *told* you," the silver woman giggled, "now be a good boy and accept your punishment."

Her fist flew towards Kazuki's face as she raised her leg – most likely in preparation for the subsequent blow. The young man instantly reacted with an upward cut towards the woman's outstretched hand, followed by a leap to his left. Although his blade once again met with ice, he managed to prevent both attacks from hitting their mark.

I need to figure out her trick, he thought as he dodged another punch. *The fire guy was just an illusion, but this ice feels very real...*

The young man quickly jumped out of the way of a spinning kick, but the silver woman anticipated his movement; as Kazuki was mid-jump, she threw a punch that landed square in his chest. The young man flew backwards from the force and hit the wall some feet behind him. He coughed heavily and watched as a few red droplets hit the floor.

"Oh dear, did I break a rib?" The silver woman smiled.

Kazuki winced as a sharp pain grew in his side. *Thundering sea snakes, that hurts!*

The silver woman slowly began to approach the young man with a playful grin on her face. She made a fist and pulled her arm back, ready to strike another blow, when suddenly a deathly scream filled the room. The silver woman turned around just in time to see smoke rise from her sister's body before it fell lifelessly to the floor.

"Sister!" She cried out.

Jun sheathed his sword and made his way towards the staircase. "I'm going ahead to deal with Silver. Come and find me when you're done playing freeze tag," the cook said to Kazuki without even once looking back at him.

How did he…? The young man was stunned at the quickness of Jun's victory over the demoness. Multiple questions about the Ryujin's cook suddenly filled Kazuki's head: *Had Jun always been that strong? Why didn't Hasunuma ever send him on missions? Was my victory during training even real, or had Jun just been messing with me?*

The young man's stream of questions was immediately broken when he realized that the silver woman had begun running towards Jun. Quickly, Kazuki chased after her and managed to leap in front of her just before she reached the stairs.

"Move!" She shouted, but Kazuki stood firm. The silver woman's rage was almost palpable.

Kazuki knew he needed to engage her in order to distract her from Jun, so he made a fast horizontal slash towards her torso. The silver woman didn't flinch. She stood, glaring at the young man, with his blade stuck in her icy gut.

"MOVE," she demanded once more.

Kazuki yanked his blade out of the ice and raised it above his head. He had planned on striking, but the young man suddenly found himself unable to move.

What the?! Kazuki watched in horror as his lower half became encased in ice.

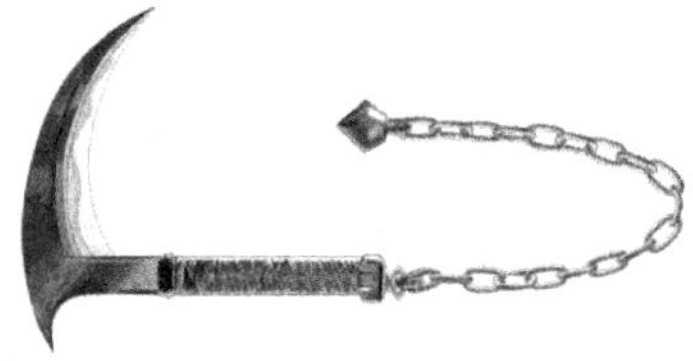

"Unbelievable," the dark, delicate woman laughed. "After all these years, all it took was a real threat to that fool's life. Ha! If only I'd known that earlier, we could have been talking like this years ago."

The ninja woman smiled. "I don't think it was that simple, but I appreciate the thought, Ni."

"Hey, you know I'd do anything for you, Ko," Ni replied. "Hasu on the other hand…" she gave the ninja woman a meaningful look and then they both burst into laughter. "Really though, what *do* you see in him?"

Kohaku blushed and looked away from her friend. Not that she needed to hide her face from the nearly blind woman.

"I mean, sure he's got an attractive voice and all, but his personality is worse than a rump rash," Ni joked.

The ninja woman giggled.

"Plus it's no fun being with a man that's too smart, because then you can't control him as easily," the delicate woman added.

Kohaku shook her head. "But I'm not looking to control him."

"What? Of course you are, Ko. If you didn't, that fool would chase every skirt within eyeshot."

...She has a point.

"Take my man for instance. He's strong, tough, attractive, and just smart enough to be capable. *But* he's also just dumb enough to fall for my tricks and traps, so I always get what I want in the end. It's perfect," Ni said with a smile.

"Yeah, but you and D have a different sort of relationship...I don't really even know what's going on between Hasu and myself," Kohaku sighed. "We started out as friends years ago, but now...well, now I want something more than that, but I'm not sure how Hasu feels."

"Um. As far as I can tell, nothing is going on between the two of you," the delicate woman bluntly stated. "Although," she added with a thoughtful pause, "I guess it says something that he *hasn't* tried anything with you. I mean, as shapely as you are, one would think Hasu would be all over you. The fact that he's not is significant in itself."

"I guess...but it's probably because he promised my mother he'd look after me," the ninja woman sighed once more. "I wish it meant what you think though."

Ni grinned mischievously. "We can always find out, you know."

"What do you mean? How?"

"You just leave that to me, Ko," the delicate woman said. "I'll sort it out."

Why do I get the feeling this won't end well?

The ninja woman thanked her friend anyways and decided to change the subject. "Ni, you seem to be holding up pretty well, despite the news that Hasu brought you."

"Oh I'm used to this sort of thing by now. My man has the worst luck," Ni said with a laugh.

"But how can you remain so calm?"

A wide grin spread across the delicate woman's face. "Because, as we speak, I know that Red Dragon is on his way to help."

Kazuki's body was quickly freezing over. The process had begun at his feet and now his legs were encased as well. If he didn't figure out a way to break it soon, the young man would be solid ice before long. But how? His katana couldn't cut through it, and Kazuki had no idea how Jun managed to kill the other ice demoness with the same kind of blade.

Gods be damned…there goes my torso!

The silver woman ignored Kazuki's distress and moved as if she would pass by him on the stairs. But the young man swung his blade towards her and the silver woman had to jump back to avoid it.

"Still feisty I see," the silver woman said, clicking her tongue. "Fine. I'll destroy you first so that I may go and seek my revenge in peace!" She yelled as she swung her leg around, aiming for Kazuki's legs.

The young man wasn't sure if her kick would shatter his body along with the ice, but he certainly didn't want to find out. Panicking, he stuck his katana out in front of him, hoping that he could deflect her attack. Right before the silver woman's kick made contact with Kazuki's katana, the young man felt a warm sensation where the ice had encased his body.

I really hope I didn't…

Kazuki looked down at his legs. To his surprise – and relief – the ice had vanished completely. He wasn't sure how exactly it had happened, but there wasn't time to think about it. Instead, the young man immediately jumped into the air, avoiding the silver woman's kick, and drove his blade downward into her skull. This time there was no ice shield. Without a word, the silver woman's body released a smoky demon into the air and then fell lifelessly at Kazuki's feet. The usual, unpleasant burning smell lingered behind.

"Oh, thank the gods it worked!" Reika exclaimed, her voice full of cheer and relief.

The young man turned and looked at the young woman, who was now running towards him. "What do you mean?"

"I used one of the sacred spells that's supposed to negate a demon's powers for a short time. I'm so glad it actually worked! I'd never used it before."

Reika was positively beaming with delight. And while Kazuki was thankful that her spell worked, he was still uncertain of her powers. He didn't like that their origin was veiled in mystery and that they seemed highly unreliable. The fact that Reika was so relieved when her spell worked only strengthened Kazuki's concern and suspicion.

"Thanks for the help," was all he could muster in response. The young man then turned back around and began ascending the stairs.

"Whaaat? No kiss for the heroine?" A voice chimed. It sounded similar to Reika's, but was different at the same time.

Kazuki whirled around and stared at the young woman.

"Ha! Totally kidding," she quickly added with an awkward smile, her voice sounding normal. "Come on, let's catch up with Jun before he gets too cranky." The young woman swiftly passed Kazuki on the stairs as she ascended them two at a time.

The young man wasn't sure what to think about what had just happened, so he decided not to.

"Oh, wait!" Reika suddenly turned around and looked down at Kazuki from the top step. "You got injured in that fight, didn't you? Here, let me see," she said as she began to descend the stairs.

"There's no need," Kazuki assured her, "I'm fine."

The young woman didn't seem convinced, but she shrugged and turned back around.

Actually, I really am fine. The young man thought as he touched the side where the silver woman had broken one of his ribs. *His powers are slowly returning...*

When Kazuki reached the top of the staircase, he found Reika staring at the sole doorway on the landing; the door had been kicked clear off its hinges.

"Wow," the young woman remarked, "for such a thin guy, Jun's a lot stronger than he looks."

Her statement could not have been more accurate. The young

man felt as if he'd underestimated the cook's abilities this entire time; although it was not the destruction of the door that had impressed Kazuki, but the quickness of Jun's fight with the demoness. He wished he could have seen it.

"Did you see any of his battle against the other silver woman?" Kazuki asked the young woman, wondering if maybe she had seen something.

Reika shook her head. "No, I…I was too busy watching you," she managed to say before abruptly walking through the busted doorway.

The young man followed the young woman, but only after he convinced himself that he was misinterpreting her words.

There's no way that she likes me, he thought. *And besides, that sort of thing doesn't happen that fast…right?*

Kazuki wished that a manual for understanding women existed. He supposed that he could ask someone for advice, but of all the people he knew, none of them seemed like a good choice. Especially Hasunuma. Kohaku might have been the best option, but Kazuki couldn't bring himself to ask her about that sort of thing.

"Please don't kill me!" A voice shrieked, interrupting Kazuki's train of thought. "I-I was only doing what they paid me to!"

"And who exactly are 'they'?" Another voice asked, this one belonging to Jun.

When Kazuki entered the room at the end of the long hallway, he saw the cook standing over Silver with his katana aimed at the man's now bald head; Silver's wig was on the floor beside him – it had been cut in half.

"I can't tell you. They'll kill me!" He pleaded.

"If you'd rather, I could kill you now," Jun replied. He lowed his blade tip so that it was level with Silver's eyes.

"N-No! Please! I'll give you money, women, supplies, you name it," he begged.

"All I want," Jun said flatly, "is an answer to the question I already asked you." The cook moved his hand forward so that the tip of his katana was now touching Silver's brow. A small trickle of red slid down the strange man's nose. "Don't make me ask you again," Jun warned.

Silver yelped and said, "The Hekigun! It was the Hekigun who paid me."

"What exactly did they pay you to do?"

"I helped them capture Red Dragon's second-in-command, and then was told to lure Red Dragon to Masayoshi Island so they could set a trap," Silver confessed.

"Well, it's too bad that your henchmen stole your thunder, Silver," Jun sarcastically remarked. "But you do realize that if the captain had come here first, there wouldn't have been enough time left for him to make it to Masayoshi Island before the execution date, right?"

"Yes, yes, whether Red Dragon makes it or not, they'll kill his second-in-command," Silver admitted, his voice shaking. "I mean, why would they let him live, after all the bases and ships that he's destroyed under Red Dragon's command?"

As the tip of the cook's sword slowly pressed further into Silver's forehead, the strange, terrified man cried out for mercy.

"The demon women," Jun continued, ignoring Silver's cries, "where did they come from?"

"Those two were part of my payment," Silver yelped, "b-but that's all I know about them. I swear!"

Kazuki wondered if Jun was satisfied with Silver's answers or not. The cook was slow to remove his sword tip from the strange man's forehead and looked as if he wanted more from Silver than a small trail of blood.

Should I intervene?

The young man contemplated stepping in, but he was more concerned about Jun's wrath than sparing Silver's life.

"P-Please don't kill me!" Silver pleaded once more.

"Idiot," Jun said as he returned his katana to its black lacquer saya. "I won't kill you. Not on this island anyways," he added as he turned towards the doorway.

Kazuki was certain that Jun's eyes were aimed at something behind the young man, so he turned around to see what it was. He nearly jumped out of his skin when he saw a man standing there silently. How long had he been there and why hadn't Kazuki sensed his presence?

The man was tall and lean with ivory skin, shoulder-length blonde hair, and eerily bright blue eyes. Women might have considered him rather handsome, but there was something about the foreign man that sent chills down Kazuki's spine.

"It's good to see you again, Jun," the foreign man said without any trace of an accent.

"Same to you, Luka," the cook replied.

Kazuki noticed that Silver froze the instant he heard Jun say the foreign man's name. Complete and total fear shone in his eyes as he stared at the man in the doorway.

"Thank you for not breaking my law," the foreign man, Luka, said with a smile. "I assure you, my Knights and I will deal with him properly."

"I don't doubt that," Jun smirked.

The young man stepped out of Luka's way as he entered the room and made his way towards Silver. Jun whispered something into Luka's ear before he headed for the exit. The foreign man's expression changed from a fake-looking smile to a rather unpleasant grin. Kazuki wondered what it was that the cook said to cause such a reaction, but he never found out. Jun motioned for the young man and Reika to follow him, and they quickly did, without a single word.

After leaving Silver's place, when the three of them were back out in the busy streets of O-kane, Reika became unable to hold back her torrent of questions.

"Who was that blonde man? Why was Silver so terrified of him? And what did he mean by the Hekigun hiring him and giving him demons to set up a trap for Red Dragon? Is this second-in-command person in trouble? What–"

"Enough," Jun said loudly as he covered his ears. "Girl, you ask too many questions."

"But we're dying to know! Aren't we Kazu?" She said as she looked pleadingly at the young man.

Kazuki, however, wasn't sure he wanted to join her side this time. Jun had a short fuse and rarely answered anyone's questions.

"And anyways," Reika continued, "we're part of the crew too, so I think we deserve at least *some* answers."

The cook sighed heavily. "Fine. But you're buying me a drink first," he said to Reika.

Again, Kazuki couldn't believe what he was hearing. Maybe Jun had a soft spot for women? Though that was hard to imagine after witnessing his attitude towards the silver women.

But soon after hearing Jun's unlikely response, the young man found himself in a dark, dingy bar, surrounded by shady-looking patrons. His companions didn't seem bothered in the least by the oppressive atmosphere. The young man could understand Jun's ease, but Reika's? It was hard to believe that she could be so comfortable in such a place. Her demeanor made Kazuki wonder if Reika really was a shrine maiden after all. He had imagined them to be more innocent and fearful of less-than-pure people and their endeavors. And while the young woman did have her innocent moments, she seemed fearless, almost brazen, when she encountered depravity.

The young man sighed heavily as he looked over at Reika. Her bright, cheerful smile lit up the room as she made her way back to their table with three drinks in hand. As much as he wanted to resist her charm, Kazuki couldn't help but become more enamored with her as the days passed. Reika was truly a beauty with a calming radiance like no other. She may have been the opposite of his first crush in many ways, but the one thing that the young woman and the ninja woman had in common was genuine warmth that could melt even the iciest of hearts.

"Alright Jun," Reika said expectantly, "we're listening."

The cook took a large swig from his mug before speaking. "I'm only going to tell you what I think you should know. The rest you can learn on your own."

Kazuki and Reika both nodded in agreement.

"First thing: the blonde guy, Luka, is the mayor of this town. He's the one who makes all the rules and is in command of the Shadow Knights."

That explains why Silver looked so terrified. "But who is he? The man looks like a foreigner but speaks our language perfectly." *Not to mention that weird feeling I got from him...*

"That's not your business, Kid," Jun responded coldly. "But I will warn you not to cross paths with him. Luka is a real piece of work..." As the cook trailed off he took another swig from his mug. "Regarding what Silver said, we already figured that the Hekigun were involved and were trying to set a trap for the captain. We're so close to the end now that they're desperate to get rid of us." Jun lowered his voice as he added, "Hiiro Genji is no idiot. He knows that the captain is the key to the rebellion against him."

"But why is Red Dragon so heavily involved? It seems odd for the King of Pirates to be on some sort of mission for justice and peace," Reika wondered aloud.

"Again, that's not your business," Jun replied, but his tone wasn't as cold as before. "What the Captain's motivations are doesn't matter one lick to me. I'm here for my own reasons, as I'm sure you are too." The cook took another swig and then set the empty mug on the table.

Reika must have decided that Jun needed more ale in order to loosen his tongue, so she hopped up from her seat to get him another serving.

While the young woman was away from the table, Kazuki asked, "Are you referring to what happened to your family?"

The cook was silent as he stared at the young man. His face was hard to read, as usual, but then, uncharacteristically, Jun replied, "I'm not out to get revenge. Even if I had been, you took care of Ammon, so that would leave me without a cause."

"Then why?"

"All I'll say," Jun slowly said, "is that this messed up cycle of revenge needs to stop."

The cook's response perplexed Kazuki. This stand-offish man, who seemed to be one of the best swordsman in Tsukigen, was unwillingly fighting for an end to fighting? How did that make any sense?

But when Kazuki thought back to the incident with Yenchi and Yanchi, the young man felt like he might be able to understand what Jun meant. If the women and children who had escaped came looking for revenge one day, for their fathers or husbands' deaths, then Kazuki would suffer their wrath. Whether he had meant to or not, the young man had been a force of evil that day.

And if someone killed Kazuki, then the Ryujin crew – or at least some of them – would take their revenge upon the killer.

So then, where does the killing end? The young man wondered.

Surely not all of the Hekigun soldiers were rotten to the core, and they, too, had families that hoped for their safe return. Would those people not also seek revenge for the deaths of their loved ones? What constitutes 'justice' then? And do the labels of 'good' and 'evil' change, depending on the perspective of the majority?

As he thought more about it, Kazuki became more confused. Justice and revenge used to be very simple to him, but now...now they were complicated and worrisome concepts.

Reika slammed the mug onto the table, startling Kazuki. "Sorry about that," she said as she smiled apologetically at the young man. "Now who is this 'second-in-command' person and what kind of trouble is he in?" She asked Jun.

The cook grinned as he took hold of the newly filled mug. "Oh he's an interesting guy," he said before chugging the ale. "And he's about to be executed."

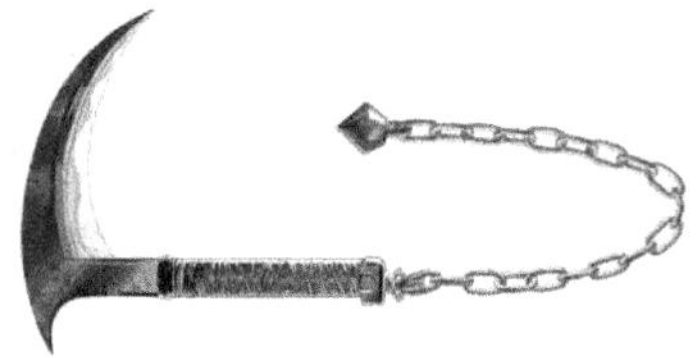

The sky wasn't particularly beautiful thanks to O-kane's brightly lit streets. Instead of an endless sea of stars, the ninja woman could only find a handful, and the varied purple and blue hues of the sky that could been seen out at sea were muted to a flat black.

"All of this unnatural brightness even messes with *my* eyesight," said the delicate woman lying next to her on the deck. "I'm surprised there haven't been more accidental fires in this town."

"Me too," Kohaku agreed.

"I wonder if Luka's icy personality keeps even the flames in line," Ni joked.

The ninja woman giggled. "That wouldn't be surprising."

Luka, the mayor of O-kane, was a man no one wanted to mess with. Although his dark and icy personality was housed in a beautiful body, there was no mistaking his true nature; Luka was cruel and calculating to his core.

I hope Kazu doesn't run into him…well, I guess Jun's at least with them. In theory.

Kohaku tried to shake the negative thoughts from her head. Worrying about 'what ifs' wasn't going to help anybody.

"I haven't heard Ami at all since I came onboard," Ni noted, "so I assume she's on a mission?"

"Yes," the ninja woman replied, "she's been so busy lately…I really miss her."

"Mmhm," Ni nodded in understanding. "They become your children in a way. I still miss my Bahst, and it's been almost four years now."

"Oh, you're right. It doesn't seem like it's been that long," Kohaku said as she thought back to her many interactions with Ni's beloved cat.

It had nearly been the same situation as Ami, where Ni had discovered Bahst as an injured kitten and took her in. She had giant paws and was larger than a Tsukigen fox, but Bahst was very sweet and had the cutest little tufts of hair on top of her ears. The ninja woman remembered how Bahst would lazily lounge on the deck of the Sphynx, or sit, still as stone, next to Ni at the shop – once someone even tried to buy Bahst thinking she was a statue.

Unfortunately, those wonderful moments came to an end nearly four years ago. Bahst's old age had finally caught up with her, and she passed gently in Ni's arms. Kohaku remembered how much her friend cried and how long it took for her to smile again afterwards. At the time, Kohaku couldn't say any words of comfort, and she had always felt bad about that.

"In Tsukigen, beloved animals are said to become gods when

they pass, so I'm sure that Bahst is still watching over you," she said softly.

Her friend sniffled and then smiled. "Thank you, Ko."

It wasn't long after that the women heard footsteps ascending the gangplank, and Kazu, Jun, and the miko walked onto the deck. It looked like they had been drinking; Kazu was supporting Jun, who was staggering, and the giggling miko clung to Kazu's waist like a belt.

"Welcome back," Kohaku said, glad to see that Kazu wasn't injured. "How did it go?"

"Scratch off two more demons from the list," Jun managed to reply. "And that idiotic Silver told me everything before I turned him over to Luka."

"Well, that's a fate worse than death," Ni said with a laugh. "But it's about time that rat got caught. He's been getting more involved with the Hekigun lately, which has been bad for business."

Ni was, of course, referring to the fact that foreigners were banned from Tsukigen by the Hekigun's ruler, Hiiro Genji. Since O-kane was the only remaining piece of Tsukigen where foreigners could go, it was a vital to keep it Hekigun-free. Not that Luka and his Shadow Knights would knowingly let a single soldier set foot on the island anyhow.

"Kazu, who's that dark-skinned woman?" the miko suddenly asked. She had meant it to be a whisper, but with her current drunken state her question was much louder than intended. Her already pink cheeks flushed a deeper shade of red when she realized that everyone had heard her.

Ni was generally a kindhearted woman though, so she simply smiled and replied, "My name is Nia. I'm Kohaku's friend from Khepria."

"Wow! All the way from Khepria!" The miko exclaimed. "I've heard about your country," she said enthusiastically, "but I've never actually met someone from there." She then looked the delicate woman up and down and added, "Your clothes are stunning. Is that a dress or a top with a skirt? Oh, is that all real gold?!"

"Yes, thank you," Ni replied. "And I'm not surprised that you haven't met anyone from Khepria before, Miss Miko, since we aren't allowed in your country at present."

"Oh, right," the miko giggled. "But my father – he's a foreigner too – told me all sorts of stories from when he visited Khepria. It sounds like such an amazing place! And he liked it too, since he wasn't shunned or imprisoned just for being different," she added.

The ninja woman was slightly surprised to hear that the miko's father was a foreigner, but it made sense when looking at her pink skin and golden hair; those weren't traits found in Tsukigen natives.

Ni smiled. "Yes, we are fortunate enough to have wise women running Khepria, which has resulted in a thriving, peaceful country that is open to different thoughts and people." Ni's pride in her country shone clearly in the way she talked about it. "Life may not be perfect, even there, but it far surpasses what Tsukigen has to offer."

"Not everyone here shares Hiiro Genji's mindset when it comes to foreigners, but there's nothing we can do about it," the miko said with a shrug. "At least we have O-kane," she added.

Kohaku shook her head. *What a careless attitude she has. And whether the miko realizes it or not, her words are rather contradictory. In fact, I wonder what her father would think of his daughter's comments?*

Ni decided to press her. "So you think that relegating foreigners to O-kane is acceptable?"

The miko cocked her head to the side and replied, "Well it's something right? I mean, better than not being able to come at all."

"But we *can't* come at all," Ni tried to explain nicely. "The only reason that we can come to O-kane is because the mayor, Luka, has basically cut the island off from Hiiro Genji and the Hekigun – in a sense declaring it separate from Tsukigen. And it's only because of Luka and his Shadow Knights' protection of the island that it has remained this way."

"Are you sure that's right?" The miko asked with a furrowed brow. "I haven't heard anything about that."

Ni shook her head. "Of course you haven't," she said with a heavy sigh, "because if you had, there would be issues on the mainland, and Hiiro Genji can't afford to have the people rise against him. Although, from my perspective, there are already plenty who would if given the opportunity."

"That's certainly true. Lately, there've been a lot of bad rumors making their rounds, and I'd say most people believe them," the miko admitted. "But is getting rid of Hiiro Genji the only way? I mean, won't another ruler take his place and then we'll be back in the same position?"

That's a surprisingly thoughtful observation coming from her.

"You have a point," Ni acknowledged, "Tsukigen can't change into a country like Khepria overnight, and installing another ruler could mean that the same awful laws and problems will continue. However," she added, "not all rulers are wicked. History shows us the bright and dark phases that each country goes through, depending on its ruler, and I am confident that Tsukigen is no different. So yes, you could have another Hiiro Genji, but you could also have someone brilliant who shines a light on your country."

The miko shrugged. "I get that, but is the hope of a better ruler really worth all of this fighting?"

Ni sighed. "To you, I suppose not."

Kohaku understood her friend well and knew that Ni's patience was at an end, but it seemed like the miko didn't get the hint. So before the miko could open her mouth, Kohaku quickly intervened.

"Kazu, can you get those two to bed by yourself? I'm sorry I can't help."

The young man shook his head. "It's alright, I can manage." He glanced over at Ni for a moment before heading towards the stairs that led below deck.

Kohaku wondered what was going through Kazu's mind. She had never heard him express his thoughts on political matters before, so she was curious as to what he thought about the issue. It was clear that he, at the very least, didn't seem to mind the fighting, but perhaps that was the Demon King's influence and not Kazu's true feelings.

The ninja woman shook her head. She would never know unless she asked, and now wasn't the time.

As the group reached the stairs, Jun grumbled something about being able to walk on his own, so Kazu let him go, but the young man had to quickly pull Jun back from the edge of the stairs when the cook nearly fell.

He still *can't hold his ale,* Kohaku thought with a sigh.

Normally she would have helped Jun back to his room, but her wounds still prevented her from moving. And, honestly, Ni would have been a worse help than Kazu, because she loved to tease people and she often took it too far for Tsukigen standards.

"That man needs a good woman," Ni said, as if on cue. "He's so handsome, I'm sure someone would be willing to put up with his personality."

Kohaku shook her head. "Just leave it, Ni. You know full well that Jun isn't ready."

Her friend clicked her tongue. "Yeah, yeah. No fun." She paused for a minute before adding with a grin, "But those two kids are ready aren't they?"

The ninja woman let out an exasperated sigh. "It's not like I can stop you, but please try to remember that your teasing is often too much for the Tsukigenese mindset."

Ni giggled with delight. "Oh, don't you worry your pretty head, Ko. In fact, I'll bet that those two figure it out on their own tonight," she snickered.

"I'm not betting on something like that. Kazu is like my little brother!" The ninja woman protested.

"Well then you'd best get ready for your little brother to become a man, because it's going to happen," Ni said matter-of-factly.

"Ugh," Kohaku groaned. "Can we please change the subject?"

"What, should we discuss Rize next? Or maybe Hanzo or Ginza?" Ni laughed.

"I'd rather stare silently at the ruined night sky," Kohaku replied drearily.

"Alright, alright," the delicate woman beside her said, still laughing, "let's talk poisons then."

Hmm. I've never seen her before…Nia, right? She seemed nice enough, but I also got an ominous vibe from her…

Kazuki shook his head. He was probably over-thinking things again. If Nia was a friend of Kohaku's, then she should be trustworthy. And the Kheprian woman seemed to be smart and worldly, like Hasunuma, so it was hard for the young man to doubt her word.

"She was really pretty, don't you think?" A lark-like voice asked.

"Uh-huh," Kazuki replied nonchalantly. He was reflecting on what Nia had said about rulers, so he was only half-listening to the young woman.

Was the bloodshed, and seemingly endless cycle of revenge, worth the chance of a better ruler? Would anything really change if Hiiro Genji was replaced? Did a candidate for the position even exist?

There were too many questions that Kazuki didn't have the answers to, so he couldn't form an opinion on the matter either way. But since he had begun to think differently about revenge, he wondered if there was another way to end the hatred and the killing.

"I wonder if she's dating one of the crew?" Reika pondered aloud, breaking Kazuki's train of thought.

"Don't think so," he replied indifferently.

"Can you two shut up for once?" Jun angrily mumbled.

Kazuki sighed. He needed to get the cook to his room as soon as possible.

Reika seemed to understand what the young man's sigh had meant, because she immediately let go of his waist and stumble-ran down the hall to open the door to Jun's room. Once it was open, she wisely positioned herself against the wall on the opposite side of the hallway. If she had gone into his room, Jun would have had a fit.

"Here ya go," Kazuki grunted as he tried to lift the cook onto his bed.

"I got it!" Jun protested, but it was clear that he did *not* have it at all.

After a minute of grunting and grumbling, the cook was in his bed and Kazuki was shutting the door behind him.

The young woman giggled. "Jun's so funny," she said, this time managing a proper whisper.

Kazuki shrugged, uninterested in starting a conversation about the cook, and then headed for his room. When they got to the end of the hall, the young man said, "You don't need help getting to your room, do you?" He wasn't really asking, since her room was next to his, but it sounded better to him than a curt 'goodnight'.

Reika twirled her hair with her finger. "Well," she said slowly, "actually I *do* need help." The young woman then reached her hand out and grabbed Kazuki's arm.

As she leaned on him, the young man felt her chest push against his skin. His pulse quickened.

OK, I'll just open the door and put her in her room, Kazuki thought to himself as he turned away from his door.

Reika giggled and rubbed her cheek against the young man's bicep.

Just open the door…

Kazuki did his best to concentrate solely on the task at hand, but his mind wanted to go elsewhere. As he turned the knob and pushed open the door, darkness greeted them. The young man reached his left arm around the doorway and felt for the flint and steel; there was a set of these, plus a candle in a ceramic holder, in each room on a shelf just inside the doorway.

"Um. I need my other hand to light this," Kazuki told the young woman after he had realized that she wasn't about to let go of his arm.

"Oh, right," Reika giggled as she released his arm.

She waited for Kazuki to light the candle before grabbing hold of him again. This time she wrapped her arms around his waist from behind, with her hands resting just below the young man's bellybutton. Kazuki's heart pounded in his chest; Reika's small, delicate fingers were dangerously close to certain things…

"Alright, well, goodnight then," the young man awkwardly announced as he turned to leave the room, with Reika still firmly attached to his back. Kazuki didn't know what was going through the young woman's head, but he knew he had to get out of there. Fast.

Suddenly Reika's fingers moved. They slowly slid up the young man's stomach to his chest and paused there for a minute before the young woman removed them.

"Are you…not interested?" She nearly whispered.

By the gods, I'm beyond interested! The young man thought, but he attempted to hide his passion in his verbal reply. "It's not that, but…well…you're um," he mumbled awkwardly, without turning to face her. "You've had a lot to drink."

A fragile punch hit Kazuki's back. When he turned around, the young man saw tears streaming down Reika's face.

"Kazu you IDIOT," she yelled before crumpling to the floor.

"Um. Wait. What's going on? Why are you crying?" Kazuki knelt on the floor next to the sobbing young woman. He had no idea what had happened or why she was so upset, nor did he have any clue as to how to get her to stop crying.

"Are you blind?! Can't you see that I care for you," she cried.

Kazuki was dumbfounded. "I…wait, you care for me as in…you *like* me?"

"Ugh! Why are men so stupid?" She asked the ceiling. "Yes I like you! It should have been obvious by now," she said as she wiped her tears on her sleeves.

"B-but you're a miko," Kazuki stammered.

"So what?"

"Aren't you supposed to stay pure and innocent or something like that?"

Reika rolled her eyes. "We miko would have died out long ago if that were the case. I mean I wasn't created out of thin air. My mother was a miko, and yet here I am."

…Good point. "But shouldn't you–"

"Look, Kazu," Reika said with a heavy sigh, cutting him off, "it's really simple. Either you like me back and we kiss, or you don't return my feelings and you leave my room. Which is it going to be?"

The young man didn't know what to do. There was a beautiful girl right in front of him, asking him to kiss her, but Kazuki didn't dare move. He was in unknown territory. What *should* he do? How was he supposed to kiss her? The young man had zero reference points besides Hasunuma, and what he learned from watching that philanderer didn't seem appropriate for this girl.

Kazuki stared at Reika. *Does she really like me?*

Tears began rolling down the young woman's cheeks once more. "I knew it," she said quietly, "you like *her* don't you?"

"What are you talking about?" The young man couldn't follow Reika's train of thought. His brain was focused on figuring out his next move.

"The ninja lady with the large breasts!" The young woman replied, sounding more than a little agitated. "You like *her* and you don't like *me*. I'm not pretty or shapely like her…" Reika said as she tried to hold back her sobs.

"Reika…" Kazuki began, but he didn't know what to say. Reika *wasn't* anything like Kohaku, but that didn't matter to him. He had fallen for the young woman the moment they had met in Giyosan. Even if she hadn't remembered, the image of her in that green kimono hadn't faded from Kazuki's mind.

The young man reached out and gently pulled Reika into him. He wrapped his arms around her and held her tightly for a few moments. Neither of them spoke or made a sound; Reika's crying gradually ceased, and then all that could be heard was the wild beating of two hearts.

Kazuki took a deep breath. *She still smells like honeysuckle,* he pleasantly noted.

"Kazu…" Reika whispered softly as her fingers began exploring his back.

The young man slowly released her from his grip, but only enough so that he could bring her face closer to his. Their first kiss was awkward and clumsy; Kazuki had moved in too quickly, so both of them had their eyes open and their teeth collided with the brusque meeting of lips. The two awkwardly separated for a brief moment in order to reset and try again. The second time their lips met, Kazuki moved more slowly and Reika closed her eyes, resulting in a soft, flat kiss. Although it lacked passion, the kiss ignited the young man's desires and he suddenly felt driven to press further. Again and again Kazuki's lips found Reika's, and each time the kiss was formed with less rigidity.

Finally, the two parted in order to catch their breaths. Reika was still nestled in Kazuki's arms, her chest pressed against his. The young man was unsure of how to progress things, so he simply followed his instincts. After meeting her lips a few more times, Kazuki's lips drifted down the young woman's neck. She let out a soft moan, which encouraged the young man to go further. When he reached her cloth collar, Kazuki gently pulled the fabric aside, revealing a small portion of Reika's small, pink breasts.

For a moment the young man halted his advance. Could he continue? Would Reika stop him if he went too far? The last thing he wanted was to hurt her, and Kazuki sensed that if he went any further, stopping would be nearly impossible for him.

Reika noticed the pause and opened her eyes. Her green orbs flickered, and the young woman grinned as she licked her lips. Then, slowly, she began to loosen the sash at her waist. Once it fell around her, Reika's top slid off of her delicate shoulders.

She was beautiful. Kazuki couldn't stop himself from drinking in the sight of her bare skin. Reika blushed and then reached out and pulled the young man's face into her neck. After an encouraging whisper in his ear, Kazuki quickly went back to work, gently brushing his lips across the young woman's soft skin.

"How much further?" The Pirate King asked as he narrowed his eyes, trying to scan the surrounding darkness.

"Not long, Captain. Once we pull around here, we'll be at the furthest dock," Rize calmly replied.

They had arrived at Masayoshi Island well before dawn. It was a difficult task, navigating solely in the light of a half-moon, but Rize had eyes as sharp as Ami's and made the job look easy. The Pirate King thanked the gods for his luck in recruiting Rize. If Hasunuma hadn't gone into Minoku that fateful day, he would never have met his helmsman. And without Rize to navigate, the Ryujin would've been lost to the sea long ago.

The Pirate King grinned as he remembered meeting the hunter. Rize was only fifteen at the time and had gone into town to sell some meat and skins from his hunts. When the young hunter overheard Hasunuma arguing with Ginza about some map coordinates, he approached the pirates, who were making quite a scene on the edge of town, and effortlessly resolved the issue by pointing to the correct location on the map.

Hasunuma had been so impressed with Rize's knowledge, and courage, that he asked him to be his navigator on the spot. The young hunter said he would love to, but that his village would starve without him, so he had to refuse. Hasunuma then offered to give a significant amount of gold to Rize's village in exchange for his service. A huge smile had spread across the young hunter's face as he readily agreed to the exchange.

"It's still hard for me to believe that you're from a remote mountain village," the Pirate King said with a grin.

The helmsman laughed. "I have gramps to thank for that. As the village elder, he held all of the knowledge and decided that I was worthy enough to share it with."

"There are rich, educated men who don't even know half as much as you," the Pirate King commended.

Rize smiled and replied, "Real, hands-on experience is the best teacher. Expensive books can only get you so far."

Hasunuma shook his head. "You say that, but every time you go into town, you buy more books."

The helmsman shrugged. "I didn't say you *can't* learn by reading. I meant that it's only a starting point for gaining true knowledge." He grinned as he added, "And not all books are made for learning."

"Ha! You're a real fox, Rize," the Pirate King laughed.

"I take that as a compliment."

Suddenly the Sphynx lurched to the right.

"Ouch," the Pirate King blandly stated as his side ran into the deck railing.

"Sorry, Captain, there're more ships than usual," Rize apologized as he spun the helm around. "Looks like some are even anchored off to the side."

"Happens every time they have their festival for the sea gods," the Pirate King sighed.

Normally, Hasunuma would avoid Masayoshi Island, especially during festival days, but he didn't have a choice this time. Festival or not, the waters around Masayoshi Island were always teeming with vessels; it had been that way ever since the Hekigun took over and converted the back half of the island into their prison. It was certainly a prime location to lock up their enemies, since the back half of Masayoshi Island consisted of numerous, tall, unscalable mountains and sheer cliffs. But the villagers living on the island hated their relatively new neighbors. And although the villagers would never have dared to pick a fight with the Hekigun, they could be counted on not to assist the Hekigun if there were, say, an escaped prisoner on the run.

"I'll tell the others to get ready," Hasunuma said as he left Rize at the helm and headed below deck.

The Sphynx was a beautifully crafted cargo ship, and the Pirate King had always wanted to acquire it someday. He loved the intricate woodcarvings that were painted with gold and bright colors; the images of which were so foreign and curious, they greatly piqued his interest. Hasunuma had once asked Nia if the Kheprians often wore animal-head masks like those in the images on her ship, and the only response he got was: "You'll have to see for yourself one day." The Pirate King didn't think he'd ever make it there, but even so he appreciated the offer.

Besides the craftsmanship, the Pirate King also loved the speed of the Sphynx. From the look of the ship, it would seem to move purely on a row of large oars that stuck out from small ports on both sides, but this Kheprian cargo ship had a secret; an underwater propelling system that was an engineer's masterpiece. According to Nia, the engineer was actually a friend of hers who offered to gift Nia the contraption if Nia let her engineer friend use the Sphynx as her experimental piece. The offer had paid off, because now the Sphynx was the fastest non-sailing ship Hasunuma had ever seen. And all it took to run the propelling system was some burly manpower – which the Pirate King thankfully had Hanzo and Ginza for.

The Sphynx's speed was actually the first reason he had asked to borrow it. While normally it took about four days for a sailing ship to get to Masayoshi Island from O-kane, with the secret underwater propeller of the Sphynx, it only took one. The second reason was that the Kheprian cargo ship wasn't nearly as recognizable as the Ryujin. And In order for his plan to work, Hasunuma needed to land on Masayoshi Island without anyone noticing.

"Cap'n we're, uh, almost ready," Ginza said as he peaked his head out from around the barely opened door.

"Good. Rize says we'll be docking soon."

"Say, Cap'n…is this *really* necessary?" Ginza nervously asked.

"Of course it is. Don't you trust me?"

"Aye, Cap'n!" Ginza shouted. "But, uh, don't tell Little Oni 'bout this, OK?" He added quietly.

The Pirate King laughed. "Don't worry, the kid won't hear about it from me. Now hurry up. I need you and Hanzo up on deck to help us dock."

"Aye, Cap'n!"

Kazuki's eyelids fluttered open, and he stared blankly at the ceiling for a while, trying to wrap his head around what had happened. Without moving his head, the young man slowly looked down at the beautiful young woman asleep in his arms. The blanket had slipped from her bare shoulders, so Kazuki carefully pulled it back into place. Reika moaned something, unwrapped her arms from around Kazuki's torso, and then turned over onto her other side. Her bare back was now resting along the young man's side and he felt himself start to rouse.

Before his baser instincts could take over, Kazuki hopped out of the bed. He then turned back and gently tucked the blanket around Reika so she wouldn't get cold. Grabbing his clothes and hastily putting them on, Kazuki left the room as quickly as he could. Instead of heading to his room, he proceeded straight for the deck of the Ryujin.

As soon as the cool night air hit his skin, the young man felt himself relax. But there remained an odd sensation inside of him; it was a sort of restlessness or excitement that he hadn't felt before. Was it because of the few hours he had just spent with Reika? Kazuki shook his head and tried not to recount the event. The whole point of leaving her room was to *not* get worked up.

The young man sat on the deck and looked up at the sky. A disappointed sigh escaped his lips when only a few stars were visible.

"Were you looking for a wishing star?" A voice suddenly asked.

Startled, Kazuki quickly turned around and saw Nia sitting with her back against a stack of crates. Kohaku was sitting next to Nia, but she had fallen asleep, with her head resting on the Kheprian woman's shoulder.

"Do you want me to get a blanket?" The young man asked, thinking that the women were probably cold sitting out on the deck.

But Nia shook her head and said, "No, thank you, Kazuki. Our blood runs hot, so this cooler air feels nice."

"Alright," the young man replied before turning his gaze back to the sky. A minute later, he remembered the Kheprian woman's question and turned to ask her what she had meant.

Nia smiled. "A wishing star is something that we Kheprians look for when we fall in love. The legend says that if you see one, your wish to be with the person you love will come true."

Love…is that what this weird feeling is?

The young man felt his cheeks grow hot and he looked away from the Kheprian woman.

He heard Nia laugh. "Young love sure is thrilling. Sometimes I wish I could go back to those early days," she said fondly, "but I'm also quite satisfied with how things are now. Well, except for this execution business." She sighed heavily as she added, "My man has the worst luck."

Huh? Execution? "Oh! Are you referring to Hasunuma's second-in-command?" The young man asked.

Nia nodded. "Yes, that's my man."

"So then why are you here?" Kazuki asked in a stern voice. "If you love him, shouldn't you be trying to rescue him?"

The Kheprian woman grinned. "I could have done that a few

years back, but my vision isn't so great now. If I went, I'd probably end up being a burden."

"Oh," Kazuki replied awkwardly. He should have realized that Nia couldn't see when he'd noticed that her eyes were closed, but for some reason he hadn't made the connection.

"It's fine though, because Hasu should be there soon to rescue my man for me," she said calmly with a wave of her hand.

Kazuki gave her a confused look. "But…the Hekigun have him on Masayoshi Island, right? Which takes about four days to get to from here."

Nia nodded.

"And Hasunuma left sometime while we were going after Silver, which means he's still got three or so days to go before–"

"Yes, normally that would be the case," the Kheprian woman interrupted. "But I lent him my ship, so he'll get there in time."

Kazuki wasn't sure what Nia was talking about, but he wasn't going to argue with her about whether or not Hasunuma would be able to save her loved one.

"You really trust him, don't you?"

Nia smiled. "Of course I do. Hasu's a strong and honorable man. If he says he'll rescue my man, then he will."

"I don't know if I'd call him honorable, but he *is* very strong," Kazuki admitted.

The Kheprian woman laughed. "Yes, well, no one is perfect."

"How long have you known Hasunuma?" The young man asked. "I hadn't heard anything about his second-in-command until recently, and I've been on the Ryujin for over three years now." Kazuki had been wondering about Hasunuma's second-in-command, but since Jun hadn't told him much, he figured this was his chance to learn something.

"That's probably because for the past three years, my man has been on a bunch of secret missions for Hasu. You know, taking out Hekigun bases and pillaging their ships and the like," she replied nonchalantly. "But we've known Hasu and Ko for…I think about seven years now."

Kazuki was shocked. This woman and her 'man' had known Hasunuma and Kohaku for longer than he had, even though, in his mind, they seemed like newcomers to the Ryujin crew.

"My man and I had traveled to Tsukigen to trade – since that's my primary business – but before we could get to O-kane, our ship was intercepted by the Hekigun. It's not that we *couldn't* take them out," she explained, "but we weren't sure if we *should* or not. You know, in case that would trigger a big war or something between our countries. But before we could make a decision, the Ryujin appeared and took out the Hekigun for us."

No surprises there.

"And then, since my man is a warrior to his core, he challenged Hasu to a battle. My man was so shocked when he lost," the Kheprian woman said with a laugh, "that he swore to serve under Hasu until the day he could defeat him. So here we are, seven years later, still hanging around Tsukigen."

"That's…not exactly what I was expecting to hear, but it also isn't surprising, knowing Hasunuma," Kazuki replied. If nothing else, Hasunuma was a formidable opponent that Kazuki never wanted to have to fight seriously, regardless of the Demon King's feelings. The Hekigun were very unfortunate to have him as an enemy.

The young man's brain then wandered back to the previous conversation that Nia had with Reika. "Can I ask you more about what you were talking about earlier? With rulers and such."

The Kheprian woman gently smiled. "I'd be delighted to share my thoughts with you, Kazuki, but it might be difficult for you to understand since you haven't traveled outside of Tsukigen."

Kazuki shook his head. "I feel like I can keep up."

Nia's smile widened into a grin. "Alright then," she said, "let's start with the basics. You know that Hiiro Genji murdered the Tsukigen Emperor and took over the country about twenty one years ago, yes?"

The young man nodded. When he lived with the old man, Kazuki had listened to the old man tell stories every night. Some were legends of gods and demons, while some were historical tales of Tsukigen. The story of how Hiiro Genji and the Hekigun took over was one of those tales he had listened to many times.

According to the old man, Hiiro Genji had once been close to the Emperor, but one day betrayed him. Instead of executing him, the Emperor chose to expel Hiiro Genji from Tsukigen; a mistake that would cost the Emperor his life seven or so years later. When Hiiro Genji returned, he had a small army with him – the Hekigun – and he stormed the palace and murdered the Emperor. He then placed himself in charge, as ruler of Tsukigen, and has been in power since.

"Well," Nia continued, "before Hiiro Genji took over, Tsukigen was a leading trader in the world. Not only that, but Tsukigenese crafts and goods were spreading like wildfire in other countries. The beauty and quality of each piece is what captivated others – or at least that's what got me interested," the Kheprian woman said with a smile. "Anyways, I suppose my point is that extreme policy changes are just part of being a country that is ruled over by one person. Whomever is in charge will make the decisions, and no one else has a say. It's an 'obey or die' sort of ruling. Whereas in Khepria, we have a group of women who make joint decisions, so that our laws do not follow the whims of one person. Or you could take Hanzo's homeland, Skövalgar, as an example of a country where there are many 'rulers'; the country is broken up into territories that are then each governed by one family. So if you don't like the laws of one territory, you can move to another."

She even knows about Hanzo's homeland?

Kazuki's stomach sank. He suddenly felt as if he were a passing stranger, rather than a true Ryujin crew member.

"Rulers may look different around the world, but the main theme is the same: with a wise, benevolent ruler, there is peace and prosperity, while a selfish, malevolent ruler will always bring calamity upon the land and its people."

"So then how do we get a good ruler?" the young man asked.

Nia shook her head. "Unfortunately with countries like this, where the people don't get to choose a ruler, it's luck of the draw. Even within family lines, you'll sometimes get a bad seed – which I'm sure Hanzo can tell you all about," she added knowingly. "However, in this specific instance, where the people have the chance to oust the ruler, the person to take Hiiro Genji's place can be chosen."

Kazuki furrowed his brow. "Won't that cause a lot of problems? I mean, more fighting?"

The Kheprian woman nodded. "Yes, normally you'd see people vying for the top spot, but in this case there is only one possible candidate."

"Please don't tell me it's Hasunuma," Kazuki said with a grimace.

"Ha ha ha!" Nia laughed aloud. "No, that would be awful," she replied. "But I take it you didn't know that the Emperor had two children: a son and a daughter."

Kazuki's eyes widened. That information wasn't a part of the story the old man had told him.

Nia nodded. "And one of them, the son, is still alive, being held captive by the Hekigun in an undisclosed location."

The young man's pulse quickened. "So if we put the former Emperor's son back in his rightful place, then you think Tsukigen would thrive again?"

"*I* think so," the Kheprian woman admitted, "but we won't know for sure unless Hasu's plan to overthrow Hiiro Genji is a success."

Kazuki stood up and walked over to the rail. He couldn't sit still; his mind was racing, trying to make sense of what Nia had just told him. Could Hasunuma's plan really work? Would reinstalling the Emperor's line really bring peace and prosperity to Tsukigen?

Although, for those following the Hekigun's laws, Tsukigen could be considered a peaceful place already.

Other than pirates, rogue samurai, and other typical lawless criminals, there were no wars being fought; only Hasunuma and his crew were actively taking on the Hekigun. And it didn't seem to Kazuki that the average villager was suffering more than usual in regards to providing for his or her family. So why did it still feel so uncomfortable, so stagnant, and so dangerous to live in Tsukigen? Ignoring the Hekigun's secret atrocities, most villages and towns were relatively safe. Was it the lack of foreigners and trade that made such a difference? Or perhaps the feeling was something that Kazuki felt as a young person, trying to find his own place in the world?

Suddenly a bright light flashed in the young man's eyes. Kazuki winced and squinted as he looked towards the horizon where the sun had just begun to emerge from its watery sleep. The image energized him, stirring a feeling of hope within the young man's soul.

"I'll admit that I'm a bit overwhelmed by all of this information," he told the Kheprian woman, "but it's like you said, there's only one way to find out." Kazuki then turned to look at Nia and grinned. "And I'm going to give it my all to make sure Hasunuma's plan is a success."

The Pirate King watched as the golden orb slowly rose from the water, breaking the dim line of the horizon. Rays of yellow and orange shattered the hazy darkness, bringing light to the world once more.

"I could never tire of that sight," he said to himself as a smile spread across his face. "It's a shame that this beautiful view is wasted on those Hekigun bastards."

The bay, hundreds of feet below, was awash with the warm glow of the rising run. A few small fishing vessels bobbed around in the relatively calm waters, not too far from the shore. It was such a warm and pleasant picture, but the Pirate King shivered as the cool mountain breeze playfully whirled around him.

"I always forget how much colder it is up high," he mumbled as he breathed into his cupped hands, attempting to warm them.

A bell rang in the distance, reminding the Pirate King of his mission.

"Have any a' you lazy, good-fer-nothin' pigs caught sight a' his ship yet?" An angry voice carried over the wind.

"Not yet, Sir!" Another voice responded.

The Pirate King peered around the edge of the boulder he had been leaning against.

"Gods be damned!" The angry man spat. He was rather large and muscular, and was wearing a distinguishable hat and coat. "Didn't he get Silver's message?"

"I believe he did, Sir," the other man, a soldier, replied. "Perhaps we should have given him more time? Normally it takes–"

"Are you sayin' my plan was wrong?!" The angry man yelled as he grabbed the soldier by his throat and hoisted him into the air.

"Gah! No, Sir!" The soldier gasped.

The angry man let go of the soldier and said, "That's right! I ain't wrong. He'll be here." He adjusted the hat on his head and commanded, "Keep yer eyes on the water, men!"

A chorus of 'Yes, Sir!' rang out from behind the angry man. There must have been at least eighty soldiers standing on the plateau that overlooked the sea.

The Pirate King whistled in awe. *Someone's getting antsy.*

"An' bring out the prisoner," the angry man shouted. "We'll

march him t' the square."

Some of the soldiers exchanged glances with each other. Hasunuma could tell that they wanted to protest the earlier-than-scheduled execution, but they were too afraid to speak up. A smaller group of about ten men responded to the order and left the plateau.

Only ten? Hasunuma grinned. *They don't know Douglas like I do.*

He hopped down from his spot amongst the rocks, above the plateau, and dusted himself off.

Well, I guess it's about time.

Without a sound, the Pirate King snuck behind the rows of men watching the horizon and made his way towards the fortress' main square.

Hasunuma arrived as the ten men were escorting the prisoner towards the gallows. There was already a modest crowd gathered around to watch the hanging. Most of them were villagers from the island's small port town, but there were also quite a few soldiers scattered throughout as well. Whether they were there for sport or duty was anyone's guess.

The Pirate King hid in the shadows between two buildings that were on the edge of the square and watched as the ten men tried to pull the prisoner up the steps to the platform. The chains around his hands, neck, and feet were tight, but no matter how hard the ten pulled, the prisoner wouldn't budge.

"Havin' second thoughts?" A familiar voice called out. It was the angry man from earlier. He sat comfortably on an elevated, covered bench that was off to the side. "'Cause I can have my men go get yer wife so she can join you, if that's whatcha want," the man threatened.

The prisoner glared at the man in charge. And then, step by step, he slowly made his way to the top of the platform where the noose swung freely in the mountain breeze.

"That's more like it," the man laughed cruelly.

The ten men now attempted to put the rope around the prisoner's neck, but he was so tall that they had to retrieve a small ladder in order to reach his head.

Before they could complete their task, the Pirate King made his entrance.

"Pardon the intrusion, but would you mind letting him go?" he asked with a smile.

The villagers gasped and backed away as the Pirate King made his way through the crowd, towards the platform.

"Heh heh," the man in charge laughed, "I knew you'd show up, Red Dragon. Even scum like you wouldn't allow yer second-in-command t' die like a dog at the gallows."

"All of this effort just to catch little ol' me…I'm flattered, Mr. Warden," the Pirate King replied. "However, I would very much like you to release your prisoner."

"Hah! I'll bet you would. But that's not happening," the warden spat.

"Even if I surrender myself to you in his stead?"

The crowd gasped once again at the sudden development. They began murmuring to each other, and even the warden looked a little shocked at the Pirate King's words.

"You what?!" The warden stood up. "This' all a trick, isn't it? Where's yer despicable crew hiding?"

The Pirate King shook his head. "It's no trick, and there's no crew. I simply want to exchange my life for his."

The warden's face turned red as he shouted, "Gods be damned, Red Dragon! I'm no fool! Men, surround an' seize 'im!"

The crowd booed at the warden's command, but they didn't dare interfere with the soldiers that advanced towards the Pirate King. As the ten from the platform joined with the soldiers from the crowd, they surrounded the Pirate King and ushered him onto the platform. Hasunuma made no move to protect himself.

As he stood next to the prisoner, the Pirate King asked the warden, "Will you not reconsider my offer?"

"T' the Demon Realm with yer offer," the warden spat. "I'm taking both a' yer heads today."

The Pirate King sighed. "If that's the way you want it, then so be it."

Without warning, the chains around the prisoner suddenly shattered as a long, trident-shaped spear flew through air, impaling five of the soldiers on the platform at once. The prisoner quickly grabbed the trident and pulled it from the bodies. Before making another move, the prisoner looked in the direction from which the weapon came. He grinned as he saw Hasunuma smiling and waving at him from a distance; another Pirate King was hiding in the shadows between two buildings at the edge of the square.

"And don't worry," the Pirate King standing next to the prisoner said calmly, "she's safe."

The prisoner's grin widened as he turned towards the Pirate King on the platform. "Then there's no reason for me to hold back," he said before swinging his trident around him. Four soldiers were knocked off the platform in an instant, and all of them had their torsos split open.

Shouts rang out from the crowd as two very ugly women rushed forward and engaged the soldiers on the ground. One wielded a large, heavy-looking blade while the other attacked with golden fists.

The Pirate King couldn't contain his laughter. "You two look lovely," he shouted at the ugly women as he dodged a soldier's blade and then sliced the man's hands off with his red dragon sword.

"Shut it, Cap'n," one shouted back as she sliced a guard in two.

"I'm never doing this again," the other grumbled as she punched a soldier's face so hard that his neck twisted around and snapped.

"Bwahahaha!" The prisoner suddenly burst into roaring laughter. "Hanzo, Ginza, why are you two dressed like that?"

"So we could sneak in with the crowd without the guards knowing," Hanzo replied gruffly.

The prisoner continued laughing. "You sure know how to plan an exciting rescue, Captain."

"I thought you'd enjoy a little extra flare," the Pirate King replied with a grin.

All of the soldiers were turned into corpses in less than one minute. All except for the warden, that is. He stood, frozen in fear, staring slack-jawed at the carnage before him.

"He's all yours, Douglas," the Pirate King said as he patted the prisoner on his back.

"Wonderful," Douglas grinned.

Kazuki made his way down the hallway towards Reika's room. He was about to knock on the young woman's door, but stopped when he heard voices coming from inside.

"…was bound to happen at some point," an unfamiliar female voice said.

"But was the timing alright? I mean, it all happened so fast," said a voice that sounded like Reika's.

"Look, sweet and innocent is nice and all, but not in bed," the other female said.

"Are you saying that I'm *not* sweet and innocent?"

"Hey, every girl has her own way – I don't judge."

"Ugh. Anyways," Reika said with disdain, "What am I supposed to do now? If he finds out–"

"He *won't* find out, so don't panic."

Kazuki's stomach dropped.

"You're right, *as usual*," Reika said with a heavy sigh.

"That's because I have a few centuries on you, young lady," the other female said with a laugh.

Something clicked in Kazuki's brain and he suddenly couldn't restrain himself any longer; he had to confirm the source of the other voice.

The young man knocked on the door. "It's me," he said softly.

"K-kazu?! Oh, uh, j-just a minute," Reika's voice called out from inside.

The young man heard a thump, then a curse, and a minute or so later the door opened.

"G-good morning," she said with a nervous smile. The young woman's cheeks were flush, and her clothes and hair were disheveled; it was clear that she had rushed to get dressed just now.

Kazuki wished he hadn't knocked.

"Morning," the young man replied as his brain conjured up images from a few hours ago. He almost let himself get distracted, but Kazuki managed to reign in his primal urges and focus on the issue at hand. He made a show of looking around the room and asked, "Where did she go?" Although he hadn't expected anyone else to be there.

"W-what?" Reika asked, sounding nervous.

"I thought I heard you talking to another woman, so I figured Nia was in here," the young man lied. He had just talked with Nia on the deck, so he knew she couldn't possibly be in Reika's room.

The young woman looked away from Kazuki and played with her hair. "O-oh, I didn't realize I was being so loud…"

Is she going to admit it?

"Um, Kazu…can you keep a secret?"

Kazuki's heart leapt in his chest. *Here it comes.* He walked into her room, closed the door behind him, and nodded.

"Well, I, um…wasn't talking to a person, per say," she said slowly. "Do you remember how I said before that I can channel spirits?"

Kazuki nodded. His heart raced.

"Well…I sort of channeled one just now," she said, still facing away from Kazuki, "and that's who you heard me talking to."

"Oh. I see," the young man replied, crestfallen. *Liar.*

"I'm sorry," she said rather genuinely, "I would have told you earlier, but I didn't think you'd believe me."

You were right about that.

"Since you don't believe in the gods and all," she hastily added.

"Don't worry about it," Kazuki said with a feigned smile.

There was an awkward silence that filled the room.

"Um, I'm sorry I, uh, didn't wake up when you left earlier," she said timidly, the pink of her cheeks turning crimson.

"It's fine," was the only response the young man could manage.

Another awkward silence took place as Reika twirled her hair and glanced sideways at Kazuki, unable to look him in the eye.

As he stood there, watching the young woman's bashful display, Kazuki's mind was racing. He wasn't sure what to ask or how to say any of the things he wanted to. It was as if every word were a tripwire that would lead to a disastrous outcome. But, in the end, his mouth betrayed him, and, as his lips parted, the question "Was last night real," escaped.

Reika froze.

It was too late to retract, so Kazuki pushed forward. "When you said you liked me, were you telling the truth?"

"Of course I was!" Reika insisted, her eyes finally meeting Kazuki's. "Do you think I'm the sort of woman who would do something like *that* with just anyone?"

"I didn't think so, but what do I know," the incensed young man grumbled. "How do I know that you're you and not some spirit or whatever?"

"Oh, so you think some spirit likes you and that I let her use my body to be with you? What kind of sick person would do something like that?!" Reika snapped.

"No! That's not what I meant," Kazuki retorted.

"Well then what *did* you mean?" Reika asked, clearly upset.

The young man knew he had already stumbled over a few tripwires, but he couldn't see how to fix the situation. He could only pull fragments of information from situations he'd seen or heard back in Mizuya or from towns he had visited with the Ryujin crew.

"Well?" Reika asked impatiently.

There was one phrase in particular that Kazuki remembered hearing often, so he decided to try it out. "I'll tell you once you've calmed down."

Reika's eyes widened and Kazuki could see within them the impending hurricane of fury. "Once I've '*calmed down*'?!" She exclaimed. "Kazu you are the most idiotic, thick-headed, and insensitive jerk I've ever met!" Reika shoved past Kazuki and opened the door. He could hear her yell, "Idiot," again after she slammed the door shut behind her.

Kazuki put his hand to his forehead and sighed heavily. "Yeah, I know."

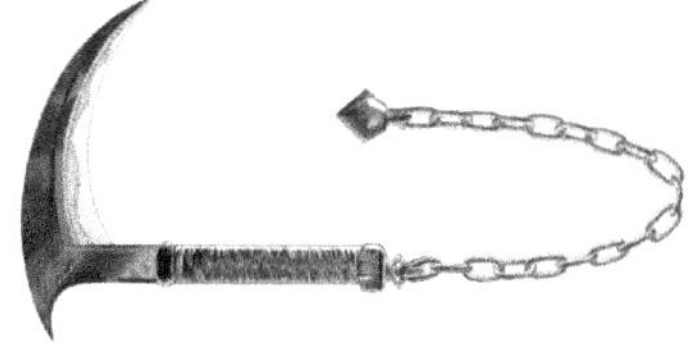

Screee!

"Yes, Ami, I'm happy to see you too," Kohaku said with a smile as she gently stroked the falcon's chest.

Ami playfully snapped her beak at the ninja woman.

"Rize should be back soon," Kohaku assured her, "so get some rest while you can."

Scree-screee!

The falcon flapped her wings, but didn't leave the ninja woman's forearm.

"Do I need to take her in?" Ni asked. She was offering to take Ami into the common room where the falcon usually stayed while she was resting on board.

Kohaku shook her head. "She'll go if she wants to."

Ami then hopped onto the ninja woman's shoulder and nipped at Kohaku's hair. It was the falcon's way of showing her affection.

"Aww, that's so swe–" Ni began to say, but she was cut off by loud, stomping feet approaching.

An angry miko stormed past the two women and headed straight for the rail. Kohaku almost thought that the miko would throw herself over, but instead she just stood there and screamed.

The people walking around the port stopped and stared at the miko for a moment. When they realized she wasn't in danger, they continued on with their business.

After releasing her frustration, the miko dropped to her knees and began to cry.

"Oh, my," Ni commented, clearly interested in what had caused the emotional explosion.

Kohaku then heard the miko mumbling, "Stupid jerk, stupid jerk, stupid jerk," between sobs.

The ninja woman wasn't exactly sure what to say to the miko, so she was thankful when Ni stepped in.

"Are you referring to Jun or Kazuki?" the delicate woman boldly asked.

The miko jumped and turned around. It was clear that she hadn't noticed the two women beforehand, and the shock stopped her tears. While furiously wiping her eyes with her sleeve, the miko said, "Oh, sorry, I'm in the way aren't I?"

She stood up as if to leave, but Ni stopped her, saying, "No, you're fine where you are."

The miko sat back down and lowered her eyes to the deck. "Okay," she sniffled.

"Your name's Reika, right? Mine's Kohaku, in case you forgot," the ninja woman said with a smile, trying to keep the miko calm. "We haven't had much of a chance to talk, but if you–"

"Look, lady, I'm not in the mood right now," the miko snapped. "Why don't you go bother Kazu instead? I'm sure he'd *love* some attention from someone like you."

Um. That was rude and totally uncalled for…but now I know who she thinks is a jerk.

"Men can be pretty thickheaded sometimes," Ni chimed in. "Even young men, like Kazuki."

Reika's demeanor immediately changed. "UGH. Seriously! What is *wrong* with him?" she vented. "I mean, you don't just accuse the girl you – well, you know – of being a whore and then tell her to 'calm down'! All because of a stupid misunderstanding!"

The ninja woman simply listened as the miko continued her rant, while Ni's grin slowly widened; she *loved* this kind of drama.

"Men are so dense!" The miko shouted as she continued her tirade. "Why can't they see when a girl is trying her hardest for the guy she likes?"

Because they're dense idiots, like you said.

"It's not like I'm this way because I *want* to be," she added with a heavy sigh, "But he'll never understand that."

"It's hard to understand someone when you haven't properly talked things through," Kohaku replied softly.

"That's true…" Reika said slowly. "Wait, why am I talking to *you* about guy problems anyways? You probably have men fighting over you like a pack of hungry wolves with a carcass."

I'm a carcass, am I? "That's not true at all," was all Kohaku said aloud.

"Yeah right," Reika huffed, "not with *that* set."

The ninja woman rolled her eyes, "Oh for the sake of the gods, it has *nothing* to do with chest size!" *You stupid, jealous bitch.* "And it's not like I *want* to have these huge things – they're always in the way!"

Scree-scree-screeee! Ami nervously screeched and flapped her wings. Ever since the ninja woman got her voice back, the falcon become agitated when Kohaku raised her voice.

"So you admit that they're huge."

That's the way you want to play it? Fine. "You know what I think? It's your attitude that's holding you back," Kohaku said as she glared at the miko.

"Well then, that's great for you, isn't it," Reika retorted. "You can swoop in and take Kazu all for yourself, you old crow!"

"What?! Okay, clearly you've misinterpreted our relationship," the ninja woman said as she folded her arms across her chest. "Kazu is like a little brother to me."

Scree-scree! The falcon called out before she took off.

Oh, sorry Ami. Kohaku briefly thought as she watched the falcon fly up and land on the rail of the crow's nest.

The miko then said in a softer tone, "Wait a minute…so, you *don't* like Kazu? In a romantic way."

Kohaku vigorously shook her head. *I don't know where she got that idea, but that's ridiculous…hopefully Hasu doesn't think the same thing!*

"Oh…oh!" Reika suddenly exclaimed. "Oh my gosh, I am *so* sorry for being so rude to you, Kohaku. I just thought…well…yeah," she said as she giggled a little to herself.

What a brat. "Whatever. I'm just glad that we got that straightened out," Kohaku said with a sigh.

Ni burst into laughter. "Ha ha ha! I'm sorry, but I've never experienced this side of Ko, and it's highly amusing."

"I'm glad that you're entertained," the ninja woman replied flatly.

Ni patted her friend on the shoulder. "You're like a sister to me, Ko. I love seeing different aspects of you," she said with a genuine smile. "Being yourself is nothing to be ashamed of."

After a nod from Kohaku, Ni then turned her attention to the miko. "So you have feelings for Kazuki," she began, "but you're unsure of how he feels?"

Reika nodded.

"Didn't last night make that clear?" The delicate woman asked with a mischievous grin.

The miko turned bright red. "Well…I, uh, I guess," she struggled to reply. "But what if it was a spur-of-the-moment thing for him?"

Ni shook her head. "I doubt it. Kazuki's as innocent as you, perhaps even more so since he's been isolated from others his age for so long."

"But what if he learned how act from Red Dragon?" The miko fretfully asked in return.

Ni started laughing so much that she couldn't respond.

Kohaku sighed, shook her head, and said, "I really hope he's not Kazu's role model."

"Agreed," the delicate woman finally managed to say. "I think Rize would make the best role model, don't you? He's the quiet, hunter type who also has the charm of a well-mannered young man."

"Jun's pretty hot too," Reika added.

"Ha! That he is, Miss Miko, but his personality is that of a stray. It would take a lot of effort to tame him," Ni replied. "In other words, Rize can show a range of emotions and can converse in a civil manner with others, even though he prefers to be alone, while Jun shuns and snaps at everyone like an alley cat."

"Oh, I see. But Jun didn't seem that bad to me," the miko offered.

Ni glanced at Kohaku. They both knew the real reason why Jun was softer towards women, but it wasn't a story that they thought should be shared freely. So the delicate woman simply said, "He mellows with each passing day."

The miko seemed to accept the answer, because she moved on and asked, "What about the two big guys?"

The delicate woman rested her chin on her knuckles. "Hmm," she said before a pause. "Hanzo and Ginza are good men, but they're a bit too old for what Kazuki needs."

Reika nodded. "Mmhmm. I can see that."

Am I the only girl who doesn't like talking about this kind of stuff? Kohaku wondered as she sat listening to her friend and the miko chattering.

"I wonder who's the most popular?" The miko pondered aloud.

"Oh it's definitely Rize," Ni instantly replied. "Jun's a close second, even with his hostile personality, but since he doesn't leave the ship that often, not as many women get a chance to see him. I think Hanzo's case is the same, but it could also be that he's too intimidatingly large for most Tsukigen women. Although he's quite popular with the women – and some men – on O-kane. And Ginza would have more fans if he didn't have such a gruff way of talking," the delicate woman summarized.

"What about the other two?" Reika quietly asked. She was either embarrassed to ask about Kazu, or she didn't really want to know how popular he was.

Ni grinned and stared pointedly at Kohaku. "How popular would you say the captain is?"

The ninja woman glared at her friend.

"I'll bet he surpasses Rize, but we'll never know, since a certain ninja woman keeps getting in his way," Ni said pointedly.

Kohaku's expression read: *'I hate you sometimes.'*

The delicate woman laughed and playfully patted her friend on the back. "As for Kazuki," she continued, gracefully deciding to drop the previous topic, "I'm not sure, since I just met him."

An audible exhale came from the miko.

"But," Ni added with a grin, "he's handsome, eligible, and innocent, so surely he has some fans."

Reika's eyes widened. She then timidly asked, "Do any of them have lovers?"

The delicate woman's grin widened. Kohaku knew what was coming and decided to intervene.

"Other than Ginza, who seems to have a favorite companion in Giyosan, none of the Ryujin men have a lover," the ninja woman quickly replied to the miko.

Ni gave Kohaku a woeful look and then sighed heavily. "Yes," she grudgingly agreed, "it's surprising, but none of them are spoken for. And, believe me, I've tried to set them up, but it seems that either the Ryujin men are too busy or just not interested," she said with clear disappointment.

I think it's because you pry too much.

"Maybe they'll change their minds when they get tired of being pirates," the miko offered with a bright tone. She must have been happy to hear that Kazu wasn't 'spoken for'.

Ni laughed. "Men never tire of freedom."

Reika rolled her eyes and replied, "Must be nice."

"Yes, well, when you live in a man's world, that's how the story is written," the delicate woman calmly offered.

Kohaku had expected her friend to go into another tirade of how awful Tsukigen was compared to Khepria, but she was surprised to see Ni show some restraint on that front. Perhaps it was because Ni realized that the miko didn't have the right mindset for that sort of discussion.

"So what should I do?" The miko suddenly asked, looking expectantly at Ni and Kohaku.

"What should you do…?"

"About Kazu! He said some mean things and then I called him a jerk and left the room…do you think he hates me now?”

Kohaku stared blankly at the miko. She knew that Reika was immature, but she hadn't realized to what extent until just then. “No,” she replied slowly, “I'm sure he doesn't hate you now.” *Although* I *might...*

Ni nodded. “Agreed. Kazuki seems like the type to easily forgive cute girls.”

The miko's shoulders relaxed and she breathed a sigh of relief.

“I don't know what you two were arguing about, but maybe it would be best to talk it through. And you should be honest with him,” Kohaku advised.

Reika made a strange face. “Well, I can't really be super honest with him…but I'll do what I can.”

“As long as you smile sweetly at him, Kazuki can't deny you,” Ni said with a laugh.

Kohaku gave her friend a look. *Don't tell her stuff like that.*

“O-okay I'll try to,” the miko responded with an awkward smile.

As Reika stood up, ready to leave, Ni stopped her and said, “Oh, and you'll need to stay in Kazuki's room for the next few days at least. When my man gets back, we'll need a room, and since there's only one empty room on this ship, we'll be taking it.”

The miko's cheeks flushed and she looked away from Kohaku and Ni.

“Might as well take advantage of the situation,” the delicate woman added with a sly grin, “since you won't have to sneak around now.”

Reika turned bright red and ran off without a word, presumably below deck.

Ni laughed, but Kohaku poked her friend's arm and said, "This is what I'm talking about. You say *too much.*"

Kazuki continued to stare blankly at the wall as his mind wandered. *What am I supposed to do? I think I love her, but what if she…no, she wouldn't…right?*

"Agh!" The young man scratched his head as he let out a frustrated sigh. Why were women so complicated? Why was life so complicated? And why couldn't he find the answers?

The young man was now under the impression that everything he thought or did was wrong. He shouldn't have taken revenge on Ammon, he shouldn't have interfered in Yamaōgi, he shouldn't have gotten Reika involved in all of this, he probably shouldn't have even joined the Ryujin crew in the first place…the list of things he regretted seemed endless as Kazuki's self-criticism continued, unchecked, in his mind.

Everyone would have been better off if I had truly died that night in Mizuya.

There was no rebuttal from the Demon King this time.

As the young man's mind spiraled out of control, there was suddenly a knock at the door. Kazuki's stomach dropped. He wasn't ready to face Reika yet, but he couldn't leave the knock unanswered, so he slowly turned around and opened the door.

"Oh, it's you," he said flatly as his eyes met Jun's.

The cook seemed surprised to see Kazuki as well. He glanced

down the hallway and then looked back at the young man. "This is the spare room, the one the miko is using, right?"

Oh, oops. Kazuki had forgotten that he wasn't in his own room. *This is awkward...*

Jun sighed, crossed his arms and said, "Look, I don't care about whatever is going on with you two, I just need help getting supplies at the market. If you two help me, I won't mention this to the captain."

The prospect of helping Jun shop wasn't great, but it was far better than being relentlessly teased by Hasunuma. "Sure," Kazuki replied with a nod.

"Then both of you meet me up on deck in five," the cook said as he turned and headed back towards the galley.

"Um...OK," a quiet voice chimed.

The young man's heart almost stopped. He hadn't noticed Reika until Jun had walked past her in the hallway.

There was so much tension in the air, it was hard to breathe.

"Sorry...about earlier. I got flustered at what you said and kinda freaked out," Reika said slowly and quietly.

"Yeah...I'm sorry too," Kazuki replied equally slowly and quietly.

There was an awkward pause before the young woman unexpectedly dashed towards Kazuki and threw her arms around his waist.

"Please don't hate me," Reika cried out.

Of course I don't hate you, Kazuki thought. He didn't say anything in response, but he placed his hand on her head and gently stroked her hair.

As she clung to him, Kazuki noticed her thin arms and small hands. She was a girl – a regular girl who shouldn't have been involved in this demon mess. But it was far too late for anyone to back out now, so what could the young man do to make it right? How could he atone for his mistakes?

Kazuki thought about Hasunuma's plan and wondered if helping the Pirate King reinstate the former Emperor's son to the throne would be a suitable way to make amends. That, coupled with winning the demon games, could be his answer.

Finally feeling more confident about the path he had chosen, Kazuki said, "Reika, I'll do whatever it takes to get your life back to normal. And I promise I'll protect you," he added with conviction.

The young woman pulled her head away so that she could look up at him. "Does that mean…that you care about me?" She asked as she blinked her big, teary eyes.

Do I have to say it out loud? Kazuki wondered as he felt his cheeks flush. "I…" the young man began, but he was far too embarrassed to say the words, so he opted for a nod instead.

Reika's face lit up with a beautiful smile. "Oh Kazu," she said with delight as she squeezed him tightly.

The young man couldn't resist her charms, so he bent his head and kissed her deeply.

Reika giggled. "You know, if you want to continue, we should go inside and shut the door…"

The young woman's offer was unexpected, but Kazuki was not about to say no. "We've only got five minutes," he said as he backed into Reika's room, pulling her along with him.

"Jun can wait," she said with a sensual grin as she shut and locked the door behind her.

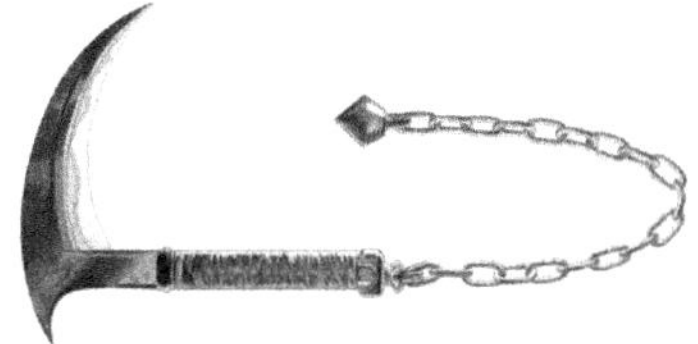

"Bwahahaha! You should have seen the look on his face after we destroyed his men," D roared with laughter.

"Well thanks t' ya, 'e doesn't have a face t' look at anymore," Ginza added with a grin as he hit his mug against D's.

The four men at the table all laughed aloud. Rize, Hanzo, Ginza and D were all on their fourth round of drinks. Hasu joined them a moment later with his fifth mug full of ale. They had all returned to the Ryujin about an hour ago, starving and thirsty. Thankfully, Jun had planned ahead and, earlier that morning, Kazu and the miko had helped him gather ingredients at the market. By the time the men returned from Masayoshi Island, Jun had heaping plates of delicious food ready for them.

The food had disappeared from the plates as if it had all been an illusion, and now the men were focused on their drinks. Which meant there would be boisterous conversations, and the topic of choice was, of course, their battle at Masayoshi Island.

"Wait a minute," Kohaku said, interrupting their cheers. "What happened to those seventy or so soldiers waiting for you on the plateau? Shouldn't they have backed up the warden?"

"Ah, that would be my fault," the helmsman responded as his

hand rose into the air. "I finally got the chance to test out my 'Rain of Arrows' – and it worked perfectly!"

The other men cheered and drank from their mugs in salute.

'Rain of Arrows'? Is that what he was working on during that month of training at Hasu's place?

Kohaku couldn't believe that Rize had taken out all of those soldiers by himself. Sure he was an amazing marksman, but to take on that many soldiers alone…perhaps the demon battles were strengthening them more than they realized.

"Men are obsessed with fighting," the delicate woman beside Kohaku said as she shook her head. "Mine especially."

The ninja woman sighed and said, "At least he's safe now."

"Yes. That's one more favor we owe Hasu," Ni smiled. She gracefully got up from the couch and approached the table of drunken men. Standing behind D, she slowly slid her fingers down his shoulders and onto his chest. She whispered something into his ear and D immediately stood up from the table.

"The lady and I have some business to attend to," he announced with a grin, "so you'll have to excuse us."

The rest of the table whistled and jeered, knowing exactly what D and Ni were up to. Before the two disappeared from the room, Ni smiled and nodded at Hasu – it was her silent way of thanking him for rescuing her husband.

"Anytime," he replied, since Ni wouldn't have seen him nod and return her smile. Hasu then drained the remainder of his mug and left the table to get a refill.

"Come join us, Kohaku!" The three remaining men at the table collectively called out.

Normally she would have joined them, but this time the ninja woman simply smiled and shook her head. Kohaku was glad that they had all made it back safely, but she didn't feel like celebrating.

"What's wrong, lovely lady?" Someone spoke softly into her ear.

The ninja woman knew it was Hasu and, without looking at him, pushed his face away with her hand.

Hasu backed away from her and laughed warmly. "Not in the mood, eh? Too bad."

Kohaku made eye contact with Hasu and frowned. "The others may not realize it, but you put yourself in a lot of danger on Masayoshi."

"What do you mean? I used my doppelganger to–"

The ninja woman held her hand out to silence the Pirate King. "No, your doppelganger was hiding in the shadows with D's trident while *you* were standing in the square."

Hasu was silent for a while before he replied, "How did you know?"

Kohaku sighed. "Because I've been watching you for over ten years, Hasu. I *know* you. And I can easily tell the difference between you and your doppelganger."

"But how? You weren't even there," the Pirate King replied quietly. It was not a conversation that he wanted the others to overhear.

The ninja woman looked at Hasu. "Promise me you won't do something foolish like that again, and I'll tell you."

The Pirate King sighed. "Fine, fine. You have my word."

Kohaku believed him and nodded. "It's rather simple, really. Your doppelganger can't speak."

A wide grin formed on Hasu's face. "Sometimes I forget how observant you are, Kohaku." He patted her gently on her head. "Thanks for the heads-up. I'll keep that in mind from now on." Hasu then returned to the table with his rowdy shipmates and continued to drink.

You'd better…before someone figures out the truth behind your technique.

"Wow, with all of this noise, you'd think we were in one of O-kane's bars," a voice chimed in from the doorway. It was the miko, and behind her stood Kazu.

"All done with your chores?" Hasu asked with a grin.

Kazu rolled his eyes. "Yes, Captain," he muttered.

Hasu laughed. "Hopefully now you've learned not to make Jun wait."

The miko blushed, while Kazu rolled his eyes again and turned his attention towards the rest of the men. The way his eyes darted around, he seemed to be looking for D.

"He just left," the ninja woman stated.

Kazu's shoulders slumped slightly, but he followed the miko into the room and joined the three drunks at the table. Hasu then pulled up a chair, making it four drunks.

"So how did you do it? How did you sneak in?" The young man asked the group.

Hanzo and Ginza looked at each other and then stared hard at Hasu. Clearly there was something they didn't want the Pirate King to reveal.

"Well, uh," Hasu began as he stifled a laugh, "we blended in with the locals."

Kazu looked at Hanzo. "Right, blended in," he commented, not believing Hasu's deficient explanation.

"What's important is we got the job done," Hanzo declared before draining the rest of his mug.

"I still don't understand how you were able to rescue someone from the Hekigun's prison. I mean, it's supposed to be impossible to escape," the miko said with a hint of awe in her voice.

"Difficult, yes, impossible, no," the Pirate King responded.

"Especially with the right people and tools," Rize added with a wink.

"Yeah, yer a pretty good tool, Rize," Ginza said as he bellowed with laughter.

"Sharp tools are the best, wouldn't you say, blacksmith?" The helmsman retorted.

Now it was Hanzo's turn to laugh. "Ha! He's calling you a dull blade, Gin."

"WHAT?!" The blacksmith roared.

Everyone at the table laughed. And then Ginza's furrowed brow relaxed, and he, too, joined the merriment.

Kohaku reveled in these cheery little scenes. There was so much hatred and violence in their daily lives that these jovial moments became her treasures to look back at when things seemed dark and hopeless.

"The party's still going I see," a deep voiced boomed.

Hanzo, Ginza, Rize, and Hasu all cheered and raised their mugs towards D as he re-entered the room. The miko's mouth hung open as she looked D up and down, while Kazu's eyes nearly popped out of his skull.

Kohaku couldn't blame them for their reaction. She remembered how she had felt full of both awe and fear the first time she encountered D. It wasn't just that he was extremely tall and muscular, or that his skin was as rich as a lacquered box, but the man was a supreme warrior; while he joked around a lot and usually wore a smile on his face, D's aura was brutally strong. Any trained fighter or swordman would instantly be able to feel D's intensity and know that he was not someone to mess with.

Kazu clearly felt that aura, while the miko was blissfully unaware of it.

"You must be Nia's husband, the second-in-command guy that was rescued," Reika stated as she continued to look D up and down.

He was only wearing a loin cloth at the time, so D's impressive physique was on full display. Even Kohaku, who was used to seeing D by now, found it difficult not to stare.

"That's me," he chuckled. "The name's Douglas."

"I'm Reika, a shrine maiden," the miko responded with a bow of her head.

"I thought you were taking care of some pressing business," Hasu said with a grin. "Done already?"

D grinned back at the Pirate King. "Oh no, not even close," he said. "Just came to get my lady some water. Hard work makes one thirsty you know."

The men all chuckled knowingly, except for Kazu, while Kohaku shook her head.

"You'd better get back to Ni before she comes looking for you," the ninja woman offered, attempting to remove D from the room before the conversation turned to accounts of debauchery.

Kohaku saw the slight shift in D's expression; she knew that he got her message.

"Right you are, Kohaku, as always," the warrior said with a smile. He quickly filled a mug with water and then headed out of the room without another word.

"Aww, but I wanted to ask him a bunch of questions," the miko sighed.

I'm sure you'll find time to pester him later.

"So *that's* the second-in-command," Kazu muttered. He seemed to be still in shock.

"Ya should challenge 'im t' a fight," Ginza suggested with a snort.

Kazu's head slowly turned to the blacksmith. "You can't be serious."

Ginza laughed. "But that's what warriors do! We all fought 'im."

"I'm surprised you're not all dead then," Kazu replied.

The blacksmith continued to laugh heartily. "Nah, 'e's honorable an' doesn't kill without reason."

"Are all Kheprian men as…impressively built?" The miko wondered aloud.

"That's what they say," the blacksmith replied with a nod.

"Of the Kheprian men that I've come across, they're all similar, but Douglas is still sizeable in comparison," Hanzo offered.

"Oh, have you been there?" The miko inquired. She was rather nosy for a Tsukigen woman.

"Sure have," the giant nodded, "many times, in fact. But that was years ago."

"Were you there for trade or…wait, where are *you* originally from, Mr. Hanzo?" Reika asked enthusiastically.

"It's just 'Hanzo,' lass," the giant said with a chuckle. "And what makes you think I'm not from Tsukigen?"

The miko cocked an eyebrow. "Are you joking? Not only are you a red-headed giant, but you have a distinctly foreign accent."

Hanzo let out a deep belly laugh. "It's true that my lovely physique is hard to miss," he said as he began to flex his muscles.

Ginza jabbed his elbow into Hanzo's ribcage. "She ain't interested in yer body, ya thick-headed lobster," he chided.

Hanzo didn't seem affected in the least as he continued to laugh.

"So…where are you from?" The miko asked again, clearly interested in getting an answer.

"A place far away from here," the giant said with a distant, longing look. "But I've got no intention of going back," he added as he turned and smiled at the miko. "I like this place."

Kohaku winced. While it was true that Hanzo liked Tsukigen, the ninja woman knew the real reason why the giant wouldn't return home, and it made her heart ache.

Reika smiled back at Hanzo. "I'm glad to hear that." She paused for a moment before adding, "Actually, my father was a foreigner too."

"Really?" Ginza and Hanzo replied simultaneously.

"Yep," she nodded happily. "My father was one of those people who came here to teach us all about their 'one true god', but when he met my mother, *he* was the one who was converted." She giggled.

"That's a much nicer story than mine," Hanzo replied after chugging the contents of his mug. "I came looking to trade, but those Hekigun bastards destroyed my ship."

"'E got 'ere soon after Hiiro Genji closed Tsukigen t' foreigners," Ginza explained.

"Oh no," the miko said forlornly, "I'm so sorry to hear that."

"Yeah," Hanzo replied flatly.

Rize refilled the giant's mug without a word. Except for Kazu and the miko, everyone in the room already knew Hanzo's unpleasant past.

The giant took a moment to himself, and a sip of his ale, before he continued. "It wasn't the loss of my goods or my ship, or even my lengthy imprisonment, that fueled my vengeance on the Hekigun." Hanzo slowly explained. "But the loss of my entire crew was unforgivable."

Hanzo…Kohaku's heart grieved for her friend.

"Thankfully the cap'n found, rescued, and recruited me," he continued, "but it sure as Freya wasn't easy for me the first few years."

The ninja woman remembered that time. It was about seven years ago that Hasu had gotten information about a detention center for foreigners and had gone to check it out. Ginza had gone with him, and when the two came back, they had Hanzo with them. Well, his name at the time was "Hans," but Ginza quickly changed it to "Hanzo," and it stuck.

The poor man was in a very dark place back then. Kohaku didn't know the particulars, but from the little she overheard, the detention center sounded like the Demon Realm – or, at least, what she imagined the Demon Realm to be like. The foreigners imprisoned there had been starved and tortured to varying degrees. He looked strong and healthy now, but back then Hanzo was a withered husk.

And his mental health wasn't any better.

It took a good year or two before Hanzo regained himself. Adding Rize to the crew and encountering D were two events that had really helped the giant to recover. But even with his recovery, Hanzo had once privately told Kohaku that he could never return home because of his guilt over the fate of his crew. He had said that facing the families of his crew, both as the captain and sole survivor, was unthinkable. In his mind, it was far better for the families to think that everyone had been lost at sea. Their ignorance would also prevent a war between Skövalgar and Tsukigen.

"I'm so sorry," the miko softly spoke. "May the gods collect and protect the souls of your crew."

It was a nice gesture on the miko's part, but all Kohaku could think was: *He doesn't believe in the same gods as you.*

Hanzo shook his head. "Although it was rough at first, I *have* grown to love this country. I've met warm, friendly people and I've learned a lot about your unique customs and traditions. Not everyone here is like your ruler, and that is a truth I've come to accept. Which is why I now fight for Tsukigen's freedom instead of my petty vengeance. And I think I've killed enough Hekigun soldiers to repay my crew many times over," he added with a hearty laugh.

"You've been through so much," the miko said, her eyes slightly watery. "Do you all have such sad backgrounds?" She asked, looking around the table.

"Life ain't all happy," Ginza said gently, "but ya gotta learn how t' move on. If ya don't, yu'll sink."

"More often than not, it's the desire for revenge that gets you through," Rize chimed in. "At least initially," he added.

"Yeah, but ya can't focus on that fer too long, or else yu'll forget how t' live," Ginza said with a sideways glance at Hasunuma.

I guess I'm not the only one who thinks that Hasu needs a new focal point...

"Alright enough with the depressing talk," the Pirate King interjected. "This is supposed to be a victory celebration, remember?"

"Aye!" Ginza and Hanzo cheered as they raised their mugs and knocked them together.

Rize grinned and raised his mug into the air.

"Oh! How about I perform another dance? There's one I know that commemorates happy occasions," the miko suggested with a giggle.

The men all gave an enthusiastic cheer. Kazu also seemed excited to see another miko dance, but Kohaku wondered if the young man secretly wanted to keep Reika's dances to himself.

Wait. Let's not go there. The ninja woman told herself.

It was very late in the evening, or very early in the morning, when the Ryujin crew finally stopped celebrating. The kid and the miko had left shortly after the miko performed her dance, while Hanzo and Ginza had both passed out on the table some time afterwards. Rize had cleverly switched from ale to water at some point early on, so he effortlessly walked away from the table and made it back to his room to sleep.

That left the Pirate King and the ninja woman.

As he stepped out of the room, carrying Kohaku in his arms, Hasunuma had to lean against the walls for support as he made his way towards the ninja woman's quarters.

"If you drop me…" she threatened.

Hasunuma laughed. "You'll do what, exactly? Miss I-can't-stand-or-walk."

Kohaku looked like she wanted to hit him, but she didn't. The Pirate King was glad for it too, because he was pretty sure he'd fall over if she did.

When they reached Kohaku's room, the ninja woman reached forward and opened the door for her escort. The Pirate King made his way inside and was able to successfully drop Kohaku onto her bed before he fell over, ending up half on the floor and half on her bed.

Spawn of a demon, I've had a lot more to drink than I thought! To the Demon Realm with those guys for keeping my mug full.

Although, despite his thoughts, the Pirate King wasn't actually mad.

There was a short whistle and a pause before Kohaku said, "You can leave now, you know."

Hasunuma's face was buried in the mattress, and he didn't feel like moving quite yet, so he simply answered Kohaku with a thumbs-up. The Pirate King heard her sigh deeply, but the ninja woman sat quietly for a long time after. Or at least it seemed like a long time…maybe it was only a few minutes…or seconds even.

"This bed's too small for both of us, Hasu," she finally said.

The Pirate King managed to push himself up long enough to answer, "Wanna move to mine then?"

When Kohaku's eyes met his, Hasunuma immediately regretted his words. Curiosity and lust swirled in those gorgeous green orbs.

"What would you do if I said 'yes'?" She asked after a moment's hesitation. Her eyes bore into him, searching for an answer.

Never thought I'd wish she were still mute.

The Pirate King didn't answer her; he averted his eyes and let his head fall back against the bed, hoping that Kohaku would think he had passed out.

The ninja woman sighed deeply. "Don't say things you don't mean," she said with clear disappointment. She then helped push Hasunuma up so that he was now sitting – or rather kneeling – on the floor beside the bed. "Do I need to yell for Rize or Jun to come get you?"

The Pirate King shook his head. "Nah."

It took him a few tries, but eventually he stood himself up and staggered out of the room, shutting the door behind him without a backwards glance.

"You look rough," came a voice from further down the hall.

Turning towards it, the Pirate King steadied himself and replied, "And you look rejuvenated."

The warrior grinned. "What can I say? I've got an amazing woman. As for you, Hasunuma–"

"Then why don't you go back to her," *and leave me the festering hole alone,* he replied frostily. Hasunuma was not about to have that sort of conversation with Douglas, especially under the circumstances.

Douglas' eyes shifted to the door that the Pirate King had exited. "I figured we could talk while she's resting…" He then returned his gaze to the man before him, "But if this is a bad time, then–"

"No. It's a perfectly good time," the Pirate King replied, welcoming the change in topic. "And I always have time for my second-in-command," he added with a grin. "What's on your mind?"

Douglas motioned towards the doors along the hall. "I think I'll escort you back to your room first."

Ah. Must be business related. "Like I need your help," the Pirate King scoffed.

He motioned for Douglas to follow him, but as he turned around he stumbled. Hasunuma heard the warrior behind him snicker and make a comment about needing to carry the Pirate King to his quarters. When Hasunuma turned and glared at him, it only made Douglas laugh more.

If I weren't so damn drunk, I'd punch him.

"Usually you're good at holding your liquor," the warrior said as he followed the Pirate King up the stairs to the deck.

"Yeah, well usually I keep tabs on how many refills I get," Hasunuma muttered.

"And I'm sure that when Kohaku pours, she keeps tabs for you."

"That too," the Pirate King admitted.

"Is she gonna be OK? For a ninja, it must be torturous not to be able to move freely."

"She's a tough one," Hasunuma said with a grin.

"I'm well aware of that," Douglas replied knowingly.

After all, Hasunuma and Kohaku's first meeting with the foreign pair had turned into an intense – and incredibly difficult – battle. Nia and Kohaku were pretty evenly matched, while Douglas could've defeated the Pirate King that night if he had been smarter about his tactics. But Hasunuma would never divulge that bit of the story.

"Nia's thrilled about Kohaku's voice though. It was so hard for them to communicate beforehand." He paused for a moment before adding with a laugh, "I suppose we've got to watch out now, Hasunuma."

"You've got that right." *In more ways than one.*

The Pirate King unlocked his cabin door and went inside. He sat himself at his desk and resisted the urge to pass out. Douglas relaxed on the couch.

"What did you want to discuss?"

"Well," the warrior began, "I'd like to get my ship and crew back. As long as they haven't been destroyed, that is."

"Makes sense," the Pirate King replied.

"But I'm gonna need your help." Douglas leaned forward. "The truth is, it wasn't just the threat of them going after Nia that got me. I mean, you know her – she's a skilled assassin who could easily nail a fly to the wall one hundred yards away."

The Pirate King grinned. He knew how formidable Nia was with her poisoned needles. But his grin quickly faded as he asked, "Was it demons?"

The warrior shook his head. "No. Even worse." He looked straight into Hasunuma's eyes and said, "He's been experimenting again. And this time he's been successful."

The Pirate King lowered his head into his hands. He had feared as much, but he had also hoped that his attacks had halted their progress. "How many?" He asked without looking up.

"From what I could tell, only a dozen or so. But I can't be sure…they found me before I got to their facility."

"Where is it?" The Pirate King asked, finally raising his head.

Douglas got up and approached Hasunuma's desk. He pointed to an island on the map in front of them. "It's here, on Rurin. They have the main port pretty well guarded, but that's not where the experimental facility is." Douglas moved his large hand to the middle of the island, where mountains dominated the landscape. "It's in a small crater here."

"Hmph. Not easy to get to I imagine."

"Definitely not. We were able to make it through to a point where we could see the wretched thing, but before my men and I could go in for a closer look, some experimental blighters caught us. They easily took out my men before I could even react. I'm only alive because they knew they could use me to get to you." Douglas made a fist and punched the table, denting it slightly. "If only I'd been more prepared," he growled, "those blighters wouldn't have stood a chance."

"Maybe not against you…" the Pirate King began, but decided it was best not to finish the sentence. "I take it the rest of your men were guarding the Chimera?"

Douglas nodded. "I only took five men with me. As long as the Hekigun didn't destroy my ship after I was captured, the rest of them should still be there. If they're not still onboard, my men will probably be locked up somewhere in the Hekigun fortress there." The warrior straightened himself and crossed his arms. "So when do we leave?"

The Pirate King shook his head – which was not a good idea. As he clutched his head between his hands, Hasunuma replied, "As soon as I get a plan together." He looked at Douglas as he added, "We can't just go barging in this time and expect an easy win."

"I know," the warrior grumbled.

The Pirate King could see the frustration on Douglas' face, but he was not about to risk everything for the sake of speed. If the Chimera and its men were still alive, they could afford to wait an extra day or two.

"Get some rest," he told the warrior. "I promise that we'll be on our way to Rurin as soon as possible."

"Yeah, I know," Douglas replied with a heavy sigh. "You're a man of your word, Hasunuma. I appreciate the help."

The Pirate King grinned. "Now you'll owe me three big favors."

A grin spread across Douglas' face in return. "Get my ship and crew back in one piece, and we'll call it four."

Kazuki awoke to the sound of someone pounding on his door.

"Oy, Little Oni! How long d' ya plan t' sleep fer? We got work t' do," Ginza bellowed.

The young man bolted upright. "What about breakfast?!"

The blacksmith laughed heartily, "Ya just missed it. Now hurry up t' the deck b'fore Cap'n's mood worsens."

He's already *in a foul mood? I wonder what happened...*Kazuki shook his head. He had to get dressed and up on deck as fast as possible. *Is it really that late?* He wondered. Even without a window in his room, the young man rarely overslept; his internal clock was well-adjusted to the rising and setting of the sun.

"Mmm just a little longer," a sleepy voice groaned.

Kazuki looked over at the young woman asleep beside him. Her golden hair was a tangled mess, but the young man found her beautiful nonetheless. He reached over and gently stroked her cheek. A smile appeared on the young woman's sleeping face. The sight warmed Kazuki's heart.

The young man wished he could stay in bed with Reika all day, but he couldn't abandon his duties as a crew member. Not only was it his way of earning his place on board the Ryujin, but Kazuki knew how hard everyone worked and would have felt useless if he didn't help them out. Especially now that Kohaku couldn't perform most of her duties due to her leg injury.

I hope she heals soon, the young man thought as he finished getting dressed. He could only guess at how frustrated and disappointed the ninja woman must have felt. For a second, he almost wished that he could somehow use the Demon King's power to heal her, but that desire quickly vanished. The power of demons wasn't natural for humans, and the cost of using those powers meant relinquishing your soul.

Wait…what will *happen to my soul at the end of all of this?*

It was a question the young man had somehow missed until now, but it was an important one. Would his soul be taken back by the gods, or would it follow the Demon King into the Demon Realm? Not that Kazuki believed the gods would actually grab his soul, but he definitely didn't want to end up in the Demon Realm – which he knew to be real.

There was no answer from the Demon King, although Kazuki could feel his presence. The young man interpreted the Demon King's silence as a refusal to answer, which only made Kazuki's apprehension worse.

As he made his way onto the deck, the young man saw Ginza and Hanzo moving huge crates around. Beads of sweat clung to their foreheads, but the two were grinning as they tried to out-carry one another. He then shifted his gaze towards the helm and saw Rize with Ami happily perched on his shoulder. His eyes then found Kohaku and Nia sitting on some barrels off to the side; the two women were smiling and laughing about something.

Kazuki felt the corners of his lips rise. He, again, sensed the warmth of happiness well up inside of his chest, and suddenly his worries ebbed. Life may have been full of hardships, but those difficulties could easily be overcome or overlooked with the support of reliable companions. At least, that's what the young man came to understand at that moment.

"Looking for your captain?" A deep voice suddenly asked.

The young man whirled around to find the colossal second-in-command towering over him.

"Uh. Yeah," was all that Kazuki could manage to say. The combination of the colossal man's extreme height and muscular build were beyond intimidating to the young man. But it wasn't his appearance that made the hairs on the back of Kazuki's neck stand up; much like Luka, the mayor of O-kane, there was something terrifying lurking behind that smiling foreign façade.

His name is…Douglas, I think.

"He's in his quarters," the colossal man said. "Oh, but you may want to watch what you say to him – he's got a massive headache from last night," he added with a booming laugh.

"That's weird. Hasunuma never gets sick from drinking," the young man noted.

Douglas continued to laugh as he said, "It just goes to show that he's no good without her."

Kazuki wasn't sure what the colossal man meant, but the young man didn't feel comfortable asking him to clarify. The only person he could have been referring to was Kohaku, but Kazuki didn't want to acknowledge that Hasunuma needed her – or vice versa. There was no way that jerk deserved her.

"You're the kid who's housing the Demon King, aren't you?" Douglas asked with a strange grin.

Kazuki slowly nodded.

The colossal man's expression revealed his thirst for battle as he replied, "Care to fight me? I'm curious to see what the King of demons can do."

The young man felt the icy prick of fear run down his spine. Douglas' aura had intensified to the point where it was hard to breathe, let alone move. But before Kazuki's consciousness was crushed, he heard a laugh escape his lips.

"I find myself curious as to what a foreign warrior can do," a voice that was not Kazuki's responded.

Douglas' brows furrowed for a moment before asking, "Am I addressing the Demon King now?"

"That you are," the Demon King replied as Kazuki's lips curled into a grin.

Kazuki could feel the auras of both Douglas and the Demon King growing stronger, and it scared him. He didn't want to fight an ally, and he especially didn't want to fight on the Ryujin or near any other crew members. The Demon King couldn't be trusted to hold back, and Kazuki didn't have the power to stop him.

"Oy," a gruff voice interrupted, "there ain't no serious fightin' on board."

Kazuki felt his head turn towards the voice. Ginza was standing there with a stern expression on his face. The blacksmith must have had an incredible fortitude to stand confidently between the Demon King and Douglas.

The young man felt himself smirk. **"And how, exactly, do you propose to uphold that rule of yours?"**

"Cap'n's rule, not mine," Ginza corrected, "an' if ya want, I can get the miko t' zap ya again."

Kazuki was impressed. Not only was the blacksmith standing his ground, but he was even *threatening* the Demon King.

"Ginza's right. The captain would flay us if we damaged his precious ship," Douglas said with a laugh. "Another time, Demon King," he added with a slight bow before turning and walking away.

The young man breathed a sigh of relief. He could feel some anger, disappointment, and perhaps a small amount of admiration coming from the Demon King as he retreated into Kazuki's subconscious.

Ginza firmly grabbed the young man's shoulders and said, "Ya gotta keep 'im in check, Little Oni."

"Are you serious? How am *I* supposed to control the *Demon King*?" Kazuki asked incredulously.

The blacksmith shook his head. "What kinda attitude's that?" He then released the young man's shoulders and sighed. "No wonder 'e pops out whenever 'e wants. Ya got no discipline."

"What are you talking about, Ginza?"

"This," the blacksmith replied as he pointed to Kazuki's chest. "Yer heart's weak."

The young man looked at Ginza with skepticism.

"What're ya livin' fer?" The blacksmith then asked.

Kazuki thought about it for a moment, but couldn't find an answer. He wasn't living for some grand purpose; he was alive because the Demon King was possessing him, and that was that. Sure, he didn't want to die again, and yes, he wanted to help Hasunuma complete his goal in order to *possibly* bring peace to Tsukigen, but neither were compelling reasons for living.

A beautiful face suddenly flashed in Kazuki's mind. *Reika...*

But was protecting her a good enough reason?

"I don't know," the young man finally admitted.

The blacksmith frowned. "Come on," he grumbled, "there's got t' be somethin' that puts the wind in yer sails."

Kazuki shook his head. "Revenge was my only motivation until recently…" The young man trailed off, not wanting to publicly declare his feelings for Reika yet.

Ginza nodded. "It's good ya've steered away from revenge. Now ya just have t' replace it with somethin' better."

The young man shrugged. "Like what?"

"By the gods, Little Oni," Ginza bellowed, "look around!"

Kazuki did as he was instructed. His eyes wandered around the deck, then up to the crow's nest, into the sky, over the clouds, and back down to the sea.

"No, no," the blacksmith said with a heavy sigh, "that's not what I meant." He scratched his head and then pointed to himself. "I want people t' live in peace. Life's hard enough without all this killin', an' if takin' out the Hekigun solves that, then I'm all fer it."

"But Ginza," the young man retorted, "how can you risk your life for strangers? I mean, not everyone is worth the effort. Think about all of the people who've spat in your face and cursed you, even after you'd helped them."

The blacksmith laughed. "I see yer point. Yeah, I can't say I'd risk m' life fer those arses."

"So then–"

"Look, Little Oni," Ginza interrupted. He then pointed towards Hanzo and said, "That man's suffered unjustly." The blacksmith's finger then moved so that it was aimed at the ninja woman. "An' our sweet Kohaku hasn't had it any easier." He then looked directly at Kazuki as he asked, "Don't they deserve some peace an' a little happiness fer what they've been through?"

Kazuki couldn't deny that. He nodded.

"The cap'n, Rize, Jun, Douglas an' Nia too. I'm surrounded by good people who've suffered terribly. Includin' ya, Little Oni," the blacksmith added as he patted Kazuki's head. "An' that sufferin's somethin' I want t' end."

"But why does it have to be *you*?" Kazuki asked, still unsure of why the blacksmith was risking his life and, frankly, wasting his time being a pirate. "There are other options for you–"

Ginza held up his hand to stop Kazuki. "No, Little Oni," he said quietly, "there's nothin' else fer me." The blacksmith crossed his arms over his chest and closed his eyes. "Not t' get too detailed, but m' family was killed by the Hekigun when m' dad refused t' forge them some weapons. First was m' mom, who they tried t' use as a hostage. Then was m' little brother, who tried t' save m' mom. An' finally m' dad, who jumped int' the fight an' died tryin' t' avenge his loved ones."

The young man's heart sank as he imagined the scene.

"I'll tell ya," the blacksmith said, swallowing hard as he opened his eyes, "not a single soldier escaped m' blade that day, but their deaths didn't stop the pain. It took years of fightin' and killin' Hekigun soldiers t' figure out that all m' rage an' hate was fer m'self fer not savin' m' family. I shoulda stepped in sooner, but I didn't. I was too scared t' lose m' own life."

Kazuki remembered his own frustration during the fight with Ammon, when fear had prevented him from moving. Although he had wanted to take revenge for the old man, the thought of his own death shook him to his core. No amount of training can prepare someone for the moment when his or her life is at stake.

"But I know what's important t' me now," Ginza continued with an unyielding tone, "an' that's what gives me strength." He then grinned and pointed to his biceps as he added, "Besides these impressive muscles a' mine."

The young man rolled his eyes. *Always about the muscles...*

"So d'ya get it now, Little Oni?"

"...I guess," Kazuki hesitantly replied.

"An' ya say *I'm* slow," Ginza said with a laugh. "I'm tryin' t' tell ya that I live t' protect the people I cherish." He swung his arm around the young man's shoulder and added, "An' that includes ya,

Little Oni. I won't make the same mistake twice."

"Gin!" Hanzo suddenly yelled from the other end of the deck. "One more crate and I'll win our bet!"

"Thunderin' sea snakes," Ginza cursed. "I'll leave ya t' think about it, Little Oni," the blacksmith uttered before sprinting to where Hanzo, looking rather triumphant, stood.

I don't have to think about it…but thanks, Ginza.

While listening to the blacksmith, Kazuki came to understand that his promise to protect Reika would be his reason for living. Just as Ginza didn't want to lose anyone else he cared about, the young man felt the same way. And, truthfully, it wasn't only Reika that he wanted to protect; Hasunuma, Kohaku, Rize, Ginza, Hanzo, and maybe even Jun made the list too. After all, the Ryujin crew was his family.

Now that he was full of new confidence, the young man knocked on the captain's door and waited for a reply. He received a gruff 'come in,' and opened the door. Kazuki stifled a laugh as he entered and saw Hasunuma slouched at his desk with his head cradled in his hands.

"Rough night?"

The Pirate King didn't move as he replied, "At least I didn't sleep in like a certain lazy kid."

"From the looks of it, you didn't sleep at all," the young man said as he noticed the plethora of charts and papers scattered around the desk. "What's our next move?"

Hasunuma lifted his head from his hands and stared at Kazuki. Dark bags clung under his bloodshot eyes. "How much can we trust in the miko's anti-demon skills?"

The young man stared back at the Pirate King; he hadn't expected him to ask about Reika. "Uh," Kazuki stalled, trying to figure out what to say. "From what I've seen, her spells have worked," which was true, "so I think you can trust in her abilities," which was not entirely true, but Kazuki didn't want to risk Reika getting kicked off of the ship.

The Pirate King slowly nodded his head. "Alright then. My plan might just work."

"What do you have in mind? Are we going after more demons?"

"Not exactly," Hasunuma said with a frown, "but I think some of her spells should work anyways." The Pirate King held out a piece of paper to Kazuki and said, "Ask her if she knows the spells to counter these abilities."

The young man took the list from Hasunuma and read it over. It was fairly extensive, with abilities ranging from regeneration to summoning the dead. Kazuki wasn't sure if all of the abilities listed were real or not, but he would ask Reika about them either way. If there was even the slightest chance that a demon could do something like raise the dead, then Kazuki wanted to know how to prevent it.

"And I'll brief the entire crew about our next mission this afternoon, so hold your questions until then," the Pirate King added as he motioned towards the door.

"Aye, Captain," Kazuki said as he left the room with the list in hand.

"Listen well! Our next mission will be our most challenging yet. Not only will we be fighting a large portion of the Hekigun army – and, most likely, a few demons – but there will also be hybrids to watch out for. We can't be certain of the abilities that the hybrids might possess, so be careful not to underestimate them. A fight with a hybrid could very well be as challenging as one with a demon."

The Pirate King scanned the faces of his crew, looking for any reaction of worry or fear. A wide grin appeared on his face when he found no trace of either emotion on any face except for the miko's.

"There will be three teams: One will stay and guard the Ryujin, a second will attempt to rescue Douglas' ship and crew, and the third will have to make their way through the mountains to find and destroy the Hekigun base hidden within. Team three has the most dangerous mission, as we believe the base to be the location for the demon experiments – meaning if there are any hybrids, they will most likely be at the base. I will give each of you your assignments shortly, but for now are there any questions?"

The Pirate King was not surprised to see the miko's hand shoot up. He gave her a nod, allowing her to speak.

"When you talk about 'hybrids,' do you mean a cross between humans and demons?" She asked.

Right to the heart of things, Hasunuma grinned. "Yes. Hiiro Genji has been experimenting with mixing humans and demons since before he took control of Tsukigen. Until recently, he's been unsuccessful." *Sort of...*

He could tell that the miko was trembling when she responded with: "What's the point of such a horrific thing?"

"Most likely he intends to build himself an unstoppable army," the Pirate King replied grimly. "After all, only demons can truly fight other demons."

"That's insane," the miko gasped.

"Sure is," Douglas said with a nod. "Which is actually the main reason why we've been trying to take down the Hekigun. If that psychotic ruler of yours succeeds, then it'll be too late for anyone to stop him."

"But you've been able to defeat some demons on your own right? Surely others can–" the miko began, but Hasunuma cut her off with a wave of his hand.

"Don't mistake us for normal humans. This crew has skills and abilities that most people can only dream of."

"Picture the average human. Even if he or she has had basic training, do you really think that person would stand a chance against a demon with accelerated speed, stamina, regeneration, and even the ability to manipulate the natural elements? It's like the Pirate King said: those of us on this ship aren't normal, and it's only because of that that we can fight the demons," Douglas said with complete sincerity.

"And even then, we don't always stand a chance," Rize added with a shrug.

There was a moment of silence, as if everyone were contemplating their own mortality, before the miko said meekly, "Why risk your lives for the sake of the country – or really the whole world? I mean, you're *pirates*."

Hasunuma looked at Douglas and the pair began to laugh. Hanzo, Ginza, and Rize joined in too, while Kohaku and Nia giggled and smiled at each other. Kazuki just shook his head like he was embarrassed.

"What's so funny?" The miko demanded as her face turned rosy.

The Pirate King chose to respond with a question. "Who exactly becomes a pirate in your mind?"

"Murderers, thieves, and other lawless monsters," the miko replied with more than a hint of disdain in her voice.

"Wow, you really think highly of us, don't you?" Rize retorted with a sardonic smile.

The Pirate King held up his hand, signaling silence. "Yes, we do have some of those unfortunates in our ranks. Not on this ship, mind you, but in general there are horrible people who become pirates. Then again, there are horrible people everywhere, even in charge of this country," he added with a darkened expression.

The silence that followed felt heavy, and Hasunuma quickly realized that his words had brought down the mood. To remedy this, he put another question to the miko, this time in a lighter tone.

"Have you ever considered that some pirates are just people who needed a job or a place to stay? Or, perhaps, a person who simply wants freedom?"

Reika shook her head. "That's what sailors – legal sailors, like fisherman – are for."

The Pirate King grinned. "So if we catch fish instead of soldiers, you'd approve?"

"No," she scoffed, "but in your case, why not sail under a different name? Your cause is just – for now – so why not be heroes instead of pirates?"

Hasunuma burst into laughter. "Heroes?! You think well of us after all," he added with a wink. "But, no, we are not heroes. Heroes don't make mistakes, heroes never fail, heroes are always just and righteous, and we are no such thing. We are merely humans, searching for justice in the name of revenge."

Reika's cheeks flushed. "There are plenty of old tales where the hero makes mistakes or fails to do something, but it's how the hero handles those situations in the end that make him a hero."

"Are we talking fables or legends?" Hanzo interjected. "Because there *is* a difference. Or, at least, there is in the stories from my homeland."

"Good point," Rize agreed with a nod of his head. "I think the miko is referring to our fables, which are used to teach children lessons about good attitudes and behavior. Whereas legends refer to historical figures or events; and in these, true heroes can be found."

Ginza chuckled. "Ya can't argue with the guy who's read e'ry book in Tsukigen."

"Not *every* book," Rize replied with a grin, "but close enough."

"Your room says otherwise," Hanzo joked.

"Hey, there's a path to my bed now," Rize countered. "And yes, I can sleep in it," he added before Hanzo could even ask.

How did we get so off topic? "Anyways," the Pirate King interjected, "the point is that it doesn't matter who we are, where we came from, or what titles we have. We are banded together by our principles, which we use as a guide to move forward. Not everyone agrees with those principles, so no matter what amount of good we achieve, we can never be considered heroes." *Nor would we want to. Being a hero is too much effort.*

The miko tossed her hair back. "Pirates with morals? I don't believe it." She shook her head to reiterate her point, but the Pirate King noticed the faintest smile begin to rise from her lips.

"Even a blind lady can see that this insanity needs to be brought to an end," Nia added with a smirk, "And who better to end it than the supposed scum of the Earth?"

"No one will celebrate you afterwards," the miko reminded them, as if it were an important point.

"Is that what should drive us to do good – the heroes' celebration and reward at the end?" The Pirate King retorted. "If that's the case, then your idea of a hero sounds more like that of a pirate to me. Or, better yet, a mercenary."

"We're not in this for the glory or any sort of monetary reward," Hanzo explained as he looked down at the miko. "We're trying to save Tsukigen, because we think it deserves to be saved."

I'd say it has every right to be saved, especially from that bastard. If it hadn't been for him, this would be a rich, thriving land. And its people wouldn't be suffering as horribly as they do now.

"You might not like our methods, but you have to admit that you agree with our goals," Kazuki added.

Hasunuma smiled. The kid didn't often speak up, so it made the Pirate King feel proud that the kid was defending his pirate family. *He's come a long way…*

"Well, of course I agree with stopping Hiiro Genji and his crazy experiments," the miko conceded. "Who wouldn't?"

Those with a thirst for power and domination, the Pirate King mentally replied, but aloud he said, "I'm glad we're all on the same page then. Especially as we're nearing the end of this long journey."

Although it had taken them years to get there, the crew could feel how close they were to fulfilling their ultimate goal. The energy on deck grew with the anticipation of the end of the Hekigun's reign. If they succeeded in their missions on Rurin, their final obstacle would be waiting for them at the capitol.

"Enough of this sea sludge already. Let's have our assignments and get to it," Jun grumbled from the stairway. He would never admit it, but Hasunuma could tell that Jun was just as excited as the rest of them were.

Playing it cool as always, huh? The Pirate King smiled and waved his hand, "Fine, fine. Here are the teams I've devised: Nia, you and Kohaku get to guard my ship."

"Oh ho, how honored we are, Captain," Nia said sarcastically. She hated being kept from the front lines.

"You won't be bored, trust me," the Pirate King replied, but Nia simply crossed her arms and looked away with a 'hmph'.

"Douglas, you and Rize are coming with me. We'll rescue your ship and crew." *Which, with any luck, are both still intact.* "Hanzo and Ginza, you two are babysitting the kids while they check out, and hopefully destroy, the experimental facility deep in the mountains." The Pirate King stared pointedly at the two pirates and added, "This will be a very dangerous mission, so I need you to be on your guard at all times…do I make myself clear?"

"Aye, Cap'n," they both shouted in response. The Pirate King could see the look in their eyes change and he knew that they fully understood what he had meant.

"Good. And as for Jun…well…you'll be taking on a solo

mission. I'll give you the details later. Everyone got that?"

The deck resounded with a mix of "Aye, Cap'n," and "Yes, Sir."

"Then get ready to depart. Douglas, assist Hanzo and Ginza. Rize, prepare coordinates for Rurin. Kid, I need to speak with you. And ladies," the Pirate King grinned, "you just relax."

He laughed aloud when he got the exact crude response from Nia that he had predicted.

"Alright, Little Oni, follow me," Hasunuma said as he led the kid to his quarters. Once they arrived, the Pirate King shut the door behind them and asked, "So, how's it look?"

Understanding what he had meant, the kid handed over a piece of paper and said, "Reika put a mark next to the ones she's confident about dealing with. The others she says she's never heard of or read anything about, so she can't be sure any of her spells would work."

The Pirate King nodded and looked at the list. He grinned when he saw that the only unmarked abilities were the ones he made-up in order to test her. "Good. I'll need her to make some charms for all of us before we get to Rurin. I don't know exactly where the demons or hybrids will be, but I'm counting on you to destroy that base and any traces of the experiments."

The kid looked straight into the Pirate King's eyes and asked, "Does that include the test subjects and any other innocent victims that may be there?"

Hasunuma stared back at Kazuki. On one hand, he was thrilled that the kid seemed to have his humanity intact – which meant that his strategy to open up Kazuki's heart by using the miko was working – but, on the other hand, Hasunuma now had to suppress that humanity in order to finish what needed to be done. "Your orders are to destroy 'any trace.' If you can't handle that, then–"

"No, I can handle it," the kid said with determination. "But," he added hesitantly, "does that mean that, in the end, I'll have to kill you too?"

The Pirate King barely managed to keep a straight face as he asked, "What does *that* mean?"

"Come on, Hasunuma," the kid said, sounding a little desperate, "I dunno about the others, but I've been suspicious of your extraordinary abilities for a long time now…and ever since you mentioned the hybrids, I knew you had to be one of them." The kid now looked away from the Pirate King and added, "I get it if you don't wanna talk about it, but…I need to know for certain."

The Pirate King's mind was racing. Was it the influence of the Demon King inside of Kazuki that triggered the kid's suspicions? Or had he just been too carefree with using his abilities in front of others? Who else suspected him? What would they do if they knew the whole truth?

Well, that's certainly not coming out.

"Alright," the Pirate King said slowly.

But before he could say more, the kid suddenly stared at him defiantly and said, "I won't kill you, no matter what your stupid orders are!"

"I could never ask that of any of my crew," Hasunuma calmly replied, "least of all you, Kid. But the situation still stands…and it's best for the world if all traces are eliminated. No exceptions."

"Why? If you keep quiet about it, no one will ever know," the kid retorted.

"It's not that simple, Kazuki. No one knows how much of an

impact these experiments have on humans. Not all hybrids may seem evil at first, but what happens to them as time goes by? Will they all become corrupted and use their abilities for foul purposes? Can these abilities that they have change over time or become more powerful? Will the demonic essence flow through their bloodlines and plague their descendants for generations to come? We simply don't know. And I don't think that we should risk the future when there are so many uncertainties."

The kid stood with his eyes downcast and his fists clenched. Hasunuma could see that he was struggling with the reality of it all, and was probably desperately trying to find a way around it.

Heh. Can't blame him for that youthful innocence.

But there was nothing else to be done, and no room for discussion on the matter. "Stop worrying about what's to come and focus on the present. You have a difficult mission ahead of you."

Kazuki nodded slowly. "I know."

"I would suggest strategizing with your team before we reach Rurin. You have a new member who hasn't worked with anyone before, and I highly doubt she's seen any real combat, so keep that in mind."

I hope for your sake that she's not too squeamish...although if she does pass out, that power of hers might unleash itself, which would be awfully handy.

"Is that all, Captain?" The kid asked flatly. His mind was clearly elsewhere.

"Yes, that's all," the Pirate King replied. As he watched the kid open the door to leave, Hasunuma called out to him, "Kazuki."

The kid turned around and locked eyes with the Pirate King.

"You had better come back."

The seriousness of the Pirate King's command got through to the kid, and Hasunuma saw the fire of determination burning within Kazuki's eyes. "We'll *all* come back, Captain," he said boldly before exiting the room.

Hasunuma chuckled. He was proud of the kid for finding his own light and fighting his way out of the darkness. It wasn't an easy task, and was something that even most adults couldn't do, which made it that much more incredible that Kazuki had managed it on his own. Those who struggle with inner turmoil either sink or swim, and the Pirate King was pleased that all of his crewmates were swimmers.

That reminds me, I need to have a chat with Jun...

The cook was in the galley as per usual, and when Hasunuma entered he was surprised that no sharp objects came flying his way. "Going soft?"

Jun narrowed his eyes and began to raise the yanagiba in his hand.

"Whoa, hold it," the Pirate King said, raising his hands in surrender, "I'd ruin the flavor of the rice."

"True," Jun replied flatly. He then returned to slicing the raw fish before him. His speed and precision were unmatchable.

"Before I give you the details of your next mission, I want to know more about your previous one," the Pirate King began.

"I thought you might," Jun replied without stopping his work.

"More to the point, I want to hear your opinion of the kid and the miko."

Jun smirked. "I figured you had something up your sleeve, letting that girl on board." He was now delicately topping bowls of rice with the fish slices he had cut. "The way I see it, she's certainly interested in the kid – though to what end, I'm not sure – and her presence seems to boost the kid's confidence – which needs all the help it can get. Overall, I'd say she's useful, but don't count on her too much," he lowered his voice as he added, "She's hiding something big from us."

The Pirate King shrugged and replied, "That's women for ya."

"You already figured out what it is, didn't you? I guess that's why you're the captain," Jun added with a smirk.

"Ever doubtful of my greatness," the Pirate King said as he shook his head. "How'd the kid do against the demon ladies?"

"Well," Jun began, "he's still got a ways to go, but the kid wasn't half bad." The cook's expression darkened as he added, "I don't think he'll make it much further without the Demon King's help though…those demons have powers that are no joke. And if what Douglas says is true – that there are hybrids on the island – then I don't think it's wise to send the kid off without either you or me with him."

The Pirate King considered Jun's warning. Although the kid exuded confidence in his ability to complete the next mission safely, there was a nagging voice in the back of Hasunuma's mind, warning him of an impending disaster.

"As much as I'd like to heed your advice," the Pirate King said slowly, "my hands are tied this time. I can't leave Douglas and Rize alone to free the Chimera and its crew, and I can't afford to substitute you out either."

The cook sighed heavily. "It'd be nice if Kohaku weren't

injured…"

"Yeah."

A moment of silence fell over the kitchen before Jun asked, "So what's this mission that only I can accomplish?"

The Pirate King grinned, "I think it's finally time to set our last player in motion."

Jun stared at Hasunuma. "You really think we're that close to ending this?"

The Pirate King nodded. "So you know what your mission is, right?"

"Of course, Captain," Jun replied with a huge grin. "You want me to free the former Emperor's son."

It was a four-day's journey from O-kane's port to Rurin. The trip would have taken less time if the Ryujin had sailed over on a straight path, however, the northern seas were very choppy, so it was more risky to sail through them. Instead, the path that the majority of Tsukigenese sailors took was one that hugged the mainland's northern coast. An extra day or two added to the journey was much preferred over the loss of a ship, its crew, and its contents.

When they set off from O-kane, Hasunuma had suggested that everyone spend their free time preparing for their mission, so the Ryujin became rather quiet. When they weren't on deck, Hanzo and Ginza used heavy crates in the storage room to strength train. During his short absences from the helm, Rize worked on making more arrows and a spare bow. Kohaku and Nia spent their time either in Kohaku's room, putting together supplies packs, or on deck soaking up the sun's rays. Jun went about his usual business in the galley. Kazuki didn't know what mission Hasunuma had given the cook, but, whatever it was, Jun didn't seem to feel the need to prepare for it.

Reika spent most of her time in Kazuki's room, drawing odd symbols and designs on slips of paper and mumbling incantations over them. The young man found the work interesting and wanted to watch, but Reika kicked him out because she said it was hard to concentrate with him around.

Douglas and the Pirate King spent much of the time in the captain's quarters; presumably planning how best to rescue the colossal man's ship and crew. A few times, Kazuki was lucky enough to witness the two men sparring on deck. Although neither man used his full strength, Kazuki couldn't help but watch them in awe. They were like gods of war that, even in their restraint, had a battle prowess that shone through and surpassed anything that the young man could ever hope to possess.

Watching the two only increased Kazuki's desire to witness Douglas fight earnestly on the battlefield. And, sooner than he expected, the young man got his wish; Two days into their journey, a ship approached the Ryujin. The red sails meant it was a pirate ship, but that didn't necessarily mean it was a friendly ship, since, being lawless by nature, not all pirates obeyed the Pirate King or the code.

Following proper protocol, the Pirate King ordered the Ryujin to a halt so that he could speak with the captain of the incoming vessel.

When the other ship was within range, Hasunuma called out to it.

A rough-looking man answered his call. "Aye, we know who ya are, Red Dragon," he spat. "We came t' challenge ya in a duel, see?"

Kazuki didn't need to use the Demon King's powers to know that the rough-looking man was housing a demon inside of him; hate, rage, and the thirst for blood were pouring out of the man as he stood on the deck of his ship, glaring at the Pirate King.

"I distinctly remember our last meeting, Izuho, which ended rather poorly for you. So which number am I speaking to?" the Pirate King replied with a grin.

The rough-looking man's demeanor immediately changed, so much so that it seemed as if his physical appearance changed as well. The same man stood before them, but he somehow looked less rough, and his eyes were now solid black.

"Seven," the man replied, his voice now sounding more intelligent. "But don't think I'll be as easy to defeat as my weak sisters, Eight and Nine."

"I didn't realize demons had families," the Pirate King shrugged.

"All it takes is a corrupt soul to become a demon. Some families are the same in life as they are in death, but there are also countless ways to become corrupted." Seven explained rather calmly. "I believe *revenge* is the most common," he added with meaning.

I'm guessing his sisters were the ones Jun and I defeated at Silver's place. Hopefully this guy doesn't have the power to freeze people too...

Kazuki glanced around for Reika and found her standing near the stairs that lead below deck. He was glad she was close by in case they needed her priestess spells.

"We aren't far from the shores of the mainland," the Pirate King announced, "so let's move our battle there."

Seven nodded in agreement and ordered his crew to head for shore. It seemed odd to Kazuki that a demon would be so quick to follow the human rules of engagement, but he was glad for it. As Hasunuma had explained to him once before, battles at sea were extremely rare because of the toll they took on the ships – which were costly to repair and maintain. So even the most lawless and ruthless pirates usually adhered to that particular rule, and would move their battles to the nearest shore.

When both ships anchored a ways off from a sandy spot of the mainland's coast, Seven and a handful of his men hopped into a rowboat and made their way to shore; the remainder of his crew remained onboard his ship. This indicated to those on the Ryujin that the demon wanted a one-on-one fight, presumably between himself and the captain.

The Pirate King followed accordingly, but before he could launch the rowboat Douglas jumped in and proclaimed that he would go too. Kazuki advanced towards the small boat, pulling a slightly unwilling Reika along behind him, but the Pirate King held out his hand to stop them.

"I appreciate the thought, Kid, but let us adults handle this one," he said with a smile.

"But Reika's skills will help even the odds of the battle," Kazuki pleaded. He didn't want to miss out on the opportunity to see the two men fight seriously. "And what if Seven's men suddenly join in?" The young man added, trying not to sound too desperate.

Hasunuma and Douglas simply looked at each other and laughed heartily in response. Then they cast off from the Ryujin and headed towards the beach where Seven and his men awaited them.

"Sorry Little Oni," Ginza said cheerfully as he patted the young man on the shoulder. "You'll just have t' watch from 'ere."

Gravely disappointed at being left out, Kazuki crossed his arms and stood silently, his eyes focused on the shore.

"If I hadn't witnessed it myself, I never would have believed that that kid houses the King of all demons."

The Pirate King smiled at the warrior before him, who was easily rowing the boat by himself across the choppy water. "He's pretty interesting, isn't he?"

"All I'll say is I hope you and Kohaku have raised him well. If something were to set him off–"

"The Kid'll be fine," the Pirate King said over the warrior's voice.

"You trying to convince me or yourself of that?" Douglas mused. When no answer came from the Pirate King, the warrior shrugged and changed the subject. "So what's our plan for once we reach shore?"

"Take 'em out as fast as possible so we can continue on to Rurin."

Douglas laughed, "You make it sound so easy. Don't you fear the demons?"

"Only those that hide within," Hasunuma replied grimly. "And anyways," he added in a more lighthearted tone, "this guy's not in the top five, so he can't be all that strong."

Douglas laughed again. "Sometimes I can't tell if you're a complete fool or an egotistical genius. Either way, I've got your back."

The Pirate King grinned. "I know."

When they reached the shore, Douglas jumped out and pulled the rowboat up onto the sand. Hasunuma stepped out of the small boat and walked towards Seven and his lackeys.

"Sorry for the wait, gentleman," the Pirate King said with an apologetic smile. He placed his hand on the hilt of his sword, but before he could draw his weapon, Douglas stepped in-between him and the demon.

"Mind if I take this one?" the warrior asked with a grin.

Seven stared at Douglas for a moment before responding, "Who is this?"

"He's my second-in-command," the Pirate King replied. "If you agree to fight him, I'll offer my head if he loses."

"More like *when* he loses," Seven's men snickered.

The demon seemed to consider the offer. It was fair and within the rules of engagement, so there was no problem as long as Seven accepted. Which he did.

The Pirate King felt the corners of his mouth rising. How long had it been since he got to sit back and watch Douglas fight? He made his way towards the dunes at the top of the beach and found a suitable spot to relax in.

"What the festering hole are you doing?!" One of Seven's men cried out in alarm.

"Just getting comfortable," the Pirate King shrugged. The man was about to retort when Hasunuma added, "Oh, and I'd step back a bit if I were you."

Seven's men's eyes shot towards Douglas's weapon: a long spear with a tri-forked blade at the tip. Although it was a unique weapon, its plain and well-worn appearance made it seem less intimidating. The men chuckled and decided not to heed the Pirate King's warning. Not that he cared.

"I know not what caliber fighter you are," Seven began slowly, "but you will not be able to defeat me."

Douglas grinned and replied, "Try me."

Seven unsheathed his sword, which looked to be an ordinary katana, and pointed its tip at the warrior before him. "Foolish human," he muttered before sprinting towards Douglas. The tip of his sword did not get within seven feet of the warrior. Instead, the demon found himself suddenly flying backwards across the sand. As Seven landed on his feet, he glared at Douglas.

"Didn't see me swing, did you?" Douglas grinned. "But you sure felt it." He had also knocked back the demon's men, who were now scattered amongst the sand dunes.

"I'll admit that I wasn't expecting that sort of speed from a human," Seven replied, "but that still doesn't compare to what a demon can do." He crouched, pausing for a split second before launching himself at Douglas once more. This time there was a distinct ring of metal-on-metal.

The remarkable and other-worldly speed at which Seven closed the distance between himself and Douglas didn't seem to bother the warrior at all. Not only had he blocked the demon's katana with his spear, but he also trapped the blade within its three prongs. Understanding his predicament, Seven quickly switched gears and kicked Douglas in his stomach. He then released his grip on his katana and delivered a series of kicks and punches to the warrior's torso before landing one final punch, powered by demonic energy, that pushed Douglas back a few feet.

The warrior patted his stomach and said, "That was a good one."

Seven's reply came in the form of another barrage of physical attacks with an increasing level of demonic power, but the warrior weathered them like a stone wall against a light breeze.

Basic attacks will never work against him, the Pirate King thought as he watched the demon struggle against his second-in-command. *He'd better pull out some fancy demon powers soon or Douglas will get bored and end it.*

As if he heard Hasunuma's thoughts, Seven suddenly jumped back several feet and a strange glow enveloped him.

Douglas glanced down at his own feet. "Am I imagining things, or is the sand suddenly very wet?"

The demon grinned, "Quite observant, strange human. I did, indeed, supersaturate the sand beneath your feet."

The warrior tried to step away, but the more he moved, the more he sunk into the waterlogged sand. By the time he realized that the best action was to be still, he was already buried up to his thighs.

"How does it feel to be helpless?" the demon taunted as he picked up his sword. "I think I'll take my time killing you. Maybe slice off little bits of flesh until I get to your bones."

In lieu of a reply, Douglas unwrapped the sash from his waist and tied one end to his spear; the other he wrapped around his wrist. The warrior then threw his spear towards Seven with all of his might, but the demon easily side-stepped out of the way. Seven almost grinned, but stopped when he saw the corners of Douglas' lips rise. He heard a cry of agony from one of his men and turned to find the pronged tips of the warrior's spear protruding from his henchman's back. As Douglas pulled on the sash, the henchman lurched forward and screamed. The other men quickly surrounded the skewered man and tried to prevent him from being pulled towards their foe.

"Let go of him, you idiots," Seven shouted, "That human is using you to pull himself out of the sand!"

But as the impaled man was dragged through the sand, flailing in pain and fear, he caught the leg of his captain and refused to let go. "No! Please, save me!"

Seven looked down at the man as if he were a disgusting insect and crushed the poor man's head into the sand with his other foot.

After seeing that horror, the rest of the men attempted to run away from their captain, only to be swallowed up by an enormous wave that crashed into them and pulled their bodies out to sea.

So he can manipulate water…no wonder he readily agreed to a fight on the beach.

"I thought those were your men," Douglas said firmly as he stood before the demon; he had freed himself from the sand trap.

"Not mine, but that of the former owner of this body. And do you really think I'd let you use them as a means of escape again? They are more useful to me dead." Seven said plainly.

Well, that settles it. Hasunuma shook his head. *Way to trigger his switch, ya damned demon bastard.*

The warrior grasped his weapon with both hands and assumed an offensive stance. "They became your men when you stole their captain's body," Douglas growled. "You have a responsibility to protect them."

Seven laughed. "What's this? You mercilessly skewered one of them to pull yourself to safety, yet you're mad because *I* killed the rest of them."

"A warrior shows no mercy to his enemy, but he *protects* his own," Douglas bellowed.

Seven laughed again. "I'm not a warrior, but a demon. And we follow a different sort of rules: namely, 'do whatever you want'."

"I don't think your king would agree with you," Douglas countered.

A shadow passed across the demon's face. "We have no king, and I obey *no one*," he growled.

I guess even the Demon King has trouble keeping his subjects in line.

The warrior and the demon were now emitting deadly auras. Douglas moved first, charging towards Seven with his tri-forked weapon aimed at the demon's throat. Seven ran to the left and circled behind the warrior. Douglas swung his spear behind him, but met no resistance. The demon had jumped high into the air to avoid the spear and was now falling towards the warrior with his sword, ready to stab through Douglas' head. The warrior sensed the demon's presence above and quickly pulled his spear over his head to block. Seven's sword hit the spear with such force that some shards broke off and flew into Douglas' chest and arms.

The warrior grunted. "That's a neat trick."

"I wasn't trying to amuse you," Seven replied.

Ah, he encased his sword in ice. That's not something I expected, but Jun did mention that Eight and Nine were ice demons, so I should have considered this a possibility. Hmm…an ice sword could be fun to wield, but I wouldn't want it sticking to my hand though.

While Hasunuma's mind wandered, Seven continued to press his sword against Douglas' spear. Neither the demon nor the warrior gave an inch. The friction between the weapons caused more ice shards to splinter off, and they found new homes in the warrior's flesh. Small trails of water mixed with blood slid down Douglas' body as the heat melted the shards.

The stalemate was broken by a large wave that crashed onto shore. While the wave split and missed Seven completely, Douglas was knocked aside. The wave rolled the warrior along the beach, towards the water. Just before he vanished beneath the surface of the sea, Douglas threw his spear. It flew past Seven, missing him completely.

The demon grinned at his apparent victory, but it was short-lived; the warrior rose from the water just shy of the shore. In his hand was one end of his sash.

Douglas coughed and spat seawater. "I was careless. I owe you one, Hasunuma."

"No, you owe me four at this point," the Pirate King corrected. "And next time watch where you throw this thing. I was almost skewered," he added as he threw the spear back to its owner.

Douglas caught it with the tip of the center prong inches from his chest. "I wanted to make sure you weren't sleeping over there."

Seven broke their interchange with a taunt, "Is pulling you out of danger all that stick's good for?"

"She's actually pretty talented," the warrior replied with a grin, "but she likes to have a big audience when she performs." He twirled the spear around in his hands and then passed it up over his chest and casually rested it on his shoulder. "You're just not enough to get her excited."

...Says the guy who was all fired-up a minute ago.

"It seems to me that you're all bark and no bite," the demon said flatly.

Douglas shrugged. "I guess I've been around you Tsukigenese too long and picked up your bad habit of chatting during a fight." He took his spear off of his shoulder, grabbed it with both hands, and assumed an offensive stance. "Get ready to feel my 'bite'."

"Another petty attempt at–" Seven began to sneer, but stopped when the warrior flew at him with such tremendous strength and speed that the demon slid backwards when their weapons met. Before Seven could counter, Douglas forced the demon to retreat further with a sweep of his spear. The warrior stepped closer to perform a thrust attack, but the demon had regained enough composure to create a sand trap between himself and his foe.

It looked as if Douglas were about to step right into the loose sand, and Hasunuma almost shouted out to him, but the warrior had either foreseen or noticed the demon's trap. Instead of stepping into it, Douglas thrust the tip of his spear into the loose sand below; he did so at precisely the right speed and angle to propel himself forward towards the demon. Sailing just above the ground, the warrior landed a forceful punch in Seven's stomach. As the demon folded from the blow, Douglas grabbed Seven's sword hand, broke the demon's wrist, and stabbed Seven through the heart with his own sword. Smoke emanated from the corpse before it dropped lifelessly to the sand.

The Pirate King stood up and made his way towards the warrior. "You had me worried for a second there," he remarked with a smirk.

"Not a chance," Douglas scoffed, "it was obvious what Seven was going to do. That demon could have used his ability in a dozen other ways, but he stupidly stuck to the same old trick."

"Yes, well, I wonder if that was intentional or not."

"What do you mean?" The warrior asked.

Hasunuma shook his head. "What we know so far about demonic powers comes from ancient texts or tales. We don't have any solid information. There could be limitations to their powers that we're unaware of, and I'm wondering if that was the case with Seven."

Douglas furrowed his brow. "You're right. And things are always overexaggerated in tales anyhow, so they can't be taken as fact."

"Exactly. However," the Pirate King added with a sigh, "it's not like we can write any of this information down in order to study it."

"Why not?"

"Because people like Hiiro Genji will make use of it," Hasunuma replied icily.

"Oh, right," the warrior awkwardly responded. He then grabbed his spear and whipped it through the air to get the sand off.

"Let's head back," the Pirate King said as he began walking towards the rowboat.

Douglas followed silently behind. It wasn't until they were casting off that he suddenly said, "I still think it would be a good idea to keep track of this knowledge we're acquiring of demonic powers. Surely there is a way to keep the accounts safe and secure so that only those fighting against the demons can use the information. We both know that these demon games will happen again in one hundred years, so why not leave something that could help?"

Hasunuma shook his head. "I know that I'm heavily biased about this, but I still can't trust that the information wouldn't somehow fall into the wrong hands. And there is no way that I can consciously take part in something that could repeat this horror for future generations."

"I understand," was all that the warrior replied. He silently rowed them both towards the Ryujin, seemingly lost in thought.

Hasunuma guessed that Douglas was trying to think of some way to create secure records for the future. He was a smart man, and rather thoughtful for someone who dedicated his life to fighting. With enough time, the warrior probably could have come up with a decent solution, but the Pirate King wanted nothing to do with it. Whether it would help future generations or not, Hasunuma had decided long ago to reject anything to do with demons. And he convinced himself that there was no need to change his mind.

Kazuki stood on the deck of the Ryujin, blankly staring at the now empty beach, unable to process what he had just seen. *That* was *a demon, right? And a number below ten at that...*

"By the gods...what is he?" The young man wondered aloud.

"He's a full-blooded warrior of the highest class," Nia answered. A devilish smile appeared on her face as she added, "Does my man intrigue you, Kazuki?"

The young man wasn't sure how to respond, so he was glad when Kohaku approached them, limping, and said, "Don't tease him, Ni."

"What?" the Kheprian woman asked innocently.

The ninja woman sighed and said to Kazuki, "D – I mean, Douglas – is a great man. And she will tell you all about him if you really want to know," Kohaku nodded towards Nia. "Just be careful," she added as she leaned in to whisper in Kazuki's ear, "that woman *loves* getting inside people's heads."

The Kheprian woman continued to smile innocently at Kazuki. "Oh, don't listen to Ko. Now, what would you like to know about my man?"

Right. Her sense of hearing is heightened because she's nearly blind...I need to keep that in mind. The young man thought about Douglas for a moment before asking, "How did he become so skilled in combat? It's like he was made for battle."

Nia laughed. "You could say that. His bloodline is that of the mightiest warriors known to our part of the world."

"So his ancestors were all part of Khepria's military?"

Nia waved her hand in dismissal. "No, we don't have a military. Or, at least, in the sense that you're probably thinking. Khepria is a large country that has the ocean nestled against its eastern edge and southern tip, but has many smaller countries bordering it's western and northern sides. Traditionally, all Kheprian boys are trained to become warriors. Those that cannot pass the physical and mental tests put before them are then switched to other professions, but, for the most part, our men are our 'military' force."

"To clarify: their men are warriors by profession, but their focus lies on the *life* of a warrior, not on the militaristic aspects," Kohaku interjected.

"Exactly," Nia nodded. "They can become our army when we need protection from our neighbors, but their man goal is to become a true warrior."

Kazuki furrowed his brow. "But what does that even mean? Aren't warriors people who fight for a living?"

"In other countries, like Skövalgar or here in Tsukigen, yes, that is the case. But in Khepria it's…hmm. How can I explain this better, Ko?" The Kheprian woman pondered.

Kohaku folded her arms over her chest. "I guess… you could compare it to how samurai used to be, before the Hekigun took over. Kazu, do you know what I'm talking about?"

The young man nodded. "The old man explained the 'samurai lifestyle' to me many times. They weren't focused on fighting as much as the way a samurai should live – like what moral code, temperament, and attitude they should have and how they should spend their time – that kind of stuff."

"Alright, yes, that sounds more like what the Kheprian warrior is," Nia said with excitement. "So, keeping that in mind, my man's family line has produced some of the most influential and skilled warriors in Khepria's long history. In fact, for as far back as we can trace his line, all of the men have been in the highest class of warrior."

"They have a ranking system that places each warrior in a class, depending on how they rank in the various aspects of the warrior life," Kohaku explained. "So, for instance, there may be a warrior who excels at battle but can't debate well; that warrior would be placed in a mid to lower class, because he is lacking in one of the aspects."

Nia nodded. "Exactly. And there are quite a few aspects in which a warrior must excel in order to be counted in the highest class. Therefore, it's not a rank many achieve, and for those that do, they are basically treated like gods."

"That's incredible," Kazuki said, genuinely awe-struck, "but it also sounds very stressful, especially for Douglas who comes from such a prestigious line. He must have grown up under enormous pressure."

"Considering that his father has sat, undefeated, in the top spot for my man's entire life," Nia said with a lighthearted laugh, "yes, there is tremendous pressure for my man to perform well. But," she continued with a warm smile, "he doesn't have some deep-seeded complex about it as you might think. My man's actually been thrilled with it his whole life. He always looks on the bright side, so to him, the day he defeats his father, he will have accomplished two goals at once: gaining the top rank and proving that he is worthy of his heritage."

Douglas must have a will of steel. I'd crumble under that pressure.

Nia then crossed her arms and sighed, "But that old man of his is beyond compare. Every time the two of them fight, or get into a debate, the gods don't even bother to place bets."

"That's…hard to believe. Especially after seeing him defeat that demon just now," the young man replied.

The Kheprian woman laughed and shook her head. "You have no idea, Kazuki. In your young eyes, Douglas may seem incredibly strong, but there are warriors superior to him in Khepria. Including his father." Nia then turned her head towards the rowboat that was nearing the Ryujin. "I have faith that one day my man will accomplish his goals, but first he needs to grow as a warrior. And the best way to do that," she grinned, "is to broaden his field of battle."

"Is that why he came here?" Kazuki asked.

Nia nodded. "I convinced him to come with me on one of my trade routes, in order to speak with people of different mindsets and to battle other warriors."

"That makes sense," Kazuki agreed, "but then why–"

"Hasunuma? Can you really not see?" Nia asked with skepticism.

The young man furrowed his brow. "He's never lost a fight that I've seen, I'll give him that, but I don't think of Hasunuma as someone to…" Kazuki paused. *No, that's not right. Hasunuma is an amazing fighter, and he's great with strategy too. I've been impressed by him ever since we first met. Why can't I admit that?*

"Hasunuma is the first man, other than his father, that Douglas has never been able to defeat. He took up the position as the Pirate King's second-in-command in order to better study Hasunuma, hoping to gain some insight into his abilities." Nia paused a moment before adding, "Did you know, Kazuki, that a man who dedicates himself solely to one thing can rise to heights unreachable by most."

Kazuki absorbed her statement before replying, "Then what about you? Where do you fit into his quest for greatness?"

Nia's small frame shook as she laughed. "I never said that you have to be alone in order to accomplish greatness. Although, I suppose it's fair to say that after we met, he did gain a second form of dedication. But, if anything, I think that has made him stronger. A man needs a reason to fight, right?"

Kazuki's heart leapt in his chest. *She's dangerously sharp...*

"Well, that was a long-winded way of answering your question. But I hope that helps you to see why my husband is so skilled. He is constantly striving to be the best. It is what he was born and raised to do."

Kazuki could hear the admiration in Nia's voice as she spoke of her husband. He still refused to honor Hasunuma with any praise, but he could see Nia's point. Her words made Kazuki think more of Jun and his dedication – or obsession – with out-mastering his father, than of the egotistical jerk that calls himself the Pirate King.

Maybe that intense level of dedication is why Jun's swordsmanship is unrivaled, the young man thought. *Despite his personality, I'd say he's a better example of a warrior than Hasunuma.*

"Now let me ask *you* a question, Kazuki," Nia said with a sly grin. She motioned for him to come to her, and, when he did, she pulled on his shoulder so that she could whisper in his ear, "How does it feel to hold your love in your arms? Does it make you feel like a real man?"

Kazuki practically jumped away from Nia and looked at her with great alarm.

The Kheprian woman laughed.

"Ni," Kohaku cautioned.

"Fine, fine," Nia said as she continued to laugh.

"Did everyone enjoy the show?" A booming voice asked.

The young man turned to find Douglas and the Pirate King standing behind them.

"You were wonderful, darling," Nia replied enthusiastically as she walked over and pulled her husband's face down to hers. "You never cease to amaze me."

The colossal man grabbed his wife around her waist and pulled her into him. She then kissed him so passionately that Kazuki grew embarrassed and looked away.

Turning to Kohaku he whispered, "She's nearly blind though, so how could she watch–"

"I'm not deaf, Kazuki," Nia interjected as she pulled away from her husband. "Ko was giving me a play-by-play."

Kazuki's face flushed slightly at his blunder. "Right, sorry," he mumbled.

"Hey, enough break time," the Pirate King interrupted, "we've got places to be, so let's get moving." He looked at the loving couple who had resumed their…physical expressions, and said, "Douglas, you're embarrassing the kid. Do that stuff in your room. And where the festering hole is everyone else?"

"Jun is where he always is, Rize is up in the nest, Hanzo and Ginza went below as soon as the fight was over, and I believe Reika went to help Jun after you left the ship," Kohaku effortlessly reported.

"Ever observant," Hasunuma said with a smile. "Douglas, tell Hanzo and Ginza to come on deck when you go below, and," the Pirate King looked up at the crow's nest and shouted, "Rize, I need you back at the helm!"

As Hasunuma made his way towards the helm, Kohaku limped over to the main mast where Rize was descending. When he reached the deck, Rize gave Kohaku a disapproving look and stopped her as she tried to ascend.

"I'm glad you can move a bit better," he said, "but there's no way I'm letting you climb up there yet."

Kohaku dropped her head with a sigh. Rize looked apologetic as he patted her shoulder. The helmsman then slowly walked the ninja woman back to the stack of crates where she had been sitting lately. He waited until Kohaku was settled before he headed for the helm.

"Feeling helpless is the worst," said deep voice from behind Kazuki. He didn't need to turn to know it was Douglas speaking.

"How much longer do you think she'll be out?" The young man asked, keeping his eyes on the ninja woman.

"My guess is another week," Nia chimed in, "but it will be longer still before she can move at full speed."

"Have you tried giving her some of your healing ointment?" Douglas asked his wife.

"No, Ko's works better than mine," Nia replied. "Although…it wouldn't hurt to add some on."

Kazuki then heard light footsteps head towards the stairs.

"I'm guessing demonic healing powers only work for the user," Douglas commented.

The young man nodded. "As far as I can tell." *Unless* you *know something else…*

Kazuki faintly felt laughter in his chest, but that was the only response he got from the Demon King.

I figured you wouldn't help, the young man thought with

annoyance. *All you care about is killing.*

For a short instance, Kazuki felt something akin to guilt or sadness and became confused. The feeling belonged to *him*, and the young man had never considered a demon capable of those sorts of emotions. But before he could delve further, Douglas interrupted his thoughts with a question.

"So, Kid, what are you going to do after this is all over?"

Kazuki turned and frowned at the warrior. "My name is 'Kazuki'," he replied flatly, "and why does everyone keep asking me all of these questions?"

Douglas laughed and firmly grasped the young man's shoulder. "Sorry, Kazuki, I didn't mean much by it."

OUCH. "It's fine," the young man replied as he tried to drop his shoulder and escape the warrior's grip.

Thankfully, Douglas seemed to understand the situation and he released Kazuki's shoulder. "If you don't have plans, you're welcome to travel with us to Khepria."

Kazuki raised an eyebrow. "You're inviting *me* to a land full of powerful warriors?"

"Is there something wrong with that?" Douglas asked with sincerity.

"Well, not really…" Kazuki trailed off. He then had a vision of encountering a whole horde of Douglases, and added, "I just don't think I'd fit in."

"Sorry, darling, but Kazuki is more interested in becoming a priest than a warrior," Nia interjected as she returned to the deck with a jar of green paste in her hand.

The young man felt his face flush at her comment, but Douglas was too busy watching Nia walk past to notice.

"But, with the proper training, you could be an elite warrior," Douglas said to Kazuki, his eyes still fixed on Nia's backside.

The young man sighed heavily. "No, that's all the Demon King's influence. Without him, I'm just..." Kazuki trailed off. He wasn't sure how to finish the sentence. What would he be after the Demon King left? If he lived, he'd just be an average young man without the Demon King's abilities. Would he still be able to protect Reika like that? Would she even want him anymore? What would his life be like?

A strong hand landed on his shoulder. Kazuki looked up to see the warrior smiling down at him.

"It's all good. Not everything has to be solved at once," he said reassuringly. "If you want to become a warrior, Demon King or not, then you're welcome to join us. But I understand that the path of the warrior isn't for everyone."

But it is *a path...*

"Your wife told me that you were born to be a warrior. Is life easier when you follow the path you've been directed down?" The young man asked.

Douglas removed his hand from Kazuki's shoulder. "That, I think, depends on the person and the circumstances. Let's say, for instance, that your father has set your path for you – to follow in his footsteps – but your passions lie elsewhere. What would you do? You could be a prince or the son of a farmer, it doesn't matter. If you chose to follow the path, your life might be easier in some ways, but you wouldn't be inspired to give it your all. And, in my mind, doing something half-hearted is a waste of time."

"But what if you can't see any other paths? What if you only learned what your father wanted you to, so there's no other choice?" The young man countered.

"There's always a choice, Kazuki. Our brains make us capable of learning new skills, and our passion drives us to strive for success," Douglas explained. "Yeah, it's easier when the path set before you aligns with your passions, but that doesn't mean you can't have an equally fulfilling life by making your own way. Plus, 'easy' usually means dull," he added with a smirk.

The young man thought about his own life; the only path he'd followed so far was the one the Demon King had carved out for him. If he really could get his life back at the end of this, then what awaited him? All he knew how to do was fight.

"So, then, has my life until now been a waste?" Kazuki asked dejectedly.

"Not at all," Douglas reassured him. "You've learned things about yourself and about the world and people around you that you wouldn't have otherwise. And not all of us are born knowing who we are and what we want to do."

"Very few are," Nia suddenly chimed in. "Sorry to interrupt, but you were supposed to summon Hanzo and Ginza to the deck, darling."

"Ah, right," Douglas replied. "You're welcome to seek me out later if you want to continue this discussion, Kazuki," he added before turning around and heading below deck.

"I'd better go too, so that he doesn't get distracted again," Nia said with a sigh, but her lips were curled into a smile. "Kazuki, you'll have plenty of time to decide what to do after we've finished with the Hekigun, so try not to worry about it too much. Take one step at a time, alright?" The Kheprian woman flashed him a radiant smile and then turned to follow her husband.

The young man stood there, thinking about what the foreign couple had said, until two shadows loomed over him, breaking his concentration.

"If ya've got time t' stare at nothin', then ya've got time t' help haul crates," Ginza said with a grin.

"And muscles gained equal enemies defeated," Hanzo added.

"Maybe for you muscle-heads," Kazuki retorted.

Ginza shook his head. "Ya can't just rely on yer blade, Little Oni."

"It seems to work well-enough for Jun," Kazuki mumbled.

"Come on, Lad," Hanzo said as he wrapped one beefy arm around the young man.

"If nothin' else, the ladies'll like ya more," Ginza added as he elbowed Kazuki in the ribs.

"I don't think he needs help there, Gin," Hanzo said with a wry smile.

Kazuki's face flushed. "Fine, I'll help you!" He yelled as he wriggled out of Hanzo's grasp. "But only for a little bit. I've got other things to do," he added.

"I'm sure ya do," grinned Ginza.

Without any further demonic interruptions, it only took a few days to reach Rurin's main port, Genin. Hasunuma hadn't been by the port in many years, but he remembered it being nearly as busy as the one on Masayoshi Island. The fisherman in Rurin caught different types of fish than what was available to the rest of Tsukigen, because of the cooler waters, so the fishing trade was usually bustling. Not only that, but there were also many mines in the mountains of Rurin that held valuable rocks and minerals used in various trades, including iron sand used in making steel for blades.

Genin was on the northeastern part of the island. The location was chosen for security; surrounded by mountains on three sides, with the sea in front of it, there was only one effective way in or out of the port. While Rurin and Masayoshi Island were similarly configured, Rurin was about twice as large. There was another section of flat land on the southern part of the island, which could also have made a nice location for the main port, but many small villages – which had been established long before commercial trade between the islands began – had already claimed the area.

It was the Pirate King's understanding that, while the locals supplied the trading goods and were appreciative of the coin it brought in, they did not welcome the new port town. Like their cold-water fish, the people of Rurin were unlike those from the mainland; not bad, just different. And they were furious when the Hekigun built a fortress on one of the mountains between Genin and the local village area. Unfortunately, the villagers were unable to force the Hekigun out.

I wonder if they'll be grateful to us after we purge the island of the Hekigun?

Hasunuma smirked and shook his head. He knew better than to expect gratefulness from anyone. In Tsukigen, all pirates, good or bad, were scum – as the miko so often loved to remind them – and that thinking was true for the people of Rurin too.

"Ready to enter the port, Captain?" Rize asked from the helm.

"Aye," the Pirate King responded.

The crew stood on deck, at the ready for an attack from any direction. But as the Ryujin pulled into the port, there were no Hekigun soldiers to be seen. In fact, there were no people of any kind, and all of the ships were docked and crewless. The shops and stalls were vacant, and the only sounds to be heard were the wind, the waves, and the seagulls.

"Somethin's not right 'ere," Ginza said grimly.

"Aye, this has 'trap' written all over it," Hanzo added.

"Precisely," the Pirate King said calmly. He had figured that the enemy would foresee their arrival and had already planned accordingly. "Does everyone remember their groups and the tasks that I assigned?"

The crew silently nodded, as no one dared to yell a word.

"Good," the Pirate King said as he looked over his crew. Everyone was on deck, including Jun. "I expect you to do your jobs well and return *safely*. Am I clear?"

Again, the crew nodded, but this time a slightly audible "Aye, Cap'n" was heard.

"Good," the Pirate King nodded solemnly. "Now let's move," he said as he stepped onto the gangplank. The rest of the crew followed behind.

Douglas and Rize immediately filed in behind the Pirate King;

they were the fastest walkers and always liked to see what was ahead of them. Normally, the kid would have come next, but he was busy watching over the miko – who walked slowly – so they ended up behind Hanzo and Ginza. Jun was last.

The Pirate King wasn't sure whether or not the cook liked being in the back for safety's sake or for anti-social reasons, but he supposed it didn't really matter. If there was an ambush from the rear, not a single enemy would get past Jun.

Hasunuma glanced over his shoulder at the two faces that hadn't moved from the Ryujin; Nia wore an unbecoming scowl, while Kohaku's expression wilted with regret. The Pirate King knew it was hard for both ladies to stay put, but the Ryujin needed to be guarded, Kohaku couldn't walk well enough to keep pace with everyone else, and he wasn't about to make her stay behind alone.

Both the ninja woman and the Kheprian assassin were smart enough to have realized Hasunuma's intentions by this point, so he didn't feel the need to explain his orders further. However, seeing Kohaku's downcast face as he walked away was more painful than he thought it would be. The Pirate King was tempted to run back, pick her up, and carry her the whole way to the base, but he knew that would be disastrous for the mission. His focus had to be on the fight, not on protecting someone.

Not that Kohaku couldn't defend herself, but the Hekigun are the type of enemy that takes advantage of their opponent's weak spot, no matter how immoral it might be. And an immobile woman, that meant more to him than he cared to admit, was not a weak spot he dared to leave exposed.

"There are soldiers hiding nearby," Rize whispered to his captain.

The Pirate King nodded. He could sense them too.

"Must be waiting to make their move until we're fully gone," Douglas added, trying to keep his voice as quiet as possible.

"Mmhmm," Rize agreed.

"Then we'd better hurry so we can stop the flow of reinforcements," the Pirate King replied with a grin as he doubled his pace.

Rize and Douglas easily kept up with their captain, while the others fell further and further behind. However, the three speed-walkers stopped when they reached the edge of town and waited for their companions to catch up. The road split into multiple paths, and Douglas was the only one who knew which to take.

As Hanzo and Ginza came into view, with the kid and the miko a few steps behind, the Pirate King waved them over.

When they were close enough to hear, Douglas pointed to the path that led North-West and said, "That's the way towards the experimental facility."

"Right," Ginza said with a nod. "Any other splits?"

"No," Douglas replied, "strangely enough, there's only one path and it takes you to a clearing where you can see the facility. How you get to it from there, I don't know."

"Sounds suspicious to me," Hanzo said as he furrowed his brow. "Are you sure you weren't led there on purpose?"

Douglas shook his head. "To be honest, I can't be sure." A serious expression formed on the warrior's face as he added, "Those hybrids are incredibly fast. Try not to let them sneak up on you…alright?"

Hasunuma was surprised at the warrior's warning. Douglas

didn't normally say things like that, and to have him say it now was…unnerving.

"If they've got any demon in them, I'll be able to sense them," the kid confidently chimed in.

Douglas looked like he wanted to say something in response, but instead he simply nodded and turned towards a different road. "This one leads to the fortress."

"Right, then I guess we'll be seein' ya later," Ginza said with a thumbs-up.

"You're in charge, Ginza," the Pirate King said as he gave the blacksmith a meaningful look.

Ginza understood what his captain meant. He nodded firmly. "Aye, Cap'n."

"Why is Gin always in charge?" Hanzo grumbled.

The Pirate King smirked. "Would *you* like to be the one to face my wrath if something goes wrong?"

Hanzo's expression immediately softened. "No, Cap'n. You're right. Gin should be in charge."

"'Ey!" Ginza yelled in complaint.

Hanzo and the Pirate King laughed together. Rize quietly joined in too.

"We need to move," Douglas interrupted.

"I know, I know," Hasunuma said with a wave of his hand. Before following Douglas' suggestion, the Pirate King made eye contact with Hanzo and Ginza and told them: "You two take care of the kids, and yourselves."

Both men nodded and replied, "Aye, Cap'n!"

"I still resent being treated like a child," Kazuki grumbled as he approached the group.

Hasunuma laughed and patted the kid on his head. "You're almost there, Kid. If you complete this mission, I'll treat you like an adult. Sound fair?"

"Nothing involving you is ever fair," the kid mumbled as he swatted Hasunuma's hand away. His eyes then shifted focus and they locked onto the Pirate King's. Worry, sadness, and a glint of gratitude or admiration reflected in Kazuki's hazel orbs. "You guys had better take care too," he said to everyone, though his eyes didn't move.

The Pirate King understood the kid's implication and smiled. "Worry about yourself for once," he replied as he put his hand on Kazuki's shoulder.

Slightly embarrassed, the kid quickly turned away. He grabbed the miko's hand and began walking briskly towards the path Douglas had set them on without another word.

Although he couldn't help teasing the kid, the warm feeling that came from Kazuki's kindheartedness lingered in the Pirate King's chest. In that moment, he felt like a proud older brother.

"Hey, Little Oni! I'll try to catch some game so we can all have a feast back on the Ryujin," Rize called out, raising his voice so that the retreating Kazuki could hear him.

Hanzo and Ginza grinned. "Sounds good t' us," they replied in unison.

"Whoever defeats the most hybrids gets a double portion," Rize offered.

The giant and the blacksmith looked excitedly at each other before turning and running to catch up with the kids.

Rize chuckled. "Hopefully that's enough motivation for them."

"If they can remember it," the Pirate King added with a smirk. He then stood there for a minute, watching as half of his crew disappeared down another path. He didn't want to admit it, but something felt off. Was it because the miko hadn't said a word since they had left the Ryujin? Maybe…or maybe not.

"We have to go, Captain," Douglas restated, this time with more urgency.

"Wait a minute, what about Jun?" Rize asked suddenly, as if he had just noticed the cook's absence.

"He's going another way," the Pirate King absently replied. And then, with great effort, Hasunuma tore his eyes from the distant figures and did his best to suppress his growing anxiety. "Right, let's go."

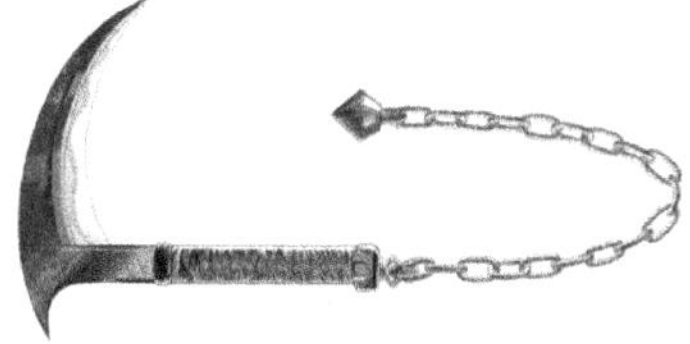

The women sat on the deck of the Ryujin, back-to-back on top of a stack of crates. From their position the ninja woman could see enough of the port to know when they would have company, but, to their dismay, not a soul had arrived yet.

"Ugh, I HATE waiting," Ni sighed heavily as she leaned her head against the back of Kohaku's.

"I know, me too," the ninja woman replied, "but that's our job this time." As she heard another sigh escape her friend's lips, Kohaku added, "And it's only been ten minutes since everyone left."

"Yes, yes," the delicate woman replied with a hint of annoyance in her voice.

The ninja woman was well aware that her friend had little patience when it came to her missions. Ni would always get so fired up that any inaction caused her mood to sour quickly. Although, in all honesty, that worked in their favor, since Ni became more deadly the grumpier she got.

Suddenly, both women sat up at attention and said in unison, "We've got company." Excitement rang in their voices.

The first group to show up consisted of about ten Hekigun soldiers – none of whom seemed to be of any notable rank. Kohaku had seen most of them emerge from a nearby storehouse.

Typical. Only weaklings wait until the perceived danger is gone.

"Tch," Ni grumbled. "Go home, little boys," she yelled to the men as they stepped onto the deck, "we're only interested in playing with the men."

The soldiers, however, didn't listen to her. Not that many men would, given Ni's size and delicate demeanor. They raised their satsumatas and surrounded the two women.

"Suit yourselves," Ni said coldly.

Not a second later, all ten men collapsed to the ground – all of them convulsing as blood seeped out of their eyes, nose, and ears.

A smile crept onto the ninja woman's face. "Your eyesight may be fading, Ni, but your speed and accuracy with those needles is still unmatched."

"But of course," the delicate woman laughed, "what good is an assassin who can't hit her target?"

The second barrage of soldiers streamed aboard the Ryujin soon after. There were twenty or so of them, but they all quickly succumbed to the same fate as those before them. Within five seconds of boarding the ship, to be precise. But this time it wasn't just Ni's poisoned needles that assailed them – the ninja woman wasn't about to let her friend get all of the action.

When the third wave appeared, the soldiers stopped and stared wide-eyed at the carnage on deck. One of them turned and vomited over the side of the ship.

"You get one chance," Ni warned. "Let's see if you're smarter than your comrades." When it came to large-scale battles, she always gave those weaker than her a chance to retreat.

It seemed that about half of the group had some brains, because they instantly fled from the ship. Unfortunately for them, they didn't get very far. The terrified men were all cut down before they left the dock.

"I won't tolerate cowards," a burly man boomed as he stepped onto the deck. He was of average height, but had a very muscular build. His hair was tied back in a knot and he had a long, knotted beard that was peppered with grey hairs.

"And I don't tolerate those that kill their own," Ni replied scornfully.

The man seemed to ignore her as he glared at the remaining soldiers and said, "Are you going to complete your mission, or do you want to end up like those cowards?"

For the first time ever, Kohaku felt some sympathy for the Hekigun soldiers. How cruel was it to be forced to choose between what was basically suicide, and death by a supposed ally.

The soldiers looked from Ni to the burly man, then back to Ni.

"*You* are the coward here if you ask me," Ni said as she pointed towards the burly man. Her words finally seemed to get his attention.

"No one asked you, *woman*," he spat. "And what does a *woman* know about cowardice?" The burly man donned a sinister grin as he added, "Oh, that's right, your kind *invented* it."

He's going to die. Slowly and painfully.

Ni stood up and motioned for Kohaku to stay seated. "Is that so?" she replied in a surprisingly calm voice. "Then you must be the founder of stupidity."

The burly man's face turned purplish-red. He raised his sword and pointed it at Ni. "You dark-skinned bitch! I'll show you what the Demon Realm is like!"

Oh? I wonder if he's one of those hybrids Hasu mentioned...

The burly man's sword began to glow red and, moments later, fire surrounded the thick, straight blade. "Ha! See what I can do? Now let's see if you're any less hideous with blackened skin," he said with a menacing laugh.

Ni simply stood where she was, unfazed by the burly man's degrading remarks.

After taking three steps towards the delicate woman, the burly man suddenly lost his grin. In fact, his face was filled with fear and surprise. Dropping his flaming sword, the burly man clutched his head between his hands and screamed. His hair began to fall out, as did his teeth and nails, before both eyes popped out of their sockets. The burly man fell to the deck, still screaming in what was assuredly unimaginable pain and agony.

The soldiers took one look at the burly man and ran off the ship without a second glance.

Ni silently walked over to the burly man, who was now rolling around on the deck as if he were on fire. She put her foot out to stop him from moving; his head ended up between her foot and the deck.

The burly man cried out, but his words were unintelligible because his tongue had recently left him, along with his nose.

"Men like you disgust me," Ni said flatly. "And just so you know, you were dead the moment you set foot on this ship. Blighters like you don't get a fair chance in a fight with a woman like me."

As she finished telling him off, Ni released a needle from her hand. It implanted right between the burly man's eye sockets, and he immediately ceased to move or breathe.

The delicate woman sighed and shook her head as she turned back to Kohaku, saying, "I should have let him suffer more. I'm still absolutely livid!"

"I hope the girls're all right," the helmsman said to his comrades as he turned and looked back down the valley below. The port town looked to be the size of a coin from where they stood.

"They're safe," the Pirate King said dismissively as he continued climbing the grassy slope. The afternoon sun was blindingly bright, and the sea winds pushed and pulled with increasing strength. On their left was a steep drop into the ocean, and to their right was a mess of overgrown bushes and shrubs. The path was dangerous, but it was the best option in order to surprise their enemy. Only the villagers knew of it, and even they didn't dare take it. Well, most of them anyways.

"Yeah, they're tough," Rize nodded. He then looked to the sky, presumably searching for Ami.

"I'd worry about your own skin," Douglas said as he paused a ways ahead of the other two. "We're not up against mere humans here."

The helmsman shrugged. "I'm with the best two fighters I know, so I'm not worried."

The warrior's booming laugh echoed down the valley.

"He's got a point," Hasunuma said with a grin. "But no amount of skill will save those already dead. Let's move."

"Aye, Captain," Rize replied as he quickened his pace.

Douglas was already ahead, but he, too, began to move faster. As Hasunuma watched him easily climb the hillside, he wondered if the warrior ever tired. Not wanting to be outdone, the Pirate King did his best to keep pace.

As they neared the top of the valley, Hasunuma ordered them to halt. From what he remembered from a previous visit, just inside of the dense forest ahead of them was a large clearing where the Hekigun base stood.

"Rize, I need you to stick to the perimeter and lend us your support when I give the signal."

"Aye, Captain," he replied, "the usual?"

The Pirate King nodded. "And make sure you're not found."

"Hold up," Douglas said as he blocked the helmsman's path. "Now don't get me wrong, Rize – I've witnessed your bow mastery many a time," the warrior then looked to the Pirate King to add, "but do you really think this is the best way? Surely the demons or hybrids waiting for us would sense him out there, even if he were hiding, and if they attacked, he'd have no backup. Rize has real ranged skills, but up close–"

The helmsman held up his hand to silence Douglas. He smiled as he looked up at the warrior before him and said, "I appreciate your concern, but trust me when I say they won't know I'm there until my arrows hit 'em."

Douglas frowned, but Hasunuma stepped in and added, "As a hunter, he had the reputation of being invisible to friend and foe alike. Let's give Rize a chance to prove himself worthy of such praise."

The warrior crossed his arms, but stepped aside. "If you say so, Captain."

In the blink of an eye, Rize was up the nearest tree. A second later he disappeared into the dense forest without a sound.

Douglas tried to hide his surprise at the helmsman's stealth and speed, but it did not go unnoticed by the Pirate King. "Let's not keep Rize waiting," he said with a grin as he crossed the boundary and stepped into the line of trees.

Contrary to the bright and airy valley, the forest was dark and silent. Thick, gnarled limbs stretched towards the sky, their foliage blocking out most of the sunlight. What little remained served as a pitiful guide to those on the forest floor. Though the trees seemed adequate for nesting, there were no signs of birds or small animals. Hasunuma thought that the lack of life was rather appropriate for a Hekigun base.

There was a sudden shower of light as the trees stood further apart and then vanished altogether. In the center of the circular clearing was a large building with a tall tower protruding from its core. The outer walls of the base were windowless, with only a set of large, iron double doors as a means of entering or exiting. It was difficult to tell whether or not the area around the tower, on the inside, was covered, though it wouldn't have mattered much since the outer walls were too high and smooth to scale. The tower itself was only open at the top, giving those in the base a perfect view of the whole island and surrounding sea.

The Pirate King had taken into account that the enemy would have known of the Ryujin's arrival in advance, which is why he planned for a surprise approach *and* some defense aboard his ship. He also figured that the enemy remained unaware of his two other missions ashore, which is why the Pirate King decided to keep the enemy's focus by attacking the base himself. The only uncertainty was whether or not the kid was being watched as well, so Hasunuma sent him to the other base, which would be closely guarded anyways, negating any chance of a surprise attack. Which, of course, left his best and least suspicious player to perform the most important mission on the island.

"You finally showed up," someone sneered in a nasally sort of voice.

"We were getting rather impatient," another, calmer voice added.

"Heh heh, at least we had ample entertainment," a third, rather rough voice snickered.

Five round objects were tossed from the top of the tower. They landed with a THUNK and rolled a short distance towards the Pirate King and the warrior. When they got close enough, it was rather clear that the objects were bloodied, severed heads.

"These do not belong to soldiers," Douglas bellowed. "These belong to women and children!"

"Yes, 'tis a pity you didn't arrive sooner," the calm voice replied. "Our orders were only to keep *your* men alive. There was nothing regarding the safekeeping of other hostages."

"There was no need for other hostages! You blighters– "

"Stop," the Pirate King said icily as he held his hand out to block the warrior's advance. "I dislike speaking to disembodied voices. Show yourselves so we may hear the terms of the release of this man's crew."

"This one has some manners," the calm voice said with a joyful undertone.

A man with long, golden hair materialized from the shadows of the looming base walls. He wore a beautiful white kimono with golden flowers embroidered on it and had a matching wooden umbrella that shielded him from the sun. His face was hidden behind a female mask, like those used in theatrical performances, and the way he moved was overtly feminine.

"I count one, but heard three," the Pirate King said, keeping his icy tone.

"Yes, come out, you brutes," the masked man calmly ordered.

"Why should we?" the nasally voice replied.

"I haven't finished playing with my toys," the rough voice complained.

Suddenly the base was covered in shadow, as if clouds had blocked the sun, but the sky remained clear and the sun was visible. Shortly after, two men appeared next to the masked man. They seemed to be cowering before him.

"That's better," the masked man said as the mysterious shadow dissipated. "The terms, my dear Red Dragon, are as follows: the underlings are free to go as soon as we remove your head from those nice shoulders of yours."

"Am I allowed to fight to keep my head?"

The masked man twirled his umbrella. "Why of course, Red Dragon, otherwise this would be a waste of my time."

"Are my men inside of this base?" Douglas asked, trying to hold back his anger.

"Might be, might not be," the nasally voice replied. It belonged to the smallest man, who was crouched next to the masked man. He had sunken eyes and the dark hair on his head was missing in patches. He looked rather weak, but the Pirate King knew better than to assess the man's strength by his appearance alone.

"Play with us," the rough voice demanded. This came from the other man who was next to the masked man. He had stood up, unlike the other one, but was still a good two feet shorter than the masked man. "And *maybe* we'll tell you where your frail human companions are." The man grinned wickedly, showing his creepily pointed teeth – which reminded the Pirate King of shark's teeth.

'Human' companions…so at least one of them isn't human. No surprise there.

"Captain, you take Blondie and I'll focus on the shorties," the warrior whispered.

"You want Sharky *and* Patches?" the Pirate King asked, feigning surprise.

Douglas grinned. "You know I fight best against multiple

enemies. And besides," he added with a more serious tone, "with the vibes I'm feeling, I'm thinking Blondie is a demon while the shorties are hybrids."

"So *I* get the toughest one? Thanks," Hasunuma replied sarcastically, but he wouldn't have had it any other way.

The warrior sprang into action first, running towards the opposite side of the base from where the enemies were. Sharky quickly took the bait and sprinted towards him. Patches seemed reluctant to move, but with a jab in the back from Blondie's umbrella, he soon followed suit. That left the Pirate King and Blondie.

"I had rather hoped that this is how things would play out," Blondie said. "I've heard a lot about you, Red Dragon, and I'm rather curious to test out the rumors."

"Then let's get to it," Hasunuma replied as he unsheathed his red dragon sword.

The masked man stepped forward as if he were making a grand entrance onto a stage. With each step he took, darkness surged forth, enveloping the ground and turning it into a carpet of shadow.

Ceasing his advance about ten feet away from Hasunuma, Blondie said, "Now, please enjoy my dance of darkness." He slowly began to move his umbrella through the air, twirling it here and there. Darkness descended from above, surrounding the Pirate King and the masked man in a sort of shadow box; the two could see one another, but the rest of the world was blocked out by the darkness. Once the masked man began to slide his feet around, the atmosphere grew thick and heavy.

Hasunuma quickly jumped to the right. Something had shot towards him, but it disappeared as soon as he dodged. Before he could think, another something came at him from the right and he twisted his shoulder just enough for the thing to miss. Again, something shot towards him from the front, and the Pirate King had to crouch to stop it from taking his head off.

"Your senses are magnificent," Blondie remarked as he continued his methodical dance. "But do not let me distract you…"

The Pirate King felt a sharp pain in his left shoulder blade. He quickly grabbed at whatever had stabbed him, but there was nothing there.

"That was a miraculous move," the masked man applauded. "I cannot decide whether or not I should be happy that I missed your head."

Hasunuma sidestepped once more as another invisible weapon came at him from the left. Immediately afterwards, he was assaulted from the right and held up his sword to block since he couldn't dodge in time. His sword, however, was a useless shield; something stabbed into the Pirate King's right bicep.

Blondie clicked his tongue. "No, no, no, Red Dragon, shadows cannot be blocked."

So I'm being attacked by shadows…sharp and pointy shadows…great.

The Pirate King jumped backwards to avoid a shadow spike from below, and then he quickly leaned to the side to avoid another from behind. He continued to duck and dodge shadows spikes as he considered his options, when suddenly the idea came to him.

Hasunuma whistled two long and one short note as loudly as he could, hoping that sound could penetrate the shadow barrier.

"Even if your companion can hear you, Red Dragon, he cannot

enter into my shadow realm," the masked man said calmly. But a few seconds later, he shouted in alarm, "This cannot be!" as an arrow pierced through his shadows.

The Pirate King grinned and ran to grab the arrow. There was a white piece of paper tied around it, and he quickly slipped it off and re-tied it to the ring on the end of his sword handle. "Right, let's give this a go," he said to himself as he crouched down to avoid a shadow spike. Hasunuma rolled forward – avoiding a shot from behind – and then sprang up and dashed towards the masked man. *This is it,* he thought as a shadow spike approached his stomach. With a flash of the red dragon, the shadow spike fell to pieces and then sunk back into the shadow floor below.

"How can you…it shouldn't be possible!" Blondie cried out.

"I know a miko," Hasunuma said with a grin as he swung the red dragon at the masked man.

Blondie blocked with his umbrella, but stumbled backwards since he had been mid-dance and his feet were un-balanced. The shadow barrier dissipated as soon as the methodical dance ceased. Not wasting a moment, the Pirate King leapt towards the masked man and slashed at him again. This time the red dragon cut through the wooden umbrella and bit into Blondie's chest.

Blood sprayed onto the masked man's kimono, and he cried out, "You ruined it, you vile brute!"

Hasunuma thrust the red dragon into Blondie's stomach and twisted it. "Where are Douglas' men?"

"Arse's stench! This path's longer than I thought," Ginza grumbled as he wiped the sweat from his brow.

"Aye," Hanzo said in agreement as he, too, stopped to catch his breath.

They had been steadily climbing the mountain path for a while now, with no end to their upwards trajectory in sight. How many times had Kazuki heard Ginza say, 'just a little further'? Too many. But it wasn't just the steep climb that stole their breath away; the air had become thinner. Frequent stops were now a requirement for all except Kazuki, as the Demon King's growing powers now prevented him from feeling tired or ill.

"Shouldn't you be used to all of this climbing, Lass?" Hanzo asked as he looked back at Reika.

She was the slowest of the group and struggled the most with the strenuous climb. Kazuki did his best to keep pace with her, but in doing so he felt like they weren't making any progress.

"Ah, sorry," the young woman apologized with heavy breaths, "but my family's shrine wasn't in the mountains."

She still doesn't trust us, Kazuki thought with disappointment.

No matter who had asked, or what the question was, when it came to her family's shrine's location or the specifics about what had happened to it, Reika wouldn't reveal anything. It was obvious that she was hiding something, but none of the crew seemed to really care. Kazuki supposed it was because they all had secrets of their own, but he still thought it was weird that the crew wasn't more wary of her. The young man deeply cared for Reika, but the only reason he could overlook her silence was because he had already figured out her secret. Meanwhile, the rest of the crew…

Maybe it's better that they don't know, the young man suddenly concluded as the fear of Reika being kicked off the ship – or worse – surfaced in his thoughts.

"Right. We're almost there," Ginza declared as he began to climb the path once more.

Hanzo followed behind, as did Kazuki and Reika. The young man walked slowly so that he could quietly talk with the young woman and not be heard by the other two.

"You haven't said much since we left the ship," Kazuki began, "is something wrong?"

Reika's eyes widened for a split second, but then she tried to cover it up with a smile. "No, not at all," she replied.

The young man's heart sank. Did she really have to lie to him too?

His face must have betrayed his feelings, because Reika suddenly stopped and said, "Oh, Kazu, I didn't mean to..." Her beautiful green eyes were full of sorrow as she trailed off, unable to finish her thoughts aloud.

Kazuki gently placed his hand on her head. The second he made contact, Reika threw herself into the young man and buried her face in his chest.

"I-I'm so scared, Kazu," she cried. "I don't want to keep going, I don't want this to end, but I don't know what else to do!"

The young man slowly wrapped his arms around her small, trembling frame. "It's alright," he assured her. "I'm here to help you."

Reika didn't respond. She tightened her grip around Kazuki's torso and continued to sob.

"Reika, I'm here for you," he gently reiterated, "and I will do what I can, but I need you to be strong. Can you do that for me?"

The young woman nodded slightly. Her sobs quieted to uneven breaths.

"That's good," Kazuki said kindly as he kissed the top of her head. The young man then slowly pulled away from Reika and took hold of her hand. "Let's go," he added with a warm smile.

The young woman wiped her tears away with her free hand. As her moist eyes met Kazuki's once more, they revealed her true feelings for him. The young man's heart skipped a beat and a warmth spread over his body like hot bath. He leaned in to kiss her lips, but was interrupted by a gruff voice.

"Ain't no time fer smoochin'! Save that fer after we finish the mission," Ginza snapped.

"That's what kids do, Gin," Hanzo retorted with a grin, "they can't help it."

"Not while I'm bustin' m' arse! Now get t' it," the blacksmith ordered as he pointed up the path.

The embarrassed couple bowed their heads and silently began walking, but Kazuki did not let go of Reika's hand.

As they trudged up the mountain path, the young man decided to ask Reika something he had wanted to ask her, ever since the same question was posed to him: "What will you do after this?"

"After what?" the young woman replied, seeming a bit confused.

"After this mess with the Hekigun is finished," Kazuki clarified.

"Is there something you want to do?"

"Of course there is," Reika said with pride. "I'll continue to be a miko at my family's shrine until I get married, and then I'll have some children who will also grow up as part of the shrine, and then I'll–" suddenly she covered her mouth with her free hand. The young woman's eyes glanced sideways at Kazuki. "I mean…I…" she trailed off.

"It's alright," the young man said with a chuckle. "I like your enthusiasm."

Her face flushed and her eyes darted away from his. "What about you, Kazu?"

"I'm not sure," the young man easily replied. He wasn't ashamed of his lack of future plans.

"Oh," Reika said quietly. She waited a moment before adding, "Well, if you *want* to, at least for a bit, you could come with me and, um, help me restore my family's shrine…But only if you really want to," she added awkwardly as her cheeks turned a deep shade of pink.

Kazuki smiled. "I might take you up on that."

"An' what about *us*?" Ginza stopped and turned to ask.

"Yeah, where's our invitation?" Hanzo asked with a sly grin.

Reika's face was practically fuchsia by this point, but she somehow managed to respond. "W-well, um, i-if you behave yourselves then I guess you both could come too."

Ginza grinned at Kazuki. "Did ya hear that, Little Oni? We get t' come too."

"Yes, Reika is being nice. But she doesn't have to, because neither of you will be joining us," the young man declared.

"Wha'd'ya mean by that?" Ginza countered.

"Come on, Gin, it's obvious that the lad doesn't want to share her," Hanzo replied with a shake of his head.

"'E just wants more one-on-one time, eh?" The blacksmith teased.

Now it was Kazuki's turn to be embarrassed. He dropped Reika's hand and looked away from her. "T-that's not true," he shouted.

"It's not? Huh. Then I guess he's not that into her," Hanzo said with a shrug.

"Maybe 'e's got someone else," Ginza added.

"There's no one else!" Kazuki countered. He knew that Hanzo and Ginza were teasing him, but he couldn't help but respond with Reika right there, listening to it all.

"Oh, so he's just shy," Hanzo continued.

"Or e's' scared. Y'know how smaller guys like him are," Ginza added.

"I don't even want to know what you're trying to imply," Kazuki retorted.

"Look, Little Oni, just 'cause yer not as big as us, doesn't mean ya can't satisfy a woman," the blacksmith began to explain. "When ya–"

"STOP NOW," the young man half-ordered and half-begged.

Hanzo's bellowing laughter was quickly joined by Ginza's, and the mountains echoed their amusement.

"You three are very close, aren't you?" Reika giggled.

"Aye," replied Ginza.

"Right you are," nodded Hanzo.

"To the Demon Realm with you both," grumbled Kazuki as he started to hike up the trail.

Hanzo and Ginza followed behind, laughing and continuing to tease the young man – though not quite as explicitly as before. Reika ran to catch up with Kazuki and did her best to keep up with his new pace. The young man glanced over at her and found the young woman smiling at him.

She really is like a ray of sunlight, he thought.

Kazuki reached over and grabbed hold of Reika's hand once more. He did his best to ignore the jerks making comments behind them. It was good that Reika, while a bit embarrassed, didn't seem to mind the teasing.

"So, what kinda repair work d' we have t' look forward to?" Ginza suddenly asked.

A large sigh escaped the young woman's lips before she replied, "For starters, the demons destroyed the front gate, sliced up half of the living quarters, obliterated the ceremonial stage, ruined the gardens and–"

"Ah, so yer family's shrine's near a city," the blacksmith interrupted with a knowing nod.

Reika's eyes went wide for a split second. "What makes you think that?" She then asked with a forced smile.

"'Cause only the bigger shrines can afford t' have ceremonial stages. An' the rural shrines, that aren't in the mountains, just have one buildin'," Ginza casually explained.

Kazuki knew that, while Ginza wasn't the smartest person, he was no fool when it came to knowing Tsukigen customs and traditions. Which, strangely enough, included the ways in which Tsukigen buildings were constructed. Maybe that particular knowledge was linked to his blacksmithing days? Or perhaps it was just a side passion. Either way, for once it was useful.

"I see," was all that the young woman decided to say in response.

Kazuki glanced over at Reika. She was clearly mulling something over.

"Gin's got craftsman skills, and I've got brute strength, so together we can do some real work at your family's shrine, Lass," Hanzo proudly announced.

The young woman stopped walking. "I don't understand. You're actually serious about helping me…why?"

"Well, why not?" The giant replied.

Reika spun around and stared at Hanzo. "But you don't know anything about me, about what I'm doing here, about anything! How can you offer to help someone like me?!"

The giant stroked his beard. "Alright, maybe I don't know everything about you," he conceded, "but here is what I *do* know: you've never looked down on me or treated me poorly just because I'm a foreigner. And for me, that says a lot about a person; enough to where I wouldn't mind helping them if they needed it."

Reika shook her head. "That's ridiculous." And then she mumbled, "You're too kindhearted."

Kazuki wasn't sure if Hanzo had heard that last part or not, but the giant smiled and added, "Well, I can also see how fond you and the lad are of each other, so there's that too."

"'E may not look it, but this guy's a big softie," Ginza chimed in as he clasped Hanzo's shoulder.

The giant crossed his arms and looked down at the blacksmith. "Stop talking about yourself, Gin. It's rude."

Ginza's grip on Hanzo's shoulder tightened. "Ya know what's

rude? Not takin' a compliment."

"That was a compliment?" The giant replied with a raised eyebrow.

"'Course it was," the blacksmith affirmed.

"Then why won't you take it?" Hanzo retorted.

"Look, I think I see the clearing up ahead," Kazuki interjected, hoping to stop their pointless arguing.

Both Ginza and Hanzo immediately turned their heads in Kazuki's direction. Looking at the path before them, some 20 yards ahead, the trees became thinner around a point where the ground seemed to reach its peak. The two rushed past Reika and Kazuki as they raced up the path. They then both came to a sudden, full halt at the top.

As the young couple caught up, Kazuki heard Hanzo say in a low voice, "Hey Gin, I thought 'clearings' were open spaces."

"They're s'posed t' be," the blacksmith responded with a snort.

When Kazuki and Reika peeked around the large pirates, they saw what the two were referring to; an army of Hekigun soldiers were occupying the clearing. The grass was barely visible due to the volume of soldiers standing at attention, and every soldier looked ready for battle. There didn't seem to be any officers though, which was strange.

A wry smile appeared on Hanzo's face. He cracked his knuckles and then reached for his steel knuckles and slid them on. "Should we tell 'em?"

"What, that they need t' clear off?" Ginza replied. After he realized what he had said he let out a quick, "HA!" before getting into an offensive stance.

Without so much as a glace back, the two large pirates sprang forward. The soldiers didn't seem remotely startled; they must have anticipated that they would be attacked as soon as they were spotted. As Hanzo and Ginza punched and sliced through the mass of soldiers, Kazuki analyzed the crowd. There didn't seem to be any non-humans present, so he stood back with Reika and waited for the other two to finish fighting.

Less than three minutes after the battle had begun, Hanzo and Ginza stood in the center of the clearing, surrounded by a sea of bodies. Not a single soldier had made it anywhere close to where the young couple stood. And Kazuki knew that that wasn't a coincidence.

"I wish they hadn't killed them," Reika murmured as she averted her eyes from the scene.

"It's kill or be killed," the young man gently reminded her.

"I know," she said with a heavy sigh, "but that doesn't mean I can't wish for things to be different."

Suddenly the sound of rustling leaves came from the other side of the clearing. Hanzo and Ginza immediately assumed defensive stances, while Kazuki positioned himself in front of Reika. A few, tense seconds passed before a small child, around eight years old, popped out from beneath the trees. He had been running at full speed, but came to a screeching halt when he saw Hanzo and Ginza.

The boy immediately cowered and covered his head with his hands as he yelled, "Please don't kill me!"

The large pirates both lowered their defenses, and Ginza called out to the boy, "It's alright, we ain't gonna hurt ya."

"As long as you're not with the Hekigun," Hanzo added in a

serious tone.

"I-I'm not! I was runnin' away from 'em," the boy called back.

"So there are more up ahead?" Kazuki asked as he joined Hanzo and Ginza in the center of the clearing. Reika followed behind, gripping his arm tightly as she tried not to stumble over the plethora of bodies.

The boy nodded. "Yeah, they've taken over the village," he added as he pointed towards the woods behind him. "C-could ya help get rid of 'em?" He tentatively asked.

Hanzo and Ginza looked at each other and then they both turned to Kazuki. The boy saw this and must have assumed that Kazuki was the one in charge, so he ran over to him and pleaded, "Please, please help me! My ma and pa and sis were taken! I…I don't know what t' doooo," he cried.

"Oh, I'm sorry…but I'm sure it'll be alright, little boy," Reika said softly, trying to calm the boy down. But she didn't try to go near or touch him.

"Is there a Hekigun building near your village," Kazuki asked as he watched the boy sloppily wipe his tears away.

The boy nodded. "That's where they took everyone."

"Alright then, let's go," Kazuki said nonchalantly as he took a step towards the boy.

The boy didn't move. It wasn't until Kazuki was right next to him that the boy sprang into action, pulling a knife out from behind him and lunging at Kazuki's side.

"Kazu!" Reika screamed.

"I'm fine," the young man assured her. His hand had shot out and grabbed the boy's, stopping the blade before it could strike.

The boy gasped. "H-how?!"

Kazuki looked down at the boy, who was struggling to get his hand free. "Your acting was decent, but you can't hide your demon from me."

"What's that supposed to mean? Are you a demon too?" The boy grumbled.

Before Kazuki could respond, the Demon King surfaced.

"Insolent fool. Are you so weak that you cannot sense the presence of your King?"

The boy's eyes widened. "No…no! I don't want to die!"

Kazuki felt his hand release the boy's.

"Then you should never have come to the Human Realm without my permission."

"B-but the humans called me here!" The boy retorted as he slowly backed away.

"You could have refused the summons," the Demon King flatly stated as Kazuki felt himself slowly unsheathe his katana.

"No! Please! Second promised that I'd be able to return!" The boy yelled as he furiously waved his arms in front of him.

Kazuki felt his brow furrow.

"You are a fool to believe the word of a demon. Especially one as tainted as Second."

With a flick of the young man's wrist, the boy fell. Before his body could hit the ground, it turned to ash and blew away with a sudden gust of wind.

"What was that all about?" Hanzo asked the Demon King.

"It is not your business," he responded coldly.

"You sound like a King who rules with an iron fist," the giant replied in an equally icy tone.

"And you would do differently?" The Demon King asked scornfully. **"You know nothing of ruling, and you know nothing of the Demon Realm. Do not act as if you are above me when you are so ignorant."**

Kazuki flinched. He was waiting for Hanzo to throw a punch at him, but the giant didn't move.

"I suppose you're right," he said gruffly. "But if that's the case, then don't assume you know everything about humans."

Kazuki felt himself grin. The Demon King then retreated into the young man's subconscious, saying no more.

After a deep exhale, Kazuki said, "Thanks for not punching me."

Hanzo chuckled. "I admit that I was tempted, but his attitude isn't your fault, Lad. I can't punish you for his ill will."

Ginza cleared his throat and then complained to Kazuki, "I thought I warned ya about lettin' 'im out like that."

"It's not as easy to control him as you think, Ginza," the young man sighed.

"An' I think yer stronger than ya think," the blacksmith retorted. "What would happen if 'e came out an' threatened us? Ya know 'is strength's buildin' up, so what's gonna stop 'im from attackin' us? Or 'er," Ginza added as he pointed to Reika.

Kazuki felt his stomach drop. The blacksmith had uncovered the one thing that the young man was most worried about. He tried to hide his insecurity by saying, "He won't do that," but the blacksmith wasn't going to let it go.

"Ya wanna bet, Litte Oni?" Ginza challenged. He was about to say something else, but stopped when he saw Hanzo hold up his hand.

The giant's expression was deadly serious. Ginza and Kazuki immediately understood and became as still as statues.

Reika cocked her head to the side. "What's wro—"

Kazuki quickly covered the young woman's mouth with his hand. When her quizzical eyes met his, he mouthed 'enemy'.

The miko immediately grabbed onto Kazuki's arm. As much as he liked it, there was no way that he could fight with her clinging onto him, so Kazuki gently unwound Reika's fingers from his arm. He then held her small, trembling hands in his for a moment before releasing them and reaching for the katana at his side. Since Hanzo and Ginza were already positioned to the front, Kazuki slowly turned to the rear, making sure to keep Reika behind him.

We'll keep her safe, the young man thought to himself as he closed his eyes. He took a deep breath and then focused on what he could hear. *There's five...no, six of them. They've got us surrounded...and none of them feel completely human. Gods be damned.*

Blondie lay in a pool of his own blood. He let out a ragged laugh before answering the Pirate King. "You want to know where those ugly, weak humans are?" He pointed the remains of his broken umbrella towards the walls of the base. "But you should hurry...my death is the catalyst to theirs," he said with a laugh as he threw his umbrella into the air with the last of his strength.

"Five's down. There's the signal," a nasally voice shouted.

"On it," a rough voice shouted in response.

As the Pirate King looked away from the masked man's smoking corpse, he saw Sharky throw something up over the base walls. There was the sound of a large explosion and, shortly afterwards, flames towered above the walls. Once Hasunuma's ears stopped ringing, he could hear the screams of many people from inside of the base.

"By the gods, Douglas, I thought you had them!" The Pirate King shouted in frustration as he ran towards the base door.

Sharky tried to stop him, but his leg was impaled from behind. He screamed and tried to pull the spear out, but it was far too heavy for him to lift.

"Sorry, Captain," the warrior replied as he pulled Sharky away from the Pirate King, using his sash as a rope. "I'm not much of a rabbit hunter."

"I hate excuses," the Pirate King shouted back as he threw open the door.

"Who are you calling a rabbit?!" Patches cried out as he dashed towards Douglas with his short sword.

The warrior reached out and grabbed Patches by his outstretched arm, breaking it instantly. "You should have kept running, little bunny."

The Pirate King crossed the threshold with one foot before being blown backwards by another explosion.

"Thundering sea snakes…they set traps," he grumbled as he picked himself up off of the ground. *How the festering hole am I supposed to save them now?* The Pirate King glanced over the base once more, looking for other possibilities, but he could find nothing.

Another explosion came from inside the base and more screams erupted.

"What now, Captain?" Rize asked grimly as he suddenly appeared next to the Pirate King.

Hasunuma was silent. He could only think of one way to *possibly* save the people inside, but he couldn't be sure that it would work. In fact, it might kill them.

"Captain?"

The Pirate King looked to Douglas, who had finally finished taking care of the two hybrids. "Get behind me," he ordered.

The warrior looked confused, but he didn't question the Pirate King.

Once Douglas and Rize were both behind Hasunuma, he took a deep breath and said, "No matter what happens, do NOT tell anyone about this. Understood?"

There was a slight pause, but both men agreed with a firm, "Aye, Captain."

The Pirate King took another deep breath and closed his eyes. He relaxed his body and tried to block out the screams. *Focus…* he told himself as he sought power from deep within. There was a growing feeling of warmth inside of his center that rose up into his chest and radiated out into his arms. He grabbed his sword with both hands and raised it above his head. *If this works…*

"Hyah!" The Pirate King swung the red dragon sword downward with all of his might. The ground split open where it hit, creating a fissure that quickly snaked its way towards the base. Once it reached the wall, there was a loud *CRACK* as the wall burst apart. The entire center section of the wall now lay in a crumbled mess of debris.

Before anyone could say anything, the people who had been trapped within the walls came pouring out from the opening. They were most likely the villagers of Rurin.

Rize quickly ran to help a young woman who was struggling to carry an injured old woman on her back, while also holding a baby to her chest. Douglas made his way to the opening in the wall in order to help the rest of the injured out, and Hasunuma joined him. Fire was still blazing inside, but some of the wall debris had squelched the sections of fire closest to the hole.

"Is there anyone else?" Douglas asked a man with horrible burns and a broken leg as he pulled him out of the hole and set him on the ground.

"I-I don't think so," the injured man breathed heavily.

Douglas frowned and looked back into the blazing base. After a moment, he turned his head away and bent down to pick up the injured man. The warrior only made it a few feet before another male villager ran over to carry the injured man.

"Don't touch him, you accursed beast!" the villager shouted as he practically yanked the injured man out of Douglas' arms.

The warrior didn't say anything in return. He was far too used to that sort of treatment to let it bother him much.

The Pirate King approached the rude villager and asked, "Were you the only ones being kept inside?"

The rude villager spat at him and then continued to carry the injured man away without a word.

"In a strange way, I feel slightly less irritated now," Douglas said as he put his hand on Hasunuma's shoulder.

"No matter where you are, or what you do, some people are just venom-spitting arses," the Pirate King said with a sigh.

"Uh, 'scuse me," a quiet voice squeaked.

The Pirate King and the warrior turned around and saw a little boy standing there. He was dirty and his clothes were a bit singed, but he didn't look like he had been injured beyond a few scrapes and bruises. He couldn't have been more than six years old.

"My ma told me not t' talk t' strangers, but…" he trailed off as he craned his neck in order to look into Douglas' eyes. "Thank ya fer savin' us," the little boy said with a big smile.

The warrior squatted down so that he and the boy were on the same level. He reached out and patted the boy's head, saying, "We appreciate that, young one. But we can't always be there to save you. That's why you need to grow big and strong like me, so that you can protect yourself and the people you love."

"I can be big like you?!" the boy asked with excitement.

Douglas laughed heartily. "Sure you can! Eat well, sleep well, and train well."

"Now go back to your ma before she gets worried," Hasunuma added as he gently tapped the boy's back.

"Kay," the boy replied as he began to walk towards the crowd of villagers that were headed into the forest.

Douglas watched the boy until he was sure that he was safe with the villagers. "It's amazing how those innocent smiles can immediately lighten your mood," he said with a smile of his own.

"Sure," Hasunuma replied blankly. His mind was elsewhere.

The warrior gazed at the Pirate King. It looked as if he wanted to ask something, but wasn't sure if he should. After a few moments, he said, "Those demonic powers sure are something."

Hasunuma didn't take the bait.

Douglas shrugged his shoulders. "It would be pretty convenient for my lady and I if I could summon a shadow box like that wherever and whenever."

The corners of the Pirate King's lips rose. He couldn't help it. "Do you think of anything other than sex and fighting?"

"Nope," the warrior responded with a grin.

Hasunuma chuckled. He knew that Douglas was a good man, and that he would never go too far for the sake of becoming stronger, but the warrior's interest in the demons was increasing, and that was worrisome. "Then, for my own sanity, can I at least remind you that demons are *not* to be admired or messed with. Whether their powers seem convenient or not."

The warrior laughed. "Under the sun's guidance, I swear I'll get a straight answer from you one day. However," he added as he playfully slapped Hasunuma on the back, "I hear you, and I promise that's not my intention. As I've told you before, a true warrior relies on himself and no one else – demonic powers included."

"Hey!" Rize shouted as he ran over to them from the edge of the forest. "Great news! According to that lady I helped, your crew's aboard your ship. It should be docked in a little inlet on the other side of this forest."

"By the will of the gods!" Douglas said as he clapped his hands in delight. "Can I borrow your expert hunter for a bit, Hasunuma?"

The Pirate King nodded. "Rize, please lead him to his ship. And watch out for traps."

"Will do, Captain," the helmsman replied.

"If what Renge told me was correct, there should have been at least two other high-ranking officers here, so be wary on your approach," the Pirate King added.

"I'll keep an eye out," Rize said before running to catch up with Douglas, who was already out of sight.

Hasunuma stood alone in the clearing, staring at the still-burning base. He glanced around at the large stone chunks that had once been a part of the towering wall before him. His heart sank as he thought: *Am I even human anymore?*

"What should we do? They haven't attacked yet, but I get the feeling that they will as soon as we move," Hanzo said in the closest thing to a whisper as he could get.

"They ain't normal humans," Ginza said in an equally low voice. "How many?"

"Six," Kazuki replied, "and it's pretty clear by their inaction that they're trained to take out intruders like us."

"What do you mean?" Reika shakily whispered.

Kazuki wasn't sure he should respond. Telling an already terrified girl: 'well, they have us surrounded in such a way that the second any one of us moves, we're dead,' didn't seem like such a good idea. What would Hasunuma say in this sort of situation?

Probably something ridiculous, Kazuki thought as a faint smile appeared on his face. "Don't worry, Reika," the young man said in a warm and calm tone, "we'll get out of this, but we're going to need your help. Can you help us?"

Kazuki couldn't see her face, but he heard her whisper a firm, "Yes."

"That's my girl," he said softly, in an attempt to bolster the young woman's confidence. He was just glad that she couldn't see his face as he said it. And that his comrades were smart enough to keep their mouths shut. "We need a protective circle – no…actually, we need a boost in power," he stated in a quiet voice that he hoped their enemies couldn't hear.

Reika didn't respond. All Kazuki could hear from her was heavy breathing. He released his left hand from his katana and reached around to grab her hand. It was cold and damp. Of course she was scared – what normal girl wouldn't be? Her life hadn't been a mess of deadly battles until now, and this was not something one got used to overnight.

Kazuki gently squeezed her hand. "Reika, we need you…*I* need you," he said softly. "You can do this. I believe in you."

He heard the young woman take a deep breath and then let it out. She gave Kazuki's hand a quick squeeze in return and then pulled her hand away. As the young man returned his left hand to his katana, he heard the faint mutterings of a miko.

We're close to the facility, but I think it's better to retreat for now. For this many hybrids, we'll need Hasunuma and Douglas, or Jun.

"Ginza, Hanzo, we've only got one shot at this," the young man stated. "We need to take the 'path of the dragon'."

"Ya can't be serious," Ginza retorted, "that tactic's based 'round the cap'n leadin' the way an' we don't have enough members fer a full dragon."

"*I'll* take the captain's place," Kazuki replied. "We can make this work. Trust me."

"Fine, fine," Ginza grumbled. "We'll be yer left n' right claws, but what 'bout–"

"No, Hanzo will carry Reika as the body and you'll be the tail," the young man directed.

"Dragons need claws, Lad," Hanzo muttered.

"This one has razor sharp teeth," Kazuki retorted.

"But this' totally different than–"

"Just trust me!" Kazuki snapped in desperation. He sensed their enemies closing in – they must have gotten tired of waiting – so there was no time to argue.

As Hanzo and Ginza both grunted a word of agreement, they were suddenly enveloped in a faint glow. The young man felt a tingling sensation throughout his body.

This is it, Kazuki thought as he positioned his sword on his left side. He held it parallel to the ground at about elbow-height. "Now!" Kazuki yelled as he rushed forward.

He couldn't see what was happening behind him, but Kazuki trusted that Hanzo had grabbed Reika and that Ginza would protect them from any close encounters with their pursuers. The whole point of the 'path of the dragon' was for the lead – usually Hasunuma – to make a hole in the enemy line that the rest of the crew could then follow through. In the typical formation, Hasunuma was the dragon's 'head', two crewmates would be the 'claws,' any non-combatants would be the 'body,' and a third crewmate would be the 'tail'. If they had the whole crew, they could add two more 'claws' near the tail, but it was rare that everyone was fighting in the same location at once. In any case, it was the only tactic that Kazuki could think to use, so that's what he went with.

The enchantment that Reika made for them was amazing. They were running so quickly that the trees were mere blurs of green and brown as they flew past them. Kazuki wasn't even sure that his feet were actually touching the ground. Other than the initial enemy that Kazuki cut down in order to make way for the others, he hadn't seen or sensed any of the other five approach them. And he had sliced clean through the enemy in one swing without feeling any resistance. Did the enchantment really make them that much more powerful than the hybrids?

Suddenly something appeared in front of Kazuki. He swung his sword at it, but the thing evaded him. Moving past the young man, it headed towards the dragon's 'body'. Kazuki whirled around in time to see Ginza block a blow that had been intended for Hanzo's head.

The 'dragon' instantly stopped.

"Impressive," the assailant said with real interest as he stood nearby.

A shiver ran down Kazuki's spine. The assailant's physical appearance reminded him too much of Ammon; they could have been twins. The only obvious differences were that this man's white hair was shoulder-length, and his face was expressionless.

"The thought never occurred to me that a miko's power could be used to enhance a human's abilities. I must study this further," the assailant commented as he reached out to touch Reika, who was being carried on Hanzo's back.

Ginza quickly knocked his hand away and growled, "Hands off."

The assailant turned his head ever so slightly towards Ginza. "For a moment I forgot about the flies. How careless of me."

Faster than even Kazuki could track, the assailant swung his weapon at Ginza. Not even with enhanced abilities could the blacksmith move fast enough to block the attack. In a flash, Ginza flew backwards, stopping only when his back made contact with a large tree. There was a loud *CRACK* on impact, and, as Ginza fell to the ground, so did the broken tree.

"Ginza!" Kazuki and Hanzo shouted in sync. But neither of them dared to move. Their assailant was far beyond them in terms of power and agility.

"Oh, but it looks like that sort of spell is rather taxing on the creator," the assailant said aloud, though he seemed to be talking to himself. "Hmm. I wonder if that has anything to do with the creator's own power level..."

Kazuki looked at Reika. Her eyes were closed and she was breathing heavily. It looked as if she would pass out any second, which meant that the enhancement spell would disappear. There was no time.

"Are you one of the numbers?" the young man asked as he took a purposeful step between the assailant and Hanzo – who was still carrying Reika on his back.

The assailant's analytical stare shifted down to Kazuki's face. "Ah, the King's vessel. That explains why one of my sentinels was destroyed." He cocked his head to the side as he added, "Strange that I'm not feeling much of your demonic aura though...but perhaps this is my chance. I am Three," the assailant said with a courteous bow, "and in order to continue with my research, I will be taking your head."

As soon as the words left Three's lips, Kazuki felt something hit his right side. A second later he was lying on the ground; a splitting pain wracking his body. He didn't have time to assess what was broken before he was hit again in the same spot.

"Lad!" Hanzo cried out.

Blood spewed from the young man's mouth when he opened it to speak. His broken ribs must have torn something inside. The pain was excruciating. In a ragged voice he managed to say, "Go…take them and go."

"Curse the gods," Hanzo growled as he dashed over to Ginza, slung him over his shoulder, and single-handedly carried both of their defenseless party members away.

"I could easily destroy them," Three said matter-of-factly as he stared down at Kazuki, who still lay broken and bleeding on the ground. "The only reason that your large friend survived is because of the miko's spell. And that won't last much longer." He prodded Kazuki's broken ribs with his weapon; it looked like a plain, wooden staff, but it was hard to believe that such a normal thing could be so deadly.

"Agh!"

"My liege, if you don't come out soon, this body will die," Three stated.

He's right, you know.

Stay. In. There. Kazuki thought as he desperately tried to hold the Demon King back.

You humans are foolishly prideful and stubborn. Though I

admit that demons are just as guilty of refusing help when it is most needed.

The young man suddenly felt a surge of power growing in him. It felt completely different than the enhancement spell; this power was overwhelming, almost nauseating, and instead of spreading warmth throughout his body, Kazuki felt a deep chill.

You have one minute.

The young man stood up and wiped the blood from his mouth. He no longer felt any pain.

"Why won't you come out, my liege? Merely sharing a portion of your power with your host will not yield results," Three stated.

Kazuki swung his sword upwards, followed by a quick reversal. He then lunged forward with a stab, withdrew his sword, brought it over his head, and tried a full-force head strike. None of his attacks hit their intended target.

Three shook his head disapprovingly. "I cannot learn anything from this ridiculous exercise."

The assailant swung his staff towards the young man's head, but this time Kazuki could see it coming. He blocked the staff with his katana and used the momentum to slide forward, change the angle of his blade, and cut towards Three's stomach. A thin, red line appeared beneath the torn cloth on the assailant's abdomen.

Three stared at the wound.

Kazuki did not stop. He charged forward again, cutting down at an angle from Three's shoulder to his hip, but the attack missed. Sensing something coming at his left side, the young man quickly put up a block. Before he could register that the staff had been there, Kazuki blocked again – this time high to the right side. He pushed against the staff and stepped forward, changing the blade angle once more and sliding it along the side of the staff towards Three's neck. The katana missed its target once more.

Tch. I'm getting the blocks now, but he's still too fast to hit.

After a few more series of blocks and missed counters, Kazuki finally remembered something that Jun had stressed many times during training: 'MOVE.' With the next block, the young man stepped through, towards Three, and then swung his back leg around; he was now positioned behind his opponent. Kazuki swung his blade towards Three's neck, but his attack was still too slow. A small, red line appeared on the back of Three's shoulder.

At least I hit him, the young man thought as he immediately angled his sword to block an attack from the side. He then pushed his weight into the block and stepped through, knocking the staff aside. As his back leg swept behind his front leg, Kazuki swung his sword over his head to his left side. He then made a horizontal cut at the same time as he stepped his right leg out, and slashed across Three's torso. Not waiting to see if he had made contact or not, Kazuki stepped his left leg forward and brought his katana around for an angled cut. Blood spewed from Three's right shoulder in a line down to his stomach.

Expressions of both surprise and curiosity appeared on Three's face as he touched the wound with his hand.

Kazuki braced himself, but, instead of feeling Three's wrath, the young man was suddenly jerked backwards. There was a blur of sights and sounds, and then suddenly Kazuki was standing next to a stream in an open meadow. He glanced around and saw both Ginza and Reika lying on the ground. Hanzo was sitting next to them with a grin on his face.

"She did it, Lad," Hanzo said, sounding incredibly relieved.

"Did what? What happened?" Kazuki asked, rather confused.

"Some sort of miko magic," the giant replied. "She mentioned demon summoning I think? But, whatever it was, it worked." He then looked at Reika and added, "The lass passed out afterwards. I think she used up all of her energy."

Kazuki sighed with relief. "Alright, well where are we? Three is extremely powerful, so we need to –"

"We're at the base of the mountains, Lad," Hanzo interrupted with a wave of his hand, "we should be far enough away."

"Wow, you made it really far," Kazuki said, genuinely impressed. The enhancement spell must have worn off shortly after Hanzo had run off, so for him to have carried the others all the way down the mountain in such a short time was incredible.

"I coulda made it further," someone moaned.

"Ginza!" Both Kazuki and Hanzo shouted.

The young man ran over to the blacksmith and helped him sit up. "Are you alright?"

"M' insides don't feel right," he grumbled. "As much as I hate t' say it, I don't think we can finish this mission."

"Agreed," Hanzo said grimly. "The cap'n couldn't have known that Three would be guarding the base."

"I think it's best t' hurry back t' the ship. Cap'n'll know what t' do next," Ginza said with a grimace. It was clear that he was trying to push through some intense pain.

Kazuki suddenly saw a shadow out of the corner of his eye. He quickly turned to see who it was, but there was no one there.

Was it my imagination, or was that…?

"You alright, Lad?" Hanzo asked.

"Yeah…wait here a minute," Kazuki replied as he began walking towards an outlying patch of trees that seemed to be swaying, beckoning him over.

"Whaddya mean 'wait 'ere'? We're not gonna – 'ey!" Ginza yelled after the young man as he suddenly ran off into the distant tree line without a backwards glance.

As the Pirate King stepped onto the deck of the Ryujin, he noticed a man speaking with Kohaku and Nia in a rather friendly manner. The man was dressed in a silky black kimono that had a symbol of two dragons intertwined, one red and one blue, embroidered on the back.

"I'm glad to see that you're alright," Kohaku said with a sigh of relief. She was always the first to notice when the Pirate King returned to his ship.

"Oh, welcome back Has-er-Red Dragon," Nia said awkwardly as she wasn't sure how to address him in front of the stranger. "I take it my husband is back on the Chimera, reuniting with his crew?"

The Pirate King nodded, though his focus remained on the well-dressed man who had turned to face him.

"Hasunuma," the well-dressed man said with a smile as he walked over to the Pirate King and embraced him. "It is wonderful to see you again." He spoke gently, but his words held power. The man released the Pirate King and looked him over. "You look well, though the years have changed you."

Hasunuma couldn't hold back his smile any longer. He clasped a firm hand around the man's shoulder and replied, "As do you, Tōichiro. Twenty long years have passed, yet you look as young as ever."

The well-dressed man laughed, "And you are as silver-tongued as I remember you being." He turned back towards the two women and added, "Even as a five-year-old this child could sweet-talk the most hardened of hearts."

Nia and Kohaku looked at each other with feigned disbelief. And then Nia asked rather slyly, "Hasunuma, could this fine, upstanding gentleman be your father? It would explain quite a lot, I think."

I truly wish he were…

Tōichiro chuckled and shook his head, "Unfortunately, I am not so blessed as to be able to call myself his father." His voice was as warm and comforting as Hasunuma remembered it being.

"This is the former Emperor's son, Tōichiro," the Pirate King explained.

"I would prefer that you refer to me as your uncle, Hasunuma," Tōichiro amended.

The Pirate King sighed as he watched Nia's reaction shift from shock to intrigue and then to understanding.

I really didn't want this out yet… "Forgive my rudeness, Tōichiro, I meant no offense," he said with a slight bow.

"So serious, this one," Tōichiro sighed. "Your tutors instructed you well with etiquette, however I am left feeling rather lonely. I had hoped that as a pirate you could address me more freely."

I see your ability to guilt me into doing your bidding hasn't changed. "You are quite right, *Uncle*," the Pirate King replied as he righted himself. "And before you begin your barrage of questions, know that I don't feel like amusing you with the answers at the moment," he said pointedly to Nia, who looked starved for information. "Come, *Uncle*, we have much to discuss," the Pirate King said while motioning for Tōichiro to follow him. "*Privately*," he added as he turned to look back at Nia, who innocently smiled back at him.

Once inside the Captain's Quarters, Tōichiro chose to sit on the couch, rather than on the chair that was offered. As he glanced around the room, a smile crept onto his face.

"King of the pirates…Now there is a title that I never would have expected you to earn for yourself."

Hasunuma grinned. "Well, the name has its advantages. It may have taken me awhile, but it's all thanks to my current position that I was able to rescue you from your confinement."

"Yes, your man – Jun, I believe – did an excellent job. Thank you, Hasunuma. I do hope he recovers quickly from his injury," Tōichiro added, sounding slightly worried.

"Injury?" the Pirate King repeated, sure that he misheard his uncle.

"Oh, I suppose you have not yet heard, my apologies for not mentioning this sooner: when Jun entered my room, he had a rather large gash in his arm. I bandaged it as best I could, but he was so insistent that we immediately return to this ship that I was unable to provide adequate care for him."

Who the festering hole did they have guarding my uncle?! Demon or hybrid, Jun shouldn't have had a problem.

"Oh, but the woman with the nice figure assured me that she would properly tend to his wound. What was her name again?"

"It's 'Kohaku,' Uncle," the Pirate King said with a sigh, "and I *know* that you remember her name."

"Whatever do you mean, my dear nephew?" Tōichiro replied with a look that Hasunuma knew well – even if it had more wrinkles than before.

The Pirate King crossed his arms. "Can we not discuss this now, please? We have more pressing matters at hand."

"Alright, alright," Tōichiro chuckled, "straight to business it is."

Hasunuma pointed to the map on his desk. "Once my men finish destroying this hidden base here, we should be able to attack the main forces at the capitol."

"So, you have finished destroying all other Hekigun bases? My, my, you are certainly an impressive tactician," Tōichiro said as he observed nearly one hundred X marks on the map.

"No," the Pirate King shook his head, "if I were truly impressive, you wouldn't have had to wait so long. Forgive me, Uncle."

Tōichiro waved his hand, dismissing his nephew's apology. "I was in no danger, and, other than the confinement aspect, I was able to live decently." His uncle smiled as he added, "And being able to see you as a grown man has been worth the wait. I know that your mother would have been equally as proud as I am, if not more so."

"She hated pirates," Hasunuma quickly replied, shielding his true feelings.

"Yumiko would not have hated your version, I think. I may have been confined, but news of your exploits reached my ears and, as much as you tried to soil your reputation, I could easily see the truth behind your actions."

Hasunuma frowned. "Kohaku sent you letters, didn't she?" *I always wondered where she kept sending Ami off to, but I assumed it was to Nia.*

"Do not be angry with her," Tōichiro said softly, "I was worried about you, and your letters never contained anything besides updates on the war with the Hekigun."

The Pirate King sighed. "Well, as usual, you are correct. I needed some way to hide my true intentions from that bastard, and becoming a pirate scoundrel seemed the best option." *And being out at sea is rather liberating.*

Tōichiro studied Hasunuma for a moment before asking, "What is it that you intend to do with Hiiro Genji?"

"I shouldn't think that I'd have to explain that to you of all people," the Pirate King scoffed.

"Then I shall once again implore you *not* to kill him," Tōichiro replied sternly.

Hasunuma frowned and said with a raised voice, "How can you say that after all that bastard has done to me, to my mother, to my grandfather, and to you. He deserves to die!"

"I agree that his actions have condemned him, however it is not *you* that should be his executioner."

Hasunuma was about to remind his uncle of his many reasons for wanting to kill that bastard, but he was silenced with one look from Tōichiro.

"Hasunuma, I am well aware of what that man has done to you

and to the rest of my family. But have you not thought of the countless other families that he has destroyed and the numerous people that have suffered under his rule? We are not the only ones who are fit to serve judgment upon that man," he explained softly.

The Pirate King gritted his teeth and curled his hands into tight fists. His uncle had a valid point, but the Pirate King was not about to let his whole life's purpose go for the sake of others.

"If you still cannot accept what I have told you, then I shall leave you to think on this: your mother gave her life so that you may *live*. As of now, you have used that life as a means of exacting revenge upon the man who stole everything from you. And while I do not think Yumiko would begrudge you for that, I *do* think that she would weep if you lost yourself to such selfishness." Tōichiro stood up from the couch and made his way to the door. Before he left, he turned back towards the Pirate King and added, "Is this truly the life that she wanted for you, Hasunuma? Is revenge all that my sister's sacrifice means to you?"

After the door was shut, the Pirate King banged his fists on the desk. *Do NOT take this away from me!* He dropped his head into his hands and desperately fought his emotions as they rose to the surface. *There's nothing left...*

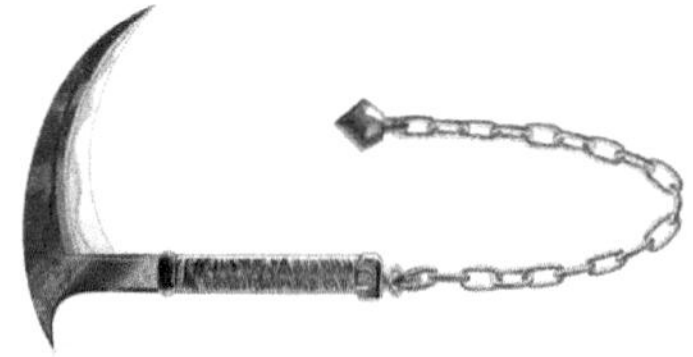

As she watched over the gangplank to the Ryujin, the ninja

woman desperately tried to avoid Ni's gaze, but the nearly blind woman was intent on getting some answers.

"Don't you dare try and sneak away from me," she warned as she revealed a tiny needle in her hand, "or I'll *make* you talk."

Kohaku knew that her friend wouldn't actually hurt her, but she also knew that Ni was the nosiest woman she'd ever met. There would be no end to the threats until her curiosity was satisfied. "But I really don't know much," the ninja woman pleaded, wishing she was still mute.

"Tell me *everything*," Ni demanded.

I'm certainly not telling you everything, but... "Fine," Kohaku sighed, "this stays between us, OK?"

The slender woman nodded, "I understand. I'll only tell my man."

"That's not what I…Oh, whatever," the ninja woman shook her head. She knew that there was no way Ni wouldn't tell her husband something, especially when it concerned Hasunuma. But both she and her husband were trustworthy people, so Kohaku determined that it wouldn't hurt Hasunuma in any way if they knew a little about his past.

"Hasu's mother was the daughter of the former Emperor, which technically makes Hasu a possible heir to the throne, *but* you should know by now that Hasu has no intention of becoming Emperor."

"Yeah, that idiot will settle for 'Pirate King' instead," Ni joked. "So is he after Hiiro Genji and the Hekigun in order to restore his uncle to the throne?"

Kohaku shrugged. "That's part of it," she said, "but I think there's another reason for why he's got such a huge grudge against

Hiiro Genji."

Ni looked at her friend with great anticipation.

Choosing her words carefully, the ninja woman said, "I'm pretty sure that Hiiro Genji murdered Hasu's mother."

"Well, yes, that would make sense," Ni said with a nod. "I mean, he betrayed and killed your former Emperor and took over Tsukigen, and since there hasn't been any recent news about the former Emperor's daughter – unlike his son – I assumed she was dead."

Kohaku nodded. "Hiiro Genji was the former Emperor's most trusted advisor, but, from what I understand, the former Emperor banished Hiiro Genji for betrayal – although what exactly that meant, no one knows." *Well, no one besides the four of us anyway.* "He then disappeared for some years before returning with a large army that he used to take over the palace and kill the former Emperor. Tōichiro was away from the palace at the time, so his life was spared, but Hiiro Genji eventually found Tōichiro and locked him away in a remote location. Hasu spent years trying to find where his uncle was located."

Ni frowned. "Why didn't he kill Hasu's uncle? Seems to me like the best way to secure your seat on the throne is to kill off the whole royal family." The slender woman's brow creased further as she added, "Which also begs the question of why Hasu is still alive."

Kohaku shook her head. "I don't know. My theory is that perhaps Hasu's mother helped him escape, but died in the process…and that Hiiro Genji has kept Tōichiro alive all these years as insurance against those that might rise against him. But those are just my thoughts. Hasu has never talked about it."

Ni spoke slowly as she tried to piece it all together. "So then…what about Hasu's father? Did he also die while rescuing Hasu from the experiments?"

Kohaku's eyes widened and her stomach dropped. "…What experiments?"

Ni sighed. "Come on, Ko. I'm not an idiot. And besides, I'm pretty sure that everyone on the ship, except maybe that priestess girl, figured out what Hasu is the moment he mentioned the hybrids."

"Oh," the ninja woman replied softly.

The slender woman reached out and hugged Kohaku. "Don't worry, Ko. We're with him all the way, no matter what. I mean we've put up with his personality flaws thus far, so what's being part demon on top of that?"

Kohaku couldn't help but smile at her friend's remark.

As Ni released the ninja woman, she wore a devious smile of her own. "Although, I now feel obliged to remind you that you have terrible taste in men."

The ninja woman sighed heavily. "Look, Hasu is who he is, regardless of what happened, and I'm well-aware of how stupid I am for lo–" Kohaku threw her hands up in front of her mouth to stop her sudden confession.

A huge grin appeared on her friend's face. "What was that last part, Ko? Sorry, I didn't catch it. Why don't you tell me again," she teased.

Oh for the sake of the gods…That woman! Kohaku bit her lip to keep quiet.

Ni laughed, "Don't worry, my sweet friend, when he is ready,

I'm sure that Hasu will reciprocate. If not," she smiled mischievously as she added, "he may find one of these babies stuck in his stubborn arse."

The ninja woman couldn't help but laugh as she looked at the rather large needle protruding from her friend's hand.

"Who are you threatening now?" A booming voice laughed.

The women turned to see D walking up the gangplank and onto the ship. *Perfect timing.*

"I'm sorry to cut your gossiping short, but we have important work to do, my love, and not a lot of time to do it in," D said as he lifted Nia up and began carrying her off the ship. "We'll catch you later, Kohaku!"

"See you soon, my sweet friend," Ni called out.

The ninja woman felt a pang of guilt for lying to her friend, but the full details behind Hasu's past needed to remain secret. "Good luck," she replied with a wave as she watched the two leave.

Kohaku could hear the two exchanging affectionate words as they went. *Such an interesting pair.* She fondly thought of them and wondered if she might one day have a similar relationship with a certain captain…the ninja woman waved her hand in the air, dismissing her thoughts. Their long years of fighting seemed to be drawing to a close faster than she expected, and Kohaku wasn't entirely sure what that would mean for her. All she knew was how to fight. Would the world without Hekigun be one without fighting? Or would there be other reasons to kill and to risk her life? And what would Hasu do? Continue being the Pirate King or would he, too, leave the fighting behind and live a quiet life?

Kohaku giggled to herself. *There's no way that man could ever lead a quiet life.* So then, she wondered as her smile faded, where did that leave her?

Not wanting to dwell on those thoughts, Kohaku made her way below deck; she wanted to check on Jun, who had apparently been injured during his mission to free Tōichiro.

"I never thought this day would come," Kohaku said teasingly as she entered the cook's room.

Jun glared at Kohaku. "Yeah, whatever," he mumbled.

The ninja woman sat next to him on his bed. His shirt was off, and she could see the deep gash in his left arm. It was a serious wound that reached to the bone. Kohaku knew that she needed to clean and bandage it before any infection set in. She reached into her medicine pouch and pulled out a small bottle.

"Hold still. This will burn a bit," the ninja woman said as she slowly began to drip the contents of the bottle onto the wound.

"Fiery blazes of the undead!" Jun yelled as the liquid began to bubble inside of his flesh. "Is there venom in there?!"

The ninja woman didn't respond. She was too busy trying to hold Jun's arm steady with one hand while continuing to steadily apply the liquid with the other. "I said hold still," she finally said with a hint of annoyance in her voice.

Jun mumbled something under his breath, but then used his other hand to hold his arm as steady as he could. It was actually rather impressive that he was able to restrain himself as well as he did, because the pain was excruciating. Kohaku knew firsthand what it felt like, as she had used the same medicine on her legs. But the results were undeniable: any wound treated with it would not become infected and would heal faster.

As the bubbling subsided, Jun's whole body began to relax. He let himself fall back onto his bed and closed his eyes. "That was awful. Next time, just cut my arm off."

Kohaku shook her head, "No, we still need you in fighting condition."

"Heh. What do you need me for when you've got the captain?" Jun smirked.

The ninja woman smacked the cook's bare chest with her hand. It was damp with sweat.

"Hey, I don't need any more injuries," he said flatly.

A long silence descended on the room. The ninja woman continued to work on Jun's wound, gently wiping away the dried blood and bits of dead flesh. She then carefully applied some salve to the raw sections and wrapped his arm with a long strip of clean cloth.

"You know, you're the only reason I'm part of this crew," Jun abruptly said.

Kohaku nodded. She knew that the Ryujin's cook had no loyalty or love for anyone on the ship besides herself. His heart had been closed off for far too long, meaning that it would take the will of the gods to open it back up again.

"Yeah, I think I told you before that you remind me of my sisters. Though I doubt any of them would have become a ninja," he added with a faint smile before letting out a deep sigh and closing his eyes.

Kohaku figured that he was probably remembering his family. She knew how hard it was to speak of lost loved ones, so she remained silent and waited for Jun to continue.

"I didn't agree to join Hasunuma in order to get revenge," he said slowly as he opened his eyes. "After losing everything, I fell into the same stupid cycle of hatred and killing that my father did. I spent years training, trying to become a master swordsman so that I could exact my revenge."

Jun shook his head, as if he were silently admonishing himself. After a moment, his handsome hazel eyes met Kohaku's. "And then I met you," he said, his eyes shining bright. "As soon as I saw you, I was reminded of my sisters. It's as if their souls spoke to me, saying 'What are you doing, you idiot? We didn't help mom raise you, just for you to throw your life away.'" Jun then smiled a rare, genuine smile. His face lit up in a way that showcased his fine features. "And they were right. I found a passion for cooking and I'm going to focus my efforts on that, instead of killing countless people for some selfish revenge that my sisters would never have wanted."

Kohaku couldn't help but return his smile. Jun had come a long way since they had met, about ten years ago.

It had only been about half a year since the incident at Hokuto when they met. She and Hasu had been moving from village to village, trying to decide what their next course of action was, when they found Jun in a remote fishing village to the north. He was fourteen at the time – one year younger than Kohaku – but he was already an amazing swordsman. His skills impressed both Kohaku and Hasu, so much so that Hasu had asked Jun to join them.

At first, Jun refused. He was like a dog that had been hurt by humans too many times to be able to coexist with them. But then Hasu beat him in a fight and told Jun that he would learn far more about swordsmanship by traveling around Tsukigen than he could alone in a small village.

However, even after joining them, it was clear that his heart had already frozen past the point of a quick thaw. Hasu and Kohaku never gave up on him, but they realized that Jun would probably spend the rest of his life that way. While it was nice that Jun thought of Kohaku as a sister, the ninja woman knew that it wasn't enough for the cook to regain his heart.

"You know," Jun said suddenly as he sat up, "he's a real idiot."

Ah. He means Hasu. "What do you think he'll do…once this is all over?" The ninja woman quietly asked.

The cook shook his head. "He won't settle down like your average man. I think you know that. In fact, I'm pretty sure he intends to–"

Kohaku quickly put her hand across Jun's mouth to silence him. She did not want to hear it. Of course she had realized long ago what Hasu would do, but she couldn't accept it. She wouldn't accept it.

Jun's fingers lightly touched her hand. They paused there for a moment before he gently wrapped his fingers around her hand and pulled it away from his mouth.

"Kohaku," Jun said softly as he cradled her hand in his. "The living are more important than the dead. And if that idiot makes the same mistake as my father…I promise that you will not find yourself alone."

The ninja woman looked at the man sitting next to her. His eyes reflected both the conviction and the deep sorrow he felt from his words. She gently caressed his face with her other hand. "Thank you, dear friend," she said with a warm smile.

The cook released Kohaku's hand. "He's such an idiot for

keeping you at a distance," he said, turning his head towards the door. "It really vexes me."

"Oh, so *that's* why you're always so frosty towards me."

Kohaku immediately pulled her hand away from Jun's face when she heard the voice from the doorway. She didn't dare look his way as she heard the familiar *thunk* of his boots against the floor, drawing nearer.

"I figured it was some sort of inferiority complex. Looks like I was right."

Jun immediately stood up from the bed.

Kohaku reached for his arm to pull him back, but she stopped in order to avoid touching his wound. "Jun, don't!" she shouted, but she knew that words alone wouldn't stop him.

"If you weren't a hybrid bastard, I'd be able to kill you easily," Jun growled.

"Not with that arm, you wouldn't," Hasu growled back. He reached for the cook's wounded arm, but his hand was smacked away by a smaller one.

"Stop this now," the ninja woman said firmly as she stood up and faced the two men, "or I'll paralyze you both." She had a needle in each hand, hovering less than an inch away from both men's necks.

"Leave it to your lover to save you," Hasu sneered at the cook.

"Should I be honored by your jealousy?" Jun said mockingly. "You know very well who her real lover would be, if he were man enough to–"

Hasu grabbed Jun's throat and yelled, "She's got no future with me! Do you want her to suffer more than she already has?"

"I SAID STOP," Kohaku loudly commanded, her voice almost

cracking from the strain.

Hasu released the cook and turned to leave, but the ninja woman stopped him by throwing one of the needles across his path. "What?" He grumbled without turning around to face her.

"Tell me the truth," Kohaku demanded, her voice shaking slightly. "After the Hekigun are finished, when it's all over," she began, her heart pounding wildly in her chest, "what…what will you do?"

An unbearable silence filled the room. It may have only lasted seconds, but it felt like hours. The ninja woman regretted asking her question and almost told him to forget it when she received a response.

"I thought I made that perfectly clear earlier," he said, devoid of emotion.

Kohaku felt like vomiting. "You…you really think that…" she had to catch her breath before continuing, "*dying* is the only option?"

There was no response.

"You're a coward," she said, her body trembling. "A selfish coward!" The rage and sorrow that had been building inside of her for some time now came pouring out. "Death is easy. Everything stops for the dead. But did you consider, even for one second, how *I* would feel if you died?! No! You've fooled yourself into thinking that your death would somehow benefit me, when in reality it would *destroy* me."

"Then what would you have me do, Kohaku?" Hasu retorted angrily as he turned to face her. "We know nothing about the hybrids. What would you do if I suddenly lost myself and became a demon? What if I end up killing you and everyone else I care about?!"

"But we *don't* know what will happen in the future. That's the point! Why do you think that ending your life now would have any benefit?"

A minute or so of silence passed before Kohaku felt Hasu's anger dissipate. His eyes never broke contact with hers as he softly replied, "Then I'll ask you again: *what would you have me do*?"

"Clearly she wants you to *live*, you idiot," Jun interrupted. "Now can you finish your lovers spat somewhere else? I want to sleep."

Hasu glared at the cook, but before he could take a step towards him, Kohaku grabbed the Pirate King's arm and pulled him out of the room. She didn't stop dragging him along until they were standing in her room, with the door shut and locked behind them.

The ninja woman's heart was still racing, but it was too late to turn back; the only option now was to press forward. "Hasu, please…give up on your quest for revenge."

The Pirate King glared down at her. "You want me to give up my whole life, my reason for existing?" He asked icily.

"No!" Kohaku shook her head. It took all of her willpower to meet his spiteful eyes. "Can't you see that revenge isn't what's keeping you alive anymore? Yes, at the beginning, when the pain was too much for you to handle, revenge was your salvation. And that was fine," Kohaku explained as calmly as she could. "But you've grown and changed since then. Even before Kazu joined our crew, you had already begun opening your heart. I know because I…I've been watching you," Kohaku slowly reached out and touched Hasu's hand. Her heart beat wildly and her throat felt dry, but she continued to speak. "You're not alone anymore, Hasu. There are people who care about you, who want you to live–"

"And what if I'd rather die than let that man take one more breath, kill one more person, hm? Does it matter what I want?"

"Revenge solves *nothing*. I would know," Kohaku tightened her grip on the Pirate King's hand. "I took my father's life in the name of revenge, and it only made me feel more lonely and more desperate for distractions. Did you know that I often think about that night? I think about how I might have saved him…if we had known the whole story, maybe we could have released him from the–"

"Don't, Kohaku," Hasunuma spoke quietly as he gently squeezed her hand. "There is nothing to be gained from reliving the past. What's happened can't be changed, no matter how horrible the circumstances." His eyes softened. "And, knowing your father, he would have killed himself when he found out what he had done."

Kohaku bit her lip, fighting back the swelling tears. Hasunuma was right – there was nothing she could have done differently. But that admission only made her current task more vital.

The ninja woman took a deep breath and slowly released it. "Hasu, I refuse to lose anyone else I care about to the Hekigun. And, despite what you said, I don't think you'd rather die. It's true, don't give me that look. You'd like to live, but you've been so focused on revenge, convinced you'll sacrifice yourself in the end, that you don't know *how* to live."

Hasu's face tensed. "Tell me then, how does a demon live?"

"Stop mentioning demons!" Kohaku fumed, pulling her hand away from his. "It's a terrible excuse and you know it."

"It's not an excuse, it's reality," Hasu retorted. "I could turn into a full one someday, and what then?"

"Then I'll kill you," Kohaku huffed, "but *until then* you are a human with a conscience who has no business destroying my happiness for idiotic non-reasons!" She suddenly grabbed hold of Hasu's face, pulled it towards hers and kissed him fiercely. He didn't resist. When she parted her lips from his, she said, "I love you, you idiot."

The Pirate King gently took hold of the ninja woman's chin and ran his thumb lightly across her lips. "Someone like me…I'm too tainted and broken. I swore to your mother that I'd protect you."

"Then protect me, stay with me, and…love me," she replied as she wrapped her arms around his neck.

A genuine smile, full of affection, spread across Hasu's face. "You know I do."

He then touched his lips to hers, tenderly at first, but gradually with more passion. Kohaku welcomed the change of pace, pulling him closer so that their bodies were in full contact. She ran her fingers through his hair as they continued kissing with shared enthusiasm.

More, more, "More," Kohaku moaned.

Hasu stopped kissing her.

The ninja woman opened her eyes and met his lustful gaze. She wanted to make her intentions perfectly clear, so she moved her lips close to his ear and whispered, "I want all of you." And then, just for fun, she licked his ear.

That was the key, apparently, to unlocking a solid hour of pure pleasure.

As he pushed open the door to Jun's room, the Pirate King paused. He saw the cook sitting on his bed, his back leaning against the wall. The Pirate King's eyes were drawn to the bandage than encompassed Jun's entire upper left arm. It was no longer purely white.

"Did you come back to gloat or to thank me?" The cook mumbled as he opened his eyes and sat up.

Smug horse's arse. "Yeah, thanks for the disemboweling."

"Any time," the cook said with a grin that quickly faded. "It was Second, in case you were wondering."

"Why the festering hole was *he* there?" The Pirate King wondered aloud.

Jun shrugged his right shoulder. "Dunno. I had just finished killing Four when out of nowhere this intense gust comes at me from the left. I thought I dodged it," Jun frowned.

I had anticipated one of the lower numbers to be there, but not Second...

"What happened next?" The Pirate King asked.

"The demonic bastard introduced himself and then said, 'Give my regards to Red Dragon,' before disappearing. I didn't even get a chance to pay him back."

So, he knew we'd be there... "I guess that means that bastard finally figured out my plans."

"Then you were right about Second working with Hiiro Genji. Good thing we've taken out most of those demons," Jun said with a smirk.

"Yeah, but we don't know if the few left are all in Chuushin or not. They may not be able to get reinforcements anymore, but having a few powerful demons might make things difficult for us..." the Pirate King trailed off as he considered the possibilities.

"You, me, and Douglas could take them out, so why not leave the others on the ship?"

The Pirate King shook his head, "No, there will be too many soldiers for us to wade through before getting to the big shots. We need the others."

"Then how about sending the kid in solo? I'm sure the Demon King could easily slaughter them all."

Hasunuma shot the cook a look and said, "Not funny."

"You're so over-protective," Jun grumbled. "That kid's stronger than you think he is."

"It's not as much a question of strength as it is willpower," the Pirate King retorted. "If the Demon King wanted to take total control of Kazuki's body, do you think the kid could fend him off?"

"What's it to you whether the kid wins or not? You've got your own agenda. The way I see it, he's just another one of your pawns," the cook said coldly.

Hasunuma glared at him. "Well aren't you a sweetheart today."

Jun looked away and mumbled, "Sorry…arm hurts…"

The Pirate King shook his head. "Get some rest. Second delivered his message, so I doubt we'll see him again until…" A thought suddenly struck Hasunuma. "By the gods," he breathed as he bolted from the room.

He ran onto to the deck of his ship and looked at the empty

gangplank. There wasn't any sign of anyone approaching the ship as far as his eyes could see.

"What's wrong?" Kohaku asked as she climbed onto the deck. She must have heard him tear through the hall and up the stairs. "Rize's on watch," she added as she pointed up to the crow's nest.

The Pirate King shook his head. *No, he should be fine. He's not alone.*

"Are you worried about Kazu?" the ninja woman asked.

She's seriously too good at reading people, Hasunuma thought. "No, he'll be fine," he said aloud. *He'll be just fine...*

I know I saw him, the young man thought as he ran into the forest. Looking around, Kazuki spotted a small clearing to his left. He slowed his pace and stepped cautiously out of the tree line. Looming overhead, the tops of the hundreds-of-years-old trees bend inward as if to hide the clearing from the radiance of the sun. The mountain grew silent as the breeze that shook the trees earlier was gone, and no birds or other creatures could be heard.

"I'm glad you came," a monotone voice called out from somewhere nearby. Even with Kazuki's heightened senses, he couldn't determine the voice's location.

"What do you want, Second?" The young man probed.

"What I always want, of course," the demon replied without emotion, "to kill Shinigami-sama and take his place." His voice seemed to emanate from every rock, tree, cloud, and blade of grass.

"That's not gonna happen," Kazuki curtly replied as he glanced around, still trying to locate Second. "I won't let the Demon King out."

"Oh, I think you will," the demon replied with a hint of amusement. "Otherwise I'll have to kill your friends, and that wouldn't be fun for either of us."

"Touch them and you die," the young man growled.

"Yes, yes, I'm well-aware of that," Second said with a bored sort of sigh as he emerged from the shadows of the surrounding trees. "And I'm not the only one. Don't you think it's worse for them because of it? I mean, if you *really* cared for your friends, it would be best to surrender your life for theirs, yes?"

Even with the underlying malicious intent, the young man felt there was some truth in the demon's words. *Wouldn't* everyone be better off if Kazuki – and the Demon King – were gone? The demon games would end, sending all remaining demons back to the demon realm, which might then give Hasunuma and the crew a fair chance of defeating the Hekigun. And would it *really* matter if Kazuki were there in the end or not?

A vision of a golden-haired beauty, smiling sweetly, flashed through the young man's mind. His heart felt heavy as he thought of leaving her behind, but surely even she would move on after a while. After all, he never should have met her, or the rest of the Ryujin crew, in the first place; if not for the Demon King, he would have remained the corpse of an eight-year-old.

Suddenly Kazuki's consciousness was roused; he thought he heard someone call his name. As his eyes regained their focus on reality, he saw Second leaping towards him with his sword held high. The young man could have help up his blade and blocked the attack, but he decided not to. Instead, he closed his eyes and resigned himself to death.

The sensation he felt next was not at all what he had expected. He had been knocked to the ground, but there was no pain from a sword wound. Slightly fearful of what he would see, the young man slowly opened his eyes.

Second had jumped back and was now standing quite a ways away – but not so far as to not be a threat – and Ginza was standing in front of Kazuki.

"Ya damned fool!" The blacksmith bellowed. "How many times d' we have t' tell ya NOT t' listen t' yer enemy!" From his reaction, Ginza must have heard what Second had told Kazuki earlier.

The young man blinked a few times before calmly saying, "But wouldn't it be better for everyone if I–"

THWACK.

The impact from Ginza's fist made Kazuki see stars.

"How the festerin' hole d'ya figure that?! 'Ere we are, bustin' our arses fightin' demons t' protect ya, an' yer about t' give up! We're givin' everythin' we have fer ya t' LIVE, Little Oni!" Ginza yelled so furiously that it almost looked like he was spitting blood.

Wait. What? The young man watched wide-eyed as the blacksmith's hand turned red after wiping his mouth.

"Fiery mountain gods, that demon's got an incredible sword," Ginza cursed as he dropped to his knees. The blade of his weapon had been shattered.

"Ginza!"

The blacksmith fell onto his back and cursed again. "Cap'n's gonna be furious." He then looked at Kazuki, who was now kneeling over him, and grinned. "But I've got no regrets."

The young man frantically searched for the source of the blood that was streaming out of Ginza's body. *No. No! This can't be happening!*

"Stop yer fussin', Little Oni," Ginza grunted, "the enemy's still 'ere."

"He's right, you know. It's rather unwise to turn your back to the enemy," Second taunted. "Although it was rather foolish of him to jump out like that, seeing as even if I had split your head open, Shinigami-sama would have simply taken over and healed your body." The demon then looked directly at Ginza and scoffed, "What a waste of a sacrifice."

A fierce wind suddenly whipped through the trees. Second braced himself, but the force of the gale began to push him backwards. Thunder rumbled overhead as the sky darkened.

"What's this?" The demon smirked. "Have you decided to let Shinigami-sama out?"

Before Kazuki could react to Second's latest taunt, a strong hand shot out and gripped his arm tightly.

"Don't give in," Ginza warned. "Don't...lose yerself...Little Oni," he added with labored breaths.

Kazuki put his hand on the blacksmith's. It was large and rough and covered in blood. The young man flashed Ginza a quick smile and said, "Got it," with a nod. Kazuki then gently removed the blacksmith's hand from his arm and stood up. "Wait here and I'll patch you up once I'm done cleaning up this horse pile."

The blacksmith grinned and gave Kazuki a 'thumbs-up'.

Grabbing his katana, the young man flew at Second with shocking speed. His opponent barely had time to block as Kazuki slashed at him repeatedly.

"Should I be impressed at how such base emotions are able to make you humans temporarily stronger?" Second scoffed. "Your pathetic 'strength' is still nothing compared to what we demons can do."

"Then why is your kind relegated to the Demon Realm?" Kazuki retorted as he cut downward across Second's shoulder. No blood was drawn, but a small tear appeared in the demon's shirt.

A scowl appeared on Second's face. "Because even demons have rules imposed upon them," he replied venomously, "and only the *King* has the ability to change things."

Suddenly Kazuki understood the full importance and implications of the demon games. It wasn't a simple power play; the one who reigned as King of Demons had *total control* over the Demon Realm. Which, theoretically, meant that if a demon king wanted to, he could allow demons to invade and take over the Human Realm.

That's a terrifying thought.

There is more to it than that, but I am glad that you finally understand the significance of what could happen, depending on which demon wins the games.

Kazuki tried to ignore what the Demon King had just told him and focus on the fight with Second, but his attention kept wavering. After another series of attempted slashes, the young man's demonic opponent recognized what was going on and decided to raise the stakes.

"Oh, there was something I forgot to mention earlier," Second stated as he grinned wickedly. "We have your precious miko."

Kazuki froze. "What did you say?"

Second laughed. "This is wonderful! I can feel your despair and rage so intensely." The demon sheathed his sword and said, "But this is not our final battlefield. I'll be waiting for you in Chuushin, Shinigami-sama." With another wicked smile, he then added, "Oh, and don't make me wait too long, or I'll have to use the miko to entertain myself."

Kazuki swung his sword in a final attempt to cut down the demon, but it was too late; Second had somehow disappeared into thin air. All that was left of him was his malicious laugh, echoing in the young man's ears.

In his mind, he was panicking, but the young man forced himself to focus as he turned back to the blacksmith lying on the ground.

"Ginza! Hey, Ginza!"

No response.

Kazuki reached for the medicine in his pack and knelt beside the blacksmith. "Second's gone now, so let me patch you up."

Still no response.

The young man put his hands on the blacksmith's shoulders and gently shook him. "Hey, Ginza, stop messing around." He grew more desperate with each silent second. "Ginza! Come on!" Kazuki yelled as he shook the blacksmith with more force.

A strong hand suddenly gripped the young man's shoulder, starling him. Kazuki glanced behind him and saw Hanzo standing there with a dark expression on his face. The giant must have joined them while Kazuki had been fighting Second, because the young man hadn't noticed him before. Hanzo had probably chased after Ginza, who had followed Kazuki into the woods. Perhaps that's when Reika, who was unconscious, had been taken. But by whom?

A deep, solemn voice interrupted the young man's thoughts as it uttered, "He's gone, Lad."

He's...what?

"No...no way...THERE'S NO WAY!" Kazuki yelled as he pushed the giant's hand away from his shoulder. He looked down at the blacksmith's bloodstained face; his eyes were closed and there was a faint smile on his lips. It seemed as if he were merely sleeping and would wake up at any second. But Kazuki took note of the stillness of the body, and the lack of breath. He reached out and put his hand over Ginza's chest, hoping that he was wrong, but he wasn't.

Kazuki's vision slowly began to blur. "It's all my fault. It's all my fault," he murmured.

"Lad..."

"I thought everyone would be better off...but they've taken Reika and now Ginza's...he's..."

I'll never hear his voice again. Or his absurdly loud laughter. He won't tease me or throw his arm around my shoulder and ruffle my hair anymore. There won't be that annoying, but comforting presence nearby...

The young man shifted his eyes to glance at Hanzo. The giant's eyes looked as if the light had been sucked out of them. His enormous hands were clenched and shaking, but the rest of his body was still as stone. Although no tears fell, Kazuki knew how much pain Hanzo was experiencing. It had been clear to the young man from the beginning that Ginza was like a brother to Hanzo. And now he was gone.

But it wasn't just Hanzo that cared for the blacksmith. The whole Ryujin crew loved him like family. How were they going to react? How could the young man face them? What would Kohaku…what would *Hasunuma* say?

The young man's stomach dropped as his mind filled with dread. *It's all my–*

No.

Kazuki was taken aback by the interruption. *But I–*

It was Second and Three who killed him, not you. They deserve the blame.

A familiar feeling began to envelop the young man. He knew where it would lead, and he knew what would happen, but Kazuki chose not to fight it. His body began to tremble as the dark feeling spread through Kazuki like wildfire.

"They'll pay…They will pay…THEY WILL PAY WITH THEIR BLOOD!" He shouted as the flames inside of him blazed.

The sudden declaration startled Hanzo. "Lad?" He inquired with a deeply worried expression on his face.

Kazuki didn't answer. His blood burned; it was agonizing, but there was no stopping it.

The giant extended his hand, as if he were about to grab onto the young man, but he abruptly recoiled it when Kazuki let out a terrifying and deafening scream.

Before he lost consciousness, Kazuki turned his eyes to Ginza's body one last time. The world was then shrouded in darkness once more.

"Hasu…Kazu and the others still aren't back yet," the ninja woman said quietly as she stared at the mountain range where the group should have been.

The Pirate King held back his worries and instead replied cheerily, "They'll be fine, Kohaku. After all, the kid has the Demon King inside of him. I doubt he'd be taken out by any hybrids."

The ninja woman didn't look convinced. "But isn't Kazu still feeling the effects from that demon sealing spell? What if he can't fully use the Demon King's powers yet? Not only that, but you sent them to destroy the experimental facility, which I'm sure has the strongest guards besides Hiiro Genji himself, and–"

The Pirate King held up his hand to stop Kohaku. Her mind was clearly running wild with all of the terrible possibilities. "He's not alone, Kohaku," he said in a reassuring tone. "Hanzo and Ginza are with him – not as bodyguards, but as sanity grounders. And that kid would do anything to keep the miko safe."

"That's part of the problem," the ninja woman said, shaking her head.

"I gave them a tough mission, so give 'em some more time," he said with a shrug, trying to downplay the situation and hide his own anxiety. Hasunuma had great confidence in his ability to consider all options and plan accordingly, but he couldn't shake the sinking feeling in his gut. After he had found out about Jun's run-in with Second – something he hadn't anticipated – the Pirate King's worries and doubts began to surface.

Maybe he should have waited and tackled the experimental facility after completing the other two missions. Maybe he should have gone with them, or sent Jun, and waited to rescue Tōichiro at the end. Maybe… no, he couldn't keep questioning the decision he made. That sort of thinking would lead him down a path with no return.

Suddenly Rize let out a sharp whistle from the crow's nest and everyone on deck let out a sigh of relief.

The Pirate King looked in the direction of the mountain range and waited for his men to come into view. *By the gods, I was actually beginning to–*

Another sharp whistle came, followed by a gasp and a, "Gods, no!"

Rize's eyes were the sharpest of anyone's by far, which meant that everyone else would have to wait to see what it was that horrified him.

The Pirate King held his breath as one figure came into view. No other figures followed. And it soon became clear that the one was carrying another over his shoulder.

"Ginza!" Kohaku cried out as she moved as quickly as she could towards the gangplank. The others followed suit.

The Pirate King did not move. He stood with his fist tightly clenched and watched as Hanzo brought his fallen crewmate aboard the Ryujin. Hanzo didn't stop until he stood a few feet away from Hasunuma. He gently set Ginza's body down before getting on his knees and hanging his head low before his captain.

A gloomy silence fell over the ship. The Pirate King stared at the two men before him – one an empty shell, the other on the verge of erupting – but he said nothing. This outcome had always been a possibility. The Pirate King had known that from the moment each member of his crew had joined his cause. And they all knew it too.

Kohaku and Rize stood a ways behind Hanzo. Deep anger and sadness vividly reflected in their expressions.

Ginza had been well liked from the moment he first set foot on the Ryujin. His jolly, boisterous nature was uplifting and helped to soften the darkness that surrounded everyone. Although he had his own dark shadow, Ginza never let it show. Instead, he locked away his personal sorrows so that he could bring joy to others. He was a rare, bright soul, which was partly why the Pirate King had assigned him to Kazuki from the beginning; in the hopes that Ginza's light would help keep the kid's enormous shadow at bay.

"Cap'n," Hanzo said softly, his voice full of emotion, "We…failed you."

Something needed to be said. Something needed to be done. But as the man who sends them to their deaths, the Pirate King was incapable of giving any consolation to those remaining. It was not his place to offer words of sorrow when he, himself, was the cause. All he could do was become their solid base from which they could continue to stand.

"Where is Kazuki?" The Pirate King asked as coldly as he could.

Hanzo's head practically hit the deck as he threw himself forward. "I'm so sorry, Cap'n! He–"

Suddenly a huge explosion assaulted their ears and all eyes turned towards the mountain range where it originated. They caught a glimpse of a column of fire shooting upwards, through the clouds, before it vanished. No one moved or spoke.

It was the Pirate King who finally broke the trance, his voice booming louder than the explosion. "Tell me everything. NOW!"

Kazuki felt like he was floating in water. Not drowning, but slowly sinking deeper and deeper into the tranquil darkness. He couldn't open his eyes, but he had the feeling that there was nothing to see anyways. How long had he been like that? And how long would he stay? He wasn't sure. If he concentrated, he could hear faint voices…

"But my liege, don't you see that all of this research I've done is for your benefit!"

"The only thing here that I can benefit from is your death."

There was a loud noise that sent ripples through to Kazuki. He stopped listening. It was difficult to concentrate. Using his brain made him feel like he was climbing a vertical rock-face while weighing two to three times more than usual – so, while possible, it wasn't worth the effort.

Kazuki felt exhausted. He lacked the strength to move.

Maybe I'll rest here for a while…

The Pirate King stood on the edge of the deck of the Ryujin. His arms were crossed and he was glaring at the kid who was walking up the gangplank towards him.

"I don't ever remember giving *you* permission to board my ship," he said coldly.

The kid looked up at him with black eyes and grinned. **"I do not need your permission, Pirate,"** he stated as he stood fearlessly in front of the Pirate King. **"You can either benefit from my return, or I will take this ship and the lives of its crew,"** the kid smiled horribly as he added, **"what say you, *Captain*?"**

Hasunuma's hand shot out and grabbed the kid by his neck.

"You would kill the boy that you have been protecting all this time?"

The Pirate King's grip tightened. "You aren't Kazuki."

"Correct. However," the kid said as he took hold of Hasunuma's outstretched arm and squeezed it, **"since I have fully awoken, you have no hope of defeating me."**

The Pirate King tried to push through the pain, but he couldn't let his sword arm get broken, so he retracted it. But not before he unsheathed his red dragon sword with his other hand and attempted to slash the demon before him.

The Demon King jumped back to avoid the blade. He grinned at the attempt, but it quickly faded when he saw that his chest had been lightly cut. **"You have become more powerful than last we met."**

"You have no idea," the Pirate King said icily as he aimed the tip of his sword at the King of demons.

A deep laugh rose from the kid's body. **"This is better than I ever anticipated. I have not felt this much excitement in centuries!"** He grabbed the hilt of his katana and began to unsheathe it.

Suddenly, an arrow flew towards the Demon King's head. He effortlessly cut it in half as he drew his blade, but a small needle snuck past the arrow and pierced the Demon King's hand. He immediately dropped his katana.

"I've paralyzed your muscles," the ninja woman explained as she appeared behind the Pirate King. "You won't be able to move your hand for at least a few minutes."

"Ah, how careless of me," the Demon King said plainly as he pulled the needle from his hand. **"Shall I reward your efforts?"**

The air grew still and cold. Hasunuma could feel the Demon King's energy pouring out of Kazuki's body. He knew what was about to happen and he had to stop it somehow.

"You mentioned that we could benefit from your return," the Pirate King blurted out. "What did you mean by that?"

The Demon King's energy lessened. He stared at Hasunuma for a moment before smiling horribly. **"I almost forgot."** His energy completely disappeared from the air around them as he picked up his katana from the ground. He then effortlessly sheathed his sword using both hands. **"This game has gone on long enough. My efforts to make this a more entertaining round have created unacceptable by-products."**

Is he referring to the hybrids?

"I will not allow Second to play around any longer. I intend to kill him and end this."

The Pirate King shook his head. "I think there's still a few more demons out there. Your game won't end with the death of Second."

"By the time I get to him, he will be the last," the Demon King said firmly.

So, he knows where the remaining demons are…although I'm pretty sure I do too. "I still haven't heard how this benefits us," the Pirate King retorted. He needed to make sure his assumptions were correct before he risked the lives of his crew on his biggest gamble yet.

"Do not play dumb, Pirate. You know that Second is working with Tsukigen's leader to make those abominations."

"Huh. That so?" Hanzo huffed as he walked closer to the gangplank. He was wearing his knuckles and carrying Ginza's broken weapon over his shoulder. "Sounds like we should pay them a visit. Right, Cap'n?"

The Pirate King was well aware of what was going through Hanzo's mind, and he didn't necessarily disagree, but he couldn't give in to the Demon King's plan so easily.

Rize then called down from the crow's nest: "Hanzo, you *really* wanna be allies with the King of demons? Lies and manipulation are his core components. He'll probably betray us and–"

"Do NOT belittle me, human," the Demon King growled. **"I am not a lowly beast, but the King of all demons. I am a ruler, and I have standards and codes that I abide by, just as you do."**

"Not all rulers are cut from the same cloth," the Pirate King retorted. "Hence our current situation."

"Then let us put an end to our problems. What we both seek hides within a fortress, guarded by an army of humans and abominations…I am willing to allow you to follow behind me as I cut through the filth and accomplish my goal."

"And what happens after you're finished?" Kohaku chimed in.

The Demon King smiled. It wasn't malicious, but it was eerie nonetheless. **"Then you will have your precious child back, and I will return to the Demon Realm."**

"And you won't try to kill us?" Hanzo asked as he tightened his grip on Ginza's broken weapon.

"Not unless you get in my way," the Demon King clarified, but he was staring at Hasunuma when he said it.

"It seems to me that you are more than capable of accomplishing your mission alone, Demon King," another voice added. "Why is it that you engage these humans?"

Hasunuma's stomach dropped. It seemed that Tōichiro had also been listening in and wanted to add his own piece.

The Demon King's brow furrowed slightly as if he was wondering who the other man was. **"That would be boring,"** he replied. **"And besides, I suppose I do owe the pirate for keeping my host alive."**

"Is there a way to guarantee your word?" Tōichiro pressed.

The Demon King shook his head. **"No. You either believe me and live, or do not and die."**

"Not much of a choice," Rize remarked.

Hanzo took a step towards the Demon King and said, "I'm thunder raving mad at what you've done to the lad, but I've also got a debt I need to repay." He nodded. "I'm in."

"I'm not one to trust a demon, but we need all the help we can get," Jun grumbled from the stairs. To the untrained eye, it looked as if the cook was casually standing there, peeling an apple, but he was more than ready to spring into action if necessary.

"If we can save Kazu *and* infiltrate the Hekigun's main base, then we should take our chances with the Demon King," Kohaku whispered. "And Hasu, you know he really could have cut us down at any point during the past few years…"

The Pirate King held up his hand to silence any more input from his crew. "While I appreciate everyone's willingness to participate in this discussion, this is *my* ship."

"What does the captain command, then?" Tōichiro said with his usual gentle prodding.

Hasunuma shook his head. "I cannot promise that we will all come out of this alive. But," he added firmly, "as your captain, it is my duty to see to it that any lives lost are not lost in vain. We *will* settle this once and for all, and Tsukigen *will* experience peace again. I can promise you that."

"That is a rather grand notion for a pirate," the Demon King remarked. **"I think it would suit you better to say that you *will* have your *revenge*."**

"You seem to forget how complex we humans are," Tōichiro replied in Hasunuma's stead. It was yet another gentle prodding that did not go unnoticed.

"I will allow you on my ship, Demon King, but only so long as you abide by our code – the pirate's code," the Pirate King warned.

The Demon King nodded. **"I agree to play by your rules for the interim, Pirate."**

"Good. Now help Hanzo ready the ship for departure," Hasunuma ordered as he turned his back on the Demon King and headed for the helm.

The Pirate King only made it a few steps before he was stopped by a strange noise. It sounded like a flock of birds flapping their wings, but there were no birds in sight. Hasunuma spun around with his sword in hand.

"I beg pardon, *Captain*," the Demon King said with a grin, **"It was not my intention to startle you."** He held out his open hands, showing the Pirate King that he was unarmed. **"I was merely following your command."**

Before Hasunuma could reply, a huge gust of wind assailed the Ryujin. Rize grabbed hold of the ropes nearby and wrapped his arms around them to keep from getting blown out of the crow's nest. Kohaku hooked her kusarigama around one of the masts and held on as best she could. Hanzo wrapped his arms and legs around the ship's rail, while the Pirate King thrust his sword into the deck and stood his ground by using all of the strength he could muster. Thankfully, Jun had already gone below deck with Tōichiro, so Hasunuma didn't have to worry about them.

The Demon King stood still on the deck, unfazed by the winds' force. **"Too much?"** Without a single movement from the Demon King, the winds lessened.

The Pirate King, now able to move, strode over to the Demon King. "I get that you're trying to put the wind in my sails," he said sternly, "but you should wait until the sails are open."

"Another mistake," the Demon King replied. He looked up at the masts for a moment and then his eyes met Hasunuma's once more. **"There. Fixed,"** he said.

A split second later, all of the sails came unfurled and opened to the wind. The Ryujin jerked forward with the sudden momentum and the gangplank splashed into the water below.

How in the demon realm did he – oh, wait. I think I know. The Pirate King shook his head. "There are steps that need to be taken before disembarking. Weren't you watching through the kid's eyes?"

"My focus was not on dull human chores."

"Fine," the Pirate King said as he turned his back once more and headed towards the helm. "Follow me and do as I command," he called over his shoulder.

The Demon King grinned and then followed Hasunuma.

"The rest of you should go below deck," the Pirate King ordered. *This is gonna be one rough ride.*

The Ryujin arrived at Chuushin in a shockingly small amount of time; a voyage that should have lasted five days minimum took less than one. As the wind steadily decreased until it became nothing more than a casual sea breeze, the ship slowed her advance.

I need to learn that wind-calling trick, the Pirate King thought to himself as he guided his ship towards an empty dock. Well, it wasn't exactly empty. There weren't any other ships, but there was a sizeable garrison standing at attention, waiting for the Ryujin and its crew.

A tall man with a long, thin mustache stood alone in front of the line of soldiers. He had a smug, self-satisfied look on his face as he said, "Well, well, it's about time you degenerates showed yourselves."

The Demon King walked to the ship's rail. Before Hanzo could drop the anchor, the Demon King jumped onto the dock that was alongside the Ryujin. It wasn't a difficult feat, in fact Hasunuma himself had done that on multiple occasions, but what was jarring was how nonchalant the Demon King seemed to be as he stood facing an entire garrison of seasoned soldiers.

"It took the great Shinigami-sama much longer to get here than I expected," the mustached man said mockingly. "Of course, you aren't a master of the winds like I, Eleven, the all-powerful wind demon."

As if in response to his declaration, the wind began to moan as it swirled around the Ryujin. The crew on deck braced themselves for another gale-force assault, but the winds quickly died down to their original breeze.

Ignoring the flashy demonstration, the Pirate King kept his eyes trained on the Demon King. Something wasn't right. Where was his haughty response? And why was his demonic aura so…relaxed?

"Oh ho, has my ability left you speechless?" Eleven happily remarked. "That is understandable, why–"

Before he could finish, the top of Eleven's head slid off to one side. It was shortly followed by a section of his face that contained his eyes and ears, then a section containing his nose and mouth, and then his neck fell from his shoulders. Subsequently the rest of his body exploded into a gory pile of bits and pieces. The garrison of soldiers cried out in alarm once their brains comprehended what had transpired. They attempted to run away, but none of them were successful since their legs had all been severed at their knees. The cries of agony that ensued were enough to drive even the sanest of men mad.

"Was that necessary?" The Pirate King managed to voice as he joined the Demon King on the dock.

"In human terms, I suppose not," he said flatly. **"But before you berate me, know that we are no longer on your ship,**

***Captain*, therefore your rules no longer apply."** The Demon King turned and began to walk away from the shrieking, screaming, bloody mess of humans. **"Follow me if you still wish to have your revenge,"** he called out to the Pirate King without looking back.

As much as he hated it, Hasunuma had no choice but to follow the Demon King. Sure, if this had happened a few years back, Hasunuma wouldn't have cared about the means as long as it meant that he got his ideal ending. But things were different now. He was different now. And the unnecessary bloodshed was more than he could tolerate.

Before he took off after the Demon King, Hasunuma quickly barked orders at his crew: "Jun stays with the ship and our guest, the rest of you come with me."

No one argued, not even Jun. Or perhaps he did, but Hasunuma didn't hear it over the screams of the soldiers. Even when the crew joined the Pirate King, none of them spoke a word. If he had to guess, it was probably the realization of the Demon King's true demonic nature that had rendered them speechless.

It doesn't help that he's parading around in Kazuki's body, Hasunuma thought grimly.

"He never moved," Rize managed to whisper after five or so minutes of silence.

"He didn't have to," the Pirate King replied in a low voice. The last thing he wanted was for the Demon King to hear them discussing his powers in awe. "He used his energy to make those cuts. Just like when he unfurled the sails, he never lifted a finger."

"You can't cut things with energy," Hanzo interjected.

"If you're human," the Pirate King added pointedly.

The crew went silent for another few minutes before Rize came to a sudden conclusion and said excitedly, "Oh! So is that how you blew that huge hole in the wall?!"

Kohaku stopped walking and asked flatly, "Who did what in where?"

Arse's stench. "Didn't I just say that humans can't do that?" Hasunuma replied quickly.

"Well, yeah, but you're–"

"And in any case," the Pirate King said, speaking over Rize, "that hole was caused by the demon's attack, *remember*?"

The helmsman looked puzzled for a moment before he finally caught on to Hasunuma's point. "Right, sorry. Got confused for a second there," he said awkwardly.

The Pirate King glanced over at Kohaku to see if she believed them. Her glaring eyes made it clear that she didn't. Hasunuma sighed and decided to keep moving, not saying anything else. Whatever he said would get shot down anyway.

"It would be more convenient if you could walk faster," the Demon King said coldly as the crew made their way past the last building on the street. He was leaning against a painted-over sign that was next to a three-way split in the road. **"Which way to the fortress?"**

"That's a pretty pathetic way of trying to stop us from coming," Rize remarked quietly.

"It almost worked," Hanzo replied in a louder voice; he was incapable of speaking in a hushed tone.

Rize tried to stifle his laughter, but the Demon King heard him and glared.

Hasunuma knew that the only reason the Demon King hadn't completely abandoned them yet was because he needed their guidance, which worked in their favor. But he agreed that they were moving too slowly. Unfortunately, with Kohaku's legs still recovering, this was the best they could do.

Suddenly, the Demon King stood before Kohaku; she was close to Hasunuma, at least fifteen feet from the Demon King, but the distance was closed in the blink of an eye. Before either the Pirate King or the ninja woman could react, the Demon King placed his hand on Kohaku's forehead. Hasunuma felt a surge of demonic energy leave the Demon King's hand. Kohaku reeled as the energy entered her, but Hasunuma was able to grab hold of her before she fell.

"What did you just do," the Pirate King asked between gritted teeth as he struggled to stay his anger.

"I-I'm fine, Hasu," the ninja woman said as she caught her breath. "I actually feel really good." She then squatted down and patted her legs where her injuries were. When she stood back up, her eyes were wide as she said, "He healed me."

All eyes shot to the Demon King. He ignored them and instead pointed back to the signpost. **"Which way?"**

"To the right," the ninja woman replied in Hasunuma's stead. "Thank you," she added softly.

The Demon King immediately began to make his way down the path on the right. After a moment, Hasunuma and the rest followed.

"What was that about?" Rize asked.

"Do you think that was the lad?" Hanzo wondered aloud.

"I'm not sure," Kohaku responded.

I doubt it, Hasunuma thought. *But it doesn't hurt to hope.*

A pensive silence fell over the crew as they continued to walk through the empty streets of Chuushin. All of the shops and stalls were closed, and there were no signs of any people. As the main port and city, Chuushin was normally bustling at all hours. But now there were no other ships or people – other than the unfortunate soldiers that had met them on the docks – to be found anywhere. It was similar to what they had encountered on Rurin.

"Do you think they evacuated?" Kohaku asked Hasunuma.

"Under whose orders?" the Pirate King replied grimly. *That man wouldn't care if the entire city was slaughtered.*

"Perhaps they were used to create an army of demons," the Demon King suggested. Apparently, he was listening, though he remained a few paces ahead of them.

The Pirate King did not reply. Although the suggestion was made as a jibe, it was not outside of the realm of possibilities. And that was a terrifying thought.

"That's ridiculous," Hanzo said with a huff. "You can't just turn people into demons."

"Oh, but you can," the Demon King replied in an eerily serious tone. **"All you need is a corpse and a way to summon a demon."**

Hanzo stopped walking. "You can't seriously be suggesting that he would kill a bunch of townsfolk and turn them into demons, just to fight us."

"You know better than I do of what your ruler is capable of," was all that the Demon King said in response.

Hanzo took a few large strides towards the Demon King. He

grabbed his shoulder and spun him around so that they were now eye-to-eye. "Firstly, he's not *my* ruler. And secondly, don't give me that horse pile answer," the giant growled. "You were at the facility in the mountains. *You saw* what was going on."

The Demon King grinned. **"I almost forgot that you never made it there yourself. Would you like to hear all of the gruesome details? I could start with the countless villagers, who were chained up like animals and were on the verge of death from a combination of starvation and mutilation. Or perhaps you would like to know about the infants I found, torn from their mothers?"**

Hanzo pulled his fist back, fully intending to strike the Demon King in his face, but Hasunuma grabbed hold of the giant's arm, stopping him.

"As much as I would like to do the same, my friend, you must remember that that is *Kazuki's* body," the Pirate King said in a firm voice, but with a gentle undertone.

The giant jerked his arm away from Hasunuma and stormed down the road. Rize ran after him, shortly followed by Kohaku.

"I strongly suggest," the Pirate King began in an icy voice, "that you remain silent until we reach the fortress."

The Demon King's grin widened into a demonic smile. **"Is that a threat?"**

"You wouldn't want to miss your chance to see the ultimate revenge carried through, would you?"

The Demon King's smile faded.

Hasunuma watched as the Demon King reluctantly turned away from him and resumed walking down the path. *How's that for disappointment? I won't let you manipulate me, you coldblooded demon.*

When they arrived at the fortress, they found the main gate standing open. It was obviously a trap, but they were past the point of returning. Hasunuma remembered the layout of the fortress from childhood; the former emperor's castle sat in the center of a labyrinth-like maze of tight passageways. After first entering a large, open section – where there would likely be an army waiting for them – they would have to navigate through the passageways, which were rigged with all manner of traps. Once they reached the castle, they would have to figure out a way to open the enormous iron doors that acted as the final barrier to any who made it that far.

Second and Hiiro Genji would be waiting for them at the castle, but getting there was not going to be easy. Or was it? It was finally time to witness the extent of the Demon King's powers. Hasunuma couldn't deny his curiosity, though he hoped that he hid it well.

As the five of them passed through the gate, it, unsurprisingly, shut behind them with a boom. Then lines of archers appeared on the battlements all around them. And, lastly, rows and rows of soldiers spilled forth from the gate at the opposite end of the enclosure, which was approximately two hundred feet away.

"Not exactly subtle, are they?" Rize remarked.

When the area was filled about halfway with Hekigun troops, all suddenly went still. One young man stepped forth from the rows of soldiers. It was Second.

"You've come at last," he said, void of emotion.

The Demon King took a few steps towards his enemy. **"Shall we**

end this?" He asked as he slowly drew his katana.

Second shook his head. "Where would be the fun in that?" He raised one hand into the air. "Part of me wants you to make it to the castle, while the other part," Second made a fist with his raised hand, "wants you to die here."

That must have been his signal to attack, because the rows of soldiers let out a battle cry and began to rush forth at once. The archers all nocked arrows onto their bows and pulled back their arms. As Second disappeared behind a sea of soldiers, the first wave of arrows came crashing down upon the five intruders.

"Down!" Hasunuma shouted as he crouched close to the ground.

Rize and Hanzo followed suit, but Kohaku and the Demon King remained standing. The ninja woman stood in the middle of the three crouching men, swinging her kusarigama as fast as possible in circles above her head. By her effort, any arrows that fell towards the group were knocked away.

Though the Demon King stood, unmoving, none of the arrows that fell towards him hit their mark. Hasunuma watched closely as the archers drew back their bows a second time. Before the volley was launched, the Pirate King noticed a sudden surge of energy emanating from the Demon King. At the precise moment that the archers released their arrows, an intense blast of wind knocked them backwards. The arrows then flew back towards their masters, striking them. The Pirate King was unsure of how many archers were unconscious and how many were dead, but none of them reappeared.

After witnessing such a grand display of power, the rows of soldiers that had been marching towards the group of five halted.

A wise choice, Hasunuma thought, *but it's too late.*

The Demon King stared at the mass of humans before him. He wore no expression on his face as he took one step towards them. And then another step. And another. With each step, the ground beneath his feet cracked as if he weighed many tons.

The soldiers began to creep backwards. They looked as if they were about to turn and run away when a lightning bolt came crashing down from the clouds, hitting the ground directly in front of the Demon King.

The Demon King paused his advance to look up. On the battlement directly above the gate stood the miko.

"Please, stop!" she cried.

There she is.

The Demon King raised his sword above his head.

"Wait, don't harm her!" Hasunuma shouted.

But the Demon King either didn't hear him or didn't care. He promptly swung his blade down with both hands. A loud CRACK sounded and a line of dust streamed out before him, stopping just before the gate, which was about one hundred and fifty feet away.

As the dust cleared, Hasunuma saw that both human flesh and ground had been cleaved. He quickly looked to the battlement, but there was no sign of the miko.

"You don't think she…" Rize trailed off.

"No," Kohaku said, sounding slightly relieved, "I lost sight of her before he swung his sword. I think someone grabbed her."

"Well, where did they go?" Hanzo asked as he squinted at the battlement.

"Maybe they've got a demon who can teleport?" Rize shrugged.

Hanzo reached over and smacked the helmsman on the back of his head. "Don't even joke about that."

"Hey, enough chatter," the Pirate King said as he stood up. "It's pretty clear that the Demon King is going to head straight for Second, destroying anyone and anything in his path. We need to be ready to move when he does."

"Aye, Captain," Rize and Hanzo replied in sync as they stood up.

Kohaku simply nodded.

The Demon King began to walk forwards once more, but this time there was no oppressive aura or cracked earth beneath his feet. Hasunuma wondered if even the fully awakened Demon King had limits to his power. He was in a human body after all.

"Let's move," the Pirate King commanded. "And stay alert," he added as a reminder. There were enemies other than human soldiers lurking somewhere in the fortress.

The two-thirds of soldiers that remained after the Demon King's first attack stood as still as stone. He had cut a literal path down the center of them and none among them was brave, or stupid, enough to challenge him. The Demon King continued towards the gate uninterrupted, but as the four pirates advanced, the soldiers came to life once more.

"Do *not* stop moving," the Pirate King commanded, "we can't lose sight of the Demon King!"

Hasunuma lead the others, with Rize directly behind him, followed by Kohaku, and Hanzo brought up the rear. The formation was such that Rize could pick off enemies at range while being protected by both Hasunuma and Kohaku. And Kohaku could focus on enemies to the sides, because Hanzo shielded her from posterior attacks. Ideally, there would be two rear guards, but…

"Captain, the gate!" Rize announced.

Gods be damned! Hasunuma watched as the Demon King passed through the gate that was slowly closing ahead of them.

"Go! We'll cover you," Kohaku said as she jumped in front of the Pirate King and swung her kusarigama, clearing the way.

"But–"

"GO!" the three crewmates yelled in sync.

Hasunuma didn't have time to argue or think, so he followed his instincts and sprinted for the gate. He barely squeezed through before the large wooden door shut with a gut-wrenching *boom*. Hasunuma stared at the closed door for a moment before forcing himself to turn and run after the Demon King.

"If any gods are listening," he said quietly, "I'm begging you to send the two missing demons and any hybrids my way."

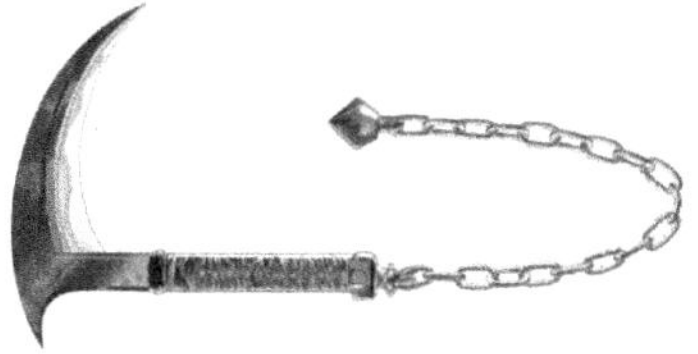

After Hasu disappeared behind the gate, the ninja woman let out the breath she had been holding in. *Just in time.* She then quickly turned her focus back to the fight at hand.

Rize had taken out the soldiers that Hasu had sprinted past, so there were none left between the three pirates and the gate, but there were still a number of soldiers that flanked them; too many for the three to take on separately.

Kohaku let out a series of whistles, telling the other two which formation to assume. She chose a defensive one where Rize would position himself with his back to the gate, while Kohaku and Hanzo would be out in front of him, covering his right half and left half respectively.

They successfully employed their defensive position, and as Rize picked off soldiers, Kohaku and Hanzo defended him from the others. As efficiently as they worked, it didn't take long for them to finish off what was left of the Hekigun battalion.

"Nice work," Rize said confidently. "Now how about we bust that gate open and catch up to the captain?"

"'We'? You mean, *me*," Hanzo corrected.

"Whatever, muscle-head, just get it open, will ya?" Rize replied with a shrug.

The giant ignored the helmsman and proudly made his way to the large wooden gate. He made a show of flexing his bountiful muscles, which made Rize roll his eyes and sigh. Just when Hanzo was about to seriously attempt opening the gate, there was a loud creaking noise behind them. The three pirates whirled around.

Opening up was the entrance gate, and, through it, Hekigun reinforcements began pouring into the battleground. This time the rows of soldiers took up more than half of the area. Bodies of their defeated comrades were shoved or kicked aside so that the soldiers could stay in formation. Once they were in their correct places, the soldiers unhooked huge shields from their backs and held them out in front. The pirates were now staring down a wall of iron.

"I could try to take them out, but it looks like the guy behind will just take the dead soldier's place in line," Rize noted. "And I don't have enough arrows for *all* of them."

"I'm not even sure that my knuckles could punch through those," Hanzo added grimly.

The ninja woman knew she didn't have enough needles for all of the soldiers. She thought it might be possible to swing her kusarigama around in such a way that she could get around the shield and strike the soldiers, but that would be too slow and inefficient.

"'Course this happens when the Demon King *isn't* here to blow them up with his special powers," Hanzo grumbled.

Too true, the ninja woman thought wistfully.

"Looks to me like you folks are in need of some assistance," a jovial voice said from behind them.

The three spun around to see a young man standing in front of the gate – which remained closed. He was wearing what looked like diver's shorts, along with a pair of diver's goggles, but nothing else. He had no weapons in his hands, and although his body looked to be one of a dedicated martial artist, his smile was very disarming.

"Who the festering hole are you?" Hanzo asked gruffly.

"Oh!" The young man exclaimed as his eyes fell on Kohaku.

"Don't ignore me, you–" Hanzo began to say, but he stopped when the man suddenly disappeared.

The ninja woman sensed someone behind her, but before she could turn she felt a hand rubbing her rear.

"Oh yes, you are quite the beauty aren't you," the young man said creepily.

She immediately drove her kusarigama backwards towards the young man's hand. Hitting nothing, she spun around to face him, but there was no one there. She then felt strong arms embrace her from behind.

"I like feisty women," the young man breathed in her ear.

He wasn't squeezing her, but his arms were locked tight enough so that she couldn't move. And when he had grabbed her, he had somehow also disarmed her; the ninja woman's kusarigama lay on the ground a few feet away.

"Hey, get your filthy hands off of her," Rize demanded as he aimed his bow at the young man.

Infuriated and mortified that a strange man was touching her, Kohaku's fighting spirit came alive. She widened her stance and dropped to a squat, freeing herself from the young man's hold. Kohaku then shifted her weight to her left leg and then swung her right leg around, tripping the young man. As he fell backwards, the ninja woman drove her elbow into his throat, causing him to cough and splutter.

The young man hit the ground and stared at the ninja woman in awe. "I think I might be in love," he said happily.

Kohaku jumped backwards, putting a few feet between herself and her admirer. "Don't touch me again," she said firmly.

The young man smiled. "But I'm curious to see how you'll react. Especially when–"

Suddenly he was gone again, and an arrow was stuck in the ground where the young man had been lying.

"Fiery mountain gods," Rize cursed.

"You can't see me," the young man's voice whispered in Kohaku's ear.

The ninja woman threw her fist towards her violated ear, but, again, she made no contact. She heard the young man laugh, but he sounded far away. When she turned to look, Kohaku found the young man standing atop the battlement above the gate.

"What number are you?" She asked icily.

The young man clapped his hands together. "Beautiful *and* smart. What a turn-on," he said with a smile. "I'm Ten."

"If you're a demon, then why were you offering us your assistance?" Rize asked flatly.

"Oh, I wasn't offering. I was simply making an observation," Ten replied jovially. "In fact," he continued as he strolled along the battlement, "all of these guys are under my command."

"So, what happens when we defeat you?" Kohaku asked, a little less icily.

The young man laughed. "I'll let you defeat me as many times as you want, Baby," he added with a wink.

Kohaku wanted so badly to shove a needle through his eye, but she knew better than to act on impulse. Especially when dealing with a demon whose movements she couldn't track.

BOOM! Crack.

The ninja woman's eyes shifted down to the gate. There was now a small, fist-sized crater in the center of it with quite a few large cracks radiating out from the crater. Hanzo turned and grinned at Kohaku. It seemed like he could punch a way out for them after all.

"Oh, that's not good," Ten said, sounding less concerned than he should have.

The ninja woman hurriedly threw a shuriken at Hanzo. The giant didn't have time to react, but it didn't matter. A split second before the shuriken hit Hanzo, Ten appeared in front of him. The projectile lodged itself in the young man's back.

"Ouch!" Ten exclaimed as he turned his head to try to see the shuriken.

Hanzo pulled back his fist and then aimed for the young man's stomach, but his fist only met air.

Ten was now standing in front of the wall of iron shields. "Pull that out will you," he asked one of the soldiers behind him. The young man grimaced as the soldier yanked the shuriken out of his back. "Yikes," he said, shaking his head as he picked up the small metal star that had been dropped on the ground. It had bits of flesh stuck to it. "Who knew there'd be a downside to fast healing?"

There's only one way to take out a slimy snake like him, the ninja woman thought as she slowly picked up her kusarigama.

"Do you do *everything* fast?" She asked in a seductive tone.

"With you, Baby, I'd take my sweet time," Ten responded with a meaningful grin.

The ninja woman began to walk towards him, making sure to sway and jiggle as much as possible with each step. "Then how about you and I do a little dance," she said as she began to swing the kusarigama rather gracefully around her body.

"Count me in," the young man said before suddenly disappearing. When he reappeared a second later behind Kohaku, he immediately had to jump back in order to avoid a blade to the groin.

The ninja woman turned her head and winked at the young man as she continued her enchanting, but deadly dance.

Ten wasn't about to give up. In fact, he looked even more eager to grab her now. He disappeared again, only to reappear to her right side. As she slung the blade towards him, Ten quickly disappeared again and reappeared on her left. His fingers reached out to grab her, but they were met with a *crack*, and he immediately jumped away from her. The young man bit his lip as he looked down at his broken fingers; he had forgotten about the round weight at the other end of the kusarigama.

"Oh my," Kohaku said with a sigh, "are you giving up already?"

Ten gave her a sly look and held up his perfectly fine fingers for her to see.

Kohaku raised an eyebrow and slowly ran her tongue along her upper lip. The young man became visibly charged. He disappeared from view for about six seconds before reappearing to her rear. Before his hand could get anywhere near her, Kohaku swung her kusarigama. Ten disappeared and quickly reappeared to her right. The ninja woman swung the other end of her weapon towards him, but he vanished before it connected. He then tried the left, but Kohaku had the blade-end waiting for him. Just as it looked as though the ninja woman had stabbed him through the heart, Ten grabbed her from the front.

Kohaku's eyes went wide.

"You stabbed my after-image," Ten said proudly. "I really am that fast," he added with a grin.

Before Kohaku could react, Ten put his mouth on hers and kissed her deeply. He was enjoying exploring her teeth with his tongue when he suddenly pulled away from her.

The young man reached up, stuck his fingers in his mouth, and pulled out a needle. "What the–" was all that he managed to say before he fell to the ground. His body began to convulse and drops of red trickled out of his pores.

After about thirty seconds, his body stiffened. Black smoke rose from the now-still corpse, but Kohaku dispersed it quickly with a wave of her hand.

The ninja woman spat on the ground and wiped her mouth on her arm. She looked over to see her two comrades staring blankly at her. "If you tell Hasu about any part of that, you'll get worse than he did," she threatened.

Rize and Hanzo nodded fervently.

"Good," she said as she turned her gaze back towards the rows of soldiers that were still standing there with their shields.

"That was rather impressive," said a gruff, but feminine voice from behind the iron wall. "Did you have that needle in your mouth the entire time?" A burly woman asked as she pushed two shields aside. After she passed by them, the soldiers closed the gap that she had made in the iron wall.

"Playboys like him are easy to read," Kohaku replied.

"They certainly are," the burly woman said with a smirk. She then stretched her neck and began swinging her arms around to loosen them up. "Well, he deserved what he got."

The burly woman was a close match for Hanzo in size, though she was a bit shorter than him. Kohaku would have assumed that the burly woman was a fellow countryman of Hanzo, except that her coloring was that of a Tsukigen native.

"Seriously, *another* demon? Haven't we killed them all yet?" Rize complained.

The burly woman chuckled. "Oh, I'm no demon. Or, at least, I'm no *full* demon, if you get my meaning."

Hanzo approached Kohaku and put his hand on her head. "You

did well," he said with a smile. "Now let me handle this one."

The ninja woman shook her head, "No, Hanzo, I can–"

"Once we get that gate open, you'll need all the strength you have to catch up to the cap'n." Hanzo said as he pointedly stared at her feet.

"But the Demon King hea–" Kohaku began, trying to remind him of what had happened earlier, but Hanzo wouldn't listen.

"Go on and sit over there," the giant said with a wave of his hand, "I got this."

The ninja woman nodded and walked over to where Rize was standing. She sat down as requested and sighed.

"You sure you're fully healed?" Rize asked quietly.

"Mmhmm," Kohaku replied with a nod.

"Well, the captain was worried, so he ordered Hanzo and I to keep an eye on you," Rize said with a smile.

"Ugh," Kohaku groaned, "that idiot."

Rize chuckled. "I agree, but I'm happy he asked. It shows how much he trusts us."

I wish he would trust me *more,* she thought, but she simply smiled and nodded at Rize. If Hasu's trust was worth that much to Rize, then she wasn't about to dampen the helmsman's spirits.

The ninja woman turned her attention back to Hanzo and the burly woman. They were standing facing each other with only a few feet between them, but nothing was happening.

Are they sizing each other up?

Suddenly Hanzo lunged forward, throwing a right hook punch at the burly woman's temple. She leaned back slightly in order to avoid the blow, and then grabbed onto the giant's wrist. Using her other hand, the burly woman pushed into the back of Hanzo's elbow.

"Agh!" Hanzo yelped as he knelt on the ground. His forearm was bent backward at an odd angle, likely meaning that his elbow had been broken.

The burly woman's foot came down hard and fast towards his head, but the giant rolled away from it. He then quickly pushed himself up off the ground and put his left hand up. The burly woman's fists flew at Hanzo, but he managed to evade or block all of her punches, even one-handed. She was strong, and a solid fighter, but her speed wasn't like Ten's.

I know that I just fought a true demon, but…I thought that the hybrids were supposed to be more powerful than regular humans. Kohaku thought as she watched the fight. Sure, Hanzo was strictly on defense, and his elbow was busted, but, other than the initial strike, the burly woman wasn't landing any hits. *She doesn't seem like much of a threat.*

Finally, the right moment came, and Hanzo managed to throw a punch with his left. But instead of the burly woman staggering backwards, it was Hanzo. He grabbed his fist and held it to his chest as he backed away. He was in great pain.

"Hanzo!" The ninja woman shouted out of concern.

"That would've been a great hit," the burly woman said with real praise, "if I was just a human." She then took one of the shield soldier's spears and jabbed it into her arm. The tip of the spear broke off, but there was no damage to the burly woman's arm. "It may not look it, by my skin's tougher than stone."

Kohaku immediately stood up. Hanzo could no longer fight with a broken elbow and a broken left hand. She took a step towards the burly woman, but Rize stopped her.

"Let me have a go," he said with only a hint of the anger he must have been feeling.

The ninja woman nodded and hurried over to Hanzo's side. She grabbed some cloth wraps and medicine from her pouch and tended to the giant as best she could, but there wasn't much she could do for broken bones.

"Subbing out, huh? I don't mind," the burly woman said as she patiently waited for her next opponent.

"Did you voluntarily join the Hekigun?" Rize asked as he grabbed one of two remaining arrows from his quiver.

The burly woman chuckled. "Does it make a difference? We'll be fighting either way."

"It makes a difference to me," Rize replied.

The burly woman shrugged and answered, "I've got a lot a' mouths to feed, so, yeah, I signed up. They said they'd pay me four times what I used to make, and that was that."

"You didn't try to go to the forest for food?"

"Ha! You mean 'nature's pantry'?" she laughed. "No way. Why would I scrounge around like some backwater hick?" She added with disgust.

"I see," the helmsman responded flatly as he nocked an arrow.

The burly woman looked at the helmsman's weapon with concern. "You *did* see what happened with the spear just now, yeah?"

"Care to demonstrate again?" Rize asked as he took aim.

The burly woman shrugged. "Not like it's gonna–"

THUNK. Rize's arrow sunk into the burly woman's right elbow.

"Agh!" She cried out in both astonishment and pain.

Rize grinned with satisfaction. "That was for Hanzo."

The burly woman tried to pull the arrow out, but her hand began to smoke as she touched it. She quickly let it go. "How is this possible?"

Rize shrugged. "You must be allergic."

Kohaku did her best not to smile. She noticed the small piece of white paper knotted around the end of the arrow. *I didn't think he had any of those left.*

Rize grabbed another arrow and nocked it, but Kohaku noticed that this one didn't have any paper tied to its end.

"You should have aimed for my heart," the burly woman said sternly. "You won't hit me again."

"You're right," Rize replied, lowering his bow.

The burly woman looked confused for a moment before she fell to the ground, motionless.

What was that?

Murmurs were heard coming from the shield soldiers. They kept in formation, but they were clearly unsettled.

Before Kohaku could ask, she heard the distinct cry of a falcon overhead. A second later, the main gate burst open, displacing a large section of the soldiers.

"The heroes have arrived!" D announced as he stepped through the gateway. He had a small army of pirates following him; some Kohaku recognized from the Chimera.

"Shut up and fight," Jun grumbled as he walked past the warrior. Without pause, he swung his katana at the nearest group of knocked-over soldiers.

Kohaku was so relieved to see her friends that she didn't even notice the slender woman standing right next to her until she said, "You could have taken care of her yourself, you know."

"Gah! Where did you come from?! Don't scare me like that," Hanzo huffed. He hadn't noticed her presence either.

"My husband tossed me up onto the battlements," the slender woman replied. "I was waiting for the right moment to assist you, but you were flailing around too much."

"I wasn't flailing!" Hanzo protested.

"Ni! How did you take her out without one of the miko's charms?" the ninja woman asked in awe.

Ni pointed to her ear and grinned. "Found an opening."

"Ouch," Hanzo grimaced.

"Oh, and thanks for the distraction, Rize," Ni said with a wave.

The helmsman waved back. "Anytime," he replied. "But next time you send me a message, try not to hit me with it," he added as he held up a tiny needle.

The slender woman shrugged. "It's not poisoned."

"ORYAH!" D thundered as he swung his spear around him in a circle, sending soldiers flying.

"Doesn't look like they need any help," Hanzo said with a grin. "Though I wish I could join 'em."

Kohaku gently patted the giant's uninjured arm and said, "You've done plenty."

Hanzo laughed and turned back towards the rear gate. "I've got one more thing to do before I can relax."

What was he doing? Without the use of either hand, he couldn't open the gate. They just had to wait for D to finish so that he could—

Crack...BOOM!

The gate split in half and exploded inward. Kohaku stared wide-eyed at Hanzo, who had just performed a complete, three-hundred-and-sixty degree spin kick on the gate.

The giant grinned when he saw the ninja woman's expression. "I've been practicing."

Rize nodded in approval. "I'm glad to see you finally putting your massive legs to use."

"Alright, Ko," Ni said as she gently shoved the ninja woman towards the broken gate, "time for you to catch up to your man."

The ninja woman sighed and shook her head. Ni wasn't wrong, but she could have said it in a better way. "Thanks," Kohaku shouted back to her friends as she cautiously ran through the opening, being careful not to trip on the huge, splintered fragments of the gate.

The ninja woman trusted that her friends could take care of the remaining soldiers without incident. Her priority now was catching up to Hasu and the Demon King. She didn't have to worry about Kazu's body coming to harm – the Demon King was too powerful – but what scared her most of all was the possibility of Hasu having to fight such a deadly enemy. And since both kings had short fuses, the probability was rather high.

As Kohaku ran through the maze of corridors, she noticed that the amount of dead bodies began to increase the further she went. It was a rather macabre path marker, but she was glad to be able to follow Hasu's trail rather easily. Kohaku was impressed at the intricacy of the labyrinth and wondered if anyone who had attempted it before had successfully made it to the center. Well, anyone who wasn't part of the imperial family. The ninja woman giggled to herself as she pictured a young Hasu running excitedly through the passageways.

Her daydream was interrupted when she rounded a corner and nearly lost her footing. She caught herself before hitting the ground, but she almost doubled over when she realized why she had slipped. The ground was saturated in blood; so much so that the ground could not be seen through the thick layer of dark red. Scraps of human flesh and bone were splattered on the walls, while the larger remaining pieces soaked in the bloody pool.

The Demon King must have done this...how awful...

Kohaku had never seen anything like it. She willed herself not to vomit, and after a few deep breaths the ninja woman slowly made her way through the sullied corridor. She chose to walk closer to the wall, where the layer of blood was thinnest, but she was careful not to touch the wall. As she neared the end of the carnage, Kohaku noticed a strange dark mark on the wall; it looked like a human-shaped scorch mark.

Ah...that means Second is the only demon remaining.

The Pirate King stared up at the enormous metal gate. It had been many years since he had seen it, but its dark beauty still fascinated him. Unlike the other gates throughout the labyrinth, this one marked the entrance to the castle, and, therefore, it was decorated accordingly. Figures painted in gold dominated the center, depicting a glorious procession of the Emperor and his army. It was meant to inspire fear and awe in all who approached the final barrier.

"Move away," the Demon King commanded.

Hasunuma silently obeyed. After witnessing the total destruction of Six and his men, in such a grisly display of the Demon King's power, he was unsettled. The Pirate King had once thought himself equal to the Demon King, but he now knew that he was wrong. No human, partial demon or not, could stand up to the might and power of the King of demons.

As the Demon King stood before the massive gate, Hasunuma could feel the energy radiating from him. *He's going to destroy it,* the Pirate King thought wistfully. But before anything happened, the enormous gate slowly began to creak open. Hasunuma felt himself exhale the breath he unknowingly had held in.

The Demon King's energy subsided as he stepped through the open gate into the main courtyard. There were only a handful of soldiers standing at attention on either side of both Second *and* Reika.

With a snap of Second's fingers, all of the soldiers charged the Demon King at once. But all it took was one sweep of his sword, and the Demon King's enemies all fell to pieces before him.

"Impressive as ever, Shinigami-sama," Second said in a sarcastic tone. "Now I wonder what you would do if I threatened your precious little plaything," he added as he grabbed the miko and held the blade of his katana to her throat.

Hasunuma watched the Demon King closely, but there was no reaction. His stomached dropped. *Come on, Kid...*

"Your threats will not work. I have already taken complete control of this body," the Demon King stated.

"So you have," Second replied, sounding slightly disappointed.

"I have grown tired of your games, Second," the Demon King said coldly. **"You have broken the rules and will pay dearly for your transgressions."**

"And how, exactly, do you intend to do that?" Second scoffed. "Even if you defeat me, I'll simply return to the demon realm and bide my time until I can continue my work here."

The Demon King grinned. **"You think you know everything, but there are some abilities that only the King can utilize."**

Second's smile immediately vanished. "You don't mean…no…that's just a myth!"

"Shall we test it?" The Demon King said with a grin as he sprinted towards Second.

The demon roughly shoved the miko aside and held up his sword, barely blocking in time. But he quickly regained his fighting spirit and returned the Demon King's attack with one of his own. It was blocked and returned in full.

Hasunuma quickly ran over, grabbed the miko, and retreated to one of the far corners of the courtyard. He put her on the ground and knelt in front of her, acting as a shield from the demonic energy pouring from the two demons. Even for a hybrid like him, it was hard to withstand the suffocating aura.

The Pirate King felt the miko's shaking hands grab onto the back of his shirt. He thought he heard her whisper 'thank you,' but it was so quiet that he couldn't be sure.

"I'm only standing in for the kid until he returns," he said plainly.

Second unleashed a devastating blast of power on the Demon King that sent him flying into the large stone wall at the back of the courtyard. The Demon King coughed up blood as he pulled himself out of the cavity his body had made in the stone.

"That was a worthy attempt," he said with a blood-spattered grin.

"How do you remain so powerful in a mere human's body?" Second asked with annoyance.

"You underestimate the powers of a King."

Second's expression remained unchanged, but his aura revealed his intense rage. The demon launched himself at the Demon King once more, slashing at him with demonic strength and speed, but all of his attacks failed.

Hasunuma noticed the grin on the Demon King's face. *He's toying with him.*

"If you thought that you could defeat me without using any of your abilities, you are more of an idiot than I realized."

Suddenly the atmosphere changed. Second ceased his attack and stood motionless. The Demon King's grin widened; he seemed to know what was happening and waited patiently with anticipation.

Second's feet slowly lifted off of the ground. He now stood in the air, as if it were solid ground, approximately fifteen feet above the courtyard. His black eyes seemed to shine while his posture relaxed; his hands hung at his sides, his right hand barely gripping his sword.

The ground began to tremble like the beginnings of a powerful earthquake, and as the Demon King stood undisturbed, the ground around him sprung forth and swallowed him.

What?!

And if that wasn't dreamlike enough, the firm ground suddenly turned to mud, and then transformed further into running brown water. The Pirate King felt both awe and terror as he watched. While he hadn't exactly expected the Demon King to drown, Hasunuma thought that he would at least struggle to stay standing. But the Demon King rose from the mess without interruption, and as his feet made contact with the ground it instantly became solid once more.

"I suppose I've tried that trick on you one too many times," Second mumbled, admonishing himself.

The wind suddenly picked up, and enormous, dark clouds appeared overhead.

"Let's try this one then," Second muttered as rain poured down.

Small cuts began appearing all over the Demon King, but he didn't seem to mind at all. Instead, he grinned and said, **"After all of these years, you finally gained a new ability."**

Curious, Hasunuma reached his hand out from under the overhang that was sheltering he and the miko from the rain. Little pinpricks and cuts appeared on his hand wherever the raindrops hit. *Ah. It's shards of ice*, the Pirate King thought, pulling his hand back under the overhang.

All of a sudden, a huge gash appeared on the Demon King's arm. Hasunuma glanced upward. Falling from the sky were no longer small shards of ice, but boulder-sized chunks. However, they only seemed to form above the Demon King, while the rest of the falling ice shards had become normal raindrops once more.

As the Demon King began to effortlessly dodge the ice boulders, one of them changed direction mid-air and hit him square in the back, knocking him to the ground. The Demon King got to his feet just as another ice boulder flew at him from the side. He jumped out of the way, but the ice boulder followed him and smashed into his left arm.

Another ice boulder dropped from the sky, falling towards the Demon King's head. He swung his right arm up and cleaved the ice boulder in two before it made contact, but he was simultaneously hit from behind by another ice boulder. The Demon King's sword flew out of his hand and slid far away, across the muddy ground.

"I'd say that disarming you deserves some praise," Second said flatly. His rage seemed to have subsided, but it was evident that his will to win was stronger than before.

Truly terrifying, the Pirate King thought as he watched the intense battle between the two most powerful demons unfolding before him.

The Demon King got to his feet once more and grinned. **"I may prefer to fight with my sword in hand, but that does not mean that I am incapable of fighting without it."**

He made his point by punching the oncoming ice boulder, which immediately broke into thousands of tiny pieces. Unfortunately for him, it seemed as though Second knew what the Demon King had planned to do and, as soon as the ice boulder broke apart, he sent the shards straight into the Demon King's body.

Now that *was a good move.*

The Demon King stumbled backwards. The tiny shards of ice weren't enough to do serious damage, but it would still hurt tremendously to be stabbed all over one's body in the blink of an eye. It was also rather discouraging to suddenly discover that even a defensive move could result in injury.

As the next ice boulder came barreling towards him, the Demon King whirled around and kicked it away. He was clearly being careful not to smash it. The Demon King managed to dodge the next few through some impressive acrobatics, but in dodging one ice boulder, he accidentally jumped right into the path of another. His only option was to block it somehow, so the Demon King pulled back his fist and punched it. Exactly as before, the ice boulder shattered into thousands of tiny ice shards. But, unlike before, as the shards changed course and charged towards the Demon King's body, they turned back into water.

"I suppose you think you're pretty clever for that," Second sneered.

"I do learn rather quickly," the Demon King replied. He was soaking wet, but his wounds from before had already healed.

Second waved his hand as if he were pulling back a curtain and the rain suddenly stopped. There were no more ice boulders either, but the dark clouds remained overhead. The demon then lowered himself back to the ground and stood facing his opponent. He slowly brought his sword in front of him, holding it with both hands as if ready to strike.

Second charged towards the still unarmed Demon King. As Second brought his sword down, the Demon King pivoted out of the way, grabbed Second's right arm with one hand, grabbed his neck with the other, and then threw him to the ground. Second somehow managed to hold onto his sword and not cut himself as he hit the ground and proceeded to roll sideways, away from the Demon King. He jumped to his feet and quickly slashed upwards with his sword in case his opponent had followed him. But the Demon King hadn't moved.

The Pirate King watched as Second initiated attack after attack.

Why did the battle still seem so one-sided? Sure, there had been some moments where it looked as though Second had the upper hand, but those were brief, and the Demon King quickly showed his true strength right after. If he was *this* powerful, even in a human body, then what was the point of challenging him in the first place? Why did the demon games exist if the outcome was already apparent?

Hasunuma thought back to when he first met Kazuki. The Demon King had barely begun to surface, so it would have been much easier to defeat him then. But, if that was the case, then why had the demons waited for so long to attack him? It seemed ridiculous to give the Demon King a handicap and then not take advantage of it. Unless there was something the Pirate King had missed…some vital piece that explained the long wait.

Suddenly a shadowy veil engulfed the two demons. The Pirate King couldn't be sure who sprung the trap, but he had encountered something similar on Rurin. He glanced down at the miko who was shaking so badly her teeth were chattering. She wouldn't be much help. Not that he *wanted* to help the Demon King, but if it would help Kazuki…

It didn't take long for the shadow barrier to dissipate. As the dark veil fell, the Pirate King could see the Demon King standing on one side with Second bent over at the other. There were new holes and bloodstains on Kazuki's clothes, but the Demon King showed no signs of pain. Instead, it was Second who seemed to be in agony. His sword lay at his feet and as he clutched his chest, his breathing was very labored.

The Demon King frowned. **"You did not gain those abilities on**

your own, did you?"

"It doesn't matter! I...will win...no matter what," Second managed to reply.

"You fool," the Demon King said, sounding mournful as he slowly shook his head.

Second grabbed his sword and lunged towards the Demon King. The attack was slow and powerless; nothing compared to what it had been like before. Disappointment, and what could have been sadness, reflected in the Demon King's expression as he easily avoided the attack. Second stumbled, barely catching himself, and as he attempted to stand once more, blood spewed from his lips. After wiping the blood from his mouth, the demon noticed that his opponent had disappeared.

A split second later, the Demon King appeared behind Second. They stood back-to-back, and for an instant it looked like a picturesque moment of friendship between two young men. However, upon closer inspection it was anything but; Second's eyes bulged as the Demon King's blade entered his back, slid through his body, and exited his chest with his heart stuck on the tip.

"It is over," the Demon King said softly as Second's body began to disintegrate and fall to the ground like bits of ash.

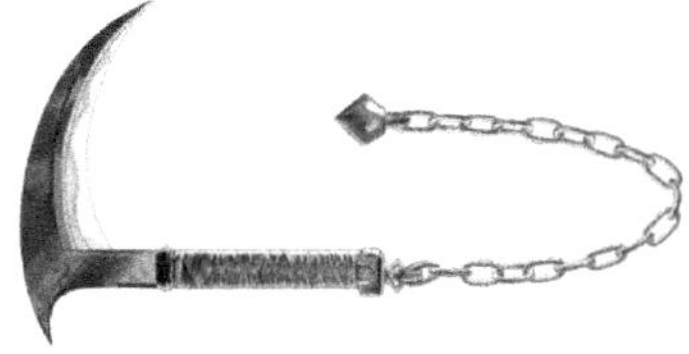

The ninja woman felt both joy and terror as she witnessed the end of Second. On one hand it meant that their deadliest foe was gone, but on the other it meant that there was no longer anyone capable of fighting the Demon King. While she had only seen the final part of the battle, from the way the courtyard, sky, and Demon King looked, it was evident that there had been an epic battle between the two demons.

Not knowing what would happen next, Kohaku hurried over to where Hasu was. She only noticed the miko huddling behind him as she approached. Reika was shaking so horribly that the ninja woman took pity on her. As Kohaku gently put her arms around the miko, she whispered, "It's all right. You're safe now."

"Where are the others?" Hasu asked in a low voice.

"They sent me ahead. Your reinforcements showed up just in time," Kohaku replied with a smile. He didn't need to know about Hanzo's injuries just yet.

"Good," Hasu said as he breathed a sigh of relief. But his eyes remained fixed on the Demon King.

Shouldn't he disappear or something?

"How disappointing," an unsettling voice said.

Everyone's heads immediately turned to the castle door. Kohaku's heart began beating wildly in her chest as her long-buried feelings of rage surfaced. As the towering, vile man emerged from the doorway, the ninja woman could only imagine how Hasu was feeling.

"After all I did for him, after so many years of my support, *this* is the result?" Hiiro Genji said with disgust. "Although, this is not the first time I've felt this way," he added as his eyes moved from the pile of ash over to Hasu. "Isn't that right, Son?"

"Don't call me that," Hasu growled as he stood up to face his biological father.

Reika gasped in astonishment, but Kohaku wasn't surprised; she had known of Hasu's true identity since she overheard a conversation between her mother and Hasu as a child; after he had escaped the very castle that they now stood before.

"I have never once thought of you as my father," Hasu added icily.

"But it is true. You are of my flesh and blood. Both you and your brother," Hiiro Genji said while wearing a wicked grin.

Kohaku watched Hasu with deep concern. Hiiro Genji was obviously goading him with every word, and Hasu was letting it affect him. The ninja woman knew Hasu was strong – stronger than anyone she ever knew – but she was worried that this long-awaited reunion with his father might be more than he could handle. To Hasu, Hiiro Genji was evil incarnate; he was darkness itself.

"You have no right to claim us as your sons. After what you did, to us and to our mother, you have absolutely NO right!" Hasu's voice thundered throughout the courtyard.

"Well now, this is going better than I expected," the Demon King said with a grin. He stood watching from the side, clearly entertained by the animosity between father and son.

"Ah, where are my manners?" Hiiro Genji said as he turned to face the Demon King. With a courteous bow he introduced himself, "I am Hiiro Genji, ruler of Tsukigen." He righted himself and added, "You must be Shinigami-sama. I have heard much about you from your subordinate. I thought to ask for your assistance with my research, but Second made it clear to that you would never accept my invitation."

"That is correct," the Demon King replied flatly. **"In fact, I intend to make sure that what you have done never happens again."**

Hiiro Genji shook his head in disappointment. "How unfortunate. I assure you that my research would be of great significance to you, as the King of all demons."

"No. It is quite the opposite. As King, I cannot allow you to meddle with my subjects. And I *will not* allow you to upset the balance between our worlds."

The ninja woman couldn't believe what she was hearing. It was rather shocking that the Demon King was in opposition to Hiiro Genji's experiments and goals. He could easily rule over both humans and demons, but the Demon King didn't seem to even consider that as a viable option.

But he is a demon...and I've seen his disregard for human life...so why is he set against this?

"Do you intend to destroy *all* of my research? Including my most successful product?" Hiiro Genji asked as he indicated towards Hasu.

The Demon King grinned. **"I thought that might be why you have some of our abilities, Pirate."** He turned his attention back to Hiiro Genji and added, **"Although, I am curious as to why he has no demonic aura, since every other hybrid that I have encountered has a distinct demonic feel."**

Hiiro Genji's eyes lit up in excitement. "That is because there is no demon inside of him. Allow me to explain," he quickly added so that no one would interrupt him. "I began my research and experiments many years ago. My first human test-subjects were my own sons. I chose their mother as my wife for two reasons: the first being that she was the Emperor's daughter, and the second being that she had a *twin* brother. When she became pregnant, and we confirmed there were two fetuses, I finally had my chance. I used an old ritual that I had discovered through my research, and summoned a demon by sacrificing one of the babies in her womb; the survivor would be host to the demon."

Kohaku did her best to hold back her emotions as she listened to the horrible account. She couldn't imagine how Hasu was feeling, or what he was thinking, as he heard his own father casually admitting to the atrocities he committed.

"I was successful in that the demon manifested in the womb, but there was an unexpected outcome: somehow the soul of the sacrificed child merged with his brother, and, through unknown means, overtook the demon," Hiiro Genji explained as he stared at Hasu.

"The soul of an unborn child is quite powerful," the Demon King added with a strange softness to his voice.

"Well, in any case," Hiiro Genji said, continuing, "the remaining child was born, and he did retain some demonic power. Unfortunately, my foolish wife told her father about what I had done, and I was forced to abandon everything as I escaped with my life. However," he grinned, "not long after, I was able to return. I then killed her pathetic father, took over the country, and continued my experiments on the child, uninterrupted. His potential was incredible, and my research thrived, but his idiotic mother could not understand what I was trying to accomplish and plotted his escape.

She succeeded, but died in the process, and, therefore, I could no longer use her to make another subject."

"And you were unable to recreate the results with other women, so you abandoned that method and tried other ways, did you not?"

"Oh yes, I have tried countless ways," Hiiro Genji admitted, "but even those that were considered to be 'successful' were nowhere near what *he* is."

Hasu...

The Pirate King brandished his red dragon sword. "How about I show you the extent of your research," he growled.

Hiiro Genji laughed. "There is no need. I have been watching you this entire time that you believed yourself to be 'free'. Your progress was much slower than it would have been if you had remained in the castle, but you finally managed to meet my expectations."

That bastard! Kohaku reached for a needle, but quickly stopped herself. This was Hasu's battle, not hers. As much as she'd like to make the bastard pay with a slow and agonizing death, she resigned herself to the sidelines.

Suddenly Hasu appeared next to Hiiro Genji. He grabbed the bastard's neck and pushed him backwards, pinning him against the castle wall. The eyes of the red dragon stared down the blade into Hiiro Genji's.

"How nice to see both of you," Hiiro Genji said sarcastically. "Such identical twins...it is no wonder that no one discovered the truth of your little 'ability'."

Kohaku bit her lip as she watched the real Hasu approach Hiiro Genji, as his twin brother's manifestation held their father in place.

She recalled the time when Kazuki had asked to learn Hasu's technique. He thought it was a cool sort of trick, but the reality was incredibly depressing. Being able to summon your deceased twin brother and have him appear, as a living being, is incredibly painful – both mentally and emotionally. Only once had Kohaku asked Hasu about his brother, and the look on Hasu's face as he described him was a mix of love, guilt, and regret; love for his sibling, guilt for surviving, and regret for using him even after his brother saved his soul from the demon.

Although Hasu felt that way, Kohaku had always seen the brother as a guardian spirit; one who protects and guides his brother out of pure love for him. But it didn't matter what sort of spin anyone put on the situation – the reality was that Hasu was alive and his dead brother's soul was stuck inside of him. And it was all that bastard's fault.

"I am curious as to why you cannot speak," Hiiro Genji said, addressing the brother. "You are more than a mere ghost, since I can certainly feel your hand on my throat, but other than the physical aspect, are you no more than a lifeless puppet?"

Hasu punched Hiiro Genji so hard in the face that some of the bastard's teeth flew out of his mouth.

Hiiro Genji laughed. "Am I to die by the hands of my sons? Will I fall to the blade of vengeance?"

Hasu angled his sword in a way that made it clear that he was aiming to decapitate the bastard.

The Demon King grinned wickedly and said, **"Yes, take your revenge,"** in a low voice.

The red dragon sword flew towards its mark.

Kohaku knew what taking revenge felt like, both the rush of the action and the emptiness that remained afterwards. Although she wanted Hiiro Genji dead, part of her wished that Hasu wouldn't be the one to kill him. She didn't want him to be the one to face the consequences of revenge – to become part of the never-ending cycle of sorrow, guilt, and hate. And then to realize that none of the pain of lost loved ones vanishes once revenge has been exacted. In fact, it only amplifies it since there is no longer any reason to keep going, to fight on and live.

Sparks flew as the red dragon bit into the stone wall. A thin line of red appeared on the left side of Hiiro Genji's neck.

The Demon King frowned. **"What are you doing?"**

As Hasu turned to face him, he returned his sword to his belt and crossed his arms. "I may have dreamed of this moment my whole life, but lately I've come to realize something: this moment is no longer mine alone." He nodded towards a hidden door on the edge of the courtyard.

Standing in the doorway was Tōichiro. He began to walk towards the castle and was followed by a group of ten elaborately dressed men, each with two swords at his side. Kohaku recognized their uniform as that of the Emperor's personal guard.

"Hiiro Genji," Tōichiro began, "for your countless crimes against this country and its people, you are hereby stripped of your title and will await public execution in the castle dungeon." He nodded to the guards and six of them surrounded Hiiro Genji.

"I see," Hiiro Genji grinned, "how clever. I wondered why you allowed me to explain the details of your past without interruption."

As the six guards grabbed hold of Hiiro Genji, Hasu's brother disappeared. The guards marched Hiiro Genji through the castle door, followed by two more guards, but Tōichiro remained behind with the final two. He faced Hasu and placed a hand on his shoulder.

"I am proud of you, Hasunuma," he said firmly but gently. "And I thank you, from the very depths of my soul, for all that you have done." Tōichiro then turned and nodded to Kohaku before entering the castle.

"You spent your entire life in pursuit of revenge against that man, but when the time came you threw it all away. You are more of a fool than I thought," the Demon King scoffed.

"I'd rather be a fool than a demon," Hasu said with a shrug. "Speaking of which, shouldn't you be leaving that body?"

"Ah, but the games have not been completed. There is one remaining demon that must be vanquished before I can win," the Demon King explained. He grinned wickedly as he turned his attention towards Kohaku.

"Um. I'm not a demon," the ninja woman said, quickly shaking her head.

"No, Twenty resides in *her*," the Demon King replied as he pointed to the miko, who was hiding behind Kohaku.

What?! The ninja woman stared wide-eyed at Reika. "Is that true?"

The miko refused to make eye contact, but she slowly nodded.

"But when? How? Why?" Kohaku asked aloud as she tried desperately to understand the entirety of what that meant.

The miko burst into tears. "I'm sorry, I'm so sorry! I didn't want to, I didn't! But they made me," she sobbed. "They took my family hostage and forced me to summon her!"

"I suppose Second grew tired of waiting. The demon games cannot begin until all of the participants have inhabited bodies," the Demon King explained. **"I asked Twenty to wait as long as possible before choosing a host, so that I would have time to gain power within mine."**

"Then the only way for Second to start the games was to find a way to summon Twenty," Hasu said as he, too, tried to gain an understanding of the situation.

"Correct. Although it would not have been easy for him to call her here," the Demon King said as he stared at the miko. **"You must be a rather powerful vessel."**

"I don't care! I never wanted this power," Reika shouted. "I just want to live in peace with the people I love! Why is that so impossible?" She dropped to the ground and continued to cry loudly and unapologetically, like a child throwing a tantrum.

The ninja woman crouched next to the miko. "The life you want doesn't just happen; life is what you make of it. You have to work hard to realize your dreams," Kohaku said in a soft, but firm tone. "And although it seems nearly impossible right now, I'm certain there's a way for you to accomplish what you seek. But *you* have to put in the effort to get there."

Reika stopped sobbing as she listened to the ninja woman's words. "But…I…don't want…to die. And I…don't want…Kazu to die," she managed to say through tearful breaths.

Kohaku smiled and patted the miko on the head. "I'm sure we can find a way to make that happen. But you need to be strong, both for you and for Kazu."

Reika sprang forward and hugged the ninja woman tightly.

"Pardon the interruption, but there is no way to avoid the death of one of these children," the Demon King said flatly.

"How can you be so sure?" Kohaku asked defiantly. "Reika summoned Twenty into her body, right? So there should be a way to un-summon her."

The Demon King shook his head. **"That method might work normally, but she is bound by the rules of the demon games. Either I cut her down or she cuts me down. That is all there is."**

"But can't we–"

"No," the Demon King snapped. **"I have wasted enough time here. I must end this and return to the Demon Realm. There is much work to be done."**

He advanced towards the ninja woman and the miko, but Hasu suddenly blocked his way.

"I'm afraid I can't let you kill the miko," Hasu said with a forced smile. "Her boyfriend would never forgive me."

Clap, clap, clap!

"Now there's a *real* man," Reika said with a smile as she abruptly released Kohaku and stood up.

No, that may be the miko's body, but that voice…she has to be–

"Twenty," the Demon King said with a hint of annoyance.

"I like your style, handsome, but you're way out-classed," the demon woman said as she patted Hasu on his back.

"It doesn't matter," Hasu replied flatly, his focus never straying from the Demon King. "This is something I have to do."

"Not to be a buzz-kill or anything, but were you even watching that battle between him and Second?" Twenty asked with a raised eyebrow.

Hasu nodded.

The demon woman burst into laughter. "Ahaha! I see, I see! Well, if that's the way you feel about it, then all I can do is give you a little boost," she said with a grin as she rested her hand on Hasu's back. There was a sudden burst of energy radiating from Twenty, but it disappeared shortly after. "Have at it," she said with a wave as she walked back towards Kohaku.

"What did you…?" The ninja woman slowly asked as she continued watching the Pirate King.

"Hahaha! Don't worry, your man's good to go," the demon woman said with a smile. "But we should back up," she added as she tugged on Kohaku's arm.

The ninja woman wasn't sure if she should trust a demon, but she didn't have a choice. She felt the energy building between Hasu and the Demon King and knew that staying clear of the battle took priority.

The Pirate King could feel energy welling up inside of him. It was beyond anything he had ever felt before. *I might be able to pull this off…*

"You are out of favors, Pirate. I will not hold back," the Demon King growled.

"Like I'd ask for that," the Pirate King replied as he darted towards his opponent, his sword ready to strike.

"Aren't you forgetting whose body this is?"

The Pirate King grinned, but didn't stop advancing. "A few cuts won't kill him," he said as he swung his red dragon sword across the Demon King's chest. A thin red line briefly appeared before vanishing as if nothing happened. "Plus, you've got that healing ability."

The Demon King scowled as more and more red lines appeared and then disappeared all over his body. He tried to block the Pirate King's attacks, but his timing was off.

"I know, I know, it's hard to fight a guy who doesn't use conventional sword techniques," the Pirate King said mockingly as he expertly brandished his sword.

"It is the power that she transferred, not your swordsmanship, that is aiding you," The Demon King grumbled.

Is that what this is? Hmm...I wonder if there are any limitations...

The Pirate King finished one more cut before jumping back a ways from the Demon King. He then focused his energy into his sword and swung it down, unleashing a massive, explosive attack on his enemy.

That was fun, Hasunuma thought as he grinned.

But as the smoke and debris settled, his expression quickly turned to a frown. There was a wall of earth in front of the Demon King that had blocked the attack. The Pirate King quickly sprinted around the side of the earthen wall, but the Demon King was nowhere to be seen.

A sharp, searing pain suddenly spread across the Pirate King's back. He spun around, but his opponent was gone once more. Another stab assailed the Pirate King from behind. Without turning, he swung his sword behind him and felt his blade make contact with steel. A second later the feeling was gone.

"That's pretty cowardly for a King," Hasunuma said through gritted teeth. The second attack had hit his spine, preventing him from moving; he needed to stall for time.

But the Demon King didn't stop his assault. The Pirate King did his best to block what he could, but without the ability to move, he was a sitting duck. He lost blood with every slash of the Demon King's sword.

I've got no choice.

Right on cue, Hasunuma's twin appeared and blocked an attack that was aimed at his brother's neck. The Demon King's momentary surprise gave the twin just enough of an opening; he forced the Demon King back, away from Hasunuma, and kept the Demon King occupied while his brother's body mended the spinal injury.

Gods be damned. I was hoping that the kid would show if I got hurt…but I guess if he didn't even come out when the Demon King revealed Reika's secret, then he's probably stuck deeper in there than I thought. I've got to try something else…

The second that Hasunuma could move, he canceled out his twin and sent another huge burst of energy towards the Demon King. This time, the Demon King redirected the blast away with a powerful gust of wind. Part of the courtyard wall collapsed in a heap of stone when the blast hit it.

"You had a better chance with the both of you fighting," the Demon King said impassively.

"Yeah, well, I'm a bit worried about what would happen if you 'killed' him," the Pirate King admitted. *Something about what*

Second said bugs me…and his death was different from the others; there was no shadowy smoke.

The Demon King grinned. **"I have said this before, but you are too clever for your own good, Pirate."**

A gale force wind came at Hasunuma from the left. It was so powerful that it knocked the Pirate King sideways. Before he could hit the ground, Hasunuma was suddenly thrust upwards by a section of the ground that had risen to meet him. The impact was so intense that the Pirate King felt a few of his ribs crack.

"Hey, handsome, you're lookin' kinda lame in front of your girl here," Twenty's voice called out. "With that kinda performance, you won't get lucky tonight."

Why am I fighting to save her?

The Pirate King blocked the Demon King's katana as it struck down towards his head. With his left foot he kicked the Demon King in the stomach, sending him backwards a few feet, but his opponent was relentless; the Demon King immediately charged forward to strike another blow to the Pirate King. Hasunuma dodged the katana blade and answered back with his red dragon sword. Sparks flew each time the blades met.

"Oi, Little Oni, wake UP," the Pirate King grunted as he and the Demon King were locked in a block.

The Demon King pushed hard against the Pirate King's sword, forcing Hasunuma to spin out of the block in order to not get sliced. As he spun around, the Pirate King swung his sword around and aimed for the Demon King's back. Unfortunately, his attack was a split second too late; the Demon King had already jumped back, away from Hasunuma.

Festering hole! I'm going to have to tap into more of Twenty's power...

Out of the corner of his eye, the Pirate King noticed that the gray clouds had finally begun floating away, allowing the sun's rays to infiltrate the courtyard once more. It gave him a strange idea.

No idea if this is a thing, but might as well give it a try.

As the Demon King charged towards him, the Pirate King attempted to jump away to give himself some distance from his opponent, but he misjudged the timing and ended up getting his shins cut.

Festering hole! That. Really. Hurts. He clenched his jaw and did his best to keep the pain to himself, but he had landed strangely and was now in a vulnerable position on the ground.

The Demon King wasn't going to miss out on the opportunity, so he lunged forward for another attack. Pushing through the pain, the Pirate King extended his legs at just the right moment to where he was able to catch the Demon King's torso and launch him through the air. The Demon King, however, did a neat flip and landed perfectly on his feet.

"Showoff," the Pirate King grumbled, but he was relieved that he now had the distance he needed. He quickly summoned as much of Twenty's power as he could and focused it towards the rays of sunlight, shining through the clouds.

Smoke suddenly began to rise from the Demon King, and small holes began appearing in his clothes. The Demon King didn't seem to notice until whatever was making the holes hit his skin. He jumped backwards, and quickly whirled around in a circle, but when he realized that the Pirate King wasn't stabbing him with anything he became puzzled.

As the Demon King glared at the Pirate King, Hasunuma grinned and pointed upwards. "Just being clever," he said tauntingly.

"You have no idea," the Demon King almost whispered in reply as he stared up at the rays of sunlight. His face began to burn wherever the sun hit him, but he did not move out of the way. **"I must eliminate you."**

The Demon King flew at the Pirate King, slashing wildly.

"Hey, Kid," the Pirate King said as he blocked and dodged the katana's blade, "if you don't come out soon, you're gonna look like a grilled meat stick."

"You are gravely mistaken if you think that you can call the child forth," the Demon King said icily as he swung his blade down at an angle, slicing a section of the Pirate King's chest.

Hasunuma winced, but he countered with a sweep of his own sword across the Demon King's shoulder. *The kid will come out. I know he will.*

The Pirate King sent a powerful gust at his opponent, knocking him off-balance. He then used another gust to propel himself towards the Demon King with his sword ready to strike. It looked as though the Pirate King would run his opponent through, but at the last second a shield of ice spread across the Demon King's body, stopping the red dragon from tasting flesh.

Hasunuma cursed and tried to retract his sword, but the ice spread too quickly; it enveloped his beloved sword, forcing the Pirate King to release it from his grasp before he, too, became encased in ice. He was now weaponless against the King of all demons.

With victory close at hand, the Demon King's demonic nature

surfaced. He grinned wickedly as he drove forward and head-butted his enemy. As Hasunuma recoiled from the impact to his head, the Demon King released his ice shield, grabbed hold of the red dragon sword, and drove it into the Pirate King's leg.

"AHHH!" Hasunuma screamed as not only the blade cut through his flesh, but shards of ice as well.

The Demon King drove the sword down so that the tip of it stuck into the ground. Hasunuma now lay on the ground, bleeding horribly from his leg that was now stuck in place by his own sword.

"Hasu! No!" Kohaku screamed. She tried to run towards him, but Twenty held her back.

"This is the end for you," the Demon King said as he held his katana high above his head.

"Come on, Kazuki!" The Pirate King yelled. He clenched his fists as he watched the katana blade drop towards him. "I trust you!"

Blood splattered all over the Pirate King, but it wasn't his; the Demon King's sword was protruding from his own gut.

Hasunuma couldn't believe what he had seen a split second before: the Demon King had stopped mid-swing, turned his sword, and eviscerated himself. The Pirate King distinctly heard some feminine screams as he tried to stay conscious, pushing through the pain and shock.

"Sorry for the late arrival, Captain," a voice said softly. It was a voice the Pirate King knew well.

"Kazuki," he said deliriously, "Kazuki, what have you done?"

"Reika, I need you to perform the demon sealing spell on me," the kid spoke quickly through gritted teeth.

"But–" the miko began to protest in her own voice, meaning that

Twenty must have switched places again.

"Hurry!" Kazuki yelled.

The miko jumped at the stern command, but she reluctantly nodded and began to perform the spell. The kid slowly backed away from the Pirate King, putting some distance between the two of them so that the spell would only affect Kazuki; the kid must have realized that Hasunuma couldn't move just yet.

Sweat was pouring down the kid's face. It was clear that he was focused on the battle with the Demon King that was going on inside of his body. Hasunuma wondered how long the kid could last like that, but he was proud that Kazuki had been able to resurface at all. His trust in the kid hadn't been misplaced.

After the miko folded her hands together and chanted some indecipherable phrases, a fierce lightning bolt crashed down from the clouds and struck Kazuki. A strange burning scent filled the air, making the Pirate King feel nauseous. He thought he saw a smoky haze surround Kazuki, but it left so quickly that he wasn't sure it had been there at all.

The kid fell to his knees. "By the gods, this hurts worse than I thought it would," he groaned.

Hasunuma watched as Kohaku caught the kid in her arms. Tears were streaming down her face as she desperately assessed his wound. However, there was nothing she could do. It was clear that the Demon King was gone, since the wound wasn't healing, and only demonic powers could put organs back where they belonged.

"No, no, Kazu, no!" the ninja woman cried out.

"Gods no, please, no!" the miko wailed, "I don't want him to die!"

The kid managed a weak smile and said, "I'm just glad that…all of you are safe. You're…the only family I've got…after all."

"Festering hole, Kazuki, were our efforts to keep you alive wasted?! What about Ginza's sacrifice?! How can you do something so idiotic?!" the Pirate King raged.

"…Says the guy…who was gonna sacrifice himself." The kid tried to laugh, but instead he coughed up blood.

Hasunuma pulled his sword out of his leg in frustration. He needed to feel a different kind of pain.

"What are you doing, you idiot?!" Kohaku yelled.

She transferred Kazuki to the miko's lap as gently as she could before she sat at Hasunuma's side and began dressing his leg wound. The Pirate King was losing blood fast, and the dressings would help to keep his loss at a minimum until his body could close the wound itself.

"Why…why did this have to happen?" The miko sobbed as she gently stroked the kid's face.

"I knew," Kazuki breathed. "I…knew about Twenty…and I decided to protect you…whatever way I could." The kid gasped as the pain wracked his body. He struggled to keep himself conscious. "I was…so tired…of watching the people…I cared for…die. I'd rather…go…and have you…live." Kazuki took a deep breath. "Don't you dare…follow me," he said, looking pointedly at Hasunuma, "and don't…make her cry…anymore."

"Even on death's door, you're a bratty kid," the Pirate King grumbled.

Kohaku slapped his leg wound and the Pirate King almost passed out from the pain. She then did her best to smile at Kazuki and said,

"He'll be the one crying."

Kazuki grinned. "I'm so glad…that we all met."

The Pirate King clenched his fists. The ninja woman continued to smile as tears streamed from her eyes. And the miko bent down and kissed the kid's forehead.

"I love you," Reika whispered.

Kazuki smiled. "Me too," he replied before closing his eyes.

The miko wailed as she called "Kazu" over and over again.

Kohaku buried her head in her hands and wept.

The Pirate King covered his eyes with his hand and lamented the conclusion of the demon games. Was there something he could have done that would have avoided this scenario? His brain refused to think. His heart ached terribly – more than his leg – as he thought of the second kid brother that he had just lost.

"Gods above," someone gasped.

The Pirate King looked up and saw Tōichiro standing with his hand covering his mouth. "I'll be fine in a minute," he assured his uncle.

Tōichiro nodded solemnly and then his eyes shifted to the kid's body, which was still being held tightly by the miko. "The Demon King is gone then?"

"Mmhm," was all the Pirate King could manage in response. He felt his jaw begin to quiver and quickly looked away.

Tōichiro placed his hand on Hasunuma's shoulder and gently squeezed it. "I am truly sorry for your loss, Nephew."

Kohaku leaned over and wrapped her arms around the Pirate King's head. With his face buried in her chest, Hasunuma normally would have had a handful of choice remarks, but this time he kept his mouth shut; he feared releasing the emotions that he desperately held back.

"Reika?!" A woman's voice screeched. It sounded like it came from the direction of the castle door.

Kohaku released the Pirate King's head as she sat back in order to see who the woman was. Hasunuma also turned his head to peer behind Tōichiro.

"M-Mom?!" The miko replied. She seemed shocked to see her.

"Oh, my sweet little girl," the woman cried as she ran towards the miko with her arms outstretched. Though this woman looked rather dirty and disheveled, she was wearing the traditional garb of a high priestess.

As the mother and daughter embraced, more surprised voices came from the doorway. The Pirate King saw a peach-skinned blonde man, who was most likely the miko's father, and a bunch of other men and women who were dressed in various traditional shrine robes. They, too, were rather grimy looking.

"Dad! Everyone!" The miko called out in excitement. "I'm so glad that you're…" she trailed off as the tears began falling from her reddened eyes once more. Of course, she couldn't bear to say the word 'alive' when she still cradled her dead lover in her lap.

Her mother may not have known the full circumstances, but she seemed clever enough to understand the basic situation. The woman held her daughter close and gently stroked her hair. "I am so sorry, my sweet," she said softly.

"The guards found these people locked in the dungeon when they took Hiiro Genji down there," Tōichiro explained. "He must have been holding them as hostages, although I am not certain as to why."

"In order to make the miko summon Twenty," Hasunuma replied.

Tōichiro looked perplexed, but instead of asking any questions, he simply said, "I trust that you will explain it to me fully in the future. For now, there is much for me to do, and I would like to invite you and your crew into the castle for a well-earned rest."

It was unprecedented, inviting pirates into the castle, but they were all headed into uncharted waters at this point. "Sure, why not?" The Pirate King responded with a shrug.

"And this young man," Tōichiro added as he motioned towards Kazuki's body, "shall have all funeral rights performed so that he may be entombed within the shrine of your choosing."

The miko and her group all gasped at Tōichiro's declaration. Kazuki would be receiving the highest honor that any person outside of the Imperial Family could obtain. Most people were cremated and their ashes either scattered or buried, while those wealthy enough could secure a ground burial inside a large wooden box. But to be entombed meant that a large structure would be built to house one's body; inside would be an altar, an ornate lacquered box that would house the body, and beautiful paintings or carvings that depicted the life of the person entombed.

"B-but isn't that sort of thing reserved for your Highness?" The miko's father timidly asked.

Tōichiro smiled politely. "As Emperor, I may do as I please, is that not so?"

The miko's father bowed his head deeply in response. Hasunuma couldn't blame him. It was extremely difficult, especially as a non-native, to speak directly and appropriately to the Emperor. After all, his position was that of a living god.

Hasunuma stood up; his leg had finally healed enough that he could walk on it. Kohaku immediately moved to support him, but the Pirate King held out his hand to signal that he didn't want any assistance. He flashed her a smile though to show that he appreciated her offer. The ninja woman nodded, her cheeks were slightly flushed and her eyes were tinged red and slightly swollen from too many tears.

As the Pirate King limped towards the kid's body, the miko's mother shifted her position in order to make room for him. Hasunuma wasn't sure if she knew exactly who he was, but she had a good sense about her, so when the miko's mother moved out of his way, he couldn't help but smile at her. The woman blushed and turned her eyes from him.

Hasunuma looked down at Kazuki's body. It was a mess and not something everyone needed to see. The Pirate King took off his overshirt and wrapped it around the kid's abdomen. He then used his red sash to tie the shirt in place.

The miko started sniffling. She ran her fingers through Kazuki's hair and tenderly traced the lines of his face. After noticing that her tears had fallen onto the kid's face, the miko gently wiped them off with her sleeve.

"I've got him," Hasunuma said softly, but confidently, as he reached towards the kid's body.

The miko seemed a bit reluctant to let him go, but she gently supported Kazuki's head so that it wouldn't fall as Hasunuma lifted the kid's body off of the ground.

He's heavier than I thought he'd be, the Pirate King reflected as he held the kid's body close. And then the corners of his lips rose ever-so-slightly. *He'd be so mad if he knew I was holding him like a princess.*

Epilogue

There was zero visibility. Simply an infinitely dark and vast space that Kazuki felt himself floating through. His soul wasn't wandering; it was being pulled towards a specific point – a particular place – and he knew exactly where that was.

As his consciousness began to awaken, he grumbled, ***Not again, Reika.***

The lovely blonde pretended to pout. "But I missed you," she whined.

Kazuki would have sighed if he could have. ***You can't keep calling me like this. It's against the rules and I'm really busy right now. Twenty is helping me get up to speed, but there's so much I need to learn about the Demon Realm that I'm a bit overwhelmed. On top of that, I have a bunch of daily stuff I'm supposed to do, but there's no one willing to help a new demon who can barely use his own powers.***

"Even though you're their King?"

Kazuki gazed at the quizzical face before him. It was a very strange setup that they had, but since Reika hadn't found another way to summon him yet, Kazuki was relegated to staring at Reika in the mirror as he shared her body with her. To anyone else, it must have looked like Reika was conversing with her own reflection.

"I thought Twenty promised to help?" The young woman wondered aloud.

And she is, Kazuki assured her, *but there's only so much that she can do. After a demon participates in the demon games and loses, that demon's powers get stripped away. So, technically, she isn't Twenty anymore.*

Reika tilted her head to the side. "Then what do you call her?"

Wen. She said she can't remember what her name was before she became a demon, and her number is so high now that it's a pain to say, so she came up with 'Wen' instead.

"She should have asked me to help her come up with something cuter," Reika pouted. It seemed as though she missed her demonic, live-in companion. Kazuki thought that it would have been nice to have his body back to himself, but maybe Reika actually liked the constant company that Twenty had given her.

Is anyone still there? The young demon asked, wondering if the young woman was feeling lonely. Last time she had summoned him, Reika had told Kazuki that most of the crew would be leaving the shrine soon.

After Hasunuma's uncle retook the title of Emperor, Hiiro Genji was publicly executed for his crimes. The rest of the Hekigun were rounded up and delt with as well. When that whole business was concluded, Hasunuma and the rest of the crew had stayed for a few weeks at Reika's family's shrine, helping to rebuild and also to recover from their injuries. But the crew's time there wouldn't last forever; each of them had their own new goals and priorities, so it was only natural that they would leave.

The crew's disbanding made the young demon's heart ache, and he imagined that it might have been hard for Reika too; after all, they were the only people who shared her connection to Kazuki.

The young woman nodded. "Hanzo's still here. Now that his injuries have healed, he's determined to follow through on his and Ginza's promise to help me rebuild my family's shrine." A small smile crept onto her face and she added, "He really is so kind…and he gets along well with my father."

I can imagine.

"Rize left a few days ago, but I think he'll come back to visit now and then. Especially if Hanzo sticks around."

Ah. He probably went to check on his home village.

"Mmhmm," the young woman affirmed, "he said he hadn't been back since he left, so it's been about 7 years. He seemed worried about his grandfather's health."

Kazuki silently hoped that the helmsman would find his grandfather alive and well upon his return.

Is Jun still missing?

Reika cocked her head to the side. "I wouldn't call him 'missing'. He just wanted some alone-time," she concluded.

I…guess you could look at it that way.

The Ryujin's cook had suddenly disappeared about a week into the crew's stay at the shrine. Not even Kohaku knew where or why Jun had gone, but Kazuki kept hoping that the cook would eventually return to the shrine. Being surrounded by people may have been an annoyance to Jun, but it was what kept him connected to the realm of the living. Without it, the young demon feared that

Jun might show up in the Demon Realm; And that was a terrifying prospect.

"Oh! That reminds me," the young woman suddenly exclaimed. "I checked again, just to make sure, and I can now completely confirm that the soul send-off ceremony for Ginza worked."

Good, Kazuki replied as a wave of relief spread through him. He had been worried that Ginza's soul would follow him to the Demon Realm, so he had asked Reika to perform a ceremony that would basically force Ginza's soul to return to the gods instead. The blacksmith had already given his life for Kazuki once, and the young demon felt that Ginza deserved the chance to be with the souls of his lost family members, instead of helping him for however-many-more-years in the Demon Realm. Although, if he'd been truly honest with himself, Kazuki *did* wish to see Ginza again…

"Red Dragon's twin refuses to leave though," the young woman added with a sigh. "I don't think Red Dragon minds sharing his body, but, at the same time, I can tell that he wishes for his brother's soul to move on." Reika then shrugged her shoulders and said, "It's complicated, but I can't do anything about it, so that's that."

Kazuki had wondered what would happen if Hasunuma and his brother were separated. He was scared that without Hasunuma's twin's soul inside of him, the Pirate King would turn into a demon, but he had no proof that it would turn out that way. Although, now it didn't matter, since the brothers weren't going to be separated after all.

"Oh, and Nia told me that she and her husband were going to take Kohaku and Red Dragon with them back to their homeland for a change of scenery," Reika rambled, continuing her report. "I think that's a good idea. So much has happened in a relatively short amount of time…Everyone needs some emotional recouperation."

Kazuki caught the slight change in Reika's voice and wished he could hold her close to comfort her. But that was something he would never be able to do, ever again.

Kazu, I…I really wish you could hold me, the young woman suddenly told him with her thoughts.

The young demon felt his heart stop. He then carefully chose his words and replied, ***Reika…you can't keep doing this to yourself. You need to move on.***

"How can you say that?! Do you even know how much I–"

"Yes," the young demon said as he took over Reika's body, silencing her. **"I *do* understand. More than you realize…but that doesn't change the fact that I'm no longer human."** Kazuki moved Reika's hand and placed it over her heart. **"This is where my heart will stay. And I will watch over you and your descendants for as long as I can. But, no matter how much either of us wishes for it, we can't be together anymore."**

Kazuki released his control and immediately saw tears well-up and fall from Reika's gorgeous green eyes. He felt her small body shake as she tried to restrain her sobs.

You're so young and beautiful…I'm sure you won't have a problem finding a good man to take care of you and to raise a family with.

"B-but..I want t-that…t-to be youuuu," she cried.

Telling the woman that he loved to forget him stung his heart painfully, but the thought of Reika mourning him for the rest of her life cut deeper into Kazuki's heart. He could never allow her to suffer like that. Especially knowing that she dreamed of having a family to pass the shrine to.

Reika, he called to her in a calm, but warm tone, *although our paths only crossed for a short period of time, being with you was the highlight of my life. My path may have ended, but yours can continue. As the years pass, your memories of me will fade, and that is when I hope that you will open your heart once more.*

There was no response from the young woman, as she continued to weep.

This will be the last time I'll allow you to summon me…

"No," she weakly rejected his words through her sobs.

…But I hope you never forget that I loved you with all of my soul.

"Please," Reika cried, "please, don't go! Don't leave me again, Kazu!"

The young demon could feel her strong emotions, and the pain of her sorrow felt as if he were cutting himself open again. As much as he wanted to hold onto her and take back his words, Kazuki knew that this refusal was in Reika's best interest.

Suddenly, he heard footsteps running towards them.

"Lass?!"

"Reika, sweetheart, what's wrong?!"

It seemed that both Hanzo and Reika's father had heard her crying and quickly ran to check on her.

Kazuki relaxed a bit, knowing that there were others that would care for Reika in his stead. The young demon took control of the young woman one last time, and placed her hand over her heart.

"Good-bye," he said conclusively, before he gathered his strength and forced his soul out of the young woman's body.

As Kazuki felt the familiar tug on his soul, now heading back towards the Demon Realm, he discovered a new sense of curiosity burning within him. What would this existence as the Demon King hold for him, and how long would it last? The young demon felt himself grin as he thought, *I wonder what Tsukigen will be like in one hundred years.*

Kazuki & Hasunuma

Kohaku & Reika

Hanzo & Ginza

Jun & Rize

Douglas & Nia

Ammon & Second

About The Author

Mary Anderson began her professional career as a lighting designer for theatre productions. After many years of working backstage, she decided to focus on the one 'job' she enjoyed more: writing stories. She now works for Curious Neko Books, alongside her silly and sweet feline assistants, and writes as often as she can – while balancing her time with her other role: full-time mom of three tiny humans.

www.ingramcontent.com/pod-product-compliance
Lightning Source LLC
Chambersburg PA
CBHW062059290726
48975CB00001B/41